Hidden Feelings

Donna Kelli

ISBN: 0-7596-6953-8

This book is printed on acid free paper.

1stBooks-rev. 02/07/02

Dedicated to the Love of my life...

Acknowledgements

My greatest fortune in life has been to meet, and love, and be loved in return, by my partner, who is absolutely incredible, and has been there for me through many exciting, wild adventures, including the writing of this novel and its sequel.

This labor of love was made easier with the help of some *very dear* friends:

Russie Tighe, an educator, has been there for me since I wrote the first rough draft.

A.J. Bassett, a retired teacher and inspiring artist, who was such a big help in designing the cover.

And my dear friend in northern Florida, you know who you are... thank-you for your insightful help since the beginning.

Dr. Karren Newman, also an educator, encouraged me so much when she told me she couldn't put the book down, and read until 4 a.m. in spite of having to work the next day.

Two, who are published writers, C. C. Teague, from Florida, and Valarie Massie, from Virginia offered their valuable assistance.

Several other friends made suggestions along the way that were extremely helpful. And, to Madeline 'Sunshine' Busch, ...bada bing!

Lori Hunter

"Wake up, Lori!" Those words rang in her sleepy mind. "Wake up, Lori! Wake up, Lori!!" ...like a terrible recording. It was her stepmother's voice...harsh and demanding...like always. With a start, she sat up in bed and looked at the clock. It said 6:25 a.m. *"Oh No!"* she thought, *"I'm going to be late for my last day of school!"*

"I'm up!" she said, dashing into the bathroom to start getting ready, and wondering why her clock didn't go off at 6:00.

Later, in the kitchen, she really didn't hear much of Maude's complaining. She tuned it out while she grabbed a quick glass of milk and some toast. She picked up her purse and her new yearbook. "Bye! Gotta go!" she said, and left, hearing, "I never saw such a mess as that girl!"

"Was she a mess?" She looked at herself and saw, neat black loafers with white socks, a navy blue full skirt with a white blouse... (the school uniform...for the last day! ...this year, at least.) *"Not so messy,"* she decided, as she briskly walked the four short blocks to school.

"Wonder if I'm very late?" she thought, as she entered the school.
"Lori! Hurry up!"
She turned to see Hattie, her best friend...red-haired and freckled, short, and always up on the latest gossip. Not at all into sports, but a true friend.
"Hi, Hattie."
"Come on! Everybody's in the auditorium, already!"

They picked up the pace, really hurrying, now. As they turned the corner of the last hall, Lori bumped head-first into the very muscular chest of 6'2" tall, Mike Warner, the school's star-wrestler.

"Sorry!" he said, quickly reaching out and grabbing her arms to keep her from falling backwards. "Are you okay, Lori?" he asked, looking down at her, and trying to see her elusive, hazel-green eyes.

"Yes, I guess so," she said, somewhat annoyed, barely glancing up at his face.

"I was running back to my locker to get my yearbook. Will...uh... you sign it for me, later?" he asked, grinning sheepishly. Unwillingly, he released his grip on her arms.

"Yeah...okay." she said, finally meeting his gaze briefly. And then she continued on with Hattie, unaware that Mike was watching her walk away. He hadn't gotten to look at her eyes long enough. He never did, and was wishing they'd have a class together next term so he could sit near her.

"Boy! He's cute! Don't you think?" asked Hattie, all excited and giggly.

"I don't know. He's okay, I guess."

"Just okay? He's tall, blonde and very good looking! And, he's exceptionally muscular!"

"Yes, he is all of that," she agreed.

"So...what kind of boy do you like?" pressed Hattie.

"I...uh..."

Just then, Julie Conners passed in front of them, and went through the open auditorium door, followed by three boys with their yearbooks and pens.

"Talk about 'tall, blonde, and very good-looking'," she thought. And then she agonized, silently, closing her eyes tight for a moment, wondering, *"Where in the world, did that thought come from?"* And then, clenching her jaw, she said, "I...uh...I don't *know* what kind of boy I like!"

"Well, don't get mad!" said Hattie. "I was just asking."

Lori realized she must have sounded grouchy, and said "Sorry... I just hate to be late."

"Don't worry, the assembly part won't start for at least a half hour."

They found several of their friends in the center of the spacious auditorium, and started passing yearbooks back and forth. After a long while, Lori was signing... "Dear Judy," to a girl she didn't know very well. "Best of luck, always. Love, Lori," but thinking, *"Dear Julie, Wish you were... were... Wish you were...What?"* She felt so weird...like somehow she was split in half... *"Maybe I should check out a book on Psychiatry...on 'split-personalities', or something,"* she thought.

Maybe she just liked the way Julie looked. So much so, that she was envious, and wished that she looked just like her. *"Yeah,"* she thought, feeling relieved... *"maybe that was it. Julie has very pretty, shoulder length, light blonde hair, and blue eyes. If I had her looks, I could...I could... what? ...have any boy I wanted? What boy? Well, there's George and Brad...the best looking football players. But they're so...so..."*

"Lori! What's wrong with you? Could you please hurry up with my book?"

"Uh... Oh, ...sorry," she mumbled to Judy. And signed "Love, Julie." *"Wha-a-t? What did I write? Oh my God!"* Her mind raced...searching. She quickly signed a 'write-over'... "Love, Jolly Lori." *"That looks really stupid,"* she thought, suddenly feeling the need for air, outside air!

"Excuse me," she said, and practically ran up the aisle and outside into the hall. *"Whew! I'm nutty today,"* she worried, continuing toward the patio. *"I hope nobody saw that!"*

"Lori! Wait!"

Hattie was scurrying after her, but pretty far back. So Lori stopped to wait. *"Lori, wait! Lori, Wake up!"* she thought. *"Tomorrow would change this existence for her. Camp Foxmore! For four weeks!"* Recently, her dad had surprised her with her fondest wish...to go to summer camp! He knew that she and her stepmother grated on each other, and he had saved up the money.

"What's the rush?" panted Hattie.

Lori chuckled at the sight of her, all falling apart. Her purse was half-open and Hattie was trying to put herself back together.

"Here, hold my yearbook for me... I dropped my lipstick in my purse, and its still open. Oh what a mess! Where are you going anyway?" And then putting one hand on her hip, she demanded, "Are you laughing at me?" Hattie paused, finally, waiting for an answer, and looking frustrated.

"I'm sorta laughing at myself. Today is strange. Let's go outside for a few minutes, okay?"

"Okay, but there are more people I want to sign my yearbook!"

"Yeah, me, too," said Lori. "We'll go back in a few minutes, okay?

They returned to the auditorium just in time for the special 'Goodbye' message from the principal.

Although the awards assembly had been held over a week ago, Mr. Anderson mentioned all the superlative winners again. After special words to each of the seniors, he began with Julie, who had been voted the *Prettiest of the Junior class*, cautioning her to be careful this summer, and to take it easy on all the boys. And when he got to Lori, who was the *Most Outstanding Female Athlete of the Junior class*, he said, "I know the boys would love to have you on their teams, Lori! It's incredible that a girl as pretty as you are can perform so well, and so easily."

Lori wasn't used to many people calling her 'pretty', and so she looked down, in embarrassment, to avoid the admiring looks from the kids seated all around her.

"Yea, Lori!" she heard from lots of different voices, all around the auditorium. Actually, most of her friends were seniors instead of her own classmates. She just kept her head down, feeling the blush creep up her neck, in spite of the cool air conditioning.

"Enjoy the summer and come back to us, safe and sound, all of you! We need your talents next year. As you know, today is only a half-day, so no lunch will be served, and you will have the rest of the time to visit with each other. The staff will be stationed at various points in the school in case you need anything. Good luck to all of you!"

3

Lori got through the rest of the school day, with only a few tearful goodbyes. She would read her yearbook comments and signatures later. She hadn't asked Julie to sign her book. Oh well, maybe next year. Hattie wanted to stay and talk to some boys, so Lori gave her a hug and said, "I'll call you as soon as I get back from camp."

"Write me! Okay?"

"Silly,... it's only for four weeks! But I'll have lots to tell you then!" she assured her.

"Okay. Have fun!" smiled Hattie.

"You bet!" said Lori, waving "bye", and hoping she would be able to do just that! She felt her spirits lifting, and she sort of floated home, promising herself that she'd avoid her stepmother as much as possible for the rest of the day. Maude tended to hang close to her whenever she was indoors, following her from room to room, and asking aggravating questions. Mainly, she tried to make Lori feel guilty about always 'playing' sports, while she had to be home, doing *all* the housework.

Later that evening, as she was packing a few last items, her dad came to her bedroom door.

"May I come in?"

She heard his deep, resonant voice, and smiled. "Hi, Dad!" She ran to hug him, and thought to herself... *"If ever I find a real boyfriend, hopefully he'll have a nice, deep voice like that."*

"Just about packed?" he asked.

"Yes," she said. "I can hardly wait!"

"I'll miss you," he said. "Lots!"

"I'll be missing you, too, Dad," she said, looking into his hazel-green eyes.

"You'll be careful, won't you?"

"Yes, ...I will. And I'll send you at least one letter."

"More! And try to call, okay?"

"I promise, especially to let you know when I get there."

"Okay, 'Pixie'."

"Dad...I'm not a little girl anymore..."

"Yeah, I know," he said softly... "but somehow you'll always be my little 'Pixie'." With that, he hugged her again, kissed her goodnight, and left quietly.

She heard, "Jon-a-than!!" ...her stepmother's voice...and she hoped that camp counselors weren't as nasty-sounding at morning wake-up call.

The Bus

The next morning, Lori sat quietly as Maude drove her to the bus station. As usual, she tried to tune her out. As she got out of the car, she managed a smile in the direction of her stepmother's rather non-descript face—one she could easily forget. But the parting words stung, as Maude grumbled, "We get no vacation at all! But you! You get four weeks of fun and games!" Lori just sighed, and closed the door.

The bus ride was long, ...six hours. But she didn't mind. It gave her time to think and daydream about what might be in store for her at camp: archery, canoeing, hiking, swimming, and even volleyball, one of her favorites. She loved just about any sport, and she was looking forward to every minute, ...even arts and crafts! Only four weeks! Six would've been perfect, since it would've taken up the whole summer. She could definitely stand to be away from her stepmother for six weeks!

As the miles flew by, she reviewed her life up until now, and except for her dad...actually, except for her dad and sports, there wasn't much she cared about in the world. School was easy and she usually made the honor roll. Sports activities were fantastic for her. She was always the captain of one team or another with the seniors. Even all the boys she grew up with in her neighborhood accepted her ability and her leadership for what it was. It just came naturally.

As far as looks, she didn't think she had much going for her except her green eyes. *"Almost like Dad's"*, she thought, *"except a little lighter...and with those little brown flecks in them."* All her life, it seemed, people had made comments about her eyes. And sometimes she found people just staring at her, into her eyes...as if they would find something there, if only they could look deeply enough. She was a very private person, deep down, and that type of continued attention made her feel violated somehow. *"There's more to me than my eyes,"* she thought.

"My social life is very lacking," she admitted to herself. *"Well, compared to a lot of girls in school that are dating, that is."* Although she knew lots of girls all around the city, because she played on the school and the park teams, she didn't really hang out with them. She competed against them or played with them, and when the games were over, she usually went home. More often than not, she got her homework done at school, but she rarely relaxed at home or had friends come over, because Maude always dreamed up chores for her to do. She

much preferred to work outside, doing the lawn, rather than working near Maude, inside. Her dad didn't have time to do it, and she enjoyed the physical exercise.

She knew lots of boys, too, because she often participated in sand-lot softball or touch football games with them. Not too many boys impressed her with their physical prowess. She could usually run faster, jump higher, catch better, both throw and bat a ball farther, and even fight, if she had to, better than most boys she knew. During her childhood years, she had fought a few boys, mainly for playing too rough around her, like ripping her favorite blouse, or some other 'important' reason. She'd always won. She had a reputation for sure, 'TOMBOY', and definitely spelled with all capital letters. Her dad had showed her a little about boxing, 'just in case'...cautioning her that she should *never, ever* hit a girl in the face. She promised that part easily, because to fight any girl she knew so far, would have been sort of a joke. He used to let her pound him in the stomach, with boxing gloves on, as hard as she could. But one day, when she was 12 years old, he stopped her. "That's enough!" he said, laughing. "You've got some punch, Pixie!"

Once, in junior high, she had dressed out in a football uniform, just to try-out for quarterback. That was her usual position in any football game she played in her neighborhood. But, even with a helmet on, her green eyes and her long black eyelashes gave her away. She'd been kidded, good-naturedly, about it ever since.

"So...there was mainly Dad, and sports...and...and...Julie." She pictured her, in her mind. *"There she is in my thoughts again! What about Hattie? Hattie is supposed to be my very best friend...yet...I hardly think about her at all."*

"And what about sex?" she asked herself. Her dad had explained a lot to her about where babies come from, when she was younger. But he was reluctant to explain much about 'how they got there'. So, she had educated herself as best she could, by reading anything she could locate in the school and public library. There weren't that many books. She had learned a lot about 'eggs and sperm'. But the books didn't show naked boys, or intercourse, or...exactly what all was involved in intimacy. She could almost picture certain things, but when she thought of her dad lying close to Maude, it made her shiver.

She was not the type of person to confide in others about personal things...especially her private misgivings and her boundless curiosity. Somehow, all the romantic books she had read so far, left her craving the feeling... but she wasn't sure she wanted to have sex with a boy just yet. She knew a few girls who 'went-all-the-way' and they had pretty bad reputations. In her senior year she would be taking sex education as an elective, but she didn't see what the big deal was...not yet, anyway...and not with the boys she knew so far. *"When I get back from camp,"* she thought, *"I'll check-out any new books I can find. I don't want to be the dumbest one in class."*

Arrival

"Camp Foxmore!" announced the driver, interrupting her daydreams. She was the only one getting off the bus. The portly grey-haired man got her large duffel bag out of the side compartment. Then, smiling, he told her, "Have lots of fun, but be careful not to drown! Good-bye," he said, waving, and slowly drove off.

There was a bench under a large shade tree, but no one else, anywhere around. And no vehicle waiting for her. *"Oh, great!"* she thought, as she walked over and sat on the bench, wondering if she'd be there for hours. After about fifteen minutes, a woman in an open-air jeep drove up.

"Hi! I'm Miss Carson. Call me Gerri...it's easier." She smiled, and said... "And you're...?"

"Lori...Lori Hunter"

"Welcome to Camp Foxmore! C'mon and hop in. Most of the girls are already here."

Lori swung her duffel bag up into the rear of the jeep, and climbed in the front seat.

You'll be in the Falcons' cabin, and I'll be your cabin counselor. If you have any problems, let me know, and I'll help you if I can."

"Thanks," said Lori. "How many girls will be here?"

"About eighty, if everyone still gets to come. Sometimes parents change their minds at the last minute," said Gerri. "There are ten girls in each side of the double-cabins. Last year we only had sixty campers, but we built a new, double-cabin last fall. Each year we hope to get a little bigger and a lot better," said the cheerful lady.

Lori decided that she liked the woman's smile, and hoped the other counselors were happy people, too. She'd had enough of bad temperament from Maude to last her for years. Smiling back at Gerri, she said, "It's good to be here! This is my first camp ever!"

Looking around, as they drove the mile and a half to the camp, Lori said "It's beautiful here! I love all these winding lanes and paths through the woods, and all these huge, shady trees!"

"Good!" said Gerri. "Just be careful when you're on horseback, not to run right into one of these trees!"

"Horseback? You mean we get to ride?"

"Yes! It wasn't in the brochure, because we weren't sure if everything would be finished for camp this summer. We just finished the barn, and the horses

7

arrive tomorrow. Everyone will need a note from home, but we've already sent them out to be signed."

"Things are getting better," thought Lori. *"Hope I can learn fast...before I make a fool of myself!"* She never liked to look stupid.

"Here we are," said Gerri. This is the parking area for parents and any other visitors. This building is the 'Mess Hall', and beyond it, you can see the lake. Over here is 'Cabin Circle.'

Lori saw a large semi-circle of cabins facing the lake. They were tucked under beautiful, huge oak trees, and looked very inviting.

"That's the new double-cabin I was telling you about...way over there..." Gerri continued, "the last one on the right... otherwise known as the Herons and the Blue jays." After making a big loop, and passing by it, she said, chuckling to herself, "This next one is a counselors' cabin, alias 'The Dirty Socks'."

Sure enough, Lori saw that each cabin had its name posted over the door...even the 'The Dirty Socks'. She smiled at the name.

"Then comes another campers' double, the Robins and the Eagles. And finally, here we are, the Falcons and the Hawks," and she pulled to a stop. "I'm in the counselors' cabin next door, to the left, called the 'The Miss Fits', between you and the first double-cabin, alias the Owls and the Ravens. As you can see, the 'counselors' cabins are interspersed between the campers' cabins. We're all on this one semi-circle."

Lori's mind was swimming with all the 'bird' names but 'The Miss Fits' sounded cute.

Gerri got out and held the screen door open wide for Lori to wrestle the duffel bag inside. "Any one of those last three bunks from the middle to the end of this row is okay. The rest of the girls have chosen their bunks, put their stuff in a locker, and are in the mess hall, checking in, and getting ready for Orientation. Why don't you take a few minutes to settle in. Check out the bathrooms and showers, maybe. Just leave your duffel bag on your bunk for now. When you're ready, come right down this dirt road, back to the mess hall." Pointing through the screen door, she said, "You can see it right there...okay?"

Lori said "Thanks," and went in to leisurely look around. The cabin was sturdily-built and spacious, with big windows at the head of each bunk. Tall lockers stood in between each bunk. *"Nice,"* thought Lori. Low bunks were lined up on opposite sides of the room, with a big aisle down the center. *"No top bunks,"* she thought. *"That's great."*

In order to check out the restrooms, she had to pass by the corner of a large side-room that had lots of shower heads, spread out all around the biggest part of three walls. *"So this is a gang shower,"* she thought. *"Yuck! Not one shower curtain to hide behind anywhere!"*

She went in the area to the left, and used the restroom. *"At least they have doors, here."* she thought, happily. Then, she walked through the center aisle of the restroom area, into the adjoining 'Hawks' cabin, and saw that it was identical, but completely reversed, to the Falcons' side. She liked the airy, rectangular rooms.

With a shrug, she went back through, and out into the dorm area, picked up her bag, and chose the first bunk of the last three. That put her in the center of the room, along the back wall. Five more bunks were lined up along the front wall, across the center aisle. She tossed the bag near her locker, flipped her doubled-over mattress to a flat position, and relaxed on the un-made mattress. *"I'll go to the mess hall in a few minutes,"* she decided.

The room was empty, and very quiet. She looked up at the ceiling and saw more of the heavy, rough-cut beams. *"Neat!"* she thought. *"Really a cabin. Not just a make-believe one. Wonder how hard it is, to actually build?"* The sound of footsteps and the screen door opening interrupted her quiet world.

"Right in here!" said a female voice. "You can pick..."

Lori sat up.

"Oh...Hi!" said the counselor. "I'm Miss Butler, and this is..."

"Julie Conners!" thought Lori, and she couldn't believe it!

"...Julie Conners." said Miss Butler. "And you are?"

"Lori Hunter. Hi, Julie."

"Hi. I didn't know you were coming here."

"Me neither...I mean...I didn't know you were coming here...too." Lori added.

Julie looked at Miss Butler and explained, "We go to the same school."

Lori noticed that she didn't say "We're friends." ...just... "We go to the same school."

Her momentary pleasant surprise suddenly turned sour, and she felt inadequate somehow.

"Well, that's nice. See you two at the mess hall in 15 minutes, for a snack, and then Orientation after that."

"Okay," said both girls.

Julie looked around the room in the opposite direction from where Lori sat, searching for an open bunk.

"I'm afraid there are only these two left." said Lori, wondering why she felt apologetic.

"Oh, ...uh...okay," said Julie, as she put her stuff by the last bunk. It was the farthest from Lori.

Lori decided to 'busy' herself, so she got up, found her linens, pillow, and blanket in her locker, and proceeded to make her bunk.

Julie copied her and the two worked silently.

"Strange," thought Lori, *"I don't know even one thing to say to her."*

"Ready to go?" Julie asked.

"Yes," said Lori, as she put her final pats to the pillow.

They didn't speak at all on the short walk to the mess hall, and Lori thought, *"I'm such a dud...so boring...and dense. What is she thinking?"*

As they entered the door, Julie spied an open seat at the first table, and said, "I guess I'll take this one," and quickly sat down.

Lori looked around, but saw that there wasn't another seat open anywhere until the fourth table, so she said "...Uh...well...okay...See you later," and made her way toward a faceless group of girls. *"What is it about me?"* she demanded of herself. *"I guess I'm just not in her league! Somebody once said that the teenage years are tough! Boy!"* she almost said aloud, *"They were right! They're downright painful!"*

New Friends

"Hi! Want to sit here?" said a smiling face, surrounded by a fluffy mop of tight blonde curls...

"What? Uh...Oh, sure," Lori said, forcing a wan smile.

"My name's Sue. And this is Jill"

"Hi," smiled Lori, a little better this time. "I'm Lori, from Grove City."

"Where's that?" asked Sue.

"About six hours south of here. And you?"

"I'm from South Hills, and Jill's from Glenside. First time here?"

"Yes. And you both?"

"Yes," they said in unison.

As she sat down, in spite of the fact that food wasn't foremost in her mind, Lori murmured, "Well, so what's for our snack?"

"We don't know for sure yet, but..."

"Ladies, may I have your attention, please?" came loudly over a crackling microphone.

A very dignified lady with perfect posture stood before them. She had short salt and pepper hair and Lori thought she looked like she had just come from the beauty salon.

"Welcome to Camp Foxmore. I'm Mrs. Zablonsky, Mrs. 'Z', for short. I've met most of you young ladies through your camp paperwork, and I will get to know each one of you personally within the next several days."

"Up at the front of this room, we have posted all kinds of information for you. Lists of everyone in your cabin, normally, nine or ten girls are in each one. A master schedule of the activities each day for each cabin is on the yellow chart. On the table, you will find your name tag, if you haven't already had a chance to pick it up. Hopefully, everything is spelled correctly. If not, please see Miss Butler, this young lady to my right, during free time, after my announcements. We're hoping these name tags will last for several days, so we can all get to know each other faster."

Lori saw that Sue and Jill were already wearing theirs. She had been so distracted by Julie's sudden parting of company, that she hadn't even paid attention.

"You may have noticed that though there are only 8 cabins, with 9 or 10 girls in each. There are 10 tables here, with only 8 per table," continued Mrs. 'Z'.

"This is so you don't hang-out with your cabin buddies only. We want you to make lots of friends here."

"At this time, I'd like to introduce some other counselors to you.

Miss Wall, Waterfront Director, whose nickname is 'Walli'.

Miss Larson, the Horseback Trainer, also known as 'Boots'.

Miss Butler, Sports Activities Director, alias, 'Fletch', for her expertise in Archery.

Miss Knowles, Outdoor Activities Director, whom you may call 'Katie'.

Mrs. Watson, Arts and Crafts, and Indoor Activities Director, who is new and doesn't have a nickname...yet!"

The only one Lori took note of, was Miss Larson, 'Boots'...who was introduced as the Horseback Trainer. She hoped to learn a lot from her. But, then they all seemed okay, and she hoped they were cheerful...not like some people she knew!

"You'll meet more of my staff later. But for now, introduce yourselves around the table. I'll be back in a few minutes."

Lori met some other girls at her table, and overall, they seemed like nice people.

Mrs. 'Z' came back to the microphone. "A snack has been prepared for you in the main kitchen, and if tables four and five, will please report this way to the side-kitchen," she said, pointing the direction, "and assist with the serving, we'll get started. Enjoy your snacks."

"That's us...we're table four," said Sue, rising. The room suddenly got noisy and lots of other girls headed for the 'name-tag' table. Lori noticed that Julie was one of them.

"Coming Lori?" asked Jill.

Lori dragged her attention toward the girls from her table. She followed Jill, a tall brunette, with shoulder length, slightly curly hair, and Sue fell in behind them. The other five were already entering the doorway of the side-kitchen.

Cookies, a banana, and juice, were the fare of the day, and as each girl picked up a tray full, Lori thought, *"I hope I don't spill any of these."* and then, setting her chin firmly, vowed... *"And I'm not going to serve her table, no matter what!"* She deliberately headed to the far side of the hall, near table six.

Mrs. 'Z' came back to the microphone, and announced, "Tables number two and six, if you please, will be responsible for clean-up, immediately after this snack-time. So, please stay here for a few minutes, after everyone else leaves."

"And, now, listen carefully! The Owls and the Ravens will be responsible for helping with dinner, and they should report to the kitchen at 5:30. Your cabin counselors will help you get organized. And... the Falcons and the Hawks will have 'clean-up' after dinner."

The room buzzed with confusion as girls figured out, that for right now, they were a certain table number, but mainly they went by their cabin names.

Mrs. 'Z' waited patiently, for them to get it straight. "Please pick up a schedule on your way out. After this snack time, your cabin counselors will be in your cabins, to help you get settled. They're very friendly people. I'm sure you'll like them!"

"By the way, if you have forgotten anything at home, something you really need, the camp store, next door, will be open for about 30 minutes. There we sell toothbrushes, tooth paste, soap, deodorant, post cards, stamps, hats, and shirts, etc. If we don't have something to take its place, come to my office, over here, in the corner of the mess hall and I'll let you call home. We plan a few, five-minute phone calls home in your tuition. So come on in, especially if you haven't made that important first call to let your parents know of your safe arrival."

"Enjoy your snacks and then, feel free to walk around and see the cabins and the paths in area right around here. Have fun, but don't walk around the sides of the lake, yet. You have free time until 6 p.m., when dinner will be served."

"We don't have any more duties right now," said Jill, finishing her last cookie. "Let's get your name tag Lori, and check out the activities."

"Good idea," said Sue.

Later, as the three girls stood by the long table, looking at their schedules, Lori said "I could really enjoy this place! Swimming at the lake, canoeing, archery, and even horseback riding."

Sue agreed, and Jill said, "I think I'll like it, too...a lot!"

"What cabin are you in, Lori?" asked Sue.

"The Falcons."

"Well, we're right next door in the Hawks cabin," said Jill. "C'mon, I want to go get my camera and walk down by the lake, okay?"

As the three girls left together, Lori looked over at Julie's table, and saw her in animated conversation with another pretty girl who had shoulder length auburn hair. *"Guess she's so used to being pretty, she doesn't feel comfortable talking to someone like me. I wonder what they could possibly be talking about?"*

The Camp

The three girls leisurely walked around the cabin areas, chatting and getting to know each other better. Lori noticed that all the cabins were built pretty much the same way, except for the counselors' cabins. They had larger lockers next to the bunks, and instead of a gang shower, there were three separate cubicles, with doors.

"Oh, sure!" said Sue, voicing Lori's own thoughts. "They get private showers!"

"Yeah," agreed Jill. "I'm going to *hate* having to shower in that big room!"

"I know just how you feel," said Lori.

When they went to cabins five-six and seven-eight, they were surprised to see that they also had individual showers, like the counselors' cabins, instead of gang showers.

"It's nice to see that Mrs. Z's getting more modern," said Lori. "Too bad we have to suffer, though."

"Yeah, that's for sure!" said Jill. "But look, they still have a big gang dressing area."

Sue added, "I hope I get used to it pretty quick. Otherwise, I'll be a basket case by the end of camp."

Next, they went to cabin four, where Sue and Jill would live as 'Hawks'. They stayed a few minutes, looking over the new faces and meeting people. Sue and Jill met their cabin counselor, 'Bigfoot', and asked her a few questions. Jill got her camera and said, "Let's go see your side Lori, and see if we know anyone else."

When they were cutting through the restroom area, Sue giggled and said, "She really does have big feet, doesn't she?'

Jill laughed and said, "Most of the staff have nicknames...but 'Bigfoot'?"

Lori said, "She seems to take it good naturedly...but I wouldn't want that to be my nickname, ever."

"Me neither," they both agreed.

As they entered her cabin and looked around the dorm area, Lori saw Gerri and waved at her. The counselor smiled and waved back.

"I already met Gerri," she said. "She's nice. C'mon, I'll introduce you."

Lori also saw that the pretty girl was moving in. And, Julie was helping her put her duffel bag on the last bunk...the one by the end window. *"Hm-m..."* she thought. *"I wonder what happened?"* Julie had already made up the last bunk before. *"Maybe the other girl needed to be by the extra window."*

Julie was moving her stuff closer to Lori...in the very next bunk.

Lori felt her breath catch, and her heart skip a beat. But then she thought gloomily, *"Now she moves closer to me. But they'll probably be talking together all the time."*

Then she thought stubbornly, *"I can find other people to talk to. I wonder who is going to be on the other side of me?"*

With her resolve up, she felt better. Although, she didn't really know why she couldn't just go in there and join their happy conversation. Then she thought, *"Maybe if I tried acting really friendly..."*

"That's my bunk right over there," she said, pointing, for her new friends' benefit, and she waved and forced a smile at Julie.

Noticing her, Julie just stopped in mid-sentence, kind of frowned, sort of waved, and went back to talking to her new friend.

"Who are they?" Sue asked.

"Come on. Let's go," said Lori. "The blonde is Julie. I don't know the other one, yet."

"Oh," the two said. Sue and Jill looked at each other and shrugged.

Outside

They went down to the lake, and marveled at how pretty it was. Everything was green and lush around the incredibly clear water. One area to the right was roped off for swimming lessons. And a wooden walkway led to a floating dock, separating the swimming area from the boating area. The camp's two row-boats were pulled far up on the beach. There was also a long, large wooden rack which held lots of upside-down canoes.

Jill asked, "Do you know how to swim, Lori?"

"Yes," she replied, "our school has swimming as a part of P.E. We get to go to the park swimming pool. Do you both know how?"

"No," said Jill.

"Me neither. I hope to learn here," said Sue.

As Lori looked off into the distance she was enchanted by the beautiful woods and paths surrounding the lake. She saw a small creek on the left side, coming down out of the hilly area and leading into the lake, and another creek on the right side, probably leading out of the lake. Each, had a small bridge over it. She was ready to explore everywhere.

"How long do you think it would take to walk around the lake?" asked Jill, having the same thoughts.

"I don't know. Maybe close to an hour."

"Look how clear that water is," said Sue. "There's no water anywhere near my house."

The trio walked around for a long time, just exploring a few short side-paths that were nearby, and taking some pictures of the beautiful majestic oak trees, and the lake, and of each other. In spite of small groups of campers walking here and there, the silence of the wilderness was becoming one of Lori's favorite things. She longed to know every part of it.

"Clang! Clang! Clang!" went the dinner bell.

"Let's go!" said Sue.

Orientation

"Hello, again," said Mrs. 'Z'. "Please be seated." The room got noisy as girls found their seats. She waited until everyone was seated and quiet.

"We have a tasty dinner for you, prepared by our kitchen staff, under the direction of Mrs. Watson. Dinner will be served immediately after this brief orientation.

"All events are scheduled by cabin names. Each of you should have gotten a brochure which tells the schedule of each daily event, cabin by cabin. Hang onto this schedule. You'll need it to refer to from day to day, week to week."

"Be on time to each activity. People who dawdle will cause the rest of the girls in the cabin to miss getting started on time. If you're used to your Mom waking you up each morning, that's okay, because, we will clang the big bell out front, to wake you up. But, if you're used to *'your Mommy'* coming back several times to wake you up, ...well, that could be a problem here."

Some girls were laughing at that, while others were looking down, trying not to 'own up' to that behavior. Lori didn't identify with that, because she didn't even want her stepmother to come into her room. She would rather rely on her own alarm clock, even though it didn't go off yesterday.

"So-o, help each other get up and out. You came here to have fun, and we want you to have the best time, ever! We'll teach you everything, including, 'how to make your bunk' properly if you haven't already done so. That will be tonight, after dinner and after the campfire.

Each cabin has its own permanent counselor, and while some of you shower and get ready for bed, she'll continue to help others get settled in. If you don't know something, just ask. Remember, we're all here for you. Cabin counselors are the people you'll get to know best. They go to all of your activities with you. They don't sleep with you in your cabins, because we feel you are old enough to have your cabins to yourselves, at night. But, if some of you are immature, we can change that arrangement for any and all cabins who seem to need the extra supervision." She waited as the campers moaned and groaned a little.

Then she introduced all of the individual cabin counselors. Lori was glad that Gerri was their counselor, because she seemed to always be happy and smiling.

Mrs. 'Z' continued. "Here are some of our rules, to help make sure you don't get hurt, or cause *us* any 'unnecessary' problems.

No going around barefoot unless showering or swimming.

No unsupervised swimming at all.

No night swimming, unless it's scheduled and supervised by us, with lights on, and lifeguards on duty.

No rough-housing. Act like 'ladies'.

17

No unsupervised horseback riding.
No leaving camp, without special permission.
We have lots more rules, but they'll be covered, later."

"All of you will need to help out in the mess hall, at breakfast, lunch, and dinner, on different days. There are ten tables in here, and we always need two girls per table to help before and after each meal."

"Will the girls from cabins #1 and #2, also known as the Owls and the Ravens, please stand up? Let's give these girls a hand. They've been here since 5:30, getting your tables ready for you."

After the applause died down, Mrs. 'Z' gave the invocation. Then, she said, "Now, if you girls will report to the side kitchen area of the mess hall, and help bring out the plates as they are passed out over the kitchen bar, and without rushing, please serve the tables. And the rest of you may begin eating, as soon as you get your plate, tonight."

There was a lot of commotion as dinner was served, but Lori didn't mind. She used the time to look around at all the faces. Julie was sitting at a different table and was facing the other direction. So Lori mostly listened to the campers at her table. It seemed to her that most of these girls were pretty immature in a lot of ways. Jill and Sue were her age, but they seemed about two years younger, somehow. *"Oh well,"* she thought, *"I'm pretty naive in a lot of ways, myself. I don't know how to go about getting a boyfriend. Jeez...I don't even know how to begin to flirt."*

Sue and Jill drew her into pleasant conversation. Dinner tasted great, and Lori felt really good being at camp, in spite of Julie.

Mrs. 'Z' interrupted during dessert, asking for everyone's attention. She explained that cabins #3, the Falcons, and #4, the Hawks, would be responsible for staying and helping to clean up, after dinner."

"That's us!" said Sue, "Both of our cabins!"

Mrs. 'Z' continued, "Mrs. Watson and her staff will be in the kitchen, at the dish washer. Your cabin counselors will help you to get organized, mostly out here, and also at the side kitchen."

"Tomorrow begins our regular schedule of all day KP duties. Please check the bulletin board for your cabin's 'KP' assignments. Your cabin counselors will make sure you get dismissed a little early from any regular camp activities in order to do this."

"Most of you have already made the call home, but if you haven't checked in with your parents yet, please come to my office after dinner. And beginning tomorrow night, we'll supply you with paper and pencils, and each of you will please, begin a letter home. Each day, during free time after lunch, or at night, before lights out, you can add a little more to the letter. We'll ask you to mail the letters in four days...sooner, if you have your letter ready. The mail comes every day except Sunday."

"Tonight is our first campfire, out at campfire circle down toward the lake. You will have about 30 minutes free time. "If you have any questions, I'll be here for awhile, along with some of the other counselors. Bye, girls...see you at the circle, at 7:30."

The room got very noisy as most of the girls started to leave.

After Dinner

After most of the girls were out of the mess hall, Gerri motioned for her girls to gather around her. Lori was glad she wasn't a yelling-type person.

Sue and Jill, were not included, because they had to go to a different part of the mess hall to meet with their own counselor, Bigfoot.

"Bye," said Lori. "Gotta go. Maybe I'll see you later."

"Bye," she heard back.

With the help of Gerri, all of them got introduced to each other. Then, she said, "Okay, Falcons, pick a partner."

Lori glanced at Julie, and wasn't surprised to see that her choice was Joann, her pretty new friend with the shoulder length auburn hair. *"Well, they both look like models...a blonde and a redhead,"* she thought, clenching her jaw.

And then Lori was thinking that two skinny girls, Liz and Nancy, looked like sisters. They both wore braids, and their blonde hair was exactly the same color. And they both even had freckles. She watched as they just naturally became a twosome.

Then a pleasant looking girl named Beth, came and stood in front of Lori, and asked, "Want to be my partner?"

Lori found herself looking at a wiry, athletic girl that was almost her own height, who had short brown curly hair and an easy smile. Lori smiled back and said, "Sure."

Within three minutes, everyone had a partner, and Gerri had the girls organized, and busily working. Beth and Lori were clearing tables. As she passed by people, Lori was trying to remember their names without looking at their name tags.

Lu, a very tall, gangly, athletic-looking girl with very short darkish blonde hair and her partner, Jen, were sweeping the floor.

Jen was sort of non-descript. She was of medium height, and had thick-brown, unruly, collar-length hair that seemed to go every which way. She also had deep-set, very small eyes. She looked somewhat flabby, yet muscular in a way, ...even 'tough'. They were a strange couple because they hardly talked to anyone, and they didn't even talk to each other as they swept the floor.

Nancy and Liz, 'the twin sisters' were sweeping the floor also. But they were talking to each other, a-mile-a-minute. Vivian and Ceil, two short, extremely 'heavy-set' girls, were busily scraping the trays into the garbage.

Beth worked well beside Lori, helping her gather up trays and silverware. Whenever Lori brought in a new stack of trays, Vivian and Ceil, who joked constantly, usually kidded with her about bringing too many, too fast.

But, it was as if Lori didn't exist for Julie and Joann, who were stacking the scraped trays and pushing them across the counter to the kitchen staff. They were in their own little world at the side-bar, and were very much absorbed in their own conversation. So, Lori decided to concentrate on Beth, and to try and have some fun. *"After all...that's what I'm here for,"* she thought.

Before long, the two partners were actually laughing and joking. And Lori realized that Beth might turn out to be her real camp buddy...that is, if she didn't already have another best friend.

Lori noticed that Lu and Jen now seemed to be sweeping the floor, close to whatever table she and Beth were clearing. And they still weren't talking to each other much at all. *"Maybe they just like listening to us, joking around,"* thought Lori.

"Do you have any other friends here, Beth?"

"Nope. This is my first camp experience."

"Yeah, mine, too. Maybe we could be partners for horseback riding, ...or swimming."

"Okay," said Beth, and Jen's broom hit the floor with a loud bang. Beth flinched and Lori looked up to see Jen looking at them with a sullen glare.

"Are you okay?" asked Lori.

"I could be better!" was the clipped reply from Jen as she picked up the broom.

Beth and Lori looked at each other, shrugged, and headed toward the side bar with containers full of silverware.

"What was that all about?" asked Beth.

"I have no idea," said Lori.

Later, everyone was almost done in the side-kitchen. Lori stretched up to put some salt shakers up on a shelf...and... Crash!

Julie bumped right into her side, causing Lori to drop three salt shakers... It also caused Julie to drop all of her dinner trays. They were plastic, and along with the shakers, made a lot of racket as they bounced all over the floor.

"Sorry!" said Julie, wide-eyed. She was not used to *ever* being clumsy or klutzy in any way. If she had ever bumped somebody like that in dance class, her teacher would've been truly amazed.

When she looked up and saw that Lori had such a look of surprise on her face, Julie said, "I'm *really sorry!* I was looking back over my shoulder at Joann, and... here,... I'll get them!"

21

But, Lori was already beginning to crouch down to retrieve the shakers, just as Julie started to kneel down, too.

Julie whacked knees really hard with Lori. Both girls bounced backwards, and landed flat on their butts. "Oh-h... Now look what I've done!" moaned Julie.

Joann and Beth couldn't help themselves, and started giggling and laughing. And pretty soon, so did everyone else who was nearby. Ceil and Vivian just naturally laughed the hardest, and the loudest.

If this had happened at school, for everyone to see, Julie would've been so mortified that she probably would've been absent the next day... Her self image was that of a graceful, ballerina dancer, not a clumsy person, and *never, never*, a buffoon. She really just wanted to crawl under the floor and hide, as she glanced from face to face.

Lori started to 'frown' at Julie for being so careless, ...but then she saw that Julie had little tears rolling down her cheeks.

Julie forced herself to look at Lori and managed to ask, "Are you okay?"

Lori's frown turned into a confused look. And, then with a sigh, she said, "It's okay. Don't worry. I'm fine, honest. Are you okay? Did you hurt yourself?"

Julie didn't answer. She just looked down at the floor.

Meanwhile, Beth reached down, to help her new partner up. And as Lori looked back down at Julie, she thought, *"She's not so... so... uppity after all...she's just..." well I don't know what she is, but at least she's not a complete snob."* And from within her, she felt a new feeling starting, ...one of self satisfaction and of being just as good as...

"You okay?" asked Beth, bending down to retrieve the shakers...

"Yeah, thanks, Beth".

Lori watched Joann help Julie up, and also help her pick up the scattered trays. Joann started kidding her, and finally, Lori saw Julie almost smile as they were leaving.

Following Beth out to the main hall, Lori sighed and said, "Guess I looked pretty silly, huh, sitting on my butt, like a 6-year old kid?"

"Actually, you looked kind of cute," whispered a raspy voice from just behind her.

Lori wheeled around to face Jen. The expression on Jen's face was strange. It made Lori almost shiver.

"Yeah, ...right!" said Lori, ...her mood changing instantly. "What's it to you?"

"Nothing, not now, anyway," said Jen, putting away her broom. "Bye, we're outta here. Let's go to the campfire, Lu."

"What did she say?" asked Beth, who had not been close enough to hear the whispered remark.

"Nothing worth repeating," said Lori. And she just stared at their backs as they walked away, trying to figure it all out. *"Lewd,"* she said in her mind. *"Not a word I've ever thought about using before, but if I did, it would probably be about a 'dirty old man'...not a teenage girl."*

"She tries to sound mysterious," said Beth.

"Yeah, I noticed..."

"Well, I've decided that she's really strange," said Beth.

"Seems that way," said Lori. "Anyway, we're done here. C'mon, I want to see if Mrs. 'Z' will let me call home. Then we'll go to the campfire, okay?"

"Sure. I'm ready."

When Lori got off the phone, Beth asked, "Did you get your dad?"

"No. I waited this late, thinking he'd be home by now, but he was at a meeting. He'll get the message, I hope."

"Who did you talk to?"

"Maude, ...my stepmother."

"Oh," said Beth, sensing that she'd have to know Lori much better before that subject would be discussed. She found herself wondering if it would ever be talked about because Lori wouldn't even tell her what Jen had said. Beth realized that she had chosen a partner that seemed to be very close-mouthed. *"Oh well, guess I'll just have to get all the gossip from other people,"* she mused.

The Campfire

All around the campfire circle, big fat logs had been placed, two-deep, providing lots of places for people to sit. Each cabin counselor sat in a special area, with her girls around her. Most of the Falcons went and sat by Gerri, but Lori and Beth went and stood by the fire. The stars were brilliant. The air was cool, and it felt good, up close to the fire, to be warm in the front and cool in the back.

Beth was telling Lori about her school and some of her friends. Lori was just looking at her, and listening. She glanced over at Julie and Joann. They were talking together, as usual. And, no doubt, about boys...because Joann was forming a 'vee' with her hands like a boy's torso, down to a small waist. And Julie made a face and flexed an arm muscle pose, as they cracked up laughing together.

Lori turned back, and chatted with Beth, for awhile, happy to find out that her partner enjoyed sports a lot. Then they went and sat with the rest of their group. After the fire settled down quite a bit, they followed several other campers and went to the food table, where they picked up a couple of coat hangers and several marshmallows to roast. They had to straighten out the hangers first, but they were soon 'browning' their marshmallows. Lori didn't want to burn hers, so she was turning it over and over.

After they had and eaten a couple, Julie and Joann came passing by them to get hangers. On the way back, Julie came up to Lori, and said, "I'm so sorry I knocked you down in there. I hope you really are okay."

"Don't worry. I'm fine. Actually, it got to be pretty funny," Lori said, smiling.

"Yeah, I guess," said Julie, but she didn't smile. "Say, how did you get your hanger undone at the top to straighten it?"

Before Lori could even start to answer, Joann said, "Here...let me show you," as she took Julie's hanger from her. They walked away, shoulder to shoulder, twisting and pulling on the hanger.

With her last marshmallow browned to her satisfaction, Lori turned to leave the fire and get some graham crackers and chocolate to make a 'some more' sandwich. Beth followed, blowing out her own marshmallow, which was in a 'ball of flame'.

"I think I'll pass on the Hershey, tonight," said Lori. "It's all just too sweet." She smushed her marshmallow between two crackers, and began to enjoy.

So did Beth, but she added the chocolate, too.

"M-m-m, that was good!" said Lori. Then, noticing a few girls and a counselor heading down to the waterfront, she asked, "Want to walk down by the lake?"

"Sure," said Beth, struggling to get crumbly, sticky stuff inside her mouth. "Just a minute... *the s'more's...* ooh...it's all over my chin!"

"C'mon, 'goo ball', the lake's not far. You can wash up there," said Lori, starting to walk, then walking a little faster, and then starting to trot. Beth started running fast, caught up, and then tried to pass her by. They sprinted around a few girls on the path, and ran to the boating area, arriving in a tie.

"It's a good thing the path is lighted," gasped Beth, slowing down as she neared the water's edge. After washing her face and hands, she said, "Boy, I wish we had night swimming here, even though this water is really cold!"

"Yeah. That *would* be neat," agreed Lori, as she gazed out over the dark water. She looked up, and could see the stars even better, away from the fire. "Do you know any of the constellations?" she asked, adding, "The only things I know are the North Star and the Big Dipper."

"No," said Beth. "But when I look up at all those stars, it makes me feel very small."

"Definitely," said Lori. "For me, it's like being in church, ...only better somehow."

They were both silent for several minutes.

"Come on," said Beth. "Don't you think we should get back to the fire?"

Reluctantly, Lori turned toward the noisy group.

When they got back, Lori glanced around to see what people were doing. She did a double-take on Jen, who seemed to be locked-in on her, just staring and glaring. She could feel Jen's eyes still on her, even after she and Beth sat down.

"Now, what?" she thought. *"I wish I could read minds. But, no, that might not be good,"* she decided, dreading what Julie probably really thought of her. She didn't look back at Jen. Instead, she got involved in the conversation right around her, with Beth, Ceil and Vivian. She found herself thinking about how certain people, like these two very fun-loving, very large girls had teamed up together, just sort of naturally.

It turned out that Bigfoot had a beautiful voice, and she started the group singing all sorts of campfire songs. Lori didn't know most of them, but lots of girls did, and all the voices blended soothingly in the crisp, cool air.

Finally, Mrs. 'Z' announced, "That's it for the campfire! For the next 60 minutes, your counselors will be in your cabins, to answer any questions you might have. Please get your showers, get your bunks ready, and be prepared for 'bed check' and then for 'lights out', in exactly one hour."

Donna Kelli

"After that, you can sit on each other's bunks, and talk all night, if you like, but we start each day, very early in the morning. The bell will be rung at 6:30 a.m., so be sure and get *some* sleep. Your counselors will be outside, around your cabin area, for awhile after lights out. Call one of them, if you need something important. After that, you'll have to go to their cabin and knock on their door. Good night, girls. Sleep well."

"Good night, Mrs. Zee-e," chorused almost eighty voices.

Shower Time

Lori and Beth walked Sue and Jill to the Hawks' side of the double cabin, said their goodnights, and then went into their own side.

"Where's your bunk?" asked Lori.

"This one," said Beth. She was in the first bunk, closest to the showers, but two bunks away from Lori. She was also directly across the aisle from the foot of Lu's bunk. As Lori glanced that way, she saw Lu and Jen at their lockers. Jen froze in place, and once again locked in on Lori's eyes.

Beth started gathering up her bathroom kit, her towel, and her pajamas. "Want me to wait for you?" she asked.

"No, thanks," said Lori, looking down at the floor. "I'll be there in a minute or two." As she walked toward her own locker, she could still feel Jen's eyes burning into her back. Trying to put the strange girl out of her mind, she watched Gerri showing Vivian how to tuck in her sheets and blanket, really tight. Lori decided that her own bunk was okay and she started gathering her stuff together. Finally, dreading having to get naked in front of everybody, she said quietly to herself, "Here goes nothing."

Just inside the gang shower was the dressing area, with four benches, placed in a double 'L' shape. Several girls had already hung up their clothes, pajamas and towels on the hooks on the walls, behind the benches. Lori saw that no one got her towel until she was *done* showering. That meant, she'd have nothing to hide behind, coming and going. *"Definitely not like showering at school,"* she thought. She sighed, sat down on the bench, and took off her sneakers and socks. The only Falcons showering so far, were 'the twin sisters', Nancy and Liz...and Beth. Lori didn't know the names of all the Hawks, yet, from next door, but there were several showering, already. Sue and Jill hadn't come in yet.

"Come on in. The water's nice and hot," said Beth.

"Be right there," she said, unbuttoning her blouse. She hung everything up, and started searching in her kit for her soap. She always liked to be clean. Especially now that she was going to... *"She was going to be right next to Julie,"* she admitted, rolling her eyes at herself, *"in the very next bunk."*

Mad at herself for having such weird thoughts, she grabbed the bar of soap, and headed to the shower next to Beth. She soaped herself thoroughly, and without thinking, even started using the bar of soap on her hair.

"Want to borrow my shampoo?" asked Beth.

"What? Oh...thanks! I forgot to bring my bottle." As she poured shampoo in her hair, Lori grumbled to herself, "Beth must think I'm a 'country bumpkin' for sure."

The noise level jumped as several other girls entered the bench area and started undressing. Soon, the shower room was full of loud whoops and hollers as naked girls tried to quickly adjust the very, very cold water, to warm. Even more girls came in, and shared shower heads.

Lori couldn't help looking at all the naked bodies...short, tall, skinny, chubby. Big butts, almost no butts...big breasts, no breasts. Some girls were brazenly uncaring if anyone looked at them. Others were trying to cover their chests with their arms. And one girl was trying to cover her chest with one arm, and her pubic area with her other hand.

This was definitely not like school, where everybody had a curtain to hide behind.

Lori was torn between hurrying out, so nobody would just stare at her, and waiting a few more minutes to see if Julie would come in. *"Why? Why do I need to see her? I'm getting really 'nuts', here,"* she thought.

Sue and Jill came in, and waved at her and Beth. Then Lori's thoughts were distracted by the silliness of several of the girls. They started throwing wet wash rags at each other and some, scored a few direct hits. Lori was beginning to enjoy the show, and had to dodge a few soggy missiles herself. She forgot, for the moment, to be embarrassed.

Turning back to Beth, she said, "Boy, this hot water feels great!"

"Yeah, just heavenly," said Beth. "But I think I'm done now."

"It's so relaxing," said Lori. "I think I'll enjoy it a bit longer." She closed her eyes and let the water pound on her face.

"Okay. See you in a few minutes," said Beth, turning off her shower.

Lori turned a little more, and watched her go across the floor to get her towel. *"She's almost as bashful as I am,"* she thought, seeing Beth, with her arms crossed over her chest, and not looking at anyone. She was just staring at the floor.

Lori saw Julie and Joann entering the dressing area, and she turned her face, quickly, back to the shower spray. *"Can't let her see me looking,"* she thought, guiltily. *"Jeez!"* she shouted in her mind, as her face scrunched up and she closed her eyes as tight as they'd go. *"I must be one of those 'peeping Tom' people! A... A voy...voy-something.!"*

She put her face even closer to the shower head, as if to wash away the new label, and stayed there for several minutes...

"Maybe it's just 'natural curiosity'," she hoped, as she felt herself turning back around to look for Julie. She squinted as the water pounded on the back of her head, and her eyes settled on a very goose-bumpy Julie, straight across from her. She was ready to turn back again, but Julie's entire face and chest were

covered with soap, and she was just letting the water pound on her back. Lori had a rare, 'unobserved' chance to look at her.

As Lori watched Julie standing under the spray, she was struck by her posture.

"She even holds herself in good posture when she's getting soaped up," she thought. *"...in fact, the way she holds herself up so straight...her back is never slouched over."*

"Her chest is always sort of 'out forward'...And the way her breasts look, so pert and all. She felt herself turning red at her own thoughts, but she couldn't turn her brain off. *"Not too big, and not too small...Her breasts are so...so... 'cute',"* she decided. *"There's so much about her I like. And, especially, I like to watch her move."* Lori sighed, and thought, *"She is definitely a picture of grace and beauty... really different from <u>any</u> other girls I know, and, somehow, as my Literature teacher would say, "something to behold."*

And then, one pink nipple peeked out from under soap bubbles at her. Lori burned even redder and glanced around quickly, to see if anyone was noticing...her...well...her 'spying'.

No one was. So she observed a few other people and saw that most girls, like herself, had brown nipples...except for Julie and a couple of others... *"And strange,"* she thought, *"she has such light blonde hair, but her...her pubic hair is black, just like her eye lashes and eyebrows."*

She watched Julie turn back around, and then she looked at her graceful shoulders, her back and her buttocks. *"Really firm, and smooth...nice,"* she thought, now ignoring her own ever present, bothersome blush. She glanced around at others.

Joann's was a little 'lumpy'. *"Funny,"* she mused. *"Joann is sort of a skinny girl...to have such a fat rear end. I wonder why Julie's not lumpy, since she doesn't seem to do any sports at all? I don't remember seeing her anywhere much during our sophomore or junior year."*

"Hi," oozed an almost syrupy sweet voice right next to her. "Remember me? My name's Jen. And this is Lu," continued Jen. She and Lu moved into Beth's empty spot.

Lori forced herself to turn around and meet their eyes. "Oh, uh, yes." she mumbled, and then she looked down at the floor, so she wouldn't be staring at their nakedness.

Lu just stood there glaring, with water pounding down on her shoulders.

Lori recognized them both, all too well. Then she felt self-conscious and turned back facing the wall.

"Boy! Are you bashful!" said Jen. And then, in a lower voice, she said, "You shouldn't be... You have a *great* body." Lu said nothing, but she sort of snorted and started getting soapy.

29

Lori could feel the burning redness creeping up her neck, and even by her ears. She turned back to the wall, thinking to herself, *"Oh God. What do you say to that? I've got to get out of here."*

"Don't be embarrassed," continued Jen. "You're better built than almost every girl at camp."

"What?" gasped Lori. "No, I'm not," she blurted.

"Oh, so you've been looking, too, huh?"

"What?"

"Nothing." Then, Jen added, "Want me to wash your back?"

"What? No, ...uh, ...No!" said Lori, turning her back on Jen. "I'm done."

And, with that, Lori turned off the water and headed for her towel. She felt anger building inside her toward Jen and Lu, for interrupting her chance to look around. *"And what comes out of her mouth!"* she thought. She started remembering the incidents in the mess hall.

She was so incensed that she didn't realize that she had dried herself off, then walked around the wall to the restroom and sink area and finished brushing her teeth, ...all, while she was totally nude. She had gone back to pick up her clothes and her shorty pajamas, at the bench, and had even gone all the way to her bunk, still in the nude, drying one last spot on her back. Finally, at her bunk, she put on her pj's, hung up her towel on the hook part of her locker, and put her stuff in the locker. Then, she sank down on her bunk and put her head on her pillow, just staring at the ceiling, still 'lost in thought'. All of a sudden, she missed Hattie, terribly, thinking, *"Good old Hattie...someone who was stable, and always there...even if she was a pain now and then."*

"That was fast," said Beth, who came up, and sat down on the foot of Lori's bunk.

Liz came over and sat down, too, saying, "I wish I could be 'un-bashful', like you, Lori. You know, to just forget anyone else is in the room, while I'm drying off and dressing."

"What?" said Lori, and thinking back, she realized she'd been walking across the room, drying that one last spot, on her back... and picturing herself, with her chest out... while she dried that spot. Her chest had been out there for all to see!

"Oh, no, I must've been a sight, looking like a 'show-off' or something," she said. Again she felt the red creeping up her neck, as she looked around quickly, to see who else had noticed her parade.

All the girls in the cabin seemed to be busy, getting dressed, or putting away their belongings. No one was looking at her, except Jen and Lu, as they started dressing by their bunks. Jen smiled warmly at her. Lu glared at her.

"They saw me!" thought Lori.

And then, Jen nodded, and winked at her.

"She thinks I was...was... 'strutting' back around the bench area, for her to see!" thought Lori. Gritting her teeth, she turned back to Beth, who was now, also looking at Jen and Lu.

Lori said, "I forgot myself. I was so mad at Jen."

"Why? What did she do?" asked Liz, as she combed out her unbraided hair.

"She just makes stupid remarks, trying to embarrass me, I guess."

"What's *not* embarrassing?" asked Liz. "There's no privacy!"

"You said a mouthful," agreed Beth.

"Amen," said Lori.

Liz added, "I have to write my name bigger on my towel. Mine got buried under two others, and it took me ages and ages to be sure I'd found the right one! It seemed like I stood there forever, absolutely naked, for all to see!"

Lori and Beth laughed at her, and Lori could just see her flustered at times like Hattie.

"Do you have a magic marker?" she asked them both.

"I do," said Beth. "C'mon." And they left to go to Beth's locker.

Julie and Joann came by, already dressed in their pajamas. Lori noticed that Julie wore 'shortys' too, and then wondered how Joann would be able to sleep in a head full of big curlers.

"Lights out in 30 minutes!" called out Gerri, in the doorway. "Bed check in 25."

31

Before Lights Out

Joann and Julie put their clothes away, and Julie got out her yearbook. The two of them sat on Julie's bunk with their backs toward Lori. Beth and Liz were still over by Beth's locker re-marking Liz's towel. There was still awhile before lights out, and Lori felt out of place being on the fringe of their conversation.

As they paged through Julie's yearbook Joann said, "Boy! You're popular! Look how many times you're in here!"

"Yeah. It was a fun year," said Julie.

"Who's your boyfriend?"

"This year it was a wrestler named Allen. Mike, probably, this next year. He's a wrestler, too. He's 6' 2", real sweet, and very, very handsome."

"You don't like any football players?"

"Well, yes. I've sort of dated three, but nothing serious.

Lori found herself thinking, *"Mike's 'okay'. At least he asked me to sign his yearbook. And, he sort of 'flirted' a little."* But, then she felt very much like an eavesdropper, so she just got up and went over to Beth's bunk, and sat at the foot. "Did you bring your yearbook?" she asked Beth.

"No. Did you?"

"No, I didn't even think of it."

Lori looked back at Julie and Joann, thinking, *"Why can't I simply join them in their conversation at any time?"* She just rolled her eyes at herself and her own stupidity. *"I should've just gone over and sat with them!"* She watched as Ceil and Vivian went over to sit on Joann's bunk, and started looking at pictures, too. "What's wrong with me?"

"I don't know," said Beth. "Half the time I don't know what's wrong with me, either."

Again Lori just rolled her eyes upwards, thinking, *"Jeez!. Out loud! ...she's got me talking to myself now, out loud."* She remembered signing 'Jolly Lori' in Judy's yearbook. *"Pretty soon they're going to start calling me 'Loony Lori' for sure,"* she thought, frowning deeply.

She glanced over her shoulder and noticed that Liz had joined Nancy and they were talking to Lu and Jen. They were looking at the camp brochures, and quietly joking around. At least Jen wasn't staring at her anymore! She looked back at Beth, who was saying, "...and then, my sister was being a real brat, because she kept sneaking my yearbook out of my suitcase."

Lori thought, *"I'm not a very good friend to Beth. I wasn't even paying attention to her."*

"Hey, Lori! Don't be hiding way over there with Beth!" shouted Ceil. "Come over here and defend yourself! What are you doing in this yearbook so *many* times?"

"Yeah," said Vivian, "what's this picture supposed to be, anyway? It looks like you're standing on this girl's back."

Jen heard the comments and immediately got up and headed to the back of the cabin to see the pictures. Lu was right behind her and said, smugly, as she passed by Lori's shoulder, "Care if I go sit on your bunk, Lori?" She didn't wait for an answer.

Beth got up also, saying, "Come on, Lori. I want to go see." Liz and Nancy were following right behind Lu, and Nancy said, "Come on Lori! Show us. Were you really standing on some girl's back?"

Lori reluctantly stood up and walked back to the little crowd of girls. As she reached the aisle between Joann and Julie's bunk, she looked down at Julie, who was right in the middle of everyone, but not smiling. She had a little frown on her face. It seemed that Julie was surprised to find out that Lori had her picture in the yearbook two more times than she did. Ceil had counted them all and announced it to everyone.

Lori decided, *"Julie doesn't really want me to come over here."* But finally she gave in to the girls who were repeating, "Come on, Lori!"

"Don't be bashful," they said, as they made room for her to sit down right in the center, between the 'large' ones, Vivian and Ceil.

"Oh, Wow!" she thought. *"Joann's bunk might break in half in the next few seconds."* Slowly, she sat down. The bunk sagged but didn't break. All ten girls scrunched together now on Julie's and Joann's bunks. Even Gerri came over to see what all the hoop-la was about.

Before long, Lori was explaining several silly-looking pictures, like the high leap she had made while doing a 'jump shot' in basketball, and it *did* look like she was standing on another girl's back.

Then she started hearing little comments, like... "I'm glad I don't have to play against you!" "I'm glad you're a Falcon!" "This cabin always gets to stay together as a team, right?" "Boy! You're really great, Lori!"

Lori wasn't comfortable with compliments, ...she had never been. She never knew what to say, or how to accept them graciously. So, the most she ever said, was, a simple "Thanks." To say anything more, would've seemed to her like she agreed with them completely, ...like she thought she was the greatest. But she didn't think that way at all.

She was very much aware of her own limitations. Her dad had always told her, "No matter how great you are, there's always somebody better. You haven't seen anyone in the high schools yet, but when you get to college, you'll meet lots of them." And Lori believed him.

For years, she had been accustomed to putting up with girls saying things like, "Oh, no!" "Not you!" "Do we have to play against you?" She accepted their rejections quietly, but sometimes it really hurt. She was even more used to 'down-playing' her own ability, in order to seem more 'normal' and to be acceptable to others.

So, tonight as usual, she occasionally said things like, "Yeah, I paid the coach five dollars to put me in the game, that day." and "That shot was just a lucky one." and "I think that other runner tripped a little in that race."

Some of her cabin mates believed her tales. Lu thought she must be a little freaky, and planned on watching Lori play sports here at camp, to see if she was really good, or not. It was possible that her high school just didn't have many 'good' girl-athletes at all, and Lori happened to be the best they had.

Lori took advantage of a lull in the comments directed at her, to look at Julie, who was telling about one of her pictures. *"She's right at home in the middle of these girls. Maybe one day I'll feel comfortable, too."* But then, the next moment she was wondering, *"Isn't anyone getting sleepy, in this crowd?"* She immediately scolded herself, thinking, *"It's not polite to be bored,"* and she turned her attention back to the hovering little crowd.

Jen showed the most interest in the yearbook. When Gerri finally announced, "Okay, Falcons, 'bed check'!" ...Jen asked Julie if she could look at her book again, the next day.

Then it seemed to Lori, like she heard "Good night," a hundred times as all the girls got up and left. She moved over on her own bunk and thought, *"I'm glad that's over."*

"Finally," thought Lori, when the lights went out. She stretched out in her bunk to get comfortable. She hoped camp was going to be more fun than this. *"Archery, in the morning,"* she told herself optimistically.

"Good night, Dad," she thought, smiling.

In spite of all the muffled conversations going on around her, Lori was asleep in less than fifteen minutes.

Morning

With her face still half-buried in her pillow, Lori sleepily forced open her left eye. As she focused it, she saw Julie's sleeping face only a few feet away, and suddenly she remembered where she was. Everything was quiet, and she wondered if she was the only one awake. Without moving, she stared at Julie, wondering how a girl who seemed to be so 'stand-offish' ninety percent of the time could look so non-threatening when she was sound asleep.

Soft blonde curls partly covered Julie's cheek. And thick, black eyelashes, ...so long that they seemed false, moved rhythmically as her eyelids twitched in 'dream sleep'. Lori knew from all her reading in Psychology class, that Julie was dreaming, and her eyes were moving under closed eyelids, 'watching the dream'. Lori wondered what she was dreaming about, but then, her eyes settled on Julie's lips. All other thoughts left her as she gazed at them. They were naturally pink, very pouty, and perfectly formed ...with a distinct outline around the edges. Her bottom lip was a little fuller, and her top lip almost came to a point in the middle. At that moment, Julie pursed her lips together as though she was getting ready to kiss someone. Somewhere in her memory, from one of the old movie actresses Maude watched on TV, she recalled the term, a 'rosebud' mouth, and decided that description fit Julie's lips perfectly.

"Funny, ...I never thought of myself as a 'lip' person'," thought Lori, *"...that is, until now."* She pictured her dad's lips and smiled...then, Maude's lips and cringed, almost saying "yuck!" out loud.

As Julie dreamed on, she pouted her lips even more, a little, 'this' way, and then, 'that' way, making funny little expressions. Lori thought to herself, *"Her lips are attractive, ...very attractive, and very...sensual."* A feeling of guilt started to creep over Lori and she decided not to look at Julie for even one more second.

But just then, in her sleep, Julie started blushing. It was intriguing to see the light red tinge creeping up into her cheek, and finally settling into a deep blush. Lori was fascinated, and found herself feeling a little enchanted by the girl. But she also felt very distanced from her...like there was an invisible wall between them. She wondered if they would ever get to be friends...

All of a sudden, a loud, clanging bell shattered the silence and she watched as Julie sat straight up in bed, looking confused.

"God that's loud!" said Joann, and Julie turned toward her and agreed with her. From the moans and groans around the cabin, it seemed that lots of girls were wishing they had gone to sleep sooner. Lori put her pillow over her head for a couple of minutes, trying to decide if this would be better than her stepmother's voice every morning. *"Oh, well,"* she thought, *"maybe I'll be able to learn to wake up every day a few minutes before they ring that gong."*

She got up, dressed quickly, and started performing her morning toilette. Beth joined her quietly at the sink, as they both brushed their teeth. The bathroom area was getting really crowded and noisy as they left. Neither of them were much for jabbering the first thing in the morning.

Later, in the mess hall, she and Beth sat with Jill and Sue. They were full of fun stories about pranks that had gone on in their cabin last night, like 'short-sheeting' one girl. And they couldn't stop talking about the eerie ghost stories that another girl had told. None of the Hawks had gotten much sleep.

Mrs. 'Z' greeted them and answered a lot of questions about the schedule for the day. Then they had breakfast. And finally, it was time to go to their first activity.

Lori looked at Beth and smiled and said, "Archery. Yes! A physical activity, at long last."

Archery I

Archery class met in front of the Falcons' cabin for the first session. Miss Butler, alias 'Fletch', asked the girls to raise their hands if they'd ever had archery, and then she assigned them to a partner who had not had any experience yet. Lori couldn't believe it when she ended up with Julie as her assigned partner, and Beth ended up with Joann.

Lori had taken P.E. every year, in school, and archery wasn't new to her. She was looking forward to shooting again, and didn't mind that they all had to go get the equipment and help carry it to the archery field. But, as usual, she could hardly wait to 'just get into the sport, and do it'... so it was very difficult to patiently listen to all of the instruction. She found herself day dreaming.

She was very much aware of Julie, next to her. And, she didn't know if Julie was 'very unhappy' at their assignment, or, just plain 'unhappy'. There was no doubt in her mind that Julie would've preferred to be with Joann.

Finally, they were assigned their alleys to shoot in. Lori didn't know how to approach Julie, or anything to say to her, so she just shot her own six arrows. Four of them hit the target on the edge of the right-hand side...

Julie, on the other hand, was a complete disaster. Fletch had been watching from nearby, and said, "Good, Lori! Maybe you can help others. Maybe, start with your partner," and she winked, and went on to the next twosome.

Lori looked around for Gerri, thinking that she'd be better at helping Julie, but the cabin counselor was at the other end of the line of girls, helping Vivian. Lori saw that Julie's arrow kept swinging out into thin air, horizontally, away from her bow. And then, usually, it fell on the ground.

"Would you like me to help you?" asked Lori.

"No!" was the abrupt reply. But then, after the next arrow fell on the ground... "Well, all right..." Julie sighed with extreme aggravation as she bent down to pick up the arrow.

Lori took a deep breath, walked closer to her and said, "Here, start like this." And she calmly notched her arrow on the string.

"That's what I did before!" Julie protested.

"And then, ...you hook your first two fingers over the string, like this, ...instead of using your thumb to grab the arrow."

"That looks really strange!" said Julie. She tried it, and after putting her fingers 'just so', she mumbled, "Feels strange, too."

Lori could feel a slight smile starting on her own cheeks, because of the funny little changing expressions on Julie's face as she concentrated so intently.

"Try it, slowly," Lori said, thinking she had seen the hint of dimples, but Julie wasn't smiling.

Julie turned toward the target and managed to pull back the string, without the arrow falling off to the side. But, she let her fingers slip off the string too soon, and the arrow shot out about fifteen feet.

"Watch out!" said Lori. "You're dan..." she almost said 'dangerous' out loud. But she stopped because she saw that Julie was cringing, absolutely humiliated. "Here...let me show you how to do the rest," she offered.

But, as she approached Julie again, the girl looked down, ...shutting her out.

"Boy...she's going to be tough," thought Lori, but she continued talking softly as if nothing had happened. "The next thing you do, after you 'notch' the arrow, is to turn your bow almost straight up, and...Wait. You don't have a 'wrist guard'. Here, ...you can use mine..."

Lori took hers off, and glanced up to see Julie, intently looking at her from only about eighteen inches away. Lori found herself looking into blue eyes, ...very clear, *light* blue eyes, with a distinct, black outline around the pretty, blue iris. *"I've never seen that before,"* she thought, more than a little distracted.

"Uh, ...here, ...give me your wrist."

Tentatively, Julie started to put out her right hand.

"No, the other one." said Lori.

Julie drooped her shoulders, in resigned failure. "I'm terrible at sports," she said.

"Don't worry, we all do dumb stuff, ...especially me."

Lori reached out in order to put the wrist band on Julie's left wrist, but as she touched Julie's skin, she jerked back as if she'd burned herself.

"What's the matter?" asked Julie. "Should I turn my hand over?"

"No...I..." Lori reached out again, forcing herself to take Julie's hand in hers, and gently, turn it back in the right direction. As she buckled the straps, she glanced up, and saw Julie looking downward, at the buckles. *"Good thing,"* she thought. *"My face has to be red. It feels like it's burning. What's wrong with me?"* she demanded of herself, frowning. *"She's not a 'goddess' or anything...so...why should I be afraid to touch her?"* Lost in thought, Lori held the last buckle in her fingers, just staring at it.

"Lori? Lori, are you okay?"

With a 'pop', she came back to the present.

"Are you sick?" asked Julie.

"No...no, I'm fine." "C'mon," she said. "Next, you do, just what I do... okay?" She forced herself to think about the mechanics of a good archery shot. And, she slowed everything down. She even spoke slowly. The next thing she knew, she had finally 'loosed' her arrow... and it found the target. *"Almost a bulls-eye,"* she thought, gratefully.

Julie shot then also, and her arrow fell just short of the target.

"Better!" said Lori. "Much better."

"This is hard!" said Julie.

"Yeah, most new things are."

"Stop shooting!" came a loud voice. "Retrieve arrows!"

The entire group laid down their bows at the shooting line, and everybody went to look for arrows. Lots of girls were complaining about the wrist bands getting in their way. Others, who had not bothered to use the bands, had red welts on the inside of their left arms, since everybody happened to be right-handed.

"Everyone toe the line! And shoot when ready!" said Fletch, loudly.

They continued shooting and retrieving.

Lori moved so that she was standing to Julie's left, and a little behind her, so she could observe her stance, and her release. "Keep your right elbow up," she coached, "and aim a little higher."

"Oops! Over the target!" said Julie.

"Well, at least you're strong enough."

"And don't forget *dangerous*!" responded Julie, sarcastically.

"Sorry I said that," said Lori. "Here, take my last two arrows."

Then, as she watched Julie aiming, she thought, *"She could be an athlete. She's got good legs, and that nice posture, and her cute figure. Cute figure! Darn! What's happening to me? This has got to stop! Why should I care one little bit about her figure?"*

"How was that?" asked Julie, with her tongue in her cheek.

"Great, ...just great!"

"Great? But I missed!"

"Oh, ...uh, ...well, your form is, ...is much better. Try the last arrow."

While Julie was pulling the string back, and aiming, Lori heard, "Oh, no! My hair!"

"What's wrong?" Lori went closer, to see.

"My hair's caught in the feathers!"

"Let's see," said Lori, softly. "Don't move... Boy, ...you really are 'tangled'. And it's not just in the feathers, ...it's caught all around the string, too."

"What a klutz I am!" said Julie.

"No, ...you're not," said Lori in her same calm voice. "Hold still."

"Everybody's looking!"

"No one is looking. Just hold still, and I'll get it undone." Tentatively, she started untangling the first few strands of hair. "Am I hurting you?"

"No...I'm fine. Sorry to be such a bother."

"No problem." Then Lori realized that she was very, very close to Julie just now, and her breath caught in her chest. She continued to gently tug on knotted hairs. Finally, as she dared to breathe, out and then in, Lori noticed the light, powdery fragrance of Julie's perfume. *"Mmm, that's so-o nice,"* she thought, as she closed her eyes and slowly, took in another long, deep breath. Then, afraid that she might get caught, she stopped breathing and finished the last few knots. "There," she said, reluctantly. "All done."

"Thanks," said Julie.

"Retrieve all arrows, and place the bows and arrows neatly along the shooting line!" came Fletch's loud voice.

"Whew!" said Julie. "I'm glad that's over."

Lori and Julie started walking back toward the cabin together, and the old silence fell between them again.

Feeling pressured to fill the silence, Lori said, "Miss your folks?"

"Uh...no...not yet, anyway."

"That was a dumb question." thought Lori. *"No wonder she doesn't want to talk to me."*

And then, Joann came running up. "Julie! You'll never guess what!"

"What?"

"There's a boys' camp down the road!"

"How far?" asked Julie.

"Only ten miles!"

"Ten miles! That's far!"

"Well," said Joann, "we'll have to figure something out. Come on. Let's go ask to see the coming events calendar, to see if there's a party, or a dance! I never thought to look up anything about that!"

Julie started off with Joann, and after a few steps, looked back and asked, "Would you like to come with us, Lori?"

Lori was tempted, but she felt like she was only an afterthought. And besides, she sensed that Joann liked to keep Julie pretty much to herself, so she said, "Umm...No thanks. I think I'll write my Dad."

"Okay! Bye!"

"Bye," she said back, softly.

Later, back in the cabin, Lori started her letter.

Dear Dad,
Camp is good. Not great yet, because we haven't had time to do much. We've had orientation a couple of times, and a campfire and singing last night.

This morning we had archery, and it was okay. It felt good to shoot again. I hope you got a permission request to sign, because I'm going to love learning how to ride horseback. You <u>will let</u> me, right? It won't cost any more...it's part of the program. It seems some of the local ranchers and farmers have loaned the camp most of the horses. We're going to see the horses this morning. But, we can't ride until the permission slips are back.

I'm meeting lots of other girls. There are about 80 here! Maybe I'll get to know most of them by camp's end. Only one girl here is from school, Julie Conners. Small world, huh? She's my partner for archery.

My other partner, my buddy, is a girl named Beth Perkins, who is a lot of fun. I think she'll be good at most sports! She's almost as tall as I am, has a few freckles, short brown, curly hair, and brown eyes. I don't think she's stopped growing yet, because she doesn't seem all filled out...if you know what I mean. She's kind of straight up and down. We do most activities together. She's really nice, and we laugh a lot!

Horses are next, and then swimming is after lunch. More later...

The Horses

As Gerri and all the Falcons walked to the stable area, Beth asked, "Do you know much about horses, Lori?"

Glancing at her, Lori said, "No, do you?"

"No, but I wish I did. I'm really looking forward to riding them."

Miss Larson came out to greet them, and said, "Hi! I'm Boots. She wore a bright yellow cowgirl shirt and blue jeans. Well-worn, scuffed black boots completed her outfit. Her shiny black hair was neatly secured in a pony tail. Her smile was so bright and cheerful that every camper just knew deep down, that this was going to be fun.

"You are here to look and listen, and pet, and learn how to groom these wonderful, intelligent animals," said Boots. "These horses are friendly, but you're just meeting them today...not riding, yet. Each horse is unique, and has its own personality. Some get afraid when they're away from their stalls, like if they were suddenly put out in a big field, all alone, for example. Some are afraid of loud noises. Others, are just shy. And occasionally, you'll find a 'leaner'. That's a horse that actually leans up against, say its big brother, or big sister, or a horse higher in the pecking order, for comfort.

"What?" several voices asked, simultaneously.

"The order of their importance in the group. Dumplin' here...is the head mare. She pushes everybody else around if she wants to eat first or drink first. And Rocky, this gelding, is next in line.

"What's a gelding?" several voices asked.

"Well, he's not a stallion, ...anymore. He, uh, can't make baby horses," said Boots, looking a little uncomfortable.

"Why not?" asked more voices in unison.

Strangely, Boots ignored their question, and continued on...about 'how to put their halters on'. Then, she led Rocky over between two posts. Each post had a rope tied to it, and the rope had a metal clip at the end. She clipped one on each side of his halter. "Now, Rocky is tied down, and ready to be attended to," she said. Half of the girls were handed grooming brushes, and then she showed the group how to brush. She started at his neck, and followed the direction the hairs fell naturally, explaining, as she went. She worked her way to his back. And then she invited a couple of girls to join her, saying, "Talk to him in a low, soothing voice. Just watch out for his feet!" she cautioned them. "If he moves around a little, he can accidentally step on you...and believe me, it *hurts*!"

The girls were taking turns, brushing Rocky, and although he was a bit nervous and fidgety at first, gradually he settled down and accepted their attention. Several girls were looking at the gelding's under-belly area, trying to figure out if he had a penis.

After a while, some giggles were heard, as Rocky relaxed his 'sheath' muscles somewhat, and his penis started dropping down a little.

"He is *too* a stallion!" said a small voice. "Look at that!"

Lori hadn't had a turn yet to brush him, so, she was standing back a little. She had a good view and was in awe of the size of the horse's organ! *"Wow!"* she thought. *"It's huge!"* She looked around to see Julie and Joann snickering, together and she wished she knew what Julie was saying.

And she also wondered what Beth thought about the penis. It seemed to be getting unbelievably longer by the minute, but she was too embarrassed to mention it. Nevertheless, she glanced at her partner and Beth's wide-eyed stare told the story.

Then Beth nudged her with an elbow, and said, "Incredible, huh?"

"Almost unbelievable," whispered Lori, hoping no one could hear them.

Boots brought Dumplin' out between two posts, farther away, and called Lori, Beth, and the others who hadn't had a turn yet.

"Here, girls," she said, handing them brushes. "Dumplin' loves to be pampered, so come close, watch out for moving hooves, and give her a good grooming!"

Beth said out loud what Lori was thinking. "I'd rather be brushing Rocky, just to see how long that penis gets. Oh, well, I guess I'll find out before camp is over."

Gerri and Boots moved around, making sure everyone was okay. The girls enjoyed doing the horses and they got to joke and kid around and know each other a little better. The time passed quickly and it didn't really seem like work. Ceil and Vivian were so busy watching out that they didn't get stepped on, that they kept accidentally bumping their big bodies into one another and bursting into laughter. It seemed there was never a dull moment around those two. Meanwhile, Joann and Julie were brushing the flanks and the tail of Dumplin, and as usual, talking about the boys that Joann either knew or would like to know.

Beth brushed out Dumplin's mane, and Lori was content to brush her neck, while she wondered just how intelligent these animals really were.

"Well, that's about it," said Boots. "Please bring your brushes over here." Then she showed them how to return the horses to their individual stalls and to make sure their water buckets were full.

43

"Feel free to come visit your favorite horse during your free time, any day or every day. Just don't go riding without the group, or without me, your 'fearless leader'." She smiled, and said "Bye, for now." And then she hung around for the 'after class' few, who would, no doubt, come to ask about stallions.

After lunch, Lori wanted to finish her letter.

Hi, I'm back,

The horses were great! We met two of them, and I think I'll love riding! The camp is as pretty as the picture in the brochure we saw at home, with all the big oak trees everywhere. And the water in the lake is so clear! The cabins are all in a big semi-circle, and almost every other one is a counselor's cabin.

I'm in cabin #3. They all have 'bird' names. We're the Falcons, and there are ten of us. My bunk isn't that comfortable, but I'm sleeping well, so far. Gang showers are 'yuck', but I guess you 'guys' don't mind things like that, right?

The biggest girl in the whole camp, is Vivian, and she's in our cabin. Dad, she must weigh about 225 pounds, and she's short! The funny thing is, her buddy is Ceil, and she must weigh almost 210. And, she's even shorter. Girls in the next cabin call them 'Chub' and 'Chubbier' behind their backs. But, I like them a lot. They're a hoot! They like to laugh, and they're always fun to be around.

Bye... gotta go and get this in the mail. I miss you!

Love, Lori

Floating

"Okay, girls!" announced the Waterfront Director. "Girls!" She waited while Gerri's campers stopped joking and splashing, in ankle deep water.

"Welcome to swimming. My name is Miss Wall, but everybody calls me Walli. Please pick a partner...a buddy, if you haven't already done so," she said.

Beth and Lori stepped sideways to be closer together.

Then Walli started explaining the importance of the Buddy System as it pertained to swimming, in case someone didn't know.

Lori glanced around and saw, not only that Jen and Lu were buddies, but that Jen was staring at her again, and so was Lu. Only, Lu's look was more of a scowl. Lori looked away, thinking *"I don't have time for this! They're so weird!"* Then, letting out a big sigh, she looked over at Julie and Joann. As their names drifted through her mind, she thought, *"Jen, ...Joann, ...Julie, ...Jill." There are just too many 'J's in my life right now!"* "Jeez!" she said aloud...and then laughed at herself because of the extra 'J'

Walli finished up her short lecture with the warning, "Remember, no matter what, you're responsible for your buddy! Stay together! Today, we're only going out as deep as that floating-rope barrier. Even the shortest person will always be able to touch bottom, so there's no reason to be afraid. Okay, the first thing we're going to do is see who can float face down, in the 'dead man's float'!"

"You mean I have to get my hair wet?" asked Joann.

"You bet!" Walli said, smiling.

Lori and Beth knew how to swim, but they waited patiently through the 8-10 minutes of directions for the three floating positions...the dead man's, the prone and the supine. Walli demonstrated each one, and then had the girls spread out and practice. She and Gerri went from pair to pair, assisting and chatting with them. Lori could hear her as she was really encouraging the novices. Meanwhile, she and Beth were trying to out-do each other, by holding their breath the longest in the dead man's float.

Walli came up to Beth and Lori, and said, "You two are very good at this! How about if I get you, to help me help some others?"

Lori and Beth looked at each other and shrugged. "Okay," they said simultaneously.

"Great! Just follow me." She started toward Jen and Lu, and said, "These two seem to be having a little trouble. And maybe, after you help them, go over and check Joann and Julie, if you will. That way, Gerri and I can stay with the others. Okay? Thanks, girls!" said Walli, and she headed back to the other four.

Jen overheard Walli, and was delighted with the instructor's suggestion and said, with sort of a 'leer' on her face, "Hey, Lori, puleeze, show me how to float! I'm not good at *this.*"

"Leer. I've read that word before," thought Lori. *"It goes right along with 'lewd' and 'lasciv...las—something."* Remembering Jen's remarks in the gang shower, Lori approached her cautiously and asked, "Which float do you need help with?"

"Well I'm having a lot of trouble with the back float. Could you help me keep my nose out of the water?"

Lori put out an arm and said, "If you'll start your float, I'll keep your head up."

With a slow, deliberate move, Jen reached out with one arm and then quickly put both arms around Lori's neck, and jumped up at her sideways. A reflex action made Lori put her arms out to keep Jen from falling back into the water, and...presto! As Jen had hoped, Lori was holding her like a baby. "What do I do next?" asked Jen, with a sly grin on her face.

And with another reflex action, Lori just dropped to a squat, holding tight, and dunking Jen thoroughly, while keeping her own head out of the water. She felt Jen let loose of her neck and try to get her feet down under her. Lori felt the adrenalin building in her own muscles, as she held her down for a few seconds. She was tempted to hold her down an extra ten seconds or so, but she finally released Jen and pushed herself backwards in an easy move.

Jen stood up, gasping and sputtering, and demanded, "What did you do that for?"

"Sorry, Jen, I guess I slipped a little," she fibbed, while treading water to get her own feet under her. She suppressed the laughter building inside her and said, "Look... let's do the prone float first. Just watch me." And she demonstrated the front float, 'face down'. "Now, you. Just hold your breath, and push off a little. Good! That's it!. And...relax...Good. Now, hold your breath longer, and see how far you can glide... get a good push off." While Jen was gliding, Lori checked to see how Beth was doing with Lu. "Good, Jen. I saw you do the dead man's float very well, before. So now let's try the back float."

Jen stood up and just grinned at her.

"She's not trying to 'embarrass' me to make me look bad... she's trying to... to... 'flirt'!" thought Lori. She froze. *"She's been trying to flirt, all along."*

Jen said, "I told you, I can't float on my back. Will you keep my nose from going under?"

Lori didn't answer, at first. She didn't trust Jen. "Are you sure you don't know how to do it?" demanded Lori.

"No. I don't. Honest!" Jen said, with a straight face.

"Okay... But no funny business!"

"Okay... Anyway, I was just kidding around."

"Yeah? Well, you 'kid around' in a weird way."

Lori glanced over at Beth. It seemed like she was getting Lu to lie back a little, even though she was still having to hold her up.

Then she looked over at Julie and Joann. Julie was trying to float on her back... as stiff as a board, with only her head and feet above the water, and bent in an almost 'pike' position. Joann was trying to help her by holding Julie's head tightly, and lifting it up high, so it wouldn't go under. They seemed comical, because it actually looked like Joann was holding Julie up by her ears.

Lori said, "Jen, if you'll do what I say, I won't let your nose get wet. Okay?"

"Okay."

Lori proceeded to get her floating. Actually Jen floated quite easily, like a bobber on a fishing line. Lori glanced at Beth, who had Lu in a nice, relaxed back float position, even though she still had to hold her up. She helped Jen to a standing position, saying, "That was great, Jen. You are a natural when it comes to floating."

Jen just beamed at her.

"Okay, you two help each other, for a while. We have to go help Joann and Julie now."

"But Lori..."

"Come on, Beth... These two seem okay now. See you later!" said Lori, already wading toward the two 'J's.

Beth said, "Wait up!" just as Lori took a little forward dive and swam a few strokes, rather than walking. Beth dove in, swam hard, and caught up.

"Hi," said Lori, standing up. "Walli asked us to...to help out. How's it going?"

"Not well," said Joann. "As you can see, we aren't exactly floating yet!"

"Yeah, ...I could use some help," said Julie, directing her comment to Lori. "I sink! ...especially my...uh, my butt."

Lori went toward Julie and Beth went to work with Joann, her archery partner.

"No...it doesn't have to sink," said Lori. "You just need to change a few things."

"How?" said Julie.

"Well, for one thing, it doesn't matter if your feet go down, ...way down! You've been trying to keep them up near the top of the water. Here, let me show you." Lori did a back float, treading water a bit. "Watch my feet," she said.

She stopped treading water and put her arms out and back, like a swan dive, arching her back. Her feet went down, ...down, ...until they sat on the bottom. "See? My feet sank all the way."

"But you weren't really floating if your feet were touching!"

47

Lori said, "Yes, ...I know... and if I go out deeper, they'll hang straight down in this fresh water because it's not as buoyant as salt water. But at least my face and nose will be out of the water, so I can breathe. And if I tread water a little, I can almost completely relax..."

"What happens if you don't tread water? ...what ever that means..."

"It means moving your hands a little, like a fin," said Lori, demonstrating for her. "And," she continued, "if I didn't paddle at all, I would find myself floating almost straight up and down, with my head about a foot under the surface."

Julie's eyes got wide open with fear. "Why do you *almost* sink?"

"Oh, ...uh, ...it's just my body type. I'm weird," said Lori, knowing that she was mostly muscle. "But don't worry, most people are able to float pretty easily, and you will, too."

"Hm-m..." said Julie. "So what do I do to keep the water out of my nose while I get to be a *great floater?* It really hurts when it runs up my nose!"

"Don't worry, ...I'll uh, ...hold you, ...uh, ...that is, ...I'll hold you *up*, so it won't happen," said Lori. She started, but then stopped herself from completely putting her hand out to touch Julie's back. "Uh, ...start to float," she said, "...like you usually do. Let me see."

And Julie laughed without smiling, and said, "I usually float like a rock!"

"Come on," Lori gently urged her, ...finally putting out her own hand. She still hesitated to touch her, as Julie leaned backwards. But then she saw Julie sinking in the middle, and saw how far her stiff chin was 'jutting out' to keep from going under. Lori finally moved closer and put her left hand under Julie's lower back, and her right hand under her head by her neck.

"I've got you," she said, and it sounded like someone else's strained voice. "Let your feet go down, ...they don't have to breathe." Then, looking at Julie's 'stricken' face, eyes wide open, and full of apprehension, staring right at her, Lori said, "But you do! Take a breath!"

Julie gasped for a quick breath. Then, realizing that her nose was completely out of the water, she almost smiled.

"Good, ...keep breathing. Now arch your back a little and let those feet go down...way down, if they want to." Lori moved her left hand to just beneath Julie's waist and continued to cradle her head. She squeezed Julie's neck a little for emphasis and said, "Relax your neck, ...it's too stiff. Let your head go back a little."

She felt Julie relax somewhat, but then tense up again. "Relax, again," she urged, "and take a few long, slow, breaths." And she thought, *"Me too, if I can."*

Julie's ears finally went under water, and she jerked her head up. "My ears feel funny when they get water in them!" she said.

"Yeah," said Lori, "but they'll be okay. They're supposed to go under. Put your ears back in and relax some more. Close your eyes and don't worry. I've got you."

Julie forcibly kept her eyes closed. Lori forcibly kept her pounding heart inside her chest. She couldn't get her heart beat to slow down.

At least, gradually Julie was doing as she was told.

"Relax even more. Let your chest come up, ...that's it. Reach your arms back a little more. Good."

Little by little, Julie's whole body was relaxing. "That's really good. Don't move, ...just relax into the float."

Lori looked down at Julie and just marveled at her face. It was *so close* to her own right now. Little dimples, ...that really did become dimples, appeared, even if she just twitched her cheeks a bit. She watched as they occasionally formed, and then disappeared again. *"And those long, jet black eye lashes, ... and light blonde hair. Like I thought in the shower, that's unusual,"* she decided.

She quickly looked back towards Beth, to see if either she or Joann had noticed her lengthy examination of Julie's face. They hadn't, but Lori was embarrassed at her own curiosity. She tried to get back to concentrating on the back float. But her eyes went right back to Julie's face. She managed to say, "You're doing great, Julie. Don't move...just relax even more."

And then, her eyes settled on Julie's lips. They looked so soft. She decided that, for sure, Julie didn't need any lipstick because they had that naturally pink color, but... their beautiful shape, was what held Lori's gaze, as she stared, and stared. She visually traced the very definite outline of her lips, around and around. *"Pouty, and full."* she thought, *"...and with the bottom lip slightly poutier."*

"You're doing great," she said, with some difficulty. "Relax even more, now. Let your shoulders relax."

She felt Julie's back lift up off her hand slightly, as Julie really relaxed and let her feet go even deeper. Lori was very reluctant to tell her she was floating all by herself, because it would end these precious seconds of closeness. So, in spite of feeling guilty, she kept a little pressure against her back, ...as if it was needed.

"You're doing just fine. Tip your head back a little more, and keep your chin up. That's it. Let your feet go down a little more."

Julie nodded again that she had heard her, even though her ears were underwater.

From her chin, Lori's focus moved gradually to Julie's chest. She saw Julie's breasts pressing tightly against the thin blue nylon tank suit. She could clearly see each nipple. Both were contracted into tight little bumps. Lori thought back to seeing Julie in the shower, all soapy. But now, here she was, ...so...*so close* to her! And Lori knew that those 'tight little buds' were pink.

49

She felt so strange. Goose bumps popped out all over on her arms and legs, and she felt a 'pulsing', almost electrical tingling feeling, going down her belly, and continuing right between her legs.

"What's that?" she thought, looking back at Julie's face to see if she'd caught her looking. She hadn't. Her eyes were still shut.

Lori watched her sort of 'purse her lips' together as she lifted her chin a little more, ...and then unexpectedly, Julie smiled, with her eyes still shut.

It was beautiful, and it made Lori catch her breath, thinking, *"Wow!"* ...and her body responded, again, with a definite 'tingling' below, and pins and needles crept down her neck and all over her back. *"...what an incredible smile. ...what incredible lips!"*

"My feet just touched the bottom."

Ignoring the intense feeling and not responding to Julie's remark, Lori was riveted to the spot... and continued to drink in Julie's 'mesmerizing looks'. She couldn't help herself, because she might not *ever* have another chance to be so near.

"She actually gets prettier, and prettier, as she smiles a little bigger. Her teeth are really beautiful and her dimples get really deep." She sighed heavily then, thinking, *"She's just incredible...I could look at her for a long... long time."* Her own thoughts and Julie's closeness caused the pulsing to surge harder.

Then, slowly, Julie smiled again, and as she watched in awe, Lori felt her own body actually begin to throb.

Julie said, "This isn't so bad! It feels good!"

In spite of her growing discomfort, Lori was still just frozen in time, gazing at Julie's soft lips, that were now looking contented and relaxed. Completely enchanted by them, she felt the unthinkable urge to...to just... bend down... and... brush them with hers. As the thought lingered, ...and became a definite picture in her mind, the 'pulsing down below' surged and throbbed even harder. Finally, the powerful, 'funny feeling' in her pubic area, began to ache.

"Ache!" she thought. *"I'm actually 'aching' for Julie! Oh, God! ...what's wrong with me?"*

She stepped back suddenly.

And when Julie felt her leave, she floundered, and splashed, trying to recover. But her feet were already touching the bottom so she stood up pretty easily, and she didn't get any water in her nose.

"You left!" she accused. "You let me go, ...just when I was almost floating!"

"Well, ...I, ...I didn't mean to!"

Just then, a big bee buzzed Lori's face and she cringed to avoid it. Reflexively, she raised her hands up to protect her face and she sort of 'flicked' at it.

Julie saw the bumble bee and said, "Uh-oh! Boy, he's a big one!"

Lori realized what Julie was thinking, and was grateful for the alibi. Then she heard him buzz loudly and felt him crash against her neck. She ducked completely under water. When she came up, blinking away the water streaming down her face, she saw the bee buzz Julie. And Julie, hiding between her hands, ducked for cover too, kneeling hard, down into the water. Lori chuckled to herself at the sight.

Julie came up with a moan. "Oh, my nose is full of water!" She wiped her eyes quickly, asking, "Is he gone? Is he going to get me?"

Lori was thinking, "She looks like she's only five years old, and so... so...afraid, and so... so 'cute'."

Lori was already chuckling to herself a little, but when she saw Julie's face so full of fear and surprise, she began to laugh softly, but loud enough that Julie heard her.

"Don't laugh *at me!*" Julie said, in a bossy way. "You looked pretty silly, yourself, *Miss Hunter!*" ...which only caused Lori to instantly laugh harder, because for some reason, Julie looked even funnier as she was making a face and getting madder at her. She looked like a real 'Miss Priss,' protesting against anyone who would dare to mistreat her.

Try as she may, Lori couldn't stop laughing. Feeling like she ought to apologize, she managed to get it down to a smothered giggle, but then, suddenly she really burst out laughing harder than ever. She had an extremely contagious laugh, and Julie hesitated, ...smiled, ...and almost started giggling, too. But when Lori's "Ha, ha, ha's," erupted into downright, hearty, "Ho, ho, ho's," Julie really frowned and started coming at her. And with vengeance on her 'scrunched up' face, she started splashing at Lori.

However, she didn't know how to hold her hands to splash very well. And to Lori, she looked a bit spastic...in fact, *very* spastic! She was all floppy wrists and elbows.

This new comical sight really tickled Lori. Already weakened, she doubled over, and in one more barely audible sound, she uncontrollably laughed out most of the air she had left. Her knees went weak, as she *still* laughed! But now it was without any sounds at all, and she sagged helplessly to a squat. It was a position too low for her to be able to splash back at Julie even if she had been able to try. Her stomach hurt, and she could hardly catch a breath *in* because the tiny amount of air she had left, was constantly being forced *out*.

51

Julie came on furiously now, with an even more determined look on her face, splashing harder and harder, faster and faster, right up to Lori. And out of frustration, at how almost completely 'un-splashed' her adversary was, she finally put her hands on Lori's defenseless shoulders and pushed her backwards as hard as she could, accidentally tripping on Lori's feet and knees. As Lori went under, falling backwards, Julie's forward motion caused her to continue right up and over on top of her, in a tumble.

Julie's chest plopped right on top of Lori's left cheek, causing Lori's entire stomach area to cramp even harder, and she laughed right down to her knees, because of the silliness of it all. And then she began thinking, *"Boy, ...I bet she's really getting mad, now."*

Lori couldn't breathe in. She couldn't breathe out. She just looked and felt like she was having some kind of seizure while watching her last bit of air, bubble out and up.

Then she realized she had to really worry about Julie's feet and legs, which were struggling and thrashing wildly! And her arms too, which were going absolutely 'nuts' all around her head. Lori covered her head with one arm, and her chest with the other one. Julie was desperately trying to get off of her, but her swimming skills weren't getting her anywhere.

Lori thought, *"She's going to get a nose-full again, ...and...I'm...I'm going to drown down here...in this very shallow water!"* Strangely, that bizarre thought only caused her to shake and tremble inside, even harder. Her stomach was contracting more and more, into just one great big, spasming, painful cramp.

Getting really desperate for air now, somehow she twisted and turned over to her stomach, and got both feet under her. Finding the strength from somewhere, she stood up, all hunched over, right under Julie!

Julie found herself unexpectedly up in the air, unceremoniously 'draped' over Lori's head and shoulders, in spite of her best efforts to escape.

A huge amount of water deluged down over Lori's face from Julie's writhing form. Still painfully convulsing, and trying unsuccessfully to wait for the water to stop streaming over her nose and mouth, Lori began choking and gasping for air.

Because of Julie's weight and the comedy of her flailing around like a weak, but enraged octopus, Lori only managed to get half-a-breath when she heard, *Miss Priss's* voice, demanding, in a very haughty manner, <u>*"Lori Hunter!! You just stop that, right now!! Put me down this minute!!"*</u>

Convulsing in laughter right down to her toes, all of Lori's strength left, and she just collapsed, sagging weakly all the way back under the water. *"For sure, I'm going to die..."* she thought, becoming alarmed. A flashback of the bus driver's warning, "Have lots of fun, but be careful not to drown," coursed through her mind. She feebly tried to duck down and walk a little and to swim forward with her arms to get away from Julie, just enough to stand up again, but she only managed to laugh in an unwanted gulp of lake water.

Finally, she felt Julie's body leaving, and a strong hand grab her under her arm and help her stand up.

"Lori! Are you okay? What are you two doing?"

Lori gasped for breath, and choked, laughed, and choked some more, looking to see who had pulled her up. *"It was Beth! Beth had saved her..."* In between choking spasms, she smiled at her gratefully, and hung weakly on her shoulder.

Then she glanced over at Julie to see if she was okay. Gerri and Joann had pulled Julie off of her, and were helping her stand up.

Suddenly Lori remembered the vivid picture of Julie coming at her, thinking she was so 'tough' and looking so funny, that her own painful stomach convulsed once again, with soundless laughter. She covered her face with both hands to try to stop giggling and shaking.

"Do you have a cramp? Where? A stomach cramp?" asked Beth.

Lori could only shake her head. Finally, she managed to say from between her hands, "No. I'm okay." And between coughs she said, "Boy...that was intense!"

Julie was still coughing and sputtering, too... "oooohh...that water burns my nose so bad!" she moaned.

Lori still had a smile on her face... She couldn't erase it. "I'm okay, now, Beth... Thanks! Thanks a *lot* for helping me up." Finally, she was able to take a deep breath without coughing. She gave Beth a big hug, and thanked her once more.

Beth shyly said, "Sure. Anytime."

Coming closer, Jen had watched the last part, and glared as Lori hugged Beth. No one but Lu noticed the intensity of her look of hatred toward Beth.

Then, Lori turned and asked, "Are you okay, Julie?" ...as she waded a little closer to her.

"Yeah... I guess..." she said, pressing both forefingers firmly against the sides of her nose. "How come you didn't get water in *your* nose?" she demanded, still mad at Lori for laughing at her. In her mind, "Lori had just deliberately picked her up, made a spectacle of her, and then dumped her back in the water, *on purpose.*"

"Okay, girls!" 'boomed' out over the group. "That's it, for floating! Everybody come over here, please, and stand in a semi-circle before I dismiss you!" Walli had seen the tail end of Julie's attack and thought she'd just let it go for now, since everyone was okay. She'd remind them of the 'no horseplay' rule, privately, after class.

Lori looked in the direction of the loud voice, and then back to Julie. "Oh well, next lesson, ...the nose trick," she said.

Julie, still pressing her sinuses, took that as an apology, and nodded, "Okay."

As they waded over, Lori asked Beth, "How'd you do with Joann?"

"Okay, but you seemed to have a lot more fun with Julie!"

"Oh, ...jeez, Beth! She was so funny!"

"Yeah? How?"

Lori, reluctant to share all of her private thoughts, said, "A big bumble bee chased us, and we dove for cover!"

"Oh," said Beth, not really understanding at all.

Arts and Crafts

Later, after swim class, the Falcons found themselves in Arts and Crafts. This wasn't one of Lori's favorite things to do, but Beth seemed to love it. So did a lot of the other girls.

They were given some paper and soft-lead pencils, and told they could draw anything they'd like. Lori started sketching a horse's head. After a while, she thought, *"Hmm, ...looks sorta like a donkey, to me."* She tried to doctor it up a little. Then after she was finished, and still unsatisfied, she took a different piece of art paper, and wrote to her dad.

"Hi, I'm here in Arts and Crafts. Not my favorite! I tried to draw a picture of my favorite horse for you. Out of pure kindness to 'Rocky', I will tear it up.

We had our first swimming lesson...well, just floating. It was kind of boring at first, but I ended up having a great time. It's too long to tell here, but when I get home, let's go somewhere and have a coke together, okay?"

More later... Tell Maude "Hello."

She walked around, looking at different girl's work. Beth was great at drawing. She'd drawn a swimmer doing a racing dive and it looked good enough to frame. Lori told her so.

Beth just shrugged and said, "It's okay, but not great."

Joann could draw a little, and had done a sketch of the lake.

Julie was still drawing when Lori looked at her paper. It was a portrait of Joann.

"Wow," thought Lori. "That's pretty incredible," she said to Julie.

Julie looked up, and seemed embarrassed. "Oh, thanks. But I, well, thanks."

That got Joann's attention and she came to see.

"Holy cow, Julie! You drew me! Wow! Nobody's ever drawn me before! Can I have that picture?" said Joann, all in one breath.

Lori turned and left, thinking, *"I'd probably feel the same way."*

That night, lying across her bunk, Lori continued her letter.

Bon jour...oops, I mean Bon soir,

Just me again. I have 'J' on the brain. In our cabin, we have Julie, and Joann, her buddy, and Jen, Lu's buddy. Next door, there's a Jill. If I forget someone's name all I have to do is start out with a 'J' sound, and I might get the rest of it.

55

Joann is one of the prettier girls here. She acts like she knows it though. She has sort of long, reddish brown hair, (that she rolls up in curlers every night). I don't know how anyone can sleep with rollers in her hair. Rory, a good friend in the next cabin, calls her the 'sink dink' because she's always hogging more than one sink with all her stuff.

Rory is great fun. She's probably the best athlete at camp, and she brought her own football. Yea, Rory! We will get to toss it around a little when we have a few minutes free. Anyway, Rory is good at giving out nicknames. She's named almost everybody in her cabin, and a couple in ours. So far, I've escaped her naming jag.

The last 'J', is Jen. She's sort of athletic. Let's see...describing her ...she's medium height, with thick-brown, scraggly... hair. (Sorry, but she doesn't seem to be able to control it.) She looks kinda tough, but I don't know yet if she really is. I think that out of all the girls I've ever met in my life, though, she's the 'most crude'. Rory calls her 'Scuz'.

Oh, well, fortunately, she's not my buddy, and I don't have to listen to her remarks very often. Guess I'll get some sleep, now. I love you Dad. Goodnight.

Girl Talk

A few minutes later, as she was pulling back the blanket on her bunk, Julie asked, "Lori, have you heard anything else from the counselors about the boys' camp coming to the dance?"

Lori was surprised to be included in Joann and Julie's normal conversation and she mumbled, "What? ...oh...uh..."

"*I* did!" said Joann. "Two girls who've been here before, said that the first regular camp dance is *definitely* on the last Friday of our first 4-week session!"

"Yes, Joann, we already found out that part from the schedule, remember? More than three weeks away," said Julie, wistfully. "But then we'll get to go to the other one, too! Right?"

"Yeah, the one at the very end of camp, if I'm here. My parents want me to go to visit my grandmother with them for the last part of summer," said Joann.

Lori decided to join in the conversation, just to see if she could be comfortable. "Yeah," she said, "seems like a long time to wait."

Joann said, "We've been wondering if there are any cute guys, or if they're mostly short, skinny, and full of pimples."

Lori chuckled. She remembered a lot of the guys at school, who looked just like that. Hardly anything to get excited about because they were so...so...*unable* to do sports. And Lori had a hard time respecting a guy who was not somewhat physically capable. *"How could a girl 'like' a guy if she didn't, at least, 'respect' him first?"*

Beth came up, and the four girls sat on Julie's and Lori's bunks facing each other.

Lori felt good at just being able to be in the little group. She was telling herself, *"to just relax, and let the other three girls carry the conversation for a while."*

But Julie 'spiked' her with, "You don't have a boyfriend at school, do you, Lori?"

"Uh, ...well, ...no, ...not a steady boyfriend," she managed.

"Oh., who have you dated? I haven't heard any sexy rumors about you," smiled Julie. "And, I've never seen you at any of the popular hang-outs."

At that moment Lori wanted desperately to have a boyfriend, ...just to say she'd dated someone, ...*anyone*. "No, ...uh, ...some boys flirt a lot, ...but I guess I haven't found the right one, yet."

"You'd better start looking harder," Julie suggested, "We only have one more year of school left."

Lori felt herself looking down, and a flush of heat starting to creep up her neck. But she forced herself to look back at Julie. "Yeah," she shrugged, ...and she forced a little smile... "Maybe I'll meet someone at this dance."

"Or, maybe...we could 'double-date' during our senior year!"

Really surprised at that...Lori mumbled, "Okay." But, in her mind, she continued, *"That could be interesting. Most likely, painful,"* she thought, *"but intriguing...and at least a chance to be near Julie."* This time, she didn't chastise herself for her fantasy, but she was more curious than ever about her hidden feelings.

That night, long after lights out, she lay staring into the darkness, going over the day's events. *"It was a 'great' day,"* she reminisced.

"It's strange, how I 'rate the day' according to 'how things went with Julie'... I should really spend more 'fun' time with Beth," she thought. Then... *"No, ...I really have to figure out why it seems Julie is the center of my life! Maybe we'll get to be best friends, ...yeah, ...Julie and Beth. Then, I'll have two best friends here."* Finally, she slept.

The Dream

The vision of Julie lying on top of her was frozen in her thoughts. And, ...she was very much aware that, ...Julie didn't have on a bathing suit...and neither did she. Somehow, Lori herself, was floating, 'face up', on her back, strangely enough, ...just underneath the water. But there was no discomfort at all. No water burned her nose, she could breathe somehow and she had her eyes wide open.

Then everything began to move in slow motion. There was no flailing of arms or legs. Julie was simply 'prone-gliding' closer toward her and Lori could feel the motion of the water. She could feel Julie, slowly sliding up higher over her, and Julie's breasts softly brushing up along her belly. Finally, their nipples touched. Her own contracted into little knobby buttons.

She wanted to hold her, ...and pull her closer, ...even entwine her legs with Julie's. But she couldn't move. She felt her nipples get even harder as Julie's smooth belly was now touching hers, and then soft breasts were touching her cheeks.

She sat up suddenly and saw darkness, and a lighted path outside the window. *"It was a dream,"* she realized. *"A dream!"* She felt the strange tightening and throbbing between her legs and shivered. Her nipples were still tight.

She tried to think of something else, ...like *"how dumb it was to be awake in the middle of the night."* But she couldn't get rid of the 'aching sensation' right in her pubic area. She put her hand between her legs gently and pressed up against her pubic bone.

"Maybe I bruised it," she thought, trying to remember if Julie had accidentally kicked her there while 'tumbling' over her. It was comforting, somehow, so she kept her hand there.

She rolled over on her side and looked at Julie's bunk. She couldn't see much, except that Julie was facing her and her blonde hair was 'all over' the pillow. Her dream came back to her, vividly. Julie's smooth body barely touching hers, ...and Julie's breasts softly brushing her cheeks, and...

She ached so bad between her legs that she pressed harder. Without warning, muscles in her pubic area started contracting. She could feel the soft part of her body moving against her hand and she 'held tighter'. Waves of pleasure began washing over her. She stretched out full-length and crossed her legs to make even more pressure on her hand. Deep, deep inside she felt muscles contracting, all by themselves. She didn't move for a long time, just 'holding onto that incredible feeling'.

Finally, she relaxed her legs. *"What was that?"* she shouted in her brain. *"Wonder if I hurt myself?"* she thought, a bit frightened. Her heart had been beating pretty fast because she could feel it slowing down. *"Guess I'm okay,"* she decided, but she felt weak. And she felt *wet* between her legs. *"Oh no! I've started my period!"*

She hurried to the bathroom. *"No blood, ...then, "What?"* Looking more closely, she saw that the toilet tissue was definitely wet, ...and, it was slippery and clear, ...and not urine.

With her mind racing, she went back to bed, trying to remember a conversation she overheard about boys... 'playing with themselves,' *"...masturbating! ...How could anyone forget that word? ...that forbidden word! I wonder if girls can do it too? ...I wonder if I...if I just masturbated myself? ...uh-h yuck, it sounds so disgusting!"* She made a face at that thought and even shivered. Then, a little voice from inside her head said, *"...but...it did feel pretty good, ...no, ...really good! ...no, ...even better!"* She couldn't think of a good 'big' word, so she just concentrated on trying to analyze what had happened.

"I was thinking about Julie, and how it would feel if she..." Lori pictured the dream, but was reluctant to put it into words... *"and then, my muscles just ...just went 'nuts'. That's what they did! And then, ...well, ...then, ...it was over! ...And, ...I feel...good! ...hmmm,"* she let out a huge sigh. *"...sort of like after a good sneeze!"*

She laughed at herself, and thought, *"Imagine! Comparing sex to a sneeze..."* And she sat up. *"Sex! By myself!"* The thought was mind boggling to her.

"Well, Julie was a big part," she admitted, *"in fact, most of it!"* She didn't understand it all, but she admitted to herself, *"that Julie, ...just thinking about Julie, had an incredible effect on her.* She remembered the powerful sensations she'd felt, just watching Julie as she'd held her, floating on her hand. *"And Julie's a girl! Wonder if I can find a boy to make me feel like this?"* She pondered that for a few minutes, then, she had a different thought. *"Wonder if I could do it again?"*

So, she touched herself, and started to press.

Nothing... no tingling... no 'ache' like before. Just a 'super-sensitive' area, telling her *"What?... 'enough already'? Well,"* she sighed, *"that was 'wonderful', ...whatever it was,"* and she turned on her stomach, wondering who she could ask about all of this.

"No wonder they call this time of life 'puberty'..." she thought, sleepily. *"It's when your pubic area gets rambunctious."* And she finally dozed off, murmuring, 'exquisite' ...that's the word, ...exquisite."

The entire next morning Lori was distracted as she thought and thought about her dream and her 'convulsive' body. Finally, just before lunch, Lori added more to her letter to see if she could concentrate and keep her mind on something besides Julie and the effect she was having on her life.

Hey, Dad...
We played a little softball, this morning. Not anything like the teams at home, but I hope it'll get better. Nancy's a real 'youngish' girl in our cabin. She wears her blonde hair in two braids, usually, and looks and acts, sometimes, like she's about twelve. The strange thing is, her buddy is Liz, who could pass for her sister. If they both wear braids, it's hard to tell them apart. Fortunately, Nancy has a quirky way of often wearing the same color socks, as the blouse she wears. So-o, I only have trouble on the days she and Liz both wear white blouses and socks. Can you guess her nickname?

Anyway, when either one of them hits the ball, it might go as far as to the pitcher. We do have one 'slugger', named Lu. She's got very short, dark blonde hair, and she's tall, ...about 5'10" I think. Now she can really whack it a ways. Rory, the best player from next door, can put it way out there, too.

Bye... Be back later...

Donna Kelli

With Beth

It was quiet time and everyone had almost an hour to themselves, to nap or read, swim, or visit the horses. Lori found Beth, sitting under a big oak tree, reading a book.

When her partner looked up, Lori asked, "Beth do you know much about boys, I mean about sex...and all?"

"What brought this on?" asked Beth.

"Well, I...uh...I had a sexy dream last night... and woke up too soon."

"You mean you didn't get to have sex with him?"

"Uh...well...yes...I mean 'no' I didn't. Uh, what about you? ...Have *you* ever... uh.... had sex at *all*, with a boy?"

When Beth didn't answer...and looked down, Lori said quickly "Oh, uh, ...never mind, I, uh, ...I didn't mean to pry! It's such a personal thing."

"No, it's okay." Beth replied in an off-handed way, "Ronnie and I have never 'gone all the way'. We've just 'petted' some."

Lori couldn't picture 'petting', because she hadn't put her hands on Julie in the dream.

"What is petting, exactly?"

Beth looked at Lori's frowning face, and felt like laughing out loud. "Look, Lori, I don't know if I can talk about this, with you looking at me so intensely. I'm too embarrassed. But, if you'll sit down and, please, look off in the distance, or look down at the ground, anywhere, but at my face, then I'll try."

Lori sat down in an easy motion and stared at the ground, and waited. She felt like a dumb little kid being punished, but she wanted some answers...She *needed* some answers.

"Petting doesn't mean like petting an animal." Beth began, "It means, well, all it means is that after you kiss him for awhile, you put your hands on him and caress him. And then, he does the same to you." Proud of herself for such a concise explanation, she took a deep breath and sighed and then relaxed.

Lori tried to get a mental picture of a guy and a girl, in a car, caressing each other. "What part of him do you caress? His face? His shoulders?"

Beth nearly choked at the question, and turned to look at Lori.

"Hasn't your mom told you anything about all of this?"

"My mom died when I was eight. I don't talk to my stepmother about anything I don't have to."

"Oh... Sorry!" said Beth. "I didn't know." She could see that this was going to be more 'in depth' than she thought. But she knew that Lori wouldn't ask such a painful, embarrassing question unless she was stupid or just desperate for information. And Lori seemed to be one of the most mature, capable people she knew. "What do you spend all of your time doing, that you haven't learned about sex yet?"

"Sports," said Lori. "I'm on a lot of different teams, and I'm always either at some practice, or at a game. I really love sports, and I hate to go home any sooner than absolutely necessary. If I have to be at home when Maude is there, it's just plain torture. She's always finding work for me to do."

"I get the picture," said Beth. "But haven't you read about it or anything?"

"I've read every book they have in our library, but the questions I have aren't even mentioned."

Well, promise not to tell any one else, and I'll tell you a little, about me and Ronnie."

"I won't ever tell. You can trust me with a secret *forever*."

And Beth looked at her face, as deep as she could into the hazel green eyes, and believed her.

"Well, like I said before, after you've been kissing for awhile, you feel like you want to get even closer. Ronnie gets really excited, really fast, you know, his penis gets hard. It's called an 'erection'. He'd like to have intercourse right away, you know, put it in me. But, I won't let him."

Lori had several questions, immediately, like, "How big was his penis when it got 'hard'? and, what, exactly, caused it to get hard?" ...but she didn't want Beth to stop talking, so she kept quiet. At least she already knew about the 'vagina' and 'intercourse' from the books.

"For one thing, I don't get as 'excited' as he does, as fast as he does. So...o, I 'slow' him down, and make him wait for me. I make him kiss me a long time." Beth took a deep breath and said, "Boy. This is tough to do. I've never talked to *anyone* about this before."

Still, no response from Lori, so Beth just went on.

"He likes to touch my breasts, and I like it too, if he's gentle, and his hands aren't too rough."

"Through your clothes?" asked Lori.

"At first," said Beth, "but then, we eventually get right down to bare skin. He's getting to be a 'pro', at unhooking my bra," she laughed, blushing a little.

Lori could picture a faceless boy with his hands on Beth's 'smallish' bare breasts, and wondered if her nipples got 'all tight', but she didn't ask.

"By this time, he's ready to 'explode', so I 'do' him," continued Beth.

Deafening silence came from Lori.

"I, ...well, ...I, ...uh, ...Damn!" said Beth.

"Look, Beth, I didn't mean to hear a confession or anything. Let's end this."

"No, it's okay...it's almost over." After taking a big breath, she admitted that next she unzipped his jeans, and 'took out' his penis.

"Then, I hold it 'pretty tight', with one hand, and move my hand up and down, for several minutes. He really likes that."

"What happens at the end of sex?" blurted Lori.

"Well, if it's really good, your body could reach a 'climax'." Beth paused and then said, "Boys almost always climax from petting, at least Ronnie does."

"What happens when they do?"

"I *knew* you were going to ask that!" Once again, Beth paused and looked away, and then almost whispered, "They sort of 'squirt'."

"Squirt? Squirt what...urine? Yuck!"

"No... No! Not urine, you nut, ...it's like a milky fluid, ...kind of sticky."

"Where does it go?"

"Well, if you're having intercourse, it goes inside you, *and* it can get you *pregnant!!* That's why I don't let him have intercourse with me. But, if you're petting, you usually use a napkin or a Kleenex, or something, and," she laughed, "if you're 'ambidextrous', you use your other hand to hold the tissue around the top of his penis, and catch it all in there. Or, sometimes, he holds the tissue."

"How much does he 'squirt'?"

Beth laughed out loud at that one. "Lori! Did anyone ever tell you, that you ask the most direct, ...the most detailed questions?"

"My dad, ...all the time," she smiled back.

"Beth scrunched up her brow, and said, "I don't know about other guys, but Ronnie squirts ...uh," and she laughed at herself. "He *'comes'* about oh, ...I guess, a couple of tablespoons full."

"Oh... Then what?"

"It's over."

"It's over?"

"For him."

"What about you, ...do you get to 'squirt'.?"

Beth started laughing harder and harder. She ended up, rolling on her side in the grass, holding her stomach, still laughing. *Come! Say...Come!"*

Lori laughed, too, in spite of herself, and said, "Okay, ...okay!"

Then, Beth stayed lying down on her side, propped her head on her hand, and looked at Lori. "Well, it depends on how nervous I am, ...you know, like if we're parked in an area where we might be discovered, or not. It also depends if his fingers are too rough, ...but if everything is just right, and he moves his fingers gently, then, ...I can 'come', too."

"Where does he..."

"...put his fingers?" Beth finished for her. "Your questions are *'too, too* much!" she moaned, shaking her head. "Well," she said, sighing, "I don't let him take off my underwear, but, I let him reach inside."

There was a long, long silence and Beth was glad it was over.

"What did it feel like, ...when you 'come', *'came'?"* she corrected.

Beth just stared at Lori for a moment, and then said, "I can't *believe* you've been asking me these things, and that I've actually been telling you all this!"

Lori just calmly looked back at her, but inside she was tense. The next answer was the one she needed most of all.

"It felt like my whole body was suddenly 'knotting up' and 'knotting up' ...but, in waves. And then, 'complete relaxation'. That's it, that's what I felt! And I think I'll die of mortification if you ever meet Ronnie, face to face!"

There was no response from Lori, except a big sigh, as she re-lived her own climax. She pictured herself last night, with her own hand pressing on the outside of her 'shorty' pajamas, ...and she definitely remembered the waves of pleasure...

"So...o," Beth asked, "ready to try 'petting'?"

"No, uh, ...I mean, ...I'm not desperate or anything, ...just curious."

"Well, maybe you'll meet someone nice, at the dance!"

"Beth, would you 'pet' on the first date?"

"No, never," she said, firmly.

"Me neither."

Lori looked off in the distance, and saw Jen, sitting under a tree, with a book. But she wasn't reading, she was looking their way. Lu was standing up, next to the tree, doing stretching exercises.

"Nope, me neither," she sighed.

Much later, Lori continued her letter.

Hello again,

Boy, it can be hot out there on the basketball court! (Even though we didn't play 'real' basketball, yet. We were just shooting for fun.) At least we can take showers, anytime. And, it's a good thing my hair is short and has a few swirls here and there. I love it that I can 'fluff' and 'go'. You wouldn't believe what

65

goes on here, at night! Hair dryers galore! You'd think they were going to a prom. I bet *that* doesn't last all summer.

Tonight is 'Storytelling', and 'the Owls' get the honors. They have one girl, named, (what else?) *Judy*, who is a natural-born actress. No doubt she'll be a main performer. Our turn comes after the week-end. It's a good thing Vivian and Ceil like to 'clown around'. They always come up with something, and save the day.

Gotta go now...our turn to set tables, and all. Miss you!

Volleyball I

The Falcons were split, five against five, for volleyball instruction. Fletch was the overall Sports Director and the girls remembered her from Archery. She realized that most girls knew how to play, at least somewhat, but she went through a quick review of the basics. She showed the girls where to stand, how to rotate, and how to hit the 'overhead' ball on the 'pads' of their fingertips, so they wouldn't break their nails or their fingers. She had several volleyballs and had the girls trying to volley the ball directly overhead, hopefully counting up to fifty, before they missed. (four was more like it.)

Remembering what a fine archer Lori was, Fletch watched her right away, to determine her skill level. Seeing her volley the ball overhead, in controlled, very high volleys, gave her the answer. Lori quit after about twenty and gave the ball to Liz, for her turn.

And, for the low balls, Fletch reviewed how to 'bump' the ball up, by putting their hands together, and using the top of both wrists and forearms, to hit the ball. That skill was usually pretty hard for almost all of the girls. So she did a few different drills with them, to get them used to hitting the ball from only waist high, and also from down by their knees.

After a prolonged set of 'how to serve' drills, she said, "Lori, you be captain on that side, please. And, Jen, you be captain on this side." Then, she assigned Joann, Liz, Nancy, and Ceil, to be with Lori. Vivian, Lu, Julie, and Beth went with Jen.

Even after all the practice, it seemed like hardly anyone knew how to serve very well, or how to really keep the ball in the air. It was very frustrating for Lori, who was used to varsity-level sports, with good set-ups and powerful spikes against determined blocks.

She knew that if she'd *had* to, she could've played the whole court, against these girls. And by using 'strategy' she could've placed the ball anywhere, at will. But, long ago, she'd learned to control herself from *ever* 'hogging' the court, and she always tried to be a 'team player'. She had seen others play as 'ball hogs', running everywhere, crashing into people and hurting them. It wasn't pretty to watch, and she didn't identify with that type of behavior, at all.

She kept on trying...setting the ball to her teammates. Gradually, some of them caught on, and Lori had some hope for the next session. She looked over at the basketball court, and saw that Fletch's two adult assistants were shooting some baskets.

"Now, if we could get all these counselors in a game, it might get to be a real challenge," she thought.

67

As if Fletch had read her mind, she came to play on Lori's side, and asked Gerri go on the other side. Things got a little better and Lori, at least, got to set up a few really high ones that Fletch actually spiked at Gerri.

The game ended on a good hit by Jen, after a set up by Beth. They won, but Lori didn't mind. At least she got to play, and it felt good.

Beth came up to her after the game and said, "Guess what?"

"What?"

"Ceil is going to change bunks with me."

"Oh yeah? Why?"

"Because she wants to be next to Vivian, since they're 'buddies' now, and I'll get to be closer to you, so we can talk. My bunk will be foot to foot with yours, but at least we won't have to talk over the top of Vivian."

"Great," said Lori.

"Want to help me move my stuff?"

"When, now?"

"Yes. Do you mind?"

"Let's go do it," said Lori.

A little later, as they were moving everything, Lu and Jen came in. It took them a minute to figure out what was happening, because Vivian and Ceil were busy, too. They didn't offer to help, or make any 'joking around' comments. Jen just sat on her bunk and glared at Beth.

Beth didn't notice. But Lori did, and thought, *"She seems to 'stare and glare' at us a lot."*

Meanwhile, Lu just sat on her own bunk, frowning.

"Such 'happy buddies'..." thought Lori.

The Crawl Stroke

At the next swim class, when all ten girls were in a semi-circle, Walli began. "All of you are checked off for the dead man's float. But I'm expecting all of you to master the prone glide, and the hardest, for some, the back float. It's important to learn to float on your back, because you can't pass this class if you don't learn how. More important, it's vital to be able to float if you get tired while you're swimming, especially, in deep water. So, practice with your buddy later today during class when you have a little 'free' time. And get checked off with me before you leave."

She reviewed the back float. Then she went over the prone glide, again.

"Hopefully, all of you have mastered the prone glide, and can hold your breath for a pretty long time. Aim for at least twenty seconds when you're practicing today. Please, spread out. You and your buddy, critique each other while I watch."

After she was satisfied that they could all do the 'glide', she called them back to a semi-circle in shallow water. "Now, we're going to try the crawl stroke. Please watch." First, she did a prone glide for a long time, and then she started a slow crawl stroke. After about ten yards, she turned around and swam back.

Next, she discussed it, breaking it down into little parts. She demonstrated how to 'cup' a hand with fingers together...to get more pulling surface against the water. Then she had all the girls stand in three feet of water, bend over, and 'swim', with just their arms, ...not really going anywhere. She demonstrated the importance of bending the arm and lifting the elbow high... and then reaching 'straight' forward with each stroke. She and Gerri corrected the ones who were 'wind-milling' with straight arms, and some others, who were reaching 'criss-cross'.

"Now, buddies, spread out, and try several 'long prone glides, and the crawl stroke. Kick your feet a little, if you can remember. Critique each other in helpful ways."

Beth and Lori headed out to a little deeper water.

"You first," said Lori.

"Okay." And Beth set out in a *very respectable* crawl stroke. She swam about fifteen yards, and then 'flipped over' and swam back.

"*That was great!* Are you on a team?"

"Yes, at school."

"You have a great crawl stroke. Is that 'your race'?"

"Yeah, that and the 'back stroke'."

"Neat! The backstroke is one of my worst," said Lori.

69

"Okay, now you," said Beth.

Lori took off with a smooth glide, and then started swimming. She 'rode low in the water' but was something to watch. She seemed to effortlessly, ...almost 'lazily' just 'cruise' along.

There was no splash anywhere, yet, each stroke took her pretty far. She stopped after going about fifteen yards, turned around, and swam back.

"Well, *I'm* impressed!" said Beth.

"Me, too," said Walli, who had waded out. You both are 'way ahead' of the other eight girls. How would you both like to be our assistants, and help us demonstrate?"

They agreed, and she called the rest of the girls back to a semi-circle.

"You Falcons are lucky! We have two girls in this class who are 'excellent' swimmers. And, they have 'graciously' agreed to be our assistants for the rest of this first camp session."

Lori and Beth just looked at each other because they both had thought she had meant 'just for now'.

"Sometimes it's hard for us to demonstrate and talk at the same time, but now we don't have that problem. Beth, would you 'demo' the crawl, mostly with 'arms only' please? Slowly, if you will..."

Beth did about thirty strokes, very slowly. Walli pointed out the way she held her hands 'cupped'...and lifted her elbows high, ...and the straightness of her forward reach.

When Beth stood up the girls clapped and said, "Yea, Beth!"

Beth didn't expect the adulation and she was embarrassed. Then Walli complimented her with, "Beth, you have a wonderful crawl stroke. Don't ever change it."

Beth turned crimson.

The girls cheered her again. Lori cheered and clapped the loudest. It made

Beth feel good. She looked around at all the smiling faces, and she smiled back. As she stepped back into the semi-circle, to 'give way' to Walli's next words, several girls gravitated to her.

"I can use all the help you've got. I'm the worst!" said Nancy.

Beth suddenly found herself being 'popular'.

"Next," said Walli, "we're going to learn about your legs. They're much heavier than your arms, and if you don't kick with them, they'll sink, and drag you down. They're much more powerful than your arms, so you need to make them work harder." She asked Lori to come 'float' on Gerri's 'outstretched arms', face down, but not 'face in the water'.

With Lori in position, she stressed the importance of letting the toes turn in, a little; not bending the knees 'more than a little'...or even not at all, and to keep the legs churning, like 'a little motor' behind you." Then she had Lori stand up and asked her to do a prone glide, and to move only her feet.

Lori pushed off, glided a long ways, and then, as she slowed down, she started her kick. She moved forward just like she *did* have a little motor pushing her.

"Look at that. She's moving pretty fast!" said Nancy.

"I never even knew you used your feet to swim," said Liz.

Lori went about ten yards, stopped, and stood up.

The girls clapped for her, too.

"Now, Lori, will you swim slowly, across in front of us, about twenty yards, or so?" "Don't demonstrate how to catch a breath, just yet, okay?" asked Walli'

Lori nodded. She moved out a little deeper, took in a breath, and started out with a prone glide. Next she got her feet going, and then she added her arms.

Everyone just stared, ...and then stared some more. Lori looked like she 'belonged' in the water. She cut it like a knife. It was beautiful to watch, and all eyes were on her, as if hypnotized. She was swimming 'slow'...and yet, moving fast.

"I could never look like that," said Liz.

"She's a 'natural'," said Nancy. "It looks like she has 'rubber fins' on her feet to help her out."

"How does she do her arms like that without splashing at all?" asked Ceil.

Walli said, "Girls, you are looking at pure, 'poetry in motion'. She is very, very special. Any thing you can learn from her, and from Beth, will help you to be a better swimmer, and then you'll really be able to have fun in the water."

"I bet she could swim across the lake," said one voice.

"...and back, ...several times," said Walli.

Lori stood up and looked back, ...to 'silence' ...and wondering faces, ...instead of clapping.

Beth and Walli and Gerri broke the silence by clapping and cheering, ...and the others joined in, and then, she heard, "Yea, Lori!" She glanced at Walli, and saw that she was motioning for her to return to the group. Automatically, she did the crawl stroke going back.

And the girls took it all in. She was heading right at them, and they could see that she didn't cross her arms over. Also, she was swimming 'to get somewhere' so she was pulling a bit harder. There was a definite little 'wake' behind her.

"Is she racing now?" asked Vivian.

"No," said Walli, "she's just swimming, and you will be too, very soon."

This time when she stood up, the girls spontaneously clapped. Lori looked down because so many eyes were on her, and then to cover her embarrassment, she did an 'exaggerated' curtsey. They clapped louder. She smiled and said, "Thank you," and headed for Beth.

"Okay, thank you, very much, Beth and Lori! Oh, ...Lori?"

Lori stopped, and headed back toward her.

"Would you mind working with these four?" She was pointing at Lu and Jen, and Julie and Joann. "Beth can stay with those four, closest to her."

"Oh, no," she thought. *"I'm doomed."* But, she said, "Okay," and with a sigh, headed toward them.

Walli said in a loud voice. "Girls, as soon as Beth and Lori have checked that you can glide well, and do the crawl for about fifteen feet, report over here to us. Gerri will work on any last little corrections, and then I want to check each of you, personally."

As Lori approached them, Jen was smiling at her, 'happy' for the turn of events. Lu glared at her, as usual. Joann was frowning, because she liked having Julie to herself. And as Lori led the group away from Walli and Gerri, and Beth's group, Julie was looking at her as if in a trance.

Julie was thinking back to all the awards Lori had won, ...and her title, over all the years in the lower grades and high school, as the school's 'Most Outstanding Girl Athlete'. Since Julie didn't have P.E. class with her, or go out for any sports after school, she hadn't ever really seen her in action. She had always thought of Lori as something akin to a 'tough girl', who played sports a lot, and was probably pretty 'rough' and 'horsey'.

Since she was 6 years old, Julie had taken ballet. She truly appreciated 'grace' and 'form'. And when Walli had said 'poetry in motion', Julie was struck by the 'truth' of it. Lori's stroke wasn't the least bit horsey...it was so-o calm, and graceful.

"I'll have to pay more attention to how she looks in Archery," she thought, *"or if it's only 'grace' in the water."*

Jen got to Lori before the others, saying, "Do us first."

"Okay," sighed Lori. "Let me see your prone glide, you know, where you add the kick after you glide ten feet. You first, Lu. Kick hard."

Jen came to stand right next to Lori, and they all watched Lu's effort.

"Good!" said Lori. "Okay, now you, Jen."

Jen did well and Lori said, "Alright! Very good!"

Jen was happy that Lori seemed 'pleased with her effort'.

"Now Lu, please do the same thing and add your arms. Lu did pretty good, and so did Jen. *"These two already know how to swim little,"* she decided. *"They might have trouble with the back float, but they've been faking quite a lot."*

So she said, "You two can swim over to Walli, to be checked off." She saw Jen's immediate frown. But she turned and said loudly, to Walli, "These two are 'good' swimmers!" And she smiled, as if she were very proud of them, saying, "Great work!"

Jen just looked at Lu, and shrugged. It wasn't what she thought was going to happen. Then they left, each doing a decent, almost 'intermediate-level' crawl stroke.

"Would you look at that," Lori murmured silently to herself, and then thought, *"Bye-bye, girls..."*

"And, now you, Joann," she said, in a pleasant voice. Nevertheless, she saw the predictable frown. "Okay?" she asked.

Joann grouchily performed, yet, did everything well. "Good!" said Lori. "You're going to do exceptionally well, because you float very high on the water, like a light-weight stick. You have a very good kick, and you do your arms very straight. You can go back and get checked off, or you can stay and wait for Julie."

"I'll stay," said Joann, feeling pretty good about her natural ability to float high.

Lori turned to Julie. "Ready?" she asked.

"No. The water burns my nose, every time. What's the nose trick?"

"Oh," Lori remembered, and smiled. She asked Julie to kneel down right in front of her, and then she got down in the water, close in front of Julie. "Watch," she said.

But before she could begin to demonstrate, Joann got restless just waiting and said, "Bye, Julie. I'm going back to get checked off!"

"Bye," said Julie, but she had her full attention on Lori.

Lori took a slow, deep breath, emphasizing that it was coming in through her mouth. Then she closed her mouth and slowly exhaled, through her nose. She took in another breath. As she was breathing 'out' through her nose, she eased down into the water, almost up to her eyes, and continued 'exhaling' for about ten seconds. Little bubbles floated up, coming only from her nose.

She came up a few inches, caught another breath, with her mouth, ducked down, and slowly, blew little bubbles again. When she finished, she asked, "Ever blow bubbles through a straw?"

Julie nodded, "Yes."

"Well, while you're blowing, ...no soda is in the straw."

"I get it," said Julie.

Lori gave a little 'nod' downward, indicating that Julie should do it.

She did, blowing pretty hard. "It works!" she said. "My nose doesn't burn at all!"

"Let the bubbles out very slowly," said Lori.

Julie did. And for ten long seconds, she concentrated very hard, on 'not letting' any water in.

For the same ten seconds, Lori looked into her eyes, ...just looking into their depths... *"like people do to me,"* she realized. *"Maybe they're not being 'as rude as I thought' ...just curious."*

"Once more," she said to Julie. "You need to make it a habit."

And as Julie was relaxing more, she noticed Lori's eyes. She had already thought to herself that, *"They were a beautiful light green."* But now, she was so close that she could see the little flecks of 'hazel brown'. Without realizing it, she was mentally counting them as she counted seconds. She lost count, when she ran out of air.

"Save a little air for the 'last bit of water' that's usually running off your face as you come up," said Lori. "You did great."

"That's it for today, Ladies!" said Walli. "Everybody out!"

About Boys

The next afternoon during free time, Lori and several others were in the cabin reading or writing letters. When there was only about ten minutes left, Lori put her book aside, and said, "Tell me more about your boyfriend, Beth. Is he cute?"

Beth looked up from her letter with a worried look and started to blush. If Lori was suddenly going to 'tell the world' about her and her boyfriend, she'd just die. And then she'd return from the grave and 'kill' Lori Hunter.

But Lori just looked at her with a calm, serious face, and said, for Beth's benefit, "You've told me a little bit about him, but you never said if he was really cute."

Beth thought, *"A little bit about him! Lord! She knows my deepest secrets! How can she say that, with such a straight face?"* Beth took a big breath and warily started describing Ronnie.

Lori was a good listener, and silently, she tried to picture him. They ended up sitting on Lori's bunk, and soon, Nancy and Liz, were sitting and chatting, too. Joann and Julie came up and joined in. Meg, Sue, and Jill even came in from next door.

Beth was saying, "And he asked me to go for a ride in his car..."

Lori thought, as she observed their faces, *"All you have to do, is talk about boys, and girls will 'come-a-runnin'. Here I am, part of my first 'natural' group, and I don't really feel part of it at all. Guess I'll just have to get a boyfriend. Then, maybe I can feel what they're so excited to talk about."*

The thought intrigued her, causing her to try and picture herself kissing Mike, the wrestler. She couldn't exactly remember what his lips looked like. She did remember that he was definitely cute. But then, the vision of Julie's lips crept into her mind.

"Darn!" she said sort of under her breath, thinking... *"Julie, Julie, ...always Julie!"*

The other girls all stopped talking, piqued by her 'curse', and all eyes were on her. A sympathetic voice said, "Don't feel so bad, Lori. You'll get a boyfriend, soon."

Nancy chimed in, "Don't go getting 'desperate' on us."

As she looked around at them, Lori thought, *"Great! Now they think I'm desperate!"* She felt the red burn creeping up her neck, and thought, *"Blushing!...darn it, I'm blushing again! I've never blushed so much in my life!"*

Nancy laughed at her. So did the others, and Lori felt very vulnerable. In her mind, she shouted at herself, *"Stop blushing! This is silly!"* But she blushed an even deeper red.

She didn't realize that it was this 'fun' little bit of vulnerability that caused the others to really like her, and genuinely feel comfortable with her. She was surprised to see Julie, looking at her, with a genuine smile. *"That beautiful smile,"* she thought, wistfully, *"If only that smile was 'just for me', instead of 'at' me. Jeez!"* she agonized internally. She had the urge to bolt out of the cabin, but she forced herself to stay. Finally, she laughed at herself and looked down, shrugging her shoulders, and said, "Okay, ...okay. You guys think you know it all... 'Wise guys'...that's what you are..." she said, still smiling as she looked up at them.

The conversation, mercifully, got back to being about boys. Lori, the 'constant observer', saw the keen interest in their faces. *"Yep,"* she thought, *I've got to try this out, ...because, ...if thinking about a special boy is as intense as thinking about Julie, ...then, 'true love' must really be worth waiting for!"*

Archery II

Ever since Walli's 'poetry in motion' comment, Julie had been trying to figure out more about Lori. She'd always thought that the only poetry in motion was in dance. But after watching Lori swim so... so very well, she had been watching her and trying to figure out if it was just her swimming that looked pretty. It was hard to tell much from volleyball, because she hadn't done a whole lot yet. In fact, Lori hadn't even spiked the ball once. *"Well, when we play again, maybe I can give her a couple of set ups."*

She didn't think Lori was a dancer. *"She doesn't move like she's had ballet training. Yet, there is something, ...but what?"* she wondered.

Today the targets were going to be moved farther away, so Julie decided that she'd better pay attention to the counselor's instructions. But, as Fletch was talking, she kept thinking, *"How will Lori look, doing this?"*

When they were allowed to go shoot, Julie said, "Lori, you shoot first, okay? I'll just watch for a few minutes. Here, shoot my arrows, too," she said, holding out her six.

Lori shrugged, and nodded her 'okay', and Julie moved behind Lori and sat down to observe.

Lori didn't seem to have any 'wasted' motion. She notched an arrow, drew, aimed, and then shot...all very smoothly. And, she usually hit the target. *"I bet that's her life."* thought Julie. *"She just does 'stuff'...easily."*

Julie checked out her posture. *"Not a dancer's posture. There was something very different. It was very graceful...but not ballet-type at all."* She couldn't even picture Lori in a 'tutu' of filmy material being lifted by a male dancer.

"No, Lori would be out of her element being held up in the air like that. She doesn't seem to be the type to 'turn over control' to someone else very easily. Now, she could probably lift me up like that," she thought, and snickered to herself at the thought of two girls 'ballet dancing'. Although, she knew that sometimes, when the 'show must go on' and there weren't enough guys, ...it happened. They dressed the part, and danced as guys.

She looked at Lori's legs. She could see the muscles, but they weren't all 'bunched up' or knotty. They were long and supple. She had very smooth, very shapely legs. *"Hmm...I wonder why she never went out for cheerleading? She's a little bit taller than I am. She could probably jump really high, and she's got a great figure."*

As Lori drew back the bowstring, Julie noted her exact stance, so she could try to copy it. *"I can do that,"* she thought, adding... *"And, she doesn't look the least bit 'horsey'. She looks more like a, ... a, ...pretty statue. Strong, for sure, but somehow, she's 'refined'...almost ...delicate."*

She went around to the other side, facing Lori, and sat down again.

Lori felt self-conscious, but she was impressed that Julie seemed really interested in learning.

As Lori pulled back the bowstring and aimed, Julie noticed her profile. *"She has a good stance,"* she decided. *"She looks like a... a... 'female Robin Hood'. No male could have a figure like that!"*

Then Julie looked down the row, one by one, at the other girls who were shooting. *"Yep...mostly they look like 'girls'...just 'trying' to shoot. But, Lori looks like a...a...mature young 'lady' who has perfected the art."* Julie surprised herself, using the term 'lady'.

"Yes," Julie thought, with a sigh. *"Walli was right. She is pretty unique."*

"Stop shooting! Retrieve Arrows!" said Fletch.

When it was Julie's turn, Lori was amazed. Julie did everything slowly and deliberately, and really 'looked like an archer'. And, she hit the target three out of six times.

"Fantastic!" said Lori, smiling. "Here, shoot my arrows, too."

And when they moved the targets back farther, she still hit the target three out of six times.

"You're really looking great!" she said, to Julie.

"Thanks...thanks for helping me," said Julie, smiling her beautiful smile...

As goosebumps burned their way down her back, Lori thought, happily, *"That smile..., 'that' smile... was just for me."*

Later, on the way back to the cabin, they still didn't have much to talk about, but Julie felt really good about herself. And Lori, was thinking about Julie's metamorphosis, from a caterpillar to a butterfly, and how it had happened so quickly. *"She could be pretty good at sports, I bet, ...if she only liked them."*

Horses II

Boots welcomed he Falcons. "Today you will get to be up on a horse, but be patient."

She showed them, again, how to bring Dumplin' out to the tie rings between two poles, and how to put on her 'regular' riding halter. Boots took her time, emphasizing how to get the bit in the horse's mouth, 'just so', and to remind them to be gentle on the reins, or the metal bit would hurt Dumplin's mouth.

"Ugh. I'd hate to have anything like that in my mouth!" said Lu.
"You need it sometimes," said Jen, sharply.
Everybody just looked at them, wondering what their problem was.
"Uh, ...to keep you quiet!" smirked Jen, as an explanation.
But no one laughed.

Lori was thinking, *"Actually, Lu is the quieter one. Jen is the real 'mouth'."*

Next they learned how to saddle a horse, making sure the cinch was tight. "You'll think it's tight," Boots said. "But the horses 'pooch out' their bellies, and fool you. So, you have to wait a minute or so, and tighten it again." She demonstrated, and the girls were amazed that she could pull the belt about two or three inches tighter than before.

"If you forget this part, your saddle will be hanging upside down between her legs. You will have been dumped out on the trail somewhere. The horse will probably break a leg trying to buck it off. You'll have to walk back, if you're able. And the horse may have to be shot."

The girls were stunned, and they were quiet. As they thought about her words, each girl knew that she didn't want to be responsible for a horse having to be shot.

Next, Boots showed them how to adjust the stirrups.

"Buddies, get together. Both of you will walk a horse around this big ring. One of you will hold the lead rope, and get used to staying to the left side, so you don't get stepped on. I'll tell you when to switch."

Boots' assistants brought out more horses and helped the girls to get them saddled, and then got them started walking around the ring. 'Checkers', a short, sturdy little mare with very fat sides was assigned to Ceil and Vivian. Beth and Lori got a nervous gelding named 'Blackie'. They walked around once with Beth holding onto the lead rope.

Joann and Julie got 'Dumplin' and they were in front of Beth and Lori. Julie was keeping her distance and letting Joann do the lead rope. Lori noticed that Lu and Jen had gotten 'Rocky'.

"Okay, change leads!" they heard from Boots.

Julie cautiously took the rope from Joann, and was very much aware of the horse's hooves. She held the rope at its very end, and stayed far away.

But Lori thought it felt pretty natural to walk next to a horse's head. She felt very relaxed and found herself talking in a low voice to Blackie.

Next, Boots showed them how to mount from the ground, always from the left side.

"Why?" asked Nancy.

"Just because it's a tradition," said Boots. "Everybody does it, and a horse might move away from you if you try the other side." Then she showed them a big rock that had been placed there for those who chose to mount, more easily, from there instead of from the ground She reminded them how to adjust the length of the stirrups and told the buddies to help each other do that.

"Okay, buddies, one will mount and sit quietly, for a walk around the ring. Keep the reins a little slack. The other person will lead the horse, like you just did."

Joann mounted from the rock. Beth mounted from the ground. Ceil used the rock and a little help from Vivian.

Every one made it around the ring, and Boots said, "Switch!"

Joann dismounted, got Julie mounted up, and then left to use the restroom. Lori looked at Julie, and noticed that she 'sat a horse' like a wooden statue. 'Dumplin' was behaving very well, and stood there, motionless.

"Twin statues," thought Lori, as she appraised Julie's profile. *"She's 'short-waisted' and 'long-legged'. She sits a horse, well, and looks better than people like me, who are more 'long-waisted'. And, with her 'perfect posture' she would look like a real 'horse-woman', if only she wasn't so scared."*

And then, Dumplin' slowly turned her head a little to the right.

"She's moving!" gasped Julie. "My horse is...moving!"

Dumplin' kept turning her head, and stretched her whole neck around farther and farther, until she was looking back at Julie, almost directly in the eyes.

"See? She moved! My horse moved! She's staring right at me! What do I do?"

Lori laughed to herself, because it did seem like a strange thing for a horse to do.

Gerri was there, in a flash, calming Julie, and reassuring her, and stroking Dumplin'.

On their next turn they learned to keep their heels down lower than their toes, in the stirrups. It felt strange, to Lori, but she could feel the difference in the ride. She could stand up in the stirrups easier, if she needed to.

Before the session ended, each girl had ridden at least three times, and they were all feeling more comfortable around the animals. Before leaving, the buddies had to water and groom their horses, and put them in their individual stalls.

"Ouch!" they heard from Jen, in the next stall. "Oh, God! Lu! Get him off me!"

Then, Lu's voice, in a quieter tone, "Maybe if you'd watch what you're doing, instead of staring at them, all the time, you wouldn't gave gotten stepped on."

"Just shut up! Just... Oh! My foot! It's killing me!"

Boots and Gerri went to check out the situation, and so did lots of others.
Lori and Beth just shrugged at each other, and headed back to the cabin.

Letter Home

Well, Dad,

Just call me 'Dusty'. The horse ring, was super dry today. I hope it rains soon. I'm loving learning to ride! It's one of the things here that I'm new at, and Boots, our instructor, is great with horses. My favorite is Rocky. As much as I like him, I haven't gotten to ride him yet.

Ceil and Vivian, (you remember...'Chub' and 'Chubbier') were assigned a very strong, short, <u>fat</u>, little horse named 'Checkers'. It was too funny! At least they weren't very high up in the air! But they couldn't bend their knees around that 'wide-barrel-belly' at all. So their legs hung almost straight out to the sides. Beth and I got the giggles every time we looked at them. They are two of my favorite people!

Some girls love horses! It's amazing how much of their free time they spend down at the stables. Seems like they just live to be near them.

Tonight is 'Charade Night'. I'll probably enjoy watching the others perform, but I'll feel sorry for them having to watch me when it gets to be my turn.

Swimming is next. We're all getting good tans, and 'lookin' good.

Ciao, for now... Miss you lots...Hugs and kisses.

                                                                        Lori

Swimming Test Day

"Welcome!" said Walli. "Today is 'Test Day'. Some of you still need to get checked off on the basics of the crawl stroke and the back float. Get your buddy and let's review everything, beginning with our 'prone glides'. Spread out a little, please. Half by me and half over towards Gerri."

Beth and Lori noticed Walli, motioning for them to please, split up, and go help people. Beth said, "Bye. See you later," and headed for her group, ...Liz, Nancy, Ceil, and Vivian.

"Yeah, okay," said Lori, and turned around to see Joann and Julie, both doing the prone float, and "Look at that," she said to herself. "Lu and Jen, are gliding perfectly, too. Now that they know I know, hopefully there will be no more faking." She noticed that Julie didn't look very relaxed because she was as stiff as a board, as usual.

"Okay, Ladies. Now, let's see your 'prone glides with a kick'," said Walli.
Lori didn't say a word. She just watched, as the girls did their glides.

"Now, let's see your prone glides, with a powerful kick," said Walli.
And Lori still just watched them all.

Next, when they were asked to add the crawl stroke, she got involved with all four of them. Each one had a different little problem that they seemed to revert to. Jen needed to put her fingers tighter together. Lu needed to straighten out her forward reach. Joann had to raise her elbows higher. And Julie needed to relax. She could float, and kick, and swim with her arms, but her back and neck were so rigid, she looked like she had a metal backbone.

"I'll try to work with her a little after class if she wants," thought Lori. *"But, at least she has conquered the 'water in her nose' problem,"* she thought, as she watched Julie, deliberately breathing out of her nose after her face had been in the water.

As each girl corrected her problem, she went to be checked off, and then came back.

"Next, is the review of the back float!" announced Walli.

All of a sudden, all four girls were wanting her attention, and Lori had to say, "Wait a minute, please. Jen, you first. And Julie, can you help Joann?"

Jen wanted her to hold her up to get her started. So, Lori did, warily. Jen was almost floating in no time, with Lori talking softly to her. Lu was right there, watching. Lori had her hand under Jen's upper back, but it wasn't really needed, finally, because Jen was 'floating on her own'.

Lori was just about to move her hand, completely, and compliment Jen, on having a nice float, when, Jen abruptly rolled over toward Lori. The roll over onto her stomach, caused her to be 'floating' in the prone position, chest down. But her head was up. And, her breast was in Lori's hand.

Lori didn't notice at first, because she was busy, catching Jen, and asking, "What's wrong? You were doing just great. Why did you stop?"

And then, when Jen just smirked at her, Lori felt the soft breast in her hand and realized what was going on. She quickly backed away from Jen, dropping her, and looked up at Lu who had fire in her eyes. Ignoring her for the moment, she looked over at Julie, to see if she had seen the 'antic'. It didn't seem like she did. She and Joann were still helping each other.

Lori clenched her jaw, and said, "You're done here Jen. If you have any questions, go see Walli." Then, she turned her back on Jen. Taking a big breath, she decided to let the incident just pass for now, and thought, *"It's a good thing it takes me a long time to get really mad."*

"Come on, Lu," she said, "and don't try anything like that."

Scowling as usual, Lu said, sarcastically, "Don't worry! I wouldn't!"

Lori began helping her to float on her back. Lu had a little problem, because she was long and lanky and had almost no body fat. She tended to sink, too. But Lori convinced her to be happy with an almost vertical float. They ended up having to go out a little deeper so that her feet wouldn't touch the bottom, and finally, Lu could do it.

"Alright, Ladies. If you've been checked off by Lori or Beth, come over here by us, please. I'll check every float. And, Gerri's going to time you, to see if you can float on your back for ten minutes. I'll decide if you pass or fail the float tests."

Julie stayed. The other three left.

As Lori went back to more shallow water, Julie waded up to her, and said, "Yes, I'm the only one left, as usual, ...and don't drop me this time." And Julie came right up to her and began to lean backwards into the float.

Lori found it was easier to reach out and touch Julie's back, this time. And when Julie felt her hand there, she almost jumped into the back float. Lori caught her weight on two hands, and she was holding Julie like a baby. *"Just like Jen wanted me to do the other day,"* she thought. *"Only... I don't mind holding Julie,"* she admitted, frankly. *"No, no..."* she commanded herself... *"Think only of floating lessons."*

Lori really concentrated on 'getting Julie to float', instead of just 'on Julie'. She removed her other hand, and just kept the one under Julie's upper back. "Julie, can you hear me?"

Julie had both eyes tightly shut, but she said "Yes."

Speaking very, very slowly, Lori said, "It will help you if you can relax. It's important not to be stiff in the water. So, just relax. Take a deep breath, and relax. Let your chest come up. Let your arms go out to the side, and back. Let your feet sink. Breathe deeper."

Julie was following each direction as Lori's soft voice reached her ears under the water. She did feel like she was relaxing. "I can do this," she said aloud.

"Yes, you can," said Lori. "You're almost floating all by yourself."

"Don't let go," said Julie, tensing up. "Don't let me go."

"Lori just looked at her worried face, and said, "I won't. Don't worry."

Julie slowly began relaxing again as her fear of being dropped, was lessening. And then, without warning, she smiled 'that' smile.

Lori felt her insides quiver and thought, *"Oh, Lord."*

Up until now, she had managed to think only about what Julie needed to do to float, better. *"Such a simple thing,"* she thought. *"Just a smile, ...a simple smile, ...and it 'captures' me."*

"Julie," she said softly. But Julie didn't hear her. "Ju...lie." she said, a little louder, and she realized she liked the sound of her name. She said it again. "Ju...lie."

"What, Lori? Are you going to let go?" she asked, tensing up.

"Please, stand up, okay?"

Julie stood up, and looked at her. "Did I do something wrong?"

"No, you were perfect," said Lori. "But, you have to be able to pass the ten minute floating test. So, this time, I'll move my hand away, after I count backward from ten to zero, okay?"

"Well, if you think I'm ready," she answered.

"You are. You're more than ready. I was 'touching' your back, but I wasn't holding you up. You actually float higher in the water than Lu or Beth."

"I do?"

"Yes. So come on now, and prove it to yourself. Remember...stay relaxed."

Lori was amazed at how natural it seemed this time to put her hand under Julie's back. She felt bad that it was going to end in about one minute, but she tried to look ahead. *"Maybe we'll get to go swimming together, soon."* she hoped.

"You're doing just great." She paused and then said, "Ten." Julie tensed up. "Relax, again." Lori waited, and then began again. "Nine, eight. You're floating, but I'm still touching you. Seven, six, ...five, four, three, two..." she paused. "one...zero." and she moved her hand just underneath Julie's back, but stayed close enough, in case she tensed up again.

"Ju-lie, you're float...ing, and you look beau...tiful, ...uh, ...floating."

"Do you think I'll sink soon?"

85

"No way. Pretend you're doing the ten minute test, right now."

"Okay, but don't leave me, okay?"

Lori rolled her eyes, and said, "I wouldn't."

Now Lori had a little while to just look at her. For the life of her, she couldn't figure out why she was so 'hung up' by this one girl. As she looked at her face, and started admiring her once again, feature by feature, she felt her own 'little friend' coming to life. *"This won't do,"* she thought. *"I can't spend so much of my time thinking about Julie."*

And then her eyes settled on Julie's breasts, in spite of her firm resolve. *"I like to look at those breasts,"* she admitted to herself. *"And the clearly outlined nipples are definitely, 'special'. "And, there you are..."* she said 'to her friend'. *"I really feel you now. You're here right on cue,"* she thought, as she felt the little waves of pleasure. *"I'm going to have to give you a name,"* she thought, chuckling to herself. *"...and of course, it will have to begin with a 'J'. Nothing else will do."* "How about 'Jerk'?"

Julie stood up and said, "What?"

"Oh, nothing. Just that you did it. You're a 'real' floater, now. You can go get tested by Walli, any time," Lori said, smiling. "I'm proud of you."

"Thanks," said Julie. Then she looked down and got very quiet. When she looked up, she looked at Lori as if she was in the midst of a big decision. Finally, she said, "You know, I didn't want to tell anyone, but I had a very bad experience when I was five years old."

Lori looked into her eyes without saying a word, and was completely attentive.

"I fell into a pond, and almost drowned. My uncle pulled me out. It was his pond. I haven't even waded in deep water, since then."

"That explains a lot," said Lori, softly. "Now I'm exceptionally proud of you."

"Really?" Julie just 'beamed' a big smile at her.

Lori felt a ripple of goose bumps go down her back. *"That's the second one, just for me,"* she thought. *"I could easily spend a lifetime looking at that smile."*

"You won't tell anyone else, will you?" asked Julie, getting a worried look on her face.

"Not even on the day I die," said Lori. "Come on," she said, smiling and reaching for Julie's hand. "Let's go tell Walli you're ready to pass her test."

Julie put her hand in Lori's, and they waded several steps together like that, hand in hand.

Finally, Lori saw Beth waving at her and felt self conscious. She let go and waved back.

Getting Somewhere

Walli told Julie that she would test her right after class. But for now, she had all the girls sit in the shallow water, while she talked.

"Now that most of you have passed most of the float tests, we'll soon be doubling up on class size. Probably, at your very next session, the Hawks, will be joining this group. That way, you'll get to swim almost every day."

The girls cheered at that because it seemed like the weather was getting hotter all the time.

Walli continued, "You'll really need to rely a little more on your buddy, and on Lori and Beth. So far, I'm pleased with this group. And before you leave today, I'd like you to swim about fifteen feet or so, doing the crawl, with your face *in* the water. When you get near me, put your head up, get a breath, and turn over into a back float. Sound easy? It is, if you know how to tread water."

She demonstrated the 'fin-like' move of an underwater hand, back and forth, pushing against the water. "Keep your knuckles up, and your palms down. Push the water downward."

Everyone had to stand in the water, chest-deep, and try to tread water hard enough to bend their knees and lift their feet off the bottom. Success meant a girl could keep them elevated a little for at least thirty seconds.

"I seem to pull myself downward," said Ceil.

Beth went over to her, to help.

"Me, too," said Liz. And Gerri headed towards her.

Everybody else seemed to get the idea.

"Now, I'd like to see you go from a prone glide into a back-float," said Walli. "As you roll over and float on your back, you can move your hands by your side, treading water a bit, and even kick your feet a little if you need to."

Lori was amazed that everybody did it the very first time, even Julie.

"Okay. Now, one at a time, swim the crawl stroke from here," she said, pointing to an imaginary line, "to out deeper, where I'll be standing. You will be able to touch the bottom, if you need to. But I'll hope you can swim, face down, for that distance, then put your face up, catch a breath, and roll over and float on your back. Stay floating, until I say 'okay'." said Walli. "Any questions?" "No? Then, okay Vivian, you first, but wait until I get out a little deeper."

As each girl tried the routine, Gerri, Lori or Beth did a follow-up with her, to work on a specific skill. Everyone but Liz finally did it well, and Beth offered to help her after class.

87

Walli said, "Everyone listen up." She waited until they got closer, and completely attentive. "See that dock out there?" she said, pointing to a little dock, floating all by itself, out near the middle of the lake. "It's a long swim to get there. Don't try it, unless I have 'certified' you, personally, to do so. To qualify, you have to swim two hundred yards without touching bottom. You can float to rest if you need to."

"From this buoy in the shallow water to the next one in shallow water is twenty-five yards. To the second buoy farther down, is fifty yards. A round trip is one hundred yards. Twice around is two hundred yards."

"Anyone who wants to get this 'special' permission, can be tested, now." She looked at Beth and Lori, and raised her eyebrows, in a silent question, directed at them.

Beth and Lori looked at each other, and agreed to try to qualify. They both looked back at Walli, with smiles on their faces, and nodded an emphatic "Yes!"

Walli sent them out a little deeper, and told Beth to go first. Lori was to follow when Beth had rounded the fifty-yard buoy and was on her way back. Beth waded out a little, and took off, swimming the crawl stroke, easily and steadily. She liked to 'breathe' on her left side, every other stroke.

Walli asked the rest of the class to sit on the beach, with Gerri, and watch. She explained, "Both of these girls know how to turn their heads a little and 'breathe' as they swim. Some people take a breath each time they bring the left arm forward. Others prefer the right side. Some people like to alternate. And some people catch a breath only after three or four strokes. It's called 'catching' a breath, because you have to do it pretty fast, breathing in through the mouth, and out through the nose, as you are swimming along."

Julie felt good that she already knew about that.

Lori finally started out, and when she began the crawl, she had everybody looking to see if she would splash much. Julie was especially interested to see if she could figure out how to copy her stroke exactly.

"Notice that she doesn't 'sling' her arms forward," said Vivian. "She 'puts' them in the water, instead of 'slapping' them in like I do. Maybe that's the trick."

"Yeah, she puts each hand in like an arrow," said Nancy.

"It's easy to see her feet churning. Man! She's got power in her legs," said Ceil.

"She leaves a little 'wake' behind her, like a swan," said Julie.

"Does she breathe on the left or right?" asked Liz.

"Hard to tell. Looks like one side and then the other," said Vivian.

When Beth crossed the 'finish line' everybody cheered for her. Lori wasn't far behind her, and they kept right on cheering.

"Congratulations!" said Walli. Whenever there is a lifeguard on duty, like now, you both may swim out to the dock if you have free time. Or, if you prefer, there is a 'short-cut' to the dock, if you walk a quarter of the way around the lake to the left. There is a sand spit, that goes almost all the way there. And unless we have lots of rain, the lake is low enough that you can touch bottom most of the way. You might have to swim for the last twenty feet or so. Beth and Lori, you two may leave now and enjoy the dock. Class is almost over for today. Thanks for all your help!"

The group watched as the two happy girls waved good-bye to everyone and dove in the water. The little audience couldn't believe they would casually swim all the way to the middle of the lake after just swimming two hundred yards.

"Who else wants to qualify for dock privileges today?"

Jen's hand shot up. And then Lu put hers up, too. "Alright, Jen, you and Lu walk out to the starting point. Lu, you go first."

Lu began her swim and made it to the second buoy before she turned over and floated. As she was resting and catching her breath, Jen passed her by. Then Jen had to roll over and float, and soon Lu passed her by.

The girls on shore were thinking that neither one would pass the test, and were betting that Lu would quit first and stand up. They also realized that neither Lu nor Jen kicked much at all.

Walli was glad that they were noticing the 'bad' skills as well as the 'good' ones. Both swimmers were getting tired and having to float a lot.

Lori and Beth boosted themselves up on the dock, and heard the whoops and hollers from the beach. They waved their 'thanks' at them, and sat down to relax.

Jen quit first, very mad at herself. Lu quit shortly afterward. The rest of the girls offered their condolences, but Jen walked up and sat down in the shallow water sulking.

Lu came and sat beside her.

Walli suggested that for the next fifteen minutes the remaining girls practice swimming as far as they could between buoys and then rolling over to float. She also told Julie she was ready to test her back float.

Meanwhile, Beth and Lori had just earned a new freedom, and it felt good.

"Camp is getting better!" said Lori, and Beth wholeheartedly agreed.

Donna Kelli

The Day Hike

After breakfast the next morning, Katie said, "Attention, please," and announced, "The Falcons, from cabin number three, have a 'Day Hike' with me. All other cabins have your regular schedule."

"Okay, Falcons, get your lunches, which have already been packed for you, in the side kitchen, and get a canteen each." After the general announcement, Katie went to the side bar and got her own lunch. All 'the Falcons' congregated there too, and she told them to meet with her outside their cabin in 10 minutes.

When they all arrived, Katie gathered them into a small semi-circle, right in front of the cabin, to answer any last minute questions. They had discussed the upcoming hike a little, after horseback riding, yesterday, and some more last night, with Gerri, before lights out. So, they knew they would be gone long enough to have an early picnic lunch, a swim, and then return. It would be a fairly short hike, ... only a mile and a half or so, each way.

"I hope you chose comfortable, sturdy shoes, and remembered to wear two pairs of socks," said Katie. "Your feet will appreciate it. And you already have your bathing suits on under your shorts, right? You should have your towel, and you can bring candy or any personal items you're willing to carry a long way."

Then Gerri passed out backpacks, along with a little garden spade, and some toilet paper, to each girl, saying, "You'll learn more about these later today."

Within a few minutes the girls were milling around outside the cabin, some, tying or re-tying shoelaces. Canteen straps needed to be adjusted, and they helped each other get backpacks strapped on comfortably. They carried their lunches in the backpacks, near the top, so they wouldn't get squashed.

"Are there any snakes?" asked Ceil.

"Some," replied Katie. "Remember, this is the woods...not civilization."

"Poisonous ones?" asked Lu.

"Yes, some of those, too," said Katie. And she produced a little book, about the size of a deck of cards. These are pictures of snakes. We're not going on a 'snake-hunt' especially, but it will be better for you if you know what they look like. As I hold this out for you to see, come closer, and really 'check out' these two pages...a 'copper-head' on the left, and a 'rattlesnake' on the right. Both are 'poisonous'."

"If you do see a snake, stop walking and *Freeze* where you are. Say, 'out loud', *"Snake!"* and decide where to step next, preferably backwards. The best defense is to look! And I mean, *really look,* where you intend to put your feet, before you take each step."

"That means, you have to learn to talk to each other, while 'looking at the trail', instead of 'looking at each other'."

"Here, on page fifteen, is a 'black snake'. They're harmless. Big, sometimes. Even four feet long, sometimes. 'Scary' but not poisonous. Look again, and remember the picture of a copperhead. They *are* poisonous."

"And here, on page eighteen, is a picture of a 'king snake', which is not poisonous. It looks a lot like the 'rattler' on page nineteen. Take a good look at these two pages for comparison."

The book was passed around, and there was a buzz of conversation.

"I hate snakes!" said Beth.

"Me, too," said Nancy.

Joann asked, "Where's the nearest hospital?"

"Twenty miles away," said Katie. "They have 'anti-venoms for snake bites, so, we would try to get you to the hospital. But, try not to get bitten, okay?" She continued, "If you come to a log, step up on it all the way, look, and then take a bigger step off of it, just in case there's a snake lying on the other side."

Lori saw Julie shiver.

"Come on, let's get started." And with that, Katie started off, saying, over her shoulder, "Buddy System."

All the girls paired off and found a place in the line. Lori, with Beth at her side, just automatically fell in behind Julie and Joann. After walking a little while, she noticed that there was something about Julie's way of walking, that was different from most other girls.

Lori kept watching her move along the trail. *"What is it?"* she asked herself. Julie didn't 'plop' her feet down, in a careless way, like some girls did. Neither did she always walk firmly, heel to toe. There was 'something' different...but she just couldn't pinpoint what it was. It didn't seem like Julie was going on a long hike. It was more like she was... 'gliding along' ...sort of 'floating' came to Lori's mind. *"No, that's ridiculous,"* she said to herself. *"But, I've seen that style of walk before, somewhere, ...but where?"* *"I guess it will come to me sometime,"* she decided and she gave up trying to figure it out.

The group had started out, along the path that went around the lake. When they got to the other side, they turned off onto a side path, that looked like it went right into the wilderness.

"Have you ever seen a snake?" asked Beth.

Her question brought Lori back to the moment at hand. "Yes, at a friend's house, once."

"Were you afraid? At first, I mean."

91

"No, just 'startled' a little... It wasn't poisonous... it was green. We just watched it awhile and then it left. It just disappeared into a hole."

"I'm scared of them!" said Beth, matter-of-factly, "...and I admit it. They give me the creeps!"

Katie was explaining about the 'flora and the fauna'. So, if you have any questions about the flowers and plants, just look for the pictures in this other little book. And now, for the 'fauna'. She named off several small animals, like squirrels, raccoons, and possums. If you see an animal, just call out, and maybe we can all see it, too."

"Are there any bears?" asked Jen.

"Probably not," said Katie. The rangers keep taking any 'strays' back to the National Park.

Beth and Lori looked at each other with raised eyebrows, and then they really began to scrutinize the woods ahead and to the sides.

"Probably not, she says!" mimicked Beth. "I can just see it all, now. 'Dear Mrs. Perkins, We're sorry to inform you, but Beth was killed by a bear. This doesn't 'usually' happen at our camp. We're glad to say, the bear was captured and killed, by the rangers. The bear wore a name tag... His name was *Probably Not.*"

Lori chuckled, appreciating all Beth's facial antics.

Gerri overheard her story, and was laughing quietly, to herself. She would tell Katie about it later.

After about an hour of walking they came to a little clearing. Katie gathered them close and said, "Check the ground for ants and such, and then sit down in a semi-circle, please."

Some girls were afraid of almost any kind of bug, so it took a few minutes, to get everybody settled. Katie demonstrated how to dig a little hole for a personal latrine. "It has to be deep enough to cover up everything, including your toilet paper. If both you and your buddy, plan to use it, dig it a little deeper. Check the area carefully before you begin to dig and before you crouch down. I now dismiss you to go 'hide in the bushes' if you need to," she said, smiling.

After about fifteen minutes, the group got going again. Soon they arrived at a wide, shallow, rocky creek that had some deep spots, wide enough to swim around in.

The cold water felt good, and after swimming and playing around in the shallow water for over an hour, they had their picnic lunch. Then several girls sat around relaxing in the shade, while others went back to wade in the water. Lori and Beth ended up sunbathing on their towels, on a very large boulder. For the past half hour they had been letting their bare feet get tan, and were just putting their dry sneakers back on.

"I have to write Dad, about this place," said Lori. "It's so pretty."

Suddenly they heard, *"Snake! Snake!"* coming from Liz. She was just across the creek and was looking down, and backing up into deeper water. She tripped on a rock and sat down hard, making a big splash.

Several people started moving. Lori headed toward Liz. Beth followed, but well behind her. Liz's buddy, Nancy, started to go help her, but changed her mind and moved away, yelling, "Help!"

Both Katie, and Gerri, who were much farther away, started toward Liz, both shouting at the same time, "I'm coming!"

Lori was the first to reach Liz, and helped her up. "Where is it, Liz? Liz, where's the snake?"

Liz finally pointed to the edge of the creek and said, "Right there! Right there, by that dead tree!"

Lori reached down, and picked up a football-sized river rock.

Katie, now coming up about twenty feet behind her, was saying, "Lori, be careful!"

Lori approached it cautiously and raised the rock high on her right hand. She saw it and set herself in case she had to throw. Then, she relaxed a little and carefully walked a little closer, still concentrating on the spot. She relaxed even more, and turned to face Katie, who was now only steps away.

"Did you see it? Which way did it go?" asked Katie.

Lori nodded "Yes," to Katie, and pointed at the ground. Then she looked over at Liz. The terrified girl watched, 'wide-eyed'. She had her hands over her mouth, as if to stop herself from screaming and stood by Beth for comfort.

Lori spoke to Katie in a pretty loud voice, for Liz's benefit... "Could've fooled me. It looks just like that picture of a copperhead," she said.

She looked back at Liz, and started speaking to her. "But, I think it's a stick. What do you think, Liz?"

Liz forgot about being completely terrified and was now only very cautious. She started walking toward Lori. Almost the whole group went to see and made a loose circle around the stick.

Katie stood mute. She had seen the stick just before the girls closed in on it. It didn't look at all like a snake. She was thinking, *"Lori handled that, better than most counselors I've known."* She looked at the girls, discussing the 'snake', as their circle got tighter. "Yeah, it could've fooled anybody!" "Boy, Liz, you're lucky it wasn't real!"

Katie had seen this type of thing happen several times, in her years of experience, and it usually turned out that the 'Liz'-type' girl, ended up being the butt of 'scaredy-cat' jokes for the rest of the day. And sometimes, it lasted for the rest of her camp time.

Lori had just walked away and returned to her boulder. She was wringing out her socks and putting them in her pockets. She already had her wet sneakers back on and was more 'ready to go' than anyone else. As Katie watched, Lori leaned back a little and got comfortable, just patiently waiting for whatever was next.

"CIT material," thought Katie. *"Just maybe I've found my next year's counselor-in-training."*

One other person looked back at Lori. It was Julie, thinking, *"That doesn't look anything like a real snake, to me. Why would Lori say it did? Well, guess if someone, like Liz, took a quick look, and expected to see a snake...she would see a 'snake'."* She thought, *"Lori wasn't afraid. Well, maybe she was, ...but she went, right away, to help Liz, and Liz isn't even her partner. Some buddy Nancy was! She went the other way!"*

Then, Julie laughed. *"I did, too! Brave soul, that I am."*

"What are you laughing at?" asked Joann. "Are you laughing, at me?"

"No," laughed Julie. "You think everything is about 'you'."

On the way back, snakes were still the main topic of conversation. Everybody was looking sharply, everywhere. Katie winked at Gerri, who was next to her, and said, "This is how they should be, very alert."

She guided them back toward the Camp by way of a different path.

They came to a big, big tree which had fallen across the path. The tree trunk, almost two feet thick, and about fifty feet long, was completely blocking their way. Katie ducked very, very low on one knee, and went under. "Go under or hop over," she said. "It's about four feet high, here in the middle. It's your choice."

Gerri stayed on the near side to help anyone who might need it. She gave the 'heavy weight' buddies her full attention. Ceil got a boost up and managed to lie on her belly. Then she seemed marooned, holding on for dear life.

Vivian started giggling and said, "You're the biggest 'bump on a log' that I've ever seen! C'mon, 'Pardner', get off that horse before you give him a backache!"

Ceil started belly laughing and rolled off sideways to Katie's helping hands.

Then, Vivian, who weighed lots more, chose to go under. She started by crawling on her hands and knees, then 'belly-whopping' part of the way, and finally rolling out from under it. She laughed every inch of the way.

Julie and Joann had fallen behind Lori and Beth because they had stopped to look at a bird's nest. But, out of the corner of her eye, Julie caught the motion of Beth hopping up on top of the tree, crouching low, and then, hopping down on the other side. Lori was calmly waiting her turn as Julie came closer and watched her with interest.

Lori casually approached the barricade, took a couple of little steps, and then looked like she 'floated' over, and landed lightly.

Being a dancer, who usually analyzed other dancers' routines, Julie automatically started thinking about Lori's move. *"Lori just put her right hand on the tree, and then, seemingly, without effort, had, with one fluid move, 'hopped' over...No. 'Jumped over' No...she just 'sailed up and over', right foot first, like a 'high jumper' going over the bar, doing a 'scissors jump'. She cleared the tree easily and smoothly, ...almost in slow motion..."* she thought to herself, *"rather like a cat."*

Julie continued to watch the others. No one else went over the tree like that. In fact, several girls had a hard time going over the tree. Even Gerri had to roll under it. 'Lanky Lu' ran slowly, put two hands on the tree, and then grunting as she went, leaped up and pushed herself over with a 'barrel-roll jump'. She made it okay.

Jen tried to copy her, but misjudged her jump and scraped her leg on the way up, stopping abruptly on top of the tree. Gerri helped her climb off, and offered her a band aid.

Julie pictured herself going over the top. It would have to be a ballet-type leap, up and over the tree without any help from her hands. *"No,"* she thought, *"Not that way. It's pretty high,"* She laughed, thinking to herself, *"and I don't do 'cat'."*

Joann boosted herself up, and swung one leg over, and climbed up on it like it was a horse. "Come on," she said to Julie, as she sat there for a moment. Then, she dismounted on the other side.

But instead, Julie ducked extremely low, in a 'sideways split, putting one foot pretty far under. She went under, in an easy move, thinking that it reminded her of her solo dance last month. Whenever she bent over, like that, she could almost hear her instructor saying, again and again, "Straight back! Straight back!"

"Show off!" said Joann.

Then, as the group started out again, and Lori started walking along with Beth, Julie thought, *"...Still moving like a cat."* ...And after looking at her shiny, jet black hair, she chuckled, and thought of a slowly undulating, black panther. *"Only panthers don't have soft curls in their hair,"* she mused.

After about an hour, Vivian said, "I see the Camp!"

That night, after lights out for the campers, Katie was in her counselor's cabin, trying to teach a lesson to all the younger counselors. She had called a meeting, and was saying, 'I think Lori decided to do it when she saw Liz's face. It was pure terror.''

"That girl put her own credibility as a leader, in jeopardy, by saying, "looks like a snake to me." What if they'd all agreed it didn't look one bit like a snake, *which, it didn't,* she would've taken the brunt of all the 'smart aleck' remarks. And then, she gave Liz the 'first right of refusal' so to speak, by asking her, "What do you think, Liz?" Liz could've gone up to that stick, and said, "Yeah, I was stupid. It doesn't look like a snake, at all.''

"And, even if she *had* called herself 'stupid' first, then the others' remarks would've only been echoes of her own idea. She still wouldn't have been the *complete* 'goat'.''

"Lori is the undisputed leader of the Falcons. I don't even think they all realize it, yet. But she is. I can still see her ready to smash that five pound rock on that 'snake'. Then, do you know what she did? She didn't hang around to collect compliments for her bravery. She left the 'cackling hens' and went off to a boulder and sat down, and calmly got ready for whatever was next.''

"Beth is lucky to have her as her buddy." said Boots.

"Yes," agreed Katie. "Lori would never leave her, if there was any trouble. Keep an eye on Lori, please, for the next several days. And if you can, give me some input that will help me decide if I want to offer her the CIT position, for next year.''

Then she told them, "Good night.''

Swimming, Breathing, and the Side Stroke

As you all can see on this beautiful day, we now have cabin four, the Hawks, with us. Thanks for being attentive," said Walli. "This is a good, big, double group."

After reviewing all the previous lessons, Walli showed the girls in detail, how to catch a breath while doing the crawl. She had Beth hold on to her hands, and had Lori hold Beth's legs out straight in the water. Beth was in a prone position now, and completely supported. Walli could show the girls in slow motion, how Beth would roll her right shoulder down a little, and catch a breath on the left side, which was her preferred side to breathe on. She turned loose of Beth's left hand, and had her demonstrate.

Walli emphasized the importance of, catching a quick breath, but *not* lifting your head out of the water, and *not* looking like your head is glued to your shoulder, with each breath.

She and Lori then held different girls, from both cabins, to do the same thing. Gerri and Beth did the same, and 'Bigfoot, got Rory to help her do the rest. Everybody seemed to be 'getting' it, although they all looked very different.

Walli assigned them to practice doing the crawl for short distances, catching breaths, and having their buddies offer helpful suggestions. Everybody spread out to get some room.

Julie remembered that she couldn't tell very well what side Lori breathed on, when Lori swam the two hundred yard test, or even the long swim out to the dock. So she waded up to her and asked, "Lori, how do you breathe?"

Passing up the temptation to make a wise crack, Lori said, "Oh, usually on my right, every two or three strokes."

"Could you show me?"

"Okay," said Lori, and she swam away from her to the left, just to get some distance between them. She began, and Julie watched for a big turn of Lori's head, to get air. But, there was hardly any turn. Lori seemed to swim with her head tipped back a little, so her forehead cut the water, instead of the top of her head. And, when she caught a breath, she seemed to pull a little harder with her left hand, and 'lunge' a little forward, instead of a definite 'roll' to her side. As she lunged, she barely had her mouth above the water. And her mouth was 'reaching to the right side' like Julie's dad did, when he shaved his left cheek.

Julie saw why she and the other girls couldn't tell, before. There was almost no sign that she'd even caught a breath. And, there was no wasted motion. *"I don't think I can do that,"* she decided, *"but I can see why it would help her win a race."*

"Could you please do it again?" she asked.

Lori was a little wary, now, wondering if Julie was playing a joke on her, and making her seem like a fool. But Julie seemed serious, so she said, "Well, okay."

This time, Julie walked out a little deeper, so that when Lori swam by, she'd be right up close to her. As Lori swam toward her, Julie noticed that Lori peeked ahead with her right eye as she caught a breath. *"Neat."* thought Julie. *"She could stay straight in her lane, in a race, but best of all, she always knows 'what's going on'. It figures. That would be Lori."*

"Thanks!" she said. "That helped me a lot."

"Sure," said Lori, still a little curious.

Then Walli said she and Gerri and Bigfoot would be testing everybody for the next twenty minutes. Beth, Lori, and Rory helped those that asked for it, and there was lots of swimming and floating going on everywhere. Best of all, the campers were passing their tests. Almost everyone could swim twenty-five yards catching a few breaths, and then turn over and float.

"Okay, Girls! Semi-circle, please. Any questions?" Surprisingly, there were none. So, Walli demonstrated the side stroke, along with the side kick, and told them it was a good, restful, stroke...almost like floating on your back. The counselors had the girls try it on their left side, and then, their right, to see which was easier, and more comfortable. Everybody caught on quickly.

Nancy asked, "Why didn't you teach us this stroke first? It's easier!"

"Because it's important for you to be able to just put your face in the water and get somewhere if you need to!" explained Walli.

Then she had them swim about twenty-five yards, from the first buoy to the second one...staying parallel with the shore line. The girls did a lot of swimming, because she had them going in small groups, one right after the other. She had them do the crawl, going one way, and the side stroke coming back.

She gathered them all together, and continued, "Do a practice test, today, swimming with your buddy. Try swimming from this first buoy, past the second one, just like we've been doing, but don't stop. Go on to the far blue one and then stop and rest for a while. When you're ready, try to swim back. Remember, it's about fifty yards each way. Don't get out too deep. Stay inside the rope. After you pass the practice test, on both strokes, you may have free time, but only in this immediate area. And during our next swim lesson, I'll be testing each one of you for the fifty yard test.

It seemed a long time, coming, to Lori and Beth, but finally, all of 'the Falcons' could be called 'swimmers'. 'The Hawks' were doing well, too. She and Beth did the practice tests and as usual, hung around a few minutes to see if they were needed. Then, they went off to the side and started relaxing, and talking. Lori happened to look up, and noticed that Jen and Lu were actually passing their test to be able to swim to the little dock. Walli was letting them do the side stroke most of the time, and letting them float a lot.

"Oh, jeez," she thought, as she closed her eyes and turned her face up to the warm sun.

The Lake

The next day Lori and Beth went for a swim during free time, at 1:15 pm. The water felt so cool and refreshing! It was a warm, sunny day, and life was good. They dove under a few times and sort of splashed each other. Other girls were swimming, too, but they were way over by the restricted, roped-off area.

It was quiet, and they could talk.

"So, what do you think about camp, so far?" asked Beth.

"Oh, I think it's great," said Lori. "Better than staying home, that's for sure," she said, thinking of her stepmother.

Beth looked up to see that Jen and Lu were sitting on a large boulder, together, down on the far side of the lake shore. They were pointing at Lori and her.

"See those two?" asked Beth. "They seem really strange. I wonder how old they are?"

Lori turned and looked over her shoulder, squinting into the sun. Sure enough, there they sat, laughing and pointing in their direction...

"Wonder what they're talking about?" said Beth.

"Us," said Lori.

"I wonder why?"

"I think they've been to some other camp, before coming here," said Lori. "They seem to know stuff, like a camp routine and all.

"Yeah, could be." After a long pause, Beth said, "Maybe they're planning some sort of stupid initiation for us..." said Beth, "like eating bugs or something, but, Yuck! I hope not!"

"Me neither," said Lori, thinking and then picturing Jen trying to force a bug in her mouth while Lu tried to hold her down. The next picture was of herself taking a big swing at Lu. Immediately she chided herself for even thinking about getting into a fight. She could just hear her stepmother when she got a call from Camp Foxmore. So, she deliberately put the whole picture out of her mind.

"Nope. Me neither," she repeated, forcing herself to turn back towards Beth. "Let's just enjoy the moment, okay?"

The two floated and played, rolling like porpoises, laughing and diving down to stand on their hands under water. Finally they decided to race to the little dock in the middle.

"Ready. Set. Go!" said Beth.

Lori got ahead easily, with Beth nearly keeping up with her crawl strokes. Out of habit, Lori slowed down a bit and let it be a 'tie' all the way.

"Yes!" gasped Beth, happily, as she touched the dock.

They boosted themselves out of the water onto the low platform. As they both sort of flopped back to relax in the sun, Beth said, "Mm-m, the sun feels wonderful!"

Lori was thinking, *"Beth is a great friend to have. She can do lots of the same things and about as well. And, ...she doesn't talk every minute!"* Everything was quiet for about three minutes. *"Yep, ...she could be a friend for life if we lived closer, or at least wrote to each other."*

"Oh, no," said Beth. "Look who's coming."

Lori looked back toward the 'now empty' boulder, and saw that Lu and Jen were walking around the lake to the small sand strip.

"Want to leave?" asked Beth.

"Yes!" was her first thought, ...but aloud, she said quietly, "No. Let's see if they act okay."

Lu and Jen waded out chest deep and swam the last few yards, toward the dock.

"Hi!" Jen said, as she grabbed on to the ladder...

"Hi," she heard back.

Jen was all smiles as she climbed up on the dock, and sat down facing Lori. "Well, girls," Jen said, smirking at Lu, who wasn't sure where to sit yet. "It looks like it's going to be just us four!"

"Oh," thought Lori, *"I hope not..."*

Beth sat up, out of courtesy.

Whatever they had in mind, Lori knew now, that Jen was definitely the leader over Lu. And she wondered if Jen had a group at camp to follow her. She doubted it, because these two always seemed to be just by themselves.

"How come you two are out here all by yourselves?" sneered Jen.

Lori didn't think the question deserved an answer, so she just lazily looked up at Jen, through her and past her.

Jen was flustered to see Lori's green eyes penetrating right to the core of her, and at the same time ignoring her...lazily blinking as though she wasn't even there. To cover the rebuff, Jen switched her fading smirk toward Beth and forced herself to not glance back down at Lori.

Beth looked over at Lori and saw that she was looking off into space as if nothing had been asked. She decided to follow Lori's lead and not answer the question. She looked down at the dock.

"Oh, not talking! Huh? So you two have secrets together, right?" accused Jen.

"Are you two 'together'?" blurted Lu.

101

"Together?" asked Beth, hating herself immediately for even answering at all.

"Yeah, ...you know, ...a pair, ...a two-some," said Jen.

Beth looked over at Lori with a questioning expression and saw the same curious frown staring right back at her. And then Lori shrugged her shoulders a bit and gave Beth a look that said, "They're crazy."

"C'mon Beth," drawled Lori. "Let's get back." She slowly stood up, stretched, and then dove cleanly into the water without so much as a 'good-bye'. She glanced back only long enough to see Beth's form already in the air, about to hit the water in a prone racing dive.

Above the sound of their swimming strokes and kicking noises, Lori heard Jen shouting. "Scared, huh? Well... Don't worry! We won't tell! ...Yet!"

Lori continued to swim with determination toward the beach. She was angry and her anger caused her to swim harder, and more powerfully. *"Beth was right!"* she thought. *"We should've left sooner!"* When she looked behind her, Beth was pretty far back, so she consciously slowed down as she neared the shore dock. She was sitting on it when Beth reached the ladder.

"Boy!" she said, gasping for air. "Were you scared of them? You swam really fast!"

"No," she answered. "Just angry."

"What's the matter with those two anyway?" asked Beth as she climbed up the ladder. "What did they mean, a 'pair' or 'twosome'? They know we're partners, right? Do they mean like 'gay'? Do they think we're 'gay'?"

"Well, who knows?" said Lori. "They are really weird." But deep down, she did know. She just replied, "I'm just sorry they're in our cabin."

"Yeah," agreed Beth. "Maybe we can just stay away from them. I came here to have fun!"

"Me, too! Let's go!" said Lori, rising to walk back to the cabin, and waiting while Beth fell in step. She half-heartedly started trying to push Beth off the narrow walkway just to get her laughing again.

Turmoil

That night in her bunk, when the lights were out and it was finally pretty quiet, Lori remembered hearing herself saying "Who knows?" to Beth. *"But, I do know,"* she admitted to herself. *"They think Beth and I like each other. No... they think we love each other. They do think we're 'gay'."* The word, *'queer'* crept into her mind.

"Boy, that's a word I'd hate to be called." When she thought of a 'queer', she thought of the man who worked at the shoe store. He had 'bleached hair' and wore lipstick. Or, she thought of one girl at the park, who always wore 'boys' jeans' and big, high-top construction shoes. She had lip hairs that she actually had to shave, or for sure she would've had a mustache.

To Lori's way of thinking, a 'queer' was somebody who looked like they should be the other sex, and would like to be. *"I don't want to be a 'guy',"* she thought.

The light was always on in the bathroom at the end of the cabin, to her left. She looked over the top of her feet toward Beth's bunk, across the aisle. In the dim light she saw her quiet form under a light blanket, probably sleeping.

She tried to picture herself approaching a romantic kiss with Beth, and it didn't seem appealing, at all! Not even a little bit! Her mind began to race, thinking, *"How stupid they were! Beth and I are just friends."* And again, from deep down, she felt the anger building toward them. Sighing, she thought, *"I should talk to Beth, I guess, and clear the air, because we are 'just friends'! In fact, ...it wasn't anything like...like... No, it wasn't anything at all like how she felt about Julie."* Suddenly she felt cold and shivered. *"Oh, God, No! I'm not really like that! I'm just not!"*

But then, she realized she *could* picture herself...getting closer...and closer to Julie, and then closer and closer to her lips, and...

Her stomach cramped brutally, with sudden nausea. She knew she'd be lucky to make it to the bathroom in time. She felt so sick!

As she raced to the end of the cabin, she passed Lu and Jen's bunks, and they spoke.

"Hey Lo-ri." said Lu, in a taunting, sing-song voice.

"Need any help?" laughed Jen.

But she couldn't have answered even if she wanted to.

Later, as she still hung over the commode, she felt weak. The anger was still there, but at whom? *"Definitely, at Lu and Jen! Boy! She'd like to do them some physical harm...with all their accusations and meddling!"*

But then gradually, she felt hopelessness and a creeping feeling of hatred toward herself. *"This is not good..."* she thought. *"Definitely, ...not good."*

Finally, she stood up, rinsed out her mouth, swallowed a little water, and dried off with a paper towel. Slowly, still feeling weak, she headed toward her bunk.

"Hey, Ba-by..." she heard, from Jen's bunk... and she 'tuned out' the rest, gritting her teeth. *"Someday,"* she thought. *"Someday..."* ...with her fists clenching.

Back in her bunk, she lay awake for a long, long time, crying silently, off and on. *"Maybe I'm homesick,"* she thought. *"But no, not really. Camp is fun! Sure, I miss giving Dad a hug! But, ...I definitely don't want to go back home yet! In spite of the harassing by Lu and Jen, I do not want to leave!"*

And her self resolve 'came to life' as she thought... *"and they're not going to make me quit camp! I'll just ignore them as much as possible and get on with my life!"*

"My life..." she thought. *"Boy, where am I headed?"* The feeling of real disappointment with herself started creeping in again... *"I just...I just...can't stand it, if I'm 'strange'...like Lu and Jen.* She tried to picture them kissing each other, and she almost, almost could. She felt herself chuckle in the middle of the tears running down her cheek, because, somehow they didn't seem like they were attracted to each other. *"So, what were they doing together? Just friends, hanging out together? More like buddies!... 'sick' buddies,"* she thought. *"Sick, like me! No! I just can't be like them!"* she demanded of herself. She muffled her sobs deep down in her pillow. She couldn't remember any other time in her life that she had hated herself.

Flashbacks of her stepmother ridiculing her for being athletic instead of dainty, ...calling her a 'tomboy'...and constantly complaining to her dad about her immersion in sports. All those times had caused her to 'doubt' her own behavior and feel ashamed. So, she tended to be more quiet and introspective than her friends. *"But, ...can I survive, ...if I actually 'hate' myself?"* she wondered.

Yet, basically, she felt pretty good about herself. She loved the feelings she got when she was playing sports. She liked it best when she had to really extend and exert herself. And she knew she *could* play hard when she needed to...when it really counted...like in a tournament, or a track meet. Somehow, her body could always respond to the needs she placed on it, like running or swimming to a finish line, throwing a baseball ball really, really far in the distance competition, ...faking and feinting to get around a pesky basketball guard, or...smashing a volleyball or a badminton shuttle-cock... And especially, she sighed, picturing and 'experiencing' the great, almost 'euphoric' feeling of watching one of her 'home-run' balls go sailing higher and higher, farther and farther, off into the distance.

Yes, she liked what she could accomplish. And she had realized, long ago, that her physical body was a special gift...like some people had, who could sing or draw well.

"It's just my mind that's messed up... Maybe I could talk about all of this, to somebody." She thought of Beth again and decided, *"No, Beth is too unsuspecting and naive for me to confide in her about how I feel about Julie."*

"Boy,...there's a word," she thought, *"naive, ...something similar to being innocent. Well, if Beth is innocent, ...am I guilty? ...no longer innocent? And, if I condemn them to Beth, how do I 'justify' my feelings for Julie? Beth might think I'm 'just as gross' as they are. No, it's too risky. I do need to talk to her about them, though."*

Her head hurt. Her stomach hurt. *"Maybe I could talk to one of the counselors here."* She pictured each one in turn, starting with Mrs. Z, and ending with Walli. Sadly, *"No,"* was the answer to each.

"Dad!" she thought. *"Hmm...maybe that's a real possibility...but not just yet. I don't want him to give me some quick, logical explanation to something I haven't really figured out, how to explain to him. No...he might end up thinking I'm silly, or insane, or something...or...that camp was really bad for me!"* She could just picture him, tending to side with her stepmother about her lack of feminine pursuits... Feminine pursuits…now there's a double meaning. *"Is that my problem? Am I pursuing Julie?"*

She took a couple of deep, deep breaths and tried to relax and think...even more deeply. *"Be honest,"* she told herself. *What is going on with me?"* she asked. *"What makes Lori happy?"*

Flashes of herself in the batter's box came to life. *"No!"* she 'corrected'...

"...about this thing with Julie! Stay on the subject," she prodded herself.

She remembered helping Julie to float...saw her face with her eyes closed...and trusting her to keep her face out of the water. She remembered those long eyelashes seeming to just lie on her cheeks... Then, her dimples that formed, ...deep dimples that got deeper as she smiled and laughed. And her lips... Lori's mind went blank when she felt the twinge starting between her thighs.

"Does this make me happy?" she asked herself. *"Does this make me happy?"* she shouted in her brain. *"No! It's agony! ...agony...because...because why? Because what? Because...she really wanted to be close to Julie...to touch her face lightly...to...to...what? ...to gently kiss her lips..."* she admitted.

As the picture became complete, her sobs began shaking her body and she put her face even deeper into her pillow. She cried until no more tears would come. *"Whatever it is, I've got it bad,"* she decided.

"If only Julie and I were stranded on an island, ...with nobody else around to see us," she thought. *"...with no boys around for her to like. Maybe we'd snuggle up together at night to keep warm ...and maybe, ...she'd learn to love me... And maybe, she'd even want to kiss me ...maybe? ...No, No!"* she thought. "Stop it," she said. "Just stop!"

Vivian, in the next bunk to the left, sat up, saying "What?" still half asleep. "What's the matter?"

"Huh?" said Lori. Then she realized she had spoken out loud and quickly looked around to see if she'd awakened anyone else. No one else seemed to be moving, not even Jen or Lu. "Uh, ...nothing," she whispered. "Just a bad dream. Sorry, 'Viv'... Go back to sleep."

Lori sighed deeply, turned over on her back and stared into the darkness.

She couldn't believe that Lu and Jen didn't seem to have heard her. They weren't that far away...just diagonally across from the foot of her bunk. As she pictured them, she wondered exactly what made them different from her...because she felt very different. She knew she'd have to get it figured out, or she'd never be able to get them off her mind. She also knew she just *couldn't* be exactly, exactly like them.

One part of her brain said *"Go to sleep, you dummy."* But her stubbornness continued. *"They don't seem to like each other...rather "love" each other. No.* In fact, she couldn't remember Lu being extra nice to any girl. She just hung close to Jen. *"Yep, 'loyal' Lu, who tags around after her. Maybe Lu loves Jen. If she did, that would explain all the glaring. Well, maybe that answered one question, anyway."*

And the only people Jen really seem to give any attention to, are Beth and myself. Some attention! Aggravation was more like it! Could such aggravating behavior be a way of saying, "We're like you two"? or, "stop denying you're gay," or "I like you.?" or worse, "I think I 'love' you?" She pictured boys pulling girls' hair for attention, and she decided that *"Maybe Jen was doing the same type of thing...to get the attention of Beth and me?"* She paused a long time... "No...it's not Beth, ...its me!" she said almost silently.

"I know it's me... A disgusting thought," she decided. *"...and deep down, I've known for some time. I've just been blocking it out."* Then, she remembered Jen, flirting, telling her she had a good body, offering to wash her back, even jumping up into her arms, and the 'turn-over' breast-in-hand trick.

Suddenly, she had an 'imagined picture' of Jen coming close, and trying to kiss her, and it caused her mind to go blank once again, as her cramping stomach doubled her up in pain.

"That will never happen!" she vowed, clenching her teeth. *"And the worst thought of the entire night is, that if Julie even* <u>suspected</u> *how I feel about her, ...she'd probably feel like throwing up, too."*

She cried dry sobs, deep into her pillow.

Gradually, her cramping eased. *"What to do?"* she wondered. *"No one to talk to...nothing to do but stay at camp, and go day by day. If only Mom was still alive... Maybe I would have been able to ask her."*

"But, it's 'special'...so very special." She wondered if she'd ever be able to talk to anyone about the intense hidden feelings she had for Julie.

She finally fell asleep, not liking herself very much.

106

Honesty

After another uneventful Arts and Crafts session, they had a while before dinner and Lori asked Beth if she'd like to walk down by the lake. On their way, Lori said, "You know, Beth, you asked me about Lu and Jen, the other day, and I said, "Who knows?" Well, I do know...at least I think I know..."

Beth just looked at her, frowning, trying to remember the conversation, exactly.

"You asked me, "What's the matter with them?" and "Do they think you and I are 'gay'?"

"And?"

"I think they *are* gay, ...and I think they believe we are, too."

"Oh, no!" said Beth. "Why?"

"Well, Jen has been making remarks to me since the first night, ...like...

"You look cute."

"Want me to wash your back?"

"Hey, Baby...,"

"...and when I put them all together, it fits."

Beth said, "Oh, I see. Now I understand why you were angry at her. But you never said anything, and so I thought you were just moody," she said, smiling. "But why do they think we're gay? I don't even know anyone who is."

"Because we're together a lot, and probably because we laugh and have fun."

"That, we do!" she said. "Don't worry, I won't let them 'get' you. Forget them! Last one to the bridge is *pitiful!*" She tagged Lori and started running.

Lori laughed, and took up the challenge, thinking, *"She's an 'okay' buddy."*

107

Letter Home

Hi Dad,

I had Arts and Crafts again this afternoon. Were you or Mom good at that? If so, you forgot to pass it on to me.

Archery is better. I'm getting some pretty good scores. My partner there is still Julie, and she's getting to be very good. I bet when we have the archery contest at the end, she'll win something.

See ya... Gotta go check on my laundry. (Hope I didn't lose the page I wrote you about the creek and the snake.)

Volleyball III

Julie had broken a fingernail the second day they had played volleyball. She had been so intent on trying to set some balls to Lori, in order to watch her spike it, that she had forgotten to use the pads of her fingers. Her nail had broken down to the 'quick' several days ago, and it was hard to get excited about maybe breaking another one. She still wanted to watch Lori, because, so far, nobody had given her any decent set ups to spike. So, she had mixed emotions about today's game.

This time, Fletch was the captain for the other side. She took Lu and Jen on her side, as well as Vivian and Ceil. She split up Joann and Julie, taking Joann, so that the sides would be even.

Gerri was captain for Julie's side. Beth and Lori, along with Liz and Nancy, made six.

Fletch was a good player and it made quite a difference. Lu and Jen were getting good set-ups from her, and they were actually getting chances to spike the ball. Lu was tall and lanky and had long arms. When she was up front, Lu spiked two hard ones right at Lori, who was on the back row. Lori got them both up in the air, but her team wasn't able to get the ball back over the net either time.

Lu gave her a smug look of 'self satisfaction'.

Later, when Lori was up front, Fletch was her awesome opponent, directly on the other side of the net. "Set it up high, if you can," said Lori. "We need points."

Beth was the best 'setter', of the girls, and after several tries, she finally set a nice, high one to Lori. Wham! Lori spiked it hard. Fletch tried to block it, but missed, and the ball hit the ground in front of Lu, on the back row.

"Point," said Beth.

Julie thought, *"Wow!"*

Lori got another high set from Gerri, and Wham! Bam! She spiked it, but Fletch blocked it with two hands, high over the net. The ball fell to the ground, on Lori's side, next to Julie.

"Oh. Sorry!" Julie said. "I should've tried harder to get that."

Later in the game, Fletch blocked Lori's spike back across the net. But this time, when the ball came at her, Julie managed to get under the ball and hit it up in the air. Beth set it to Lori, and Wham! She spiked it at an angle, very hard toward the back row. It hit Lu in the knees.

"Point," said Beth, in a taunting way, causing Lu to scowl intensely at her.

Meanwhile, Julie was thinking, *"Boy! I'm glad she isn't spiking it at me, that hard. I'd have ten broken nails."* Then she thought, with a little smile, *"Nah, I would've just dodged them, or ducked..."*

The other side won, finally, due to Fletch's spikes. As they changed sides, Lori said to Beth, "What are you doing, taunting Lu? Trying to aggravate her?"

"Yes, aren't you? I told you I wouldn't let them 'get' you. Don't worry."

"Beth, please don't. Things could get nasty. Okay?"

Beth just looked at her.

"Okay?" Lori insisted.

"Well...okay."

The second game got more intense, as the girls really got into it. Everybody was trying harder, and they were doing their best to get the ball to their spikers up front.

Lori was having a great time. Beth and Gerri were giving her some good high ones, and she was spiking them powerfully. If Fletch hadn't been on the other side of the net, blocking them, Lori would've toned down her efforts. But this was great, because she had to try hard, and that was the best she ever hoped for, ...just being allowed to play without restraint.

Julie had never gone to a varsity volleyball game, or even watched girls her age playing at this level of ability, and for her, it was a real 'eye opener'. For sure, she knew now, that Lori was an incredible athlete. She had an amazing sense of presence, and rarely missed anything that was hit to her. One thing that caught Julie's attention was how Lori could leap high in contorted ways to reach a ball, then, somehow manage to hit it while she was up in the air, and then land gracefully. More than once, Lori had to change direction in mid-air, because Liz or Nancy inadvertently ran under one of those high leaps.

Julie knew that she, herself, wasn't a very good player at all, but she was having fun, because she was right in the middle of it all. Today, she *always* had to be ready for the ball to come to her, or right at her, and it was exciting. Mostly, whoever got the first hit, tried to get the ball up in the air, and then, if Lori was the spiker for the front row, either Gerri or Beth would try to get a decent set up to her. This time Julie watched Lori take some little steps, and then leap up higher than ever, and spike the ball almost straight down. Fletch tried to block it, but the ball bounced on her upper arm, and then hit the floor.

Julie was impressed. She cheered, "Yea Lori!" along with the other girls on her side. Lori didn't strut or even acknowledge the cheer. She was totally into the competition, and was already looking back to watch Gerri serve the next ball. Gerri signaled 'time out', and bent down to tie her sneaker.

Julie walked three steps, right up close to Lori, and said, in a low voice, "Lori?" And when Lori glanced up at her, she looked her directly in the eyes and said, "That was a *great* spike."

Lori said, "Oh, uh..." and started looking down.

To Julie's amazement, Lori seemed embarrassed, at her compliment, instead of being proud. And she knew she was right, when Lori murmured, "Thanks," and slowly started turning a little red.

"Service!" said Gerri. And the game went on.

Julie was puzzled. Most athletes she knew were guys, and they usually acted like 'they were good, and they knew it'. Here was an athlete, a really good one, and she was, of all things, 'humble'. Julie's thoughts would have to wait, because suddenly she was in the middle of all the action.

Beth hit the ball up to her, and she did her best to set the ball high to Lori. It worked, and she admired her high set going toward the net. As if in slow motion, she caught the last part of Lori's upward leap, and the precise skill it took to powerfully deflect the ball downward, without touching the net. She watched the ball bounce hard, in front of Jen on the back row. Fletch had been there to block it, but Lori had changed the direction of the ball so drastically, that it angled completely past her outstretched arms.

Lori came up to her and said, "That was an incredible set, Julie. Thanks."

Julie mumbled, "You're welcome." But she was still thinking about how hard the ball had hit the ground in the middle of the other team's court. *"If I stood on a step ladder, and threw the ball or hit the ball downward with my fist, I know I couldn't do it that hard. Yet, Lori had done it, easily. No big deal, to her,"* she thought.

Jen brought her back to the present, with "Hey Lori! That was a lucky hit. You couldn't do that again, on your best day."

Something in the snide tone of voice, touched Julie. She wasn't usually 'into' volleyball, especially the low caliber of game she was used to in PE. But Jen caused her to want to spike it at her, hard. And Julie wasn't even a spiker. She surprised herself, even more, by thinking, *"...right in the mouth."*

She looked at Lori, expecting her to give some smart retort, but Lori only gave Jen, a body language reply. It was a little smile, with a slight 'tip back' of her head, along with a chuckle, which Julie easily interpreted...It meant, "You might be right."

But, as Lori was watching Gerri's serve go over the net, Julie knew somehow, by the calm, determined look on her face, that Lori had accepted the challenge. The ball went over the net and came back several times, in an extended volley. Julie, on the front row next to Lori, was getting dizzy going round and round keeping track of the ball. People were trying to place the ball between players, aiming for open spots on the court, and hitting 'long balls' to the back row. She had never, ever been in this kind of a volleyball game.

Fletch got a good set up and spiked it down at Julie's knees. Amazingly enough, she dived downward and got her fist under it. The ball went into the net, hard, and when the net snapped it out, it went far to the right of Beth, on the back row. Beth lunged sideways and forward, and somehow managed to 'fist' it into a very high set up, that was going toward the net, but almost straight up, over Julie's position.

From her knees and elbows, Julie turned onto her right side, and watched Lori coming right at her. Julie couldn't move out of the way, because Beth had fallen to the ground, right behind her.

Meanwhile, Lori ran along the net, did a little leap, landed on two feet, and then went almost straight up in the air. The effort took her high above the net. She 'side-swiped' the ball with her open hand.

Julie watched from almost directly below her, with the blue sky as a background. And to her absolute amazement, Lori's hand, and her wrist, and every other part of her, stayed on her own side of the net. The ball, however, took off like a shot, and was directed past Fletch's block.

Julie followed its path, and watched it hit Jen in 'ready to volley' hands. The ball bent her fingers, 'way back', and 'bam' ...it hit her, ...right in the mouth ...knocking her backwards! She landed flat on her butt and bounced twice.

"Hah!" thought Julie as her heart soared. *"Take that!"* she almost said out loud.

"Yes!" she heard Beth say, from her own sprawled out position.

And Julie was aware that her whole team was laughing. She heard, "It serves her right!" and "What a shot!"

But then she saw Lori, already under the net and half way to Jen. Glued to the spot, she watched, as Lori was saying, "Are you okay, Jen? I'm sorry. I didn't mean to hit you in the face." Lori knelt down by Jen, and was trying to peek between her hands, that were tightly covering her whole face. She had gotten to Jen, a few steps ahead of Fletch.

Julie got up and went to see, along with everyone else.

When Jen finally moved her hands, those closest to her could see that she had a bloody lip. Lori reached in her pocket, and pulled out a folded tissue and handed it to Jen. She was saying, "Here. Your lip is bleeding a little, but we can go get some ice. Let me help you up." And she took Jen's free hand, and helped pull her to her feet.

Fletch had watched everything happen, just like everyone else. She was thinking, "That girl *can* handle herself, and things that happen, too. I really didn't even have to be here. Guess I'll let Katie know the good news."

Lori looked at her and asked, "May I take her to the mess hall, to get some ice? And, is the Nurse here, today?"

Fletch just smiled and nodded, 'Okay', and said, "Yes, she is," because Lori had taken the words right out of her mouth.

Curious, and in a teasing mood, Fletch said, "Lori?"

When Lori paused and looked back at her, Fletch asked, "Do you always carry new, folded tissues in your pocket?"

Lori just smiled, and tipped her head back slightly, acknowledging the verbal jab, shrugged, and started walking away with Jen.

The game went on, with five against five, but, Julie was thinking, *"It just isn't the same, now."* Lu was thinking the same thing. So was Beth, and so was Fletch.

With Jen

Lori was feeling bad about her spike. *"It could've hit someone else, and really hurt them."* *"But, no,"* she had to admit, *"the ball went where I aimed it,"* and then, she felt even worse.

"Does it hurt bad?" she asked.

Liking the attention, and still letting Lori 'help' her along, Jen said, "Yes, it does. Very bad." She planned to 'cry', and get Lori to hold her close, and give her 'lots of comfort' before they got to the mess hall.

"I'm sorry, Jen. I didn't mean to make your lip bleed," said Lori, thinking, to herself, *"I definitely shouldn't have done that. She's not a 'varsity-level' player."* She said, "Here, let me see. I hope you didn't break a tooth."

Jen willingly stopped and let Lori look. It was the closest she'd ever been to Lori, and was thinking, *"It's time to cry."* But she couldn't, just yet. She was hypnotized by the cool green eyes with the little hazel flecks in them.

As she checked Jen's front teeth, Lori was wondering if there was something she could teach Jen, that would keep that from happening to her again.

Lori started re-living the event in her head. Definitely, Jen's hands had been a little too wide apart. She could at least teach her to keep them closer together. She started to make a suggestion, but then she pictured the part where Jen plopped down on her butt and bounced, ...and suddenly the unthinkable happened, ...she felt little giggles starting in her stomach. Since she was only inches from Jen's face, she cleared her throat and swallowed hard to keep them there. But it was no use. Lori finally choked on the soft muffled laugh as it rolled up, and out. She had no excuse for her actions, but her entire belly was shaking and quivering. She just couldn't make it stop.

Jen looked at Lori with unbelieving eyes, and she got a shocked expression that soon changed to scowling at her, accusingly. Lori tried to apologize, but ended up laughing out loud.

This wasn't going like Jen planned, at all.

Finally, when the girl started getting a lopsided look that made her face seem grotesquely deformed, Lori 'lost it' completely. She couldn't even look at her anymore, and laughed harder and harder until she was crying.

"It's not funny!" said Jen.

Lori nodded "Yes," and forced herself to try and get a straight face. Brushing aside the tears she said, "I know. It's *not*, ...but," she grabbed her stomach, "you were, ...you...you... actually *bounced* a few times." And her contagious laughter bubbled up all over again.

Jen remembered landing clumsily on her butt. She definitely didn't want to laugh but she couldn't help herself, and finally, she started chuckling, too.

Lori, by now, was hopelessly in her 'laughing zone', and sagged lower and lower. Finally, she just fell all the way down on her knees and one elbow. Then, oblivious to the entire world, Lori rolled on the grass with her knees up, still laughing, and holding onto her cramping abdomen.

Jen thought Lori looked like a dying roach, and laughed harder, too. She finally sat down beside her, thinking, *"This is better than crying, I guess."*

She just watched Lori, thinking how cute she was, and how much she liked her. Finally, when Jen, herself, could stop laughing, she said, "Lori, we could have lots of good times together...I want you to be my girlfriend."

That sobered Lori, immediately. She stopped laughing, cleared her throat, and sat up. She wasn't positive she'd heard, correctly. "What?"

"I want you to be *my girl*."

She looked right at Jen. Then, she brushed away the 'happiness' tears, and said, slowly, "I...can't, Jen."

"Why?" asked Jen, in an impatient voice.

"Because, ...it's just not *in* me, to be your 'girlfriend'.

"You could try."

"Will you settle for 'friend'?" asked Lori.

Before Jen could consider her answer, they heard, from off in the distance, "Jen! Jen! Are you alright?" Lu came running toward them. The game was over, and she had trotted ahead of the rest. She was hollering from far away, down the path.

"Here comes your real 'girlfriend'," said Lori, softly. "You know, I think she likes you a lot."

Jen just stared at her.

"What happened, now?" demanded Lu, in a loud voice, from about 50 yards away. She was still running fast. "As she got closer she yelled out, with a mean look on her face, "Did you let her fall down?"

Jen yelled, "No! It's okay, Lu! We're just talking!"

Both Lori and Jen started to get up.

From far away, back down the path, the front half of the volleyball group came around the bend, into view. When Beth saw Lu running at Lori and Jen, she said, "Uh, oh. Trouble!" and took off running toward them.

Fletch and the others saw Lu running, full tilt, right at Lori. Lori hadn't quite gotten to a standing position yet when Lu dived at her, tackling her hard. The impact caused them both to roll over and over in the grass.

Everyone was running, now. Julie surprised herself that she was out in front with Fletch, who could really move.

Jen was yelling, "Lu, stop it! Lu, I'm okay!"

Lori had the breath knocked out of her, and Lu ended up sitting on top of Lori's stomach, and was trying to punch her in the face. Lori was busy ducking and blocking the hard blows. She finally managed to grab one of Lu's wrists, and then the other. At least she didn't have to worry so much about getting punched in the face now, and she took a couple of deep breaths.

"I'll make you sorry you were ever born!" vowed Lu, trying to jerk free.

Lori pulled hard on one wrist, and pushed on the other, and rolled Lu to the side. She kept her rolling, and ended up on top, pinning Lu on her back, and holding her wrists down on the ground, up near her ears.

Lori was calmly sitting on her 'bucking' stomach holding her down when Beth arrived.

There was nothing for Beth to do.

And Jen was still screaming at Lu.

Lu didn't hear anything Jen was yelling, but she saw Beth looking down at her. She said, from flat on her back, "I'm going to get you, too. You just won't know when."

"No-o, Lu! You don't need to be 'getting' anyone," said Fletch, coming to a stop. "What's going on, here? I thought you two were going to see the nurse."

Lori loosened her grip gradually, because she didn't know if Lu was going to still try to fight. Lu was glaring up at her, but she didn't try to hit her any more.

"Come on, both of you, stand up, now. Well, what *did* happen here?" asked Fletch.

Lori brushed herself off, and looked at Jen, knowing that it was important for her to explain, and for Lu to hear.

"We were just resting, Fletch," said Jen. "Lu thought Lori had dropped me, or hit me or something. So, she attacked," said Jen. And then, shrugging her shoulders, she said, "Lu has a bad temper." Then, she looked at Lu, and said, "Don't you!"

"Well, its over, now," said Fletch. Seems like it was just a misunderstanding. Are either of you hurt?" "No? Okay, then Lu, how about if you come with me and Jen, to get her some ice? Lori, I'll see you later... That's all the excitement for today, girls!"

Everybody gathered around Lori, asking "What really happened?"

Lori said, "I think you guys saw it all. She just came running."

Feeling troubled by the day's events, Lori added to her letter.

Hi Dad...I'm back. Today was volleyball, ...and wrestling. Funny, huh? Well, I spiked a ball, and it hit Jen in the hands. Then, it went through them and bopped her in the mouth. Her 'buddy', Lu, thought I did it on purpose, and tackled me later. We ended up wrestling a little. I had to sit on her stomach, until the counselor got there.

Hope I don't get in trouble over it. Maybe they'll call you. Oh well, all I can do is hope for the best.

Maybe I can get this in tomorrow's mail.

I think I'm a little homesick today...Bye...

Lots of love,
Lori

The Cave

Lori was feeling especially good, this morning, because she hadn't gotten in any trouble yesterday over Lu. Last night, before lights out, Fletch had quietly spoken to her and even complimented her on keeping her cool in a bad situation, by not 'punching back'.

And now their destination was a distant cave, and this hike was to last all day.

The girls carried backpacks, well loaded with food, a jacket, a poncho, extra socks, a towel, a small spade, and any extra essentials that they were willing to carry. Katie and Gerri checked each girl and made sure she had her own canteen and that she was prepared to hike long and far.

After about two hours into the hike, Katie stopped in a shady area, that had lots of short tree stumps in a circle, as seats. The campers didn't know that there was a dirt road that led from the main camp to just behind some short scrub oak trees nearby.

"Check around for snakes, ants, and any other 'critters', before you sit and rest," said Katie.

The girls started searching all around the bases and tops of the stumps. Warily, some girls sat down. Others flopped on the grass. Almost everyone reached for their canteens.

"If you need to use the 'restroom' you can go behind a bush, and dig your own latrine, or you can wait for our 'group latrine'." After they had rested for about five minutes, Katie took a small folding shovel out of her backpack and said, "Follow me for our next project."

She led them behind a couple of bushes and she proceeded to dig a little trench, about ten inches deep, in the soft ground. "There," she said, when it was a couple of feet long. She jammed the point of the shovel into the mound of dirt, beside the ditch. Next, she took a roll of toilet paper out of her backpack, and hung it on the handle of the shovel.

"Okay, girls...please remember to bury your toilet paper under a little dirt, always, even if you are only hiding behind a bush, somewhere. When we leave here, this little trench should be all filled in."

"Great!" said Nancy. "May I go first?"

"All right," said Katie, "and, let's give her a little privacy, okay?"

As they left, Vivian kidded her, saying, "Careful, Nancy! You wouldn't want to accidentally pee on those purple socks, now..."

Amid whoops and hollers, the group followed Katie back to Stump Circle where they all rested and chatted for a short while, joking and checking everybody's socks, as they emerged from the bushes...

Later, the hike took them up to a very long, narrow 'hanging bridge' over the Little Foxmore River. Katie explained to them that it was about ninety feet in length, and was stretched between two high banks, attached to four stout poles. The forestry service maintained it for hikers, and it was best if only four people at a time got out on the bridge.

"Single file!" said Katie, "with lots of space between you. And the last two girls here, please pull tight on the ropes while you're waiting, in order to 'steady' the bridge as much as possible."

Beth said, to Lori, "Let's be last."

Lori nodded, "Okay." And they moved down the bank a little, and held onto the bottom part of the bridge, on both sides. Lori noticed Gerri talking quietly with Vivian, who was having doubts about crossing.

Katie went first, as everyone watched intently. They were wondering if each slat of wood would hold her next step. When she reached the other side she heard, "Yea, Katie!" She smiled, waved, and set about 'steadying the bridge' from her side, too. "Okay! Next!" she yelled.

One by one, they crossed, 'hanging on for dear life'. Katie chuckled to herself because the water was only four feet deep, and they all could have waded across. Of course, everybody would've gotten wet, from their armpits down to their boots or sneakers. And also, the bridge hung only about 6 feet high above the water, but the first two girls, Liz and Nancy, acted like they were in danger of falling into the Grand Canyon. The bridge did move and sway a lot and so, after Liz and Nancy arrived, Katie got them to help her steady the bridge. With lots of encouragement, especially to Ceil and Vivian, the first eight girls arrived safely.

Lori and Beth made it across easily, after having watched all the others do their hesitations and 'near miss-steps'. Gerri brought up the rear, and crossed quickly.

And from there, it was only a short distance to a cave. The cave had been used by Indians years ago. As they entered, Katie allowed them to explore all its nooks and crannies. The cave was fairly deep and it had been a comfortable place for the Indians to live. Then, while the girls ate their sandwiches and fruit for lunch, she gave them a history of the cave and the surrounding area.

After lunch they went outside and learned about the berries they could safely eat that were nearby. And they all gathered firewood, and stacked it in the cave.

Katie came in and showed them a tiny little nook where she kept a 'water-proof' box containing lots of matches. Then she taught them how to build a fire in a circle of rocks. And even though it was summer and very hot outside, they all sat around the tiny fire inside the cool cave. Time passed quickly with Katie and Gerri entertaining them with several Indian tales.

All of a sudden, a bolt of lightening and a crash of thunder boomed somewhere off in the distance. Katie and Gerri immediately went outside to see how close the storm was to the cave.

"Do you think we should go back?" asked Gerri.

"Yes," said Katie. "The storm's pretty far away. Zee will bring the bus to meet us at Stump Circle as soon as she knows it's going to rain. It's happened before. We won't have to walk very far." She headed back inside, with Gerri right behind her.

"Pack up!" she ordered. "Let's start hoofing it back. Maybe we can beat the rain."

Everyone scrambled to get their stuff together. Gerri put out the fire, by scattering the few remaining chunks of wood and sprinkling water on them from her canteen, and then covering them with dirt. She then signaled Katie that she was ready to leave.

"Buddy system," Katie reminded, and started outside.

The group walked very quickly toward the bridge. When they arrived, they were all amazed at the difference in the river. The water was rising at an alarming rate.

"But it's not even raining yet!" said Vivian.

"Look backward over the cave formation," said Katie. Clouds, so dark gray that they looked purple, loomed in the distance. "It's been raining upstream. This usually happens if the rain comes in from the west. Let's go!"

The group hurried along, looking forward to crossing the hanging bridge as quickly as possible. But they had to approach the bridge cautiously, because the river was coming out of its 'trough', and getting wider and deeper.

Then, they all heard a tremendous roar, and Katie yelled, "Get away from the river! Run!" And she pointed up hill from the riverbed. Once she was sure that everyone was running in the right direction, she ran behind them. Gerri also made sure there were no stragglers.

They all made it to a rock ridge and watched in awe as a deluge of water came down the small, 'creek-like' waterway, turning it into a wildly churning river. The water level rose higher and higher, until the hanging bridge was only a few inches above the raging current.

They waited and watched for about twenty minutes. Finally the water level started to recede a lot. And after another twenty minutes, the water level had dropped down to about two feet under the bridge.

"The water must've gotten 'dammed up' somewhere," said Katie, "but the big surge seems to be over, now. Let's get back to camp! We don't want to get stranded here overnight, if we can help it."

The group started trotting down toward the bridge, each person wanting to get across *right away!* Vivian was 'wide-eyed', and feeling panicky, and took off in a frantic race to the bridge. Ceil was more cautious, and hung back.

Katie was afraid that Vivian would be careless and make a 'misstep' so she raced in front of Ceil, and shouted, "Wait up, Vivian! Wait for me!"

The girl slowed down.

She caught up with Vivian, and told her, "It's okay. I'm right here with you. Hold on tight, as you go!" Then, she looked back at Ceil, and said, "Wait until Gerri tells you to *Go!* ...okay?"

Vivian frantically groped along, not really watching her feet. Katie had to hurry on the bouncing bridge just to keep close to her. And all the while, she kept speaking calmly to the exceptionally heavy-set girl, trying to get her to be more careful.

Gerri stayed by the bridge, calmly encouraging each girl in line, to hold on tight, and to keep moving, with little steps. Beth and Lori hadn't even lined up to start across. They brought up the rear, and were helping to steady the 'wobbly' bridge. Both were knee deep in rushing water.

Ceil started out slowly, but then hurriedly began picking her way over the individual slats.

Next came Jen, and then Lu, each steadily groping her way across. There were five people spread out on the bridge, now, instead of four, but it seemed to be strong enough to hold even more.

Meanwhile, across the river, when Vivian and Katie got off safely on the other side, Vivian went down the bank a little to help tug on the bridge, to keep it as motionless as possible.

Gerri gave Nancy the 'go ahead', and she began the trek carefully, with little baby steps.

After a few minutes more, Liz got to go, and followed her 'pig-tail buddy' out on the shaky bridge...

It started to rain lightly. Everyone had to hold on tighter, as the bridge slats got very slippery.

When it was Joann's turn, she looked back and said, "Gerri, I'm really, really scared. Will you go with me?"

Gerri said, "Sure." But first, she looked at Lori and Beth, and asked, "Are you two going to be all right, by yourselves?"

They both nodded, "Yes."

And Gerri said, "Be Safe! See you in a few minutes!" The counselor started to move in front of Julie. "Will you be okay, Julie?" she asked.

Julie nodded "Yes," and let her pass.

Gerri looked back at Julie, and said, "Julie, don't start until we're almost half way across, okay?" And she smiled a big smile at her, saying, "Because, I'm kind of heavy, okay?"

Julie smiled as best she could back at her and said, "Okay." She watched them leave and let out a big sigh.

Lori was watching Julie closely, and knew she was probably just as afraid as Joann, but she hadn't asked Gerri to help her. She was just waiting quietly, but it was easy to see that she was very tense. Lori thought, with some admiration, *"She's terrified, but at least she's trying to be brave."*

It seemed like forever, but Gerri and Joann were making good progress and arrived in the center. Finally, Julie started out very, very carefully.

Lori and Beth still held onto the bridge, trying to steady it. Joann, and Gerri, were now almost three-fourths of the way across. And then, there was Julie, who had only taken about twenty-five steps out onto the bridge. Everything was going well and soon, it would be their turn.

Katie looked back, upstream and started yelling, "Watch Out! A *tree!* A tree, is floating down the river, at you! Get off the bridge! Come on, hurry up, Nancy!"

Nancy, who was only a few steps away, didn't even look at the tree. She hurried and made it to the end. Katie grabbed her arms and helped her off the bridge.

"Come on Liz, you can make it, too!" shouted Katie. Liz had already looked up at the tree and was scrambling toward the counselor.

Julie, Joann and Gerri, had all stopped dead in their tracks and were looking at the menacing sight in awe, trying to decide what to do. Gerri was wondering if the tree had helped dam up the river, before. The on-rushing tree loomed like a big barge, racing downstream right at them. The entire root-system was huge and 'grotesquely bare', with no soil left on the roots.

Lori was already shouting, "Julie! Come back!"

And Gerri started yelling, "Joann! Go! Go!"

Joann looked back at Gerri, and then at the tree. She turned and started frantically clawing her way toward Katie and the others.

Julie still stood there, frozen... just staring at the tree.

"Julie! ...*Ju-lie!*" screamed Lori.

Julie finally looked back at her.

"Come back! Julie! Come back! Hurry!"

Julie still just looked at her.

"Move, Julie! This way!"

Julie took two steps on the 'now, shaking' bridge...and nearly fell off. The tremors were being caused by Joann's wild scramble toward the other side, with Gerri close behind her.

"Hang on! Keep moving, Julie!" shouted Lori. Julie was slipping and sliding, but she was getting closer back to the bank.

The tree roots hit the bridge closest to the other side, just as Joann and Gerri were being pulled ashore by lots of helping hands.

When the bridge lurched terribly, Julie's feet slid off. She was now hanging onto the rope handrails.

"Help!" shouted Julie.

"Hold on! Don't let go!" different voices kept yelling.

Her legs were dragging in the fast moving water.

"Help! Help me! I can't swim good yet!"

Only Lori knew about Julie's previous fear of the water. She was desperate to help her, and had already removed her backpack and moved up the bank. Just as Lori was beginning to venture out on the bridge, it suddenly started bucking up and down wildly. The rampaging current was causing the tree roots to push hard against the bridge with tremendous force, and making the bridge heave up and down at the same time.

Suddenly the bridge ripped in half, dumping Julie into the turbulent water.

Everybody was screaming at Julie. She was hanging on to the rope for dear life and there was terror in her eyes...

Lori yelled, "Hang on Julie! You can almost touch bottom! Look, you're getting closer to shore!" She and Beth had begun moving downstream to intercept Julie's 'drift' toward the bank.

"Try to touch bottom!" yelled Beth.

The girls with the counselors were running and stumbling along on their side and shouting, "Julie! Keep swimming! You can do it! Swim towards shore! Get your pack off!"

The huge tree, with its roots still entangled in the ropes, was closer to Katie's side. It was just beginning to swing around a little and the branches were eventually, going to crash shore on Lori's side of the river.

Lori, with Beth behind her, ventured out a bit from the bank, reaching for Julie, who was still hanging on to the 'now-taut' hand-rail rope. *The current's going to bring her into the bank,"* thought Lori, *"and then I can reach her."*

"Ow-w!" said Julie, as her knee crashed into an unseen rock. Her drift toward shore was slowed. It was getting more difficult for her to hang on against the drag of the water, in spite of all the encouragement she heard being yelled at her.

Meanwhile, the tree had been careening around, slowly at first, and then faster, as it turned broadside to the current. Its branches were coming toward Julie, with ever increasing speed. Lori saw it and said, "Oh my God!" She screamed, "Julie! Watch out!"

"Watch out!" screamed everybody, from both sides of the river.

Julie didn't see the danger and a branch banged her on the side of her head. She went completely under the water, swept away by the tree.

Lori was lunging downstream along the bank, in the water. But she couldn't move very fast because of the treacherous footing. The water was swirling around her ankles and dragging her downstream, and she would've been 'out of control' in an instant, if she took a wrong step. She finally climbed up and out onto the steep, rocky shore and stumbled along as fast as she could, trying to catch a glimpse of Julie. She could only guess where she might be in the huge crown of the tree, which was moving downstream and swinging toward the far bank. Lori was terrified that Julie was trapped underwater.

On the other side of the water, Katie, Gerri and the girls were also stumbling down-river along the bank. The terrain was more open on their side and they could move more freely.

It started raining harder.

Oblivious to the rain, Lori was rushing through tall brush and in and out between trees, under low-hanging branches, and stumbling over big roots. Beth, after shedding her pack, was slipping and sliding along right behind her.

"There she is!" someone cried, from the opposite bank.

"Where?" yelled Beth and Lori, at the same time.

"There!" yelled lots of voices. And the group was pointing a little farther downstream.

The tree, with its roots still 'hung up' on the tail end of the broken ropes, was now temporarily anchored, and floating with its branches pointing down the river. When the current veered it to the left a little, Lori could see Julie's blonde hair near a huge rock, not too far from shore. She was 'free' of the tree, for the moment, and, about twenty feet farther downstream than the branches. Lori pushed herself harder to get downstream.

"Hold on to that big rock near you, Julie!" shouted Lori, racing toward her.

"Yeah! Hold on, Julie!" yelled the other group.

When she reached the spot, Lori looked around for Beth and saw her about six feet behind her. "Hurry, Beth! Hold onto my hand! I'll try to reach her!"

Lori waded out, and so did Beth, up to her knees.

Julie saw them, but didn't try to reach out for Lori's outstretched hand. She was wedged up against the boulder by the fast moving current.

"Reach out! Grab on!" Lori shouted, but, Julie seemed to be too weak, in spite of all the encouraging voices from the other bank.

"Watch out!" they all yelled. "The tree's broken loose!"

Lori saw the that the roots had finally pulled free, and now the current was swinging that ugly end of the tree around to her side of the river.

Beth hollered out, "I've got the branch of this other big tree to hold on to...Go out deeper!"

Lori felt the bottom disappear, with her first step. But then, she felt a swirl of rocks around her ankles with her second effort, and she found a 'semi-firm' spot. She reached out and grabbed Julie's hand and pulled, with all her strength.

Julie was limp, like a 'rag doll'...but she managed to keep her own head up out of the water.

"Hurry!" "Watch out!" "The tree!" "THE TREE!" voices screamed.

Beth held on to the branch with all her might.

And through sheer determination, Lori kept searching for 'foot-holds' as she dragged Julie slowly toward her. Finally, Lori could stand on both feet in thigh-deep water. She gave one last 'Herculean' pull, and dragged Julie up close enough to grab the back of her collar. Beth pulled harder, too, and it brought both girls to a sitting position, in shallow water against the steep bank... The tree roots rushed by, just brushing their feet.

They heard loud cheers from the other side of the river.

Lori tried to get Julie up, out of the water, but Julie was a 'dead weight', and Lori was dead tired. Beth came farther into the water and they finally got Julie's arms up on their shoulders and grabbed her around the waist. They half-carried and half-dragged her up the slippery bank, until they reached a little flat spot and sat her down, slowly. Lori collapsed down next to her, still holding onto Julie's arm.

Julie didn't even try to stay sitting up, ...she just 'limply' sagged down, flat on her back. She looked around, but it didn't seem like her eyes were really focusing. Her eyelids fluttered, and then, didn't open again.

"Julie!" said Lori. "Julie! Can you hear me?"

Beth demanded, "Open your eyes, Julie! Don't go to sleep! Wake up!"

From across the river, Katie and the others were yelling, "Is she all right?" "Is she breathing?" "Is she okay?"

Lori put her ear by Julie's nose, but couldn't hear anything because of the noise of the rain and the river. She put her ear closer, and 'felt' a breath, and then heard a faint, little moan.

"Yes! She's breathing." said Lori. Beth yelled it back across to the others.

The rain started coming down more, in huge droplets. It pounded them harder and harder. Within a couple of minutes they could hardly see Katie or the others. And the rain on the river was almost deafening.

"Can--you--hear--me?" shouted Katie.

"Yes!" Beth shouted back.

"Can--you--make--it--back--to--the--cave?"

"I--think--so!

"Then,--Try! And--stay--there! We'll--go--get--help! --Okay?"

"Okay!" shouted Beth.

"Bye!" was heard from many voices.

Shadowy figures, mostly in ponchos, turned and left the water's edge. As the group was leaving, Lori felt a sudden, 'cold, hard fear'. As she sat on the slippery bank, she stared after them, thinking... *"What if we... if we...? What?"* she shouted, in her head. She noticed that she was doing a lot of 'that' lately. *"We're 'okay',"* she thought, *"and we're not going to drown. And, the others are okay... And they'll get help, and be back...When? Oh, by late tonight, or tomorrow morning, ...but they'll probably have to go around, and reach us from this side of the river."*

She looked up, and Beth was trying to keep the rain off of Julie's face, by bending over her. "Boy, this rain is cold! I'm freezing!" said Beth. "...and, it hurts!"

"Yeah. Let's see if we can get her up, and get started."

They managed to get her up to a standing position. And, as Lori was raising Julie's arm up and over her own right shoulder, she saw a nasty bruise on her left temple.

"Beth! Look at this bruise! She hit her head on that tree, or something!"

Shouting, Beth said, "At least it's not bleeding!"

Finally they had her in between them and stumbled along, trying to find a path. There wasn't one, so they endured thorny branches and other underbrush for about 20 minutes. It was very slow going. They didn't talk, because they had no extra breath.

Julie moaned every once in awhile, but for the most part, she seemed almost unconscious. At least she moved her legs, and helped to keep her feet going.

"Boy, she's really shivering!" said Beth. Maybe we'll see my backpack. I have a poncho and a jacket in it. After struggling along several more minutes, Beth said, "I guess the river took my backpack, too. And Julie's was probably ripped right off her by the current."

Finally, after what seemed like hours, "There! There's the bridge!" said Lori, squinting into the teeming rain.

"Or what's left of it!" said Beth. The broken and twisted bridge was still tied to the posts on both sides of the river, with the severed, 'ragged middles', weaving like two sea serpents along each bank. "Look how high the water is, now! It came back up," she added.

"Yeah, from all this rain. I don't see my pack, either," said Lori. "It's gone in the flood, too."

After only a couple of minutes more, Lori said, "And there's the path!"

"Boy! I'm tired!" gasped Beth.

"Me, too," said Lori. "But if we put her down, she'll be too hard to lift up again."

"Okay. But, let's rest a minute."

The 'ungainly' three-some, leaned up against a large oak tree.

Lori looked at Julie, thinking, *"Dear God, Please let her be alright...please!"* There was no break from the relentless rain. It pounded them.

"C'mon...let's go." said Lori, wearily.

"Yeah," said Beth, "but let's change sides, okay?" "And, besides, I have a rock in my sneaker."

"Okay," said Lori, "but how do you want to do this?"

"You hold her up for a few seconds, and I'll come over to the other side." Beth helped turn Julie so that she was facing Lori, and said, "Can you hold her?"

Lori leaned back against the tree, and put both hands around Julie's waist, mostly behind her back, to support her full weight. "Yes," said Lori, as she let Julie lean forward on her, even more. The half-drowned girl seemed almost lifeless. *"Dear God,"* she prayed, again, *"Please, please let Julie be 'okay'."*

It seemed like Beth was taking forever. Then, as her own shoulders sagged, Lori thought, tiredly, *"It looks like we're dancing."* Just then, Julie started to slide down.

Lori leaned away from the tree, bent her knees, tightened her grip, and boosted Julie up a bit. *"Good thing she's pretty' light..."* she thought, *"...and boy, her waist is tiny."*

Julie's head tipped forward, and as it came to rest on Lori's right shoulder, the injured girl began shivering violently. Lori wrapped her arms around her and held her tighter. She felt Julie's cheek next to her own, and looked quickly, to see if Julie's eyes were open. They weren't. And Beth was busy shaking out her sneaker. Next, Lori realized she was tightly pressed up against two, very soft breasts. She closed her eyes and just stood there, in her own little world, oblivious to every discomfort, including the almost deafening, relentlessly pounding, rain. Her usually active brain was numb, but, somehow, her heart felt happy.

"Okay. I can take her left arm, now," said Beth. "Sorry, but that rock was killing me."

"Oh, ...okay," said Lori, opening her eyes, "...but she seems to be shivering more." Lori reluctantly turned Julie away from her as Beth took her new position and the three started forward. The path was easier now, but a muddy mess.

They trudged along and Julie's head just hung down, and her feet were dragging more. "Is she unconscious?" asked Beth.

"I don't think so," said Lori. "She at least keeps her feet moving some of the time." *"Oh, No!"* thought Lori. *"Not unconscious? I wonder if she felt me so close to her? What if she thought it was gross?"*

They pushed on for 'long' minutes, and then Beth announced, "There it is!" They both felt the same surge of energy, walked faster somehow, and made it into the entrance of the cave. "We made it!" she said.

It was such a relief to be out of the freezing, bruising rain. They continued inside for about ten more feet, and started letting Julie down.

"Go easy," cautioned Lori. "Watch her head. She might bump it hard on the ground."

They laid her back, gently. Then, they both took deep breaths and let out big sighs, as they each collapsed down to the ground.

"I'm so-o tired," said Beth, sprawling backwards from where she sat.

"Yeah, me too," said Lori. "And, I have so many scratches and bruises, that tomorrow I'll probably look like I've been in a war, ...Julie too, and you, three."

"Do you think she'll be all right?" asked Beth.

"I don't know. I sure *hope* so. But, look at her shiver! We have to get a fire started."

Beth said, "I'll do it. Good thing Katie made us gather all that firewood before we left the cave." She forced herself up to a standing position. Wearily, she groped around and found the waterproof match box on the ledge, and then went to select some kindling. Next, she settled down at the fire circle, and started searching in the dirt for any warm remnants of the earlier fire and arranging the new little twigs.

Lori said, 'I wish I had a jacket or a blanket to put over Julie."

"Yeah, but there's nothing like that, here," said Beth, "and we're so wet! Maybe we should take off our clothes..."

"Wha-at?" said Lori.

"Well, if I can get this fire going, we can get warm first, ...and dry our clothes later. It would be quicker than trying to dry them against our wet bodies, ...don't you think?"

Lori felt very cold in spite of the fact that she had labored so hard getting to the cave. But Julie was so cold that her teeth were actually making noise, 'chattering'.

Beth looked up and said, "She probably has a fever. Does she?"

Lori felt Julie's forehead, and said, "No. She's 'ice cold'! Her *arms*, too."

"Can you get her shoes and socks off?" asked Beth. "I'll have this fire going in a few minutes."

Lori untied Julie's sneakers and removed them. Then she took off each sock and said, "Even her *feet* are like *ice!*"

"Maybe we can rub them," suggested Beth. "I'll be there in a few minutes."

Lori tentatively put her hands around the foot she still held, then looked at Julie's eyes and asked, "Julie, are you awake? Can you answer me?" Lori blew warm breath on her icy toes. Julie moaned slightly as Lori began to massage some circulation into her foot.

Beth fanned the beginning tiny flames and they caught the kindling on fire, bit by bit. She cupped her hands over the tiny fire, and warmed her fingers. "Ah, ...that feels good! If you get her clothes off, ... we'll move her a little closer, okay? Just let me add these larger twigs, to really get this going. It's hard because Gerri dumped water here before, and she buried all the little pieces of wood..."

Lori took a deep, deep breath and thought, *"This can't be happening...to Julie, to me."*

She moved up by Julie's shoulders, sighed, and started unbuttoning Julie's blouse from the bottom. She remembered Julie's bathing suit, ...and how she could see two, very distinct, little nipples through it. "I can't do this," she murmured.

"By yourself? Okay, I'll be there in a minute to help you," offered Beth. "It looks like she even lost her canteen in the river. I didn't notice before."

"Me neither," said Lori.

Beth came closer, knelt down and unbuttoned the rest of Julie's blouse. Then she helped Lori get Julie up to a sitting position. "Hold her, while I get her arm out of this sleeve," she said, leaning Julie's shoulder sideways, over against Lori. She got the blouse off her arm, and un-hooked her bra, and then slid the strap down off her shoulder. "Okay, lean her over on me, now."

Lori did, and then moving as if she were hypnotized, she pulled the soggy clothes off of Julie, keeping her eyes averted from her chest.

"Okay, now we can lay her back, easy," said Beth.

Lori did her part, but kept her eyes on Beth. Her good intent didn't help at all. In her peripheral vision, she saw Julie's form. "Boy, these clothes are really wet," said Lori, not knowing what else to say, and being very uncomfortable with Julie's bare figure, just 'right there'.

"Yeah, I can hardly wait to get mine off," said Beth. "Let's get her bottoms off, now." She began undoing the zipper. "Help me roll her up on one side."

Lori helped roll Julie, first to one side, and then the other, while Beth fought the wet garments. "There," said Beth, "they're finally off. Let's see if we can move her real close to the fire. Boy! She's got goose bumps on top of her goose bumps!"

"Okay," said Lori, and she moved to pick up Julie's shoulders, keeping her eyes on the fire... Beth picked up Julie's ankles and they moved her about 5 feet closer to the small flames.

"And now, me!" Beth smiled. "I can't stand to be wet any longer."

Lori watched her undoing her canteen strap, shoe laces, and buttons, and decided, *"It's not much different than being in the gang shower, I guess."* And she started getting undressed too, but slowly.

As self conscious as Lori was today, Beth seemed to be completely indifferent to it all, and liked taking charge. She was especially enjoying having Lori follow her suggestions. Quickly she set about wringing out her own clothes, and then Julie's.

Lori, in a trance-like stupor, just watched Beth moving around, thinking, *"She looks kinda funny, walking around naked. I'll probably look just as funny. It's not really the same as being in the gang shower, where we deliberately ignore everybody else. Besides, back there we have our towels to hide behind, at least in the bench area."*

Next, Beth walked over to the firewood and found several long, skinny branches about three feet long. She said, mumbling to herself, "And now I can hang up all these things on these sticks to drip dry.

Lori was thinking, *"Jeez... Beth's walking around completely naked, as if she just 'usually' dresses that way."*

After Beth leaned the sticks with wet clothes against the wall, she looked at Lori and asked, "Want me to do yours?"

"No, ...uh, ...no, ...thanks. I'll do them." But Lori was very, very conscious of Julie, who was definitely, also stark naked, lying so close, right there, on the floor of the cave. She felt like running away, ...outside, anywhere. Instead, she turned and went over to the pile of kindling and selected some prop sticks. Then, acting like everything was normal, she began to hang up her own clothes to drip dry.

As she busied herself, she gradually forgot to be self-conscious every minute. Beth wasn't watching her. She was tending the fire, and adding some big chunks of wood. Julie was still lying by the fire, with her eyes closed, really shaking. "She's still shivering!" Lori said, aloud.

"I'd like to build a big 'bonfire' to really warm up the cave, but we might be here all night, so I'd better save some wood," said Beth.

Lori forgot about everything else, went to Julie and moved her feet as close to the fire, as she dared. Then she warmed her own hands over the fire, and rubbed them together, to dry them. When they were warmer, she began on Julie's shoulders. After several minutes, she thought Julie should've been warmer, but she was still shaking violently. Lori said, "Beth, I can't get her warm enough. Can you come help me?"

Beth said, "Okay. Let's both lie close-up beside her, and try to get her to stop shivering. We can all keep our feet by the fire, and just lie back."

"It might work," said Lori.

They moved Julie a little and then they got settled. Soon they were pressed up against her on either side. Each girl held one of Julie's hands, rubbing warmth into the bluish looking, icy fingers. They stayed like that for a long time, without a sound except the crackling fire.

"This is better," said Lori, and she meant it. She was glad, *not* to be walking around and she was getting warmer. "Julie doesn't seem to be shivering so bad."

"Yeah, finally!" said Beth. "What a day this has been. I'm exhausted!"

"Me, too."

Beth squirmed around, trying to get more comfortable. Thunder and lightening crashed outside the cave. Julie jumped a little, and tensed up.

Lori said, "It's okay, Julie," and reached over and ran her hand lightly over her forehead. *"Funny,"* she thought, *"if she were wide awake, I'd be afraid to just touch her face, ...but asleep, she looks like such a little girl, ...and so helpless."*

Beth said, "Yeah, Julie, don't worry. We're here." And then she put her arm, very naturally, across Julie's stomach, to reassure her.

"That's the way I should be," thought Lori. *"I'll probably get over these silly feelings and be just like Beth by the end of camp. I hope so,"* she added.

After awhile, Beth rolled onto her back. "Boy, it's dark outside, already," she said, "but that lightening really lights up the sky. Look at that rain come down. Do you think they'll come for us tomorrow?"

"Sure," said Lori, with more confidence than she felt. She secretly wondered if the lake and the whole campground area was flooding so badly, from it's own little creeks, that it would take them longer. "At least we're safe, ...and we're dry."

"Yeah," agreed Beth, "but when we get back to camp, I hope they don't make me tell my parents. They might make me come home. They might not even let me come back next year."

"I know, I probably won't tell mine, anything," said Lori, thinking of her stepmother.

They talked softly for awhile, and then Lori realized that Beth had fallen asleep. She heard her breathing, deeply, and evenly, ...almost a light snore.

Lori stretched her arms over her head, and then moved her hands under her head, like a pillow, to get comfortable.

Another loud clap of thunder boomed outside, and all three jumped. Beth turned on her side, away from Julie. Julie turned more toward Lori and draped

131

her arm over Lori's waist. Lori froze, and then felt her heart skipping a few beats. After several seconds, she realized she had momentarily stopped breathing.

Slowly, and 'afraid', she drew in a deep breath. *"Afraid of what?"* she asked herself. *"...That Julie would wake up and be 'appalled' at touching her, ...or...afraid that Julie might turn back the other way?"*

She realized that she was still not breathing normally, and her heart was beating pretty fast. She tried to relax. Then, she was aware with sudden clarity, that part of her physical discomfort was due to a growing sense of uneasiness, ...deep within herself.

Julie 'twitched' again, but not due to thunder. She just moved in closer to Lori, and Lori's heart went 'berserk'. She could hear it pounding in her own ears.

"My heart's going to come right out of my chest!" she thought. Lori felt Julie's softness against her, and then felt the slight 'tightening' of the muscles between her own legs. She felt guilty having Julie pressed up against her so intimately, and started to roll away from her.

But Julie, seeking the warmth, rolled closer, nestling on Lori's shoulder with her forehead under Lori's chin.

As Julie's soft breasts moved against her, they felt cold, yet 'so smooth' on her own skin, and Lori's ache started to intensify. She began to picture how they would look to anyone who saw them... *"...like we're hugging,"* she thought, and shivered as she felt her own nipples contract.

Her mind was racing. *"Poor Julie, her head 'might' be messed up...but mine is 'really' messed up."* Lori didn't move, ...she just stared ahead, straight up.

The fire was a bright warm glow and the dancing flames made designs on the ceiling of the cave. Lori lifted her head a little to look at the fire and to move her hands out from under her head. She noticed Julie's rounded hip, and how the soft glowing light accented the curve down to the shadow of her little waist. The unexpected beauty of it made her think, *"If only I was good at art, I'd paint this, ...especially the shadow effect, ...and keep it forever to remember this night."*

She could smell the rain and river water in Julie's hair. She drew in a very, very slow breath, letting the scent permeate her nostrils, and there...there it was, ...faintly, ...like she remembered, the pleasant aroma that was Julie's own.

Julie moved, again. To Lori's disbelief, she put her knee, up over her hips, and snuggled even closer.

"Don't wake up!" she urged, silently. *"What if she wakes up,"* she thought, *"...and thinks that I pulled her, ... half-way over on top of me?"*

Lori was torn between fear and excitement. Julie's bare skin felt like it was burning hers. Her 'friend' was going wild. Minutes passed and her body was aching, terribly. She remembered how she had 'pressed' her hand against herself when she was in her bunk, and felt almost desperate to 'touch herself' now. But Julie's bent leg was 'right there'.

As she was thinking *'right there'*, she felt another twinge, 'right there'. She consciously contracted her own muscle, and the twinge deepened. *"Yes, ...it's right in 'that' spot,"* she decided. She caused the muscle to contract again, and she felt aching pleasure.

Without thinking, she put her hand on Julie's bare back, and she felt the same aching pleasure. *"Hm-m, strange...all I did, was touch her, and look what happened."* She gently moved her hand over Julie's smooth shoulder, and she felt deep aching once again. *"If I could only touch myself,"* she agonized, as her lower body just throbbed and throbbed...

Slowly, she put both arms around Julie, and held her closer. She felt inner muscles dancing. She forgot to be afraid, ...and went into a little 'world apart', contracting her own muscles deliberately, over and over, ...causing pleasure to move through her in little waves. It would be intense for a few seconds, and then fade away. Her mind was drifting with the feelings, thinking, *"...mm-m, ...oh-h, ...yes..."* and then as it faded, *"...oh... where did it go...?"* If she contracted them again, the pleasure would surge once more. Then she'd relax, and feel the 'wonderful wave', sort of rippling through her, deep, deep inside.

Without realizing it, she began slowly caressing Julie's back.

When it finally came, the explosion in her body was deep and powerful. Her body jerked uncontrollably, and for several moments, Lori was in a different part of the universe.

As she began to re-enter the 'here and now', she realized she was holding Julie tightly with both arms. Lori felt 'melted', all over. *"Oh, Ju-lie,"* she thought, *"this feels so-o right."* And she lay perfectly still for some minutes until her body finally stopped spasming, and her breathing calmed down. She thought, *"This would be such a wonderful way to live, ...and love, ...with Julie beside me each night."* She sighed heavily, relaxed her arms and let her elbows rest on the ground. Julie didn't move. She was sleeping peacefully, 'innocently unaware'.

"Oh-h ...Julie," sighed Lori, now silently chiding herself, *"this is so ...wrong. What would...you think...if you woke up? You'd think I was the very worst..."*

Then, yawning tiredly, she thought, *"I should...move you over. But, ...it feels...so-o...comfortable, ...and...if Beth...sees us... 'this way', I'll just...just explain...<u>something</u>. I'm too...tired to think of 'exactly what' ...right now, ...but..."*

She was still murmuring to herself, as she slipped deeper and deeper into a sound sleep.

Rescue

"Oh-h, ...my head," moaned Julie softly, lying on her back with her eyes closed.

Both Lori and Beth sat up, startled out of their sleep.

"Julie! You're awake!" said Lori. "I'm *so-o* glad!" She was relieved that Julie seemed okay.

Lori looked at Julie's nakedness, and then her own, and was very thankful that Julie woke up, lying by herself, instead of 'how they slept most of the night'. However, she was afraid that Julie might remember the close embrace they'd shared.

"Oh-h..." Julie said, holding her head. "What happened?"

"You fell in the river! Don't you remember?" said Beth.

"River?" asked Julie.

"Yes! said Beth. The bridge broke and you fell off when the river flooded. Don't you remember, ...the tree?"

Lori got up and went to gather her clothes, and Julie's. She put on her own damp blouse and shivered. Then, she stepped into her underwear, and her shorts.

"Sort of...," replied the sleepy girl. "Mainly, I remember being so-o cold. And then, warm." Julie slowly sat up, holding her head.

"Yeah. We made a fire and kept you warm," said Beth.

Lori came up and said, "Here, Julie, here's your blouse and stuff. We tried to dry all of our clothes."

"Where's everybody else?" asked Julie, taking her clothes, but making no move to put them on just yet. "Oh, my head! It hurts so bad!"

"Yeah, we think a tree branch whacked you," said Lori. "And everybody else made it across the river, okay. They went back to camp to get some help."

Then, Lori was thinking, *"Maybe if I stay away from her, right now, it will be better."* She turned back to the wall, saying, "I'll get yours, Beth." She handed Beth's clothes to her and then, after putting on her own cold, wet sneakers, said, "It has stopped raining. I'm going to go outside and find a bush. Be right back."

She stayed outside awhile, searching for enough berries for the three of them. They were scarce, because yesterday, the girls had picked most of them. When she returned, Julie was dressed, and saying, "...and you two saved my life, huh, and then, carried me all the way back here? Wow! Bet I was heavy, huh!"

Beth said, "Yep, through all the briars and low branches. We all have lots of scratches everywhere, to prove it."

"I do remember the tree, now. It broke the bridge! And I was so scared. I couldn't hold on to the rope any longer. The water was pulling me and pulling me, and it was so cold! Julie paused, thinking, rubbing her temple. I don't remember anything else, much."

"Well, thank goodness, you seem 'all right'. Can you see okay? Is anything blurry?" asked Beth.

"Yes, I can see just fine, ...nothing's blurry."

"Do you think you broke anything?"

Julie said, "No. Nothing hurts except my head."

"Do you think you have a fever?" asked Beth.

Lori had finally sat down with them and just listened. She almost put her hand out to feel Julie's forehead, but Julie felt her own head, and said, "I don't know."

Beth reached out, and said, "Here, let me feel your head. I can tell." Julie leaned toward her. "No fever. Good," said Beth. "But you'd better not move around too much. You might have a concussion. Do you feel nauseous?"

"No, just very tired."

"Want me to help you outside, to go to the bathroom?"

Julie let Beth help her up, and they left.

Lori was beginning to feel relief, that maybe, Julie wouldn't remember anything about last night. Then, as they came back in and were sitting down, Julie asked...

"Were there any boys here, last night?"

"No, why?" said both Beth and Lori together.

"Oh, while I was 'out, or whatever, I must've been dreaming," she said, and she blushed, slightly.

"What about?" asked Beth.

Lori's heart started pounding and skipping beats and she held her breath.

"Well, I was with, uh, ..hm-m, I can't see his face. But, we were at the beach. It was cold, and he held me close, ...not rough, you know. Very, uh, ...tender. Yes, ...he had a nice touch. He caressed my back, and my shoulder, and held me closer."

Lori still held her breath.

"Well, maybe you have a concussion," said Beth. "We'll get you to a doctor, when they rescue us."

"Oh, I'll be okay," Julie said. Then she turned toward Lori. "Beth told me everything you did."

Lori quickly looked down, ashamed.

"I'm sure I'll remember more," said Julie.

135

Lori started turning red.

"Thanks."

Lori looked up at her, really confused.

"Honest. I'm better, now," she said, looking intently into Lori's eyes.

Lori still gave her a very strange look.

Thinking Lori's weird look was one of doubt, Julie crossed her eyes, looking silly, and smiled a big smile, and said, "See?"

Lori said, "Whew," slowly letting out her breath, and smiling a bit, in spite of herself, thinking, *"She's not talking about...rather she's talking about... Boy...am I ever lucky."* Her mind went blank for a second, but her next thought was, *"She really should smile like that more often, and for me, very often. That's number three, for me."*

She finally smiled back, and said, "Feel like eating a few berries?"

Before Julie could answer, they heard, "Hello-o! Lori? Beth? Are you here?" Katie's voice was far away.

"We're saved! They're here!" said Beth, running to the entrance.

Lori stayed by Julie, telling her not to jump up quickly, yet.

"But, I'm okay," insisted Julie.

"Please?" asked Lori. "I just want you to be better than, 'okay', okay? Please let them check you, first."

Julie was calmed back down, by the sincerity in Lori's voice, thinking, *"She's not trying to be a 'know it all', like Joann said. She really seems to be concerned about me."*

Katie entered, along with Mrs. 'Z', the nurse, and a ranger. Right behind them were two ambulance guys, and they had a stretcher. The nurse and the two paramedics went immediately to Julie and did all sorts of checks on her. Zee and Katie asked Lori and Beth about a hundred questions, and then the medical group checked them out, too.

When all was said and done, Julie seemed okay, but got a 'stretcher' ride, through the woods, around to the left of the cave, for almost half a mile. There sat the ambulance, the camp's jeep, and the ranger's jeep. Zee and the nurse went in the ambulance with Julie, to get her checked out by the hospital, and to telephone her parents, to bring them 'up to date'.

Lori and Beth went back to camp with Katie, while the ranger stayed to survey the remnants of the hanging bridge.

Phone Home

"Hi, Dad."

"Yeah, I'm okay. They called you yesterday afternoon, huh? No, Beth's okay, too. Yeah, it was scary! The whole bridge broke. No, I wasn't on it. Julie was. Yeah, she's at the hospital because she got knocked out with a bump on the head, ...maybe a concussion. We should be hearing from the hospital soon, now."

"No, Dad, tell her it wasn't *anybody's* fault! No, they're *very* careful. But who could know a giant tree would be coming along?"

"Yes. I'm sure. I'm definitely sure. No, tell her I do *not* want to come home. In fact, I wish I could stay longer. It's great here!"

"Okay, Dad. I will. I love you, too. Bye."

"That Maude," she thought, walking back to the cabin. *"She's always butting into my life."*

The next morning, Mr. Hunter called to check again on Lori.

"Hi, Dad, what's up?"

"No...I'm fine, honest. Yeah, I slept really well. The whole thing isn't even that big of a deal anymore. Julie didn't even have to stay at the hospital overnight. No, no concussion, just a hard bump, and fatigue. We're getting ready to play horseshoes and Beth and I will be playing against Joann and Julie, so you can see that everybody's okay."

"What? No. No, I didn't get in any trouble about that. No, in fact, I received a compliment from my counselor. Yeah, she said I did well. You told Maude about the 'wrestling'? Why, Dad? Why did you have to tell her that? Oh. No, I guess not. I don't expect you to hide my letters from her." Then, making a face, Lori said, "Give Maude...my regards."

"Okay, Dad, I will. I love you, too. Bye."

"I wonder what nickname Rory would come up with for my stepmother if she ever met her?" Lori thought as she left Zee's office.

Trail Ride

After lots of practice, the campers were obliged to pass a test before they could go out on a trail ride with Boots. They had to make their horses go forward and backward, go left around the ring, and then reverse, and go right around the ring. Next, they had to get the horses to trot and then canter.

Every single Falcon had passed, and today was Trail Ride Day. Boots led out, and one of her assistants brought up the rear. Gerri rode somewhere in the middle. They all had their horses walk for about fifteen minutes and then they came to an open field.

"Okay, girls, here's a chance to run the horses a little," said Boots. "You first four come with me. The rest of you, control your mounts until Gerri sends you." She left, with Nancy, Liz, and Ceil and Vivian. They enjoyed a slow canter, and soon reached the end of the field.

Next came Lori, Beth, Julie and Joann. Beth was doing very, very well. Joann was hanging on for dear life. Julie wasn't completely comfortable with her horse's canter. Lori was ecstatic. She had Rocky today and he had such a smooth, slow canter, that she felt like she was sitting in a rocking chair. Her hips 'flowed' with his rhythm. She had strong legs so she could take a little weight on her feet, when needed. As a result, she didn't 'slap' up and down in the saddle. She felt like she wanted to ride for miles.

Last came Gerri, with Jen and Lu. Lu was the best rider of the three. She rode very well, looking like she belonged in the saddle and should be on a cattle drive. Jen bounced a lot and rode with a frown on her face. Gerri bounced, but enjoyed it all.

After everyone cantered the small field, Boots had them 'trot' the horses back across. This was a harder gait to master, for Lori. But when she looked at Julie, she decided that *"Julie most definitely 'had it' for this gait. She looks like a really elegant 'horsewoman' with her incredible posture, and the way she 'sits' a horse. And look at her, 'posting' with the horse."* As she looked around, no one, not even Boots, who wore a bright pink cowgirl shirt today, looked as 'picture-perfect' as Julie. Lori was pretty impressed.

When they got to canter the small field, once more, Lori felt even better. She shut out the rest of the world and 'became one with Rocky'.

They walked the horses to Stump Circle and it didn't seem nearly as far as when they had hiked there. After a break, they headed to the river.

The new bridge was under construction but all the slats weren't finished, yet. Boots led them upstream where they crossed the river, and then let the horses drink. Next, they followed a narrow trail up to a bluff that overlooked a lot of the valley and the winding river. It was a beautiful sight and Lori wished she had borrowed Jill's camera.

"I'll be back here," she vowed. "Somehow, I'll be back."

The ride back to camp was pleasant and peaceful. By the time the trail ride was over, a lot of girls were happy campers.

Donna Kelli

Test Day in Swim Class

Today was test day for both the basic crawl stroke 'with breathing' and the side stroke. To pass, each girl had to swim twenty-five yards up, and twenty-five yards back. Lots of girls were afraid, ...not of drowning, but of not being able to finish.

Lori and Beth were asked to do one last demo so the campers could watch, once more, what they were expected to do. Lori went first and a hush fell over the girls from the Hawks' cabin, followed by comments, like "Would you look at that!" This was really the first time they were seeing her swim with a purpose, other than the little 'demos' that she did for individual girls.

Bigfoot waded up to Walli, and quietly said, "Okay, Walli! Now I know why you want her for Waterfront C.I.T. How many people do you know with a crawl stroke like that?"

"Only one. A graceful, powerful woman I saw training for long distance swims. That was in France about five years ago."

When Lori was done, Walli gave Beth the 'go ahead', and asked, "Okay, who's the next 'brave one'?"

Vivian stepped up and then everyone lined up.

"You can rest as long as you want once you get to the buoy. Then, do the side stroke all the way back. If you get in trouble just stop, walk back, and start over."

Lori and Beth watched as everybody swam. Julie did extremely well, especially after what had happened to her in the river. When she swam all the way to the far end, she jumped up and down for joy. She was especially happy that she hadn't gulped in any water accidentally.

Later, as she finished doing the side stroke all the way back, she smiled when Walli announced, "Julie Conners, ...Pass!"

But then, Julie looked for Lori and headed for her, still smiling. When she got close enough, she said, "Thanks, Lori, for all your help, and for putting up with me. You're the greatest!" And she gave Lori a completely unexpected hug.

Lori was dumbfounded, and didn't know whether she should hug her back, or not. Before she could move, Julie was turning away looking for Joann to see if she had passed, also.

Beth was hugging some of her campers, too, ...those that she'd helped, and Lori thought, *"I've never thought much about hugging, except to hug Dad. Guess I'd better get used to it though, because here comes Joann, all smiles, too."* Sure enough, Lori got another hug.

Everybody was hugging everybody it seemed, and then Lori saw Jen, heading her way. She felt like turning away and racing to the little dock, but she steeled herself to endure Jen's hug, if that was why she was coming over.

Sure enough, Jen smiled, put her arms up all the way around Lori and gave her a full body hug. She held on tight, and said, "Thanks for helping me." Lori started to step back because the hug should've been over by now. But Jen asked, "Aren't you going to hug me too, and congratulate me? I passed a long time ago!"

Lori could see that this could end up being really weird, ...so to end it quickly and tactfully, she put her hands on Jen's back and gave her a tentative hug and a few pats on the back and said, "Congratulations, Jen. I knew you could do it."

Jen finally turned loose and stepped back, saying, "See, now was that so hard?"

Lori just looked at her, for a second, and then said, "Excuse me, Jen. Hey! Sue! Congratulations!" And she left Jen standing there. For about three steps, Lori felt herself shivering and thinking, *"Yuck!"*

Walli called them together, and had them sit in the shallow water. "Almost everyone has passed," she announced, "and I'll work with those who didn't, every day until they do. Congratulations to all of you for your effort."

The testing hadn't taken very long and Walli used the rest of the session to teach them the Breast Stroke.

While they were still sitting, she demonstrated the arm motions and the frog-type kick. "This is an easy stroke, and if you keep your head out of the water you'll be floating and swimming. When we have Canoeing soon, you'll be using this or the side stroke to practice bringing the canoe back to shore," she said.

Liz asked, "How come you didn't teach us that stroke first?"

Walli smiled, and said, "Like I've said before, because it's important for you to be able to put your face in the water and swim and not be afraid."

And later, when she was ready to end the session, she asked, "Okay, now, who else wants to earn their privilege to go to the dock?"

About four girls raised their hands, who had never been brave enough before. Sue and Jill were two of them.

Beth said, "Boy, I'm not even motivated to go out there as much anymore. Since Rory and all those girls from the other cabins have been qualifying, it's getting too crowded to be comfortable."

"You're so right," said Lori.

Touch Football

The Hawks challenged the Falcons to a game of touch football, and excitement was in the air.

Lori was glad that Rory remembered to bring a football, because it was one of her favorite sports. She had always played it with the neighborhood boys, growing up. She didn't go in for 'tackle' because she didn't want to get a crunched chest, so she had always made the boys play 'touch', whenever she played. They didn't seem to mind.

Here at camp during free time, a few of them had played catch with Rory from time to time, but now this was going to be a real game, with a referee, and all. Some girls from the other cabins were even coming to watch.

Lu and Jen were excited to play. Beth wanted to play, too. Joann was willing to learn and Julie had mixed emotions. Liz and Nancy just wanted to watch, and so did Ceil and Vivian.

They headed toward the softball field, and started tossing the ball around. Gerri agreed to be the referee and she put out some markers to indicate the four corners.

Lori threw a few short passes to the girls who wanted to play in order to warm them up and to see who could catch. She was glad it was a soft, squishy, football so that her girls wouldn't be afraid to catch it. Hopefully, no one would get any broken fingers.

Gerri said, "This game will start in one minute. Captains come here for the coin toss." Joann was holding the ball and she automatically handed it to Lori, their captain by silent assent.

They lost the coin toss, however, and Lori's group had to kick off to the other team. Lori got them together in a huddle, and said, "Now, when one of their girls tries to run past us and through us for a touchdown, somebody tag her, below the waist, with one hand." Then she gave the ball to Lu, and said, "I'm guessing you can punt pretty well."

Lu kicked it very far to the Hawks team and Sue got it. Jill was running 'interference' for her. Sue was running slowly, hiding behind Jill as they ran down the sideline trying for a TD. Sue was fast, and when she saw the chance, she left Jill and took off on her own. She made it all the way. "Touchdown!" she yelled from the end zone. "Yea, it's 6-0!"

Lori smiled, and said, "See? That's what we have to do. Now, when they kick off to us, whoever gets it, try to run straight ahead, as fast as you can, until you get tagged. By the way, that was a great kick, Lu."

Lu started to smile at the compliment, but then just looked down and murmured, "I know."

The ball came bouncing on the ground to Joann. She picked it up and started to run forward. Lu came up beside her, grabbed the ball out of her hands and ran it about fifteen yards before she got tagged.

Joann said, "I don't like this game."

Lori heard her and said, "I don't blame you. Come on, everybody. Huddle up." In the huddle, Lori said, "Look, Lu, this is a team sport. No more 'grandstanding' and no more 'grabbing the ball' away from anyone. You could've blocked for her and we might have gotten lots more than fifteen yards."

"Yeah, but she wasn't going to run."

"Yes, ...she was." said Lori. "Okay. Lu, you center the ball to me, and then, go out for a pass. You go out, too, Jen. Beth, Julie, and Joann, you stand right here and 'push against anyone who tries to come tag me. 'Block them like this, with your forearms up to protect your chest. Okay?"

"Set. One, two, hup!" Lori got the ball and watched the mad rush coming at her. She 'focused' in on Jen who was looking back at her and threw a nice, soft pass to her.

Jen caught it, and ran all the way for a touchdown.

"Tie score, 6-6!" yelled Jen, all smiles.

Lori extended her arms overhead and clapped to show Jen her appreciation for a good run.

"Is that what we're supposed to do?" asked Joann.

"Yes," said Lori. "And when we get another set of four turns, I'll throw it to you."

Jen kicked off to the other team. Rory got it but couldn't run it all the way for a touchdown because Lori tagged her pretty quickly. Then, on their first down, Jill caught a pass from Rory and ran for a TD for the Hawks.

"We're winning now, 12-6!" yelled Jill.

On the next kick off, the ball came to Lori. She handed it to Beth, and said, "Run! Follow me!" She blocked Rory and Beth made it halfway down the field before she got tagged.

"Great run, Beth!" she said

143

In the huddle, Lori said, "Okay, everybody, if you ran out for a pass last time, this time you stay back and block for me. She looked at Joann, and said, "When Beth centers the ball to me, you run over that way, three steps, and then look at me. Catch my pass, and run!"

"Ready. Set. One, two, hup." Lori got the ball, and ran to her right, a little, and waited for Joann to look at her. She threw a nice easy pass to her. Joann caught it with stiff fingers, but she held on, and everybody yelled, "Run!" She ran about ten yards and then got tagged.

"Good catch! Good run, Joann." said Lori.

Lori set her team, again. Lu and Jen were up on the line to 'go out for a pass'. Lu wasn't 'open' so Lori threw to Jen, who 'bobbled' the ball, and couldn't catch it.

"That's okay." said Lori. "Good try. Let's huddle up."

"Okay," she said, "Beth and Joann go out for a pass, Julie, center the ball."

"Set. One, two, three, hup. Lori threw a pass to Joann, who caught it and ran all the way.

"This is fun!" she said. "I never scored a touchdown ever in my life before! What's the score, now?"

Lu answered, "It is 12-12, but I'm not having much fun! Throw me a pass when we get the ball again!"

It wasn't very long before Rory made a touchdown for the Hawks and the score was 18-12, their favor.

On the next kick off to Lori's team, Jen picked up the ball, and got tagged immediately, by Rory. Now, the Falcons would have to start way back near their own goal, so they had a long, long way to go. Lori didn't have to tell them anymore who was blocking or who was running out for passes. They all knew, go out for a pass... then, next turn, stay back and block; go out, stay back.

"Joann, you center the ball. Lu, go straight up the middle for about ten steps, just like Joann did, then stop, and look back at me, okay?"

"Hut, hut." Lori got the ball and ran to her left, a little. She watched Lu, and watched Lu, and watched Lu some more, waiting for her to stop and turn around.

Lu kept running straight ahead. Lori kept running around behind her blockers, avoiding the 'taggers' who were 'rushing' her. *"She'll turn around soon,"* she thought. *"She has to!"*

Two opponents, Rory and Sue, were reaching out to tag her, when she finally threw the ball. Since Lu was really far away now, Lori had to throw a pretty long pass. It kept going up and out, higher and higher. It had a nice spin to it, which helped it sail along.

Gerri, refereeing, looked up, squinting, and thought, *"what a great spiral."*

Lori thought, *"She'll look back, for sure!"* But, Lu just kept 'chugging along'.

"Lu! Turn around!" yelled Lori. "Lu!" Lori watched the ball coming down, right *at* Lu. "Oh, no!" she said aloud.

Bam! The ball hit her square in the back of the head, and knocked her off balance, forward. She landed flat on her stomach with her arms outstretched, and slid pretty far on the grass.

"Jeez! ...lucky that's a very soft football," said Lori to herself, running quickly toward Lu to see if she was okay.

No one but Lori and Gerri knew exactly what had happened, and Gerri was chuckling to herself as she trotted closer. She hoped Lu wouldn't start a fight.

Lu got up completely 'irate', hollering from far away, "You did that on purpose!" And, as she was walking back, she yelled, "Why did you do that?"

Lori met her, and said, "Sorry, Lu. I thought you'd be ready. Are you all right?" She didn't know what else to say and figured Lu was in no mood to listen anyway.

Lu didn't give her the courtesy of an answer. She just mumbled to herself all the way back.

In the huddle, Lori said, "Okay Julie, for the next play, you stand back here. I'll run in front of you and hand you the ball. You run that way, to the left, as far as you can get."

When Lori handed off the ball to Julie, she thought she'd probably run a short way and then get tagged.

But Julie took off like the wind.

Lori watched, thinking, *"I didn't know she could run so fast. And would you look at that, that... 'girlie-girlie-type-run'..."*

Julie had her elbows in tight, her wrists up, and her right palm very delicately 'outward', in utter femininity, ...like she was 'testing the temperature of the air' as she passed by. She held the football up against her heart with her left hand.

To Lori, who now stood mutely watching her, she was an 'elf-like' figure' just floating down the field. *'Tinker bell'* came to mind. Her feet didn't seem to touch the ground.

Four different girls tried to tag her, but she 'zigged' or 'zagged' so easily, that it seemed like she was born for it. She ended up running the whole length of the football field, because not even Rory could catch her. Julie was all by herself the last half of the way. Everybody was watching her, and cheering loudly.

"It looks like she runs almost on her 'tippy toes'," said Beth as she walked back to Lori.

Lori, shaking her head, thought to herself, *"Was that really a 'football' romp? It looked so fragile. And I wouldn't be surprised if she was giggling all the way."*

Smiling with pride and clapping her hands overhead, Lori motioned her back.

Julie 'floated' back not even winded. "Great run! Julie! You're pretty fast!" Lori said, as everybody cheered her again.

Julie wasn't sure she wanted to be identified as a *'football player'* exactly, but that was fun! ...Definitely! And it was *great* fun dodging all the people who wanted to tag her.

Vivian got up, and said, "Okay, I'll play, too."
Liz said, "Yeah, me too!"

Lori thought, *"Things are looking up."*

Canoeing

It had been fun swimming every day for the past week with the girls from the Hawks' cabin. The Falcons had progressed quickly and were all feeling good about their swimming skills. But today, only the girls from their cabin gathered at the lake, not too far from the swimming area. They sat in a small group and listened while Walli explained...

"Now that you've all mastered the crawl, the side stroke, and the breast stroke, and have passed your tests, Welcome to Canoeing! You won't have to swim twenty-five yards, or even fifteen, in either creek to get to shore, but it's comforting to know that you could, if you had to. Mostly you could just walk to the bank. There are only a few really deep spots in the creeks."

"You might tip over in the lake, however, and then you would have to swim and float to the dock or to shore. One nice thing is the canoe floats, even when it's full of water. And you can hold onto it a little, for support."

"Canoeing," she continued, "can be so much fun. It's peaceful and relaxing. It can also be exciting, like when we have the races next week. It can also be dangerous. Canoes tip over easily because your upper body weight tends to be up too high. But, if one person were to lie down in a canoe, it would be very hard to tip it over."

She showed them how to kneel-sit in the canoes, to reduce their chances of tipping over. They took turns, two buddies at a time. While one was learning how to climb into a canoe in shallow water, the other held the canoe as steady as possible.

For the next skill, the entire group helped hold onto the sides to keep the canoe from tipping over. Then, one partner had to bend down, hold onto the sides, and walk the length of the canoe on the middle floor 'seam' without tipping over. After both partners had a turn, then they went with Gerri, to the canoes nearby, and practiced by themselves, right near the beach in shallow water...

Next, Walli had each twosome sit in the canoe in water about waist deep, and deliberately tip it over, just to feel 'what it felt like'. Then, they had to 'swim' the canoe to shallow water, turn it sideways to the beach, and tip the water out. "Lift the canoe to empty the last few drops." she said. "Dragging the canoe can damage the bottom, so try not to ever do it."

147

Lori and Beth thought tipping over was great fun. Julie was apprehensive, until she did it twice. Then Lori saw her smiling.

For 'their next trick', Walli had them do the same thing in water up to their necks. They got accustomed to the canoe staying buoyant, even though it was upside down or full of water right-side-up. It could actually hold them up a little. They put their swimming skills to work since they weren't supposed to touch the bottom unless they had to, bringing the canoe back to shore. When it was their turn, Lori and Beth got back in the 'mostly' sunken canoe, sat inside, and 'hand' paddled back.

Before any of them ever touched a paddle, the girls had to practice walking the length of the canoe, out in a little deeper water. Then, they were supposed to walk the length with their partner still in the canoe. Climbing over her was going to be the hardest part.

Walli said, "You all know how to float and swim. All of you have passed several tests. So, if you should 'accidentally' tip over and you can't touch bottom, don't panic. Hold onto the canoe and float or swim it back in, just like you've been doing."

Everybody stood in water, chest deep, watching. Ceil and Vivian, with their canoe out beyond the group, went first. Since both were extremely chubby, they knew they had to be extra careful. Vivian got down as low as she could kneel, and she still presented a formidable object to step over. Ceil, the shorter of the two, inched along, trembling slightly, holding onto the sides of the canoe with such tight grips that her knuckles were white.

With a grunt, she managed to get one leg up and over Vivian, but as she went to put her foot down on the bottom, she missed the seam, and tipped the canoe to the right, a little. She leaned left, and tried to scoot her foot closer to the seam, but she had very short legs, and was 'hung up' across Vivian's back and shoulders.

Vivian was saying, "Hurry up, Ceil!" in a muffled voice.

"I'd like to, but I'm stuck!"

Their 'audience' started laughing and snickering, but didn't make any smart alecky comments, because they didn't want to miss anything these two said to each other.

"Well, go on over!"

"Easy for you to say!"

"Ceil, just push with your back foot and lean on your hands and go on over!"

Ceil tried harder, but she couldn't move forward, at all.

"Then, Go back!" yelled Vivian.

Ceil really tried, but she was tiring from holding her weight on her hands so long.

Vivian could feel her trying to lean backwards, but as Ceil was doing that, she was putting more weight on her back. "What are you doing up there? I'm dying under here!"

Ceil saw the problem from Vivian's perspective and realized her painful predicament. She really felt bad for her, but then, she started laughing, out loud.

"It's not funny! You're squashing me, you 'tub'!"

Ceil had tears running down her cheeks now, she was laughing so hard. Her arms lost all their strength, and she just sagged more on Vivian.

"Help!" said a croaking voice.

Ceil felt herself leaning a little too far to the right and she couldn't do anything about it, except shake all over laughing... Slowly, very slowly, the canoe tipped to the side. Ceil couldn't see much through her tears, but as she felt her elbow going in the water, she heard a weak, but indignant voice...

"You're going to regret this! Just wait 'til it's my...glub"

Walli and Gerri had moved to each end of the canoe, in case either girl had trouble after they tumbled out. Walli, herself, was still laughing hard and she hoped she didn't have to 'save' either one of them right this minute.

Both girls untangled themselves in the water. Ceil managed to hold onto the canoe, still laughing, while an 'irate' Vivian was doing all the work 'swimming' both the sunken canoe and Ceil to shore. "My fat Aunt Tillie could do this better than you!"

Lori, still laughing, said, to Beth, "They're a great pair. I like them a lot."

"That's for sure," said Beth.

Lori knew what it felt like to be laughing as hard as Ceil. She automatically looked over at Julie. She and Joann were wiping tears from their own eyes, when Julie suddenly looked directly at Lori.

Their eye contact held, and Lori wondered, *"...what...?"*

Julie, still smiling, nodded her head up and down slightly, and with a gently moving wrist and a bent elbow, pointed her finger at Lori. Her motions said, "I remember what you did to me in swim class, and don't think I'm going to let you off easy. I'll get even. Count on it."

Lori just tipped her head back a little and laughed in resignation. She knew if people really believed something, it was hard to change their minds. Then, looking back again at Julie, she lifted her shoulders a little, cocked her head to the right, and turned her palms up.

Julie read the motions to mean, "I know you think I 'dumped' you on purpose...but it was an accident..."

To which she replied, with a 'No' motion with her head. Then, she smiled bigger, and slowly, and deliberately repeated her 'Yes' nod, and with a limp wrist, wagged her forefinger up and down at Lori.

149

Lori knew it meant, "I don't think so...and I *am* going to get you back."

"Okay, who's next?" asked Walli.

Joann started tugging on Julie's shoulder. The two of them headed back to shore to do the climb-over each other 'canoe thing'.

Lori was thinking, *"Our first, 'purely personal, fun' conversation, and it was 'wordless'."*

Comes the Dawning

It was very early in the morning. Lori sat up in bed, and looked around. Julie's bunk was empty. *"Probably in the bathroom,"* she thought. Everyone else was still asleep.

But, when she got in there, the only sounds she heard, were her own, echoing through the empty stalls, and there was no one in the showers. *"Probably at the mess hall,"* she thought. She went back and put on her sneakers.

Lori deeply appreciated and valued the beauty and serenity of early morning. She headed outside to go down by the lake. It made her feel good to watch the birds out and about so early. And, far off in the distance, she spotted a deer getting a drink at the water's edge.

It was very still as she breathed in the cool morning air. She liked the way the morning dew glistened everywhere. She especially loved the effect of the sun's light rays, streaming down through the branches of all the oak trees, like a striped, misty, diagonal curtain. *"If only I could draw and paint well,"* she thought, *"but, I can't. I really do need to get a camera."* As she moved along quietly toward the campfire ring, suddenly she stopped dead in her tracks.

There, under a huge oak tree by the canoe rack, was Julie, in her shorty pajamas, stretching and apparently doing some morning exercises. Lori didn't want to disturb her. But, on the other hand, she didn't want to go back inside, either.

She just stood there like a statue, watching, as Julie moved. The morning sun's rays were shining down through the trees on Julie, too, and it was as if she was shrouded in a veiled, 'make-believe world' of mist, golden sunlight and shadows.

Julie bent over slowly, and touched her toes. Only it wasn't like Lori was used to watching most girls do in P.E. class. It was more deliberate and controlled, and she bent over and down, extremely low. One of the main differences was, that Julie's body bent at the hips, not so much at the waist. As Lori watched, Julie's upper body went over, and down so far, that her stomach was actually touching her upper legs, and her chest touched her knees.

Lori frowned, because most people weren't so limber. And Julie's shoulders weren't 'rounded over'. She still had good posture, with a straight back, even though she was 'bent in half'.

"She...looks...like a..."

Next, Julie lifted a leg, and hooked her heel over one of the rungs of the canoe rack, and stretched out into a 'split', with her fingers extended 'artistically' toward her toes.

"a...dancer...a...ballet dancer," thought Lori, still glued to the spot.

After stretching one leg, and then the other, Julie started doing the basic positions, bending at the knees, and pointing her toes 'just so' and putting her arms 'just so'. She didn't seem to 'swing' her arms heavily. They just floated, from one 'picturesque' pose to another, effortlessly.

"I never really noticed her arms that much, before." thought Lori. *"They're so graceful."* She watched Julie's hands and wrists do delicate, dainty little moves, that were completely foreign to her. Lori tried to move her own wrists the same way. Frustrated, she realized that her motion was different, the way she did 'loop-the-loop' with a yo-yo, ...and not even close to what Julie was doing.

Then, Julie did some sideways bends, with flowing, elegant, arms, reaching over her head. *"She looks so-o-o graceful."* she thought, once again. *"There's no other word for it."*

"Ah, ...that explains her 'walk'." Lori remembered how ballerinas walk across a stage...like they were putting their pointed toes down first, instead of their heels. *"Julie, doesn't walk that way every step,"* she decided, *"...it just shows up every once in awhile."*

Then, Julie did some 'plies'. *"Funny,"* she thought, *"how some words you've heard somewhere stick in your brain."* And then, as she continued to watch, in fascination, Julie did some little runs and some little leaps.

"Julie's 'girlie girlie' way of running like an elf," she thought, smiling at the recent memory. *"Of course..."*

After warming up with several, Julie ran in a different direction, and leaped incredibly high in the air, over an upside down canoe.

The picture seared itself into Lori's brain. At the top of her leap, it was as if an invisible cord was holding her up in the air, for a long, long time. Julie's head was up, and her posture was exquisite. Her arms were outstretched to the sides, with her fingers and wrists, 'just so'. And, her legs were extended beautifully, forward and backward in a split, with her toes dramatically pointed.

Lori didn't remember Julie landing. She only saw her form frozen in mid-flight. *"I have to get a camera,"* she thought. *"I'd like to have that picture to look at, for the rest of my days."* She took in a long, slow breath, and then sighed. *"It was, ...sheer beauty."*

And Lori knew, that in spite of all her own 'natural ability', she would never look like that, leaping over anything. *"And that explains her figure,"* she thought, as she remembered Julie in the showers and in the cave.

She finally turned to go back to the cabin. After walking a few steps, she stopped and closed her eyes for a moment. There was the 'picture'...still embedded in her brain. She smiled. *"Just checking,"* she thought.

More Arts and Crafts

After drawing a picture of their cabin tucked back under the shady trees, Lori returned to her favorite subject.   But she was having a hard time drawing anything that resembled Rocky's beautiful, elegant head. She loved his big light-brown eyes, but she couldn't do them justice, either.

Mrs. Watson came over, because she could tell that she wasn't 'in to it'. Lori held her head, leaning on her hand.

"Problem?" asked the instructor.

"Yes," sighed the normally happy girl. "I don't have a knack for drawing."

"Oh, what do you like?"

"Well, ...I think I'd like to do photography. There are some really beautiful things that I'd like to remember, ...just as they were, ...not how I try to draw them. What I try to create doesn't even come close..."

That was the most Lori had said in class, ever, and Mrs. Watson knew that she must've felt strongly about it all.

"Well, we're going to do 'clay-molding' in our next class. How about if you try that? And, if you don't like it, maybe you'd rather be at team sports instead, during this couple of hours."

Lori brightened. "Really?"

"Yes," said Mrs. Watson, smiling, "Really."

"Even today?"

"Yes."

"You're not insulted that I don't like Arts and Crafts so much?"

"No, Lori. Not at all. See you next time, okay?"

"Yes! For sure. Thanks. Excuse me, please. Bye."

Quietly, she stopped for a second near Beth, to say, 'Good-bye' and then Lori was gone. She headed for the stables.

Quiet Beauty

After their third canoeing lesson, Lori waited to speak with 'Walli' quietly and privately,

"May I please have permission to take a canoe for an early morning ride tomorrow morning, if the weather is nice?"

Walli looked at her for a minute, deciding. Then, she said, "Fletch and I are planning to do the same thing, tomorrow. So, yes, you may. Go only with a buddy, not alone. Take life vests. Go upstream. Don't pass the second sharp curve and be back before breakfast."

"Thanks, Walli," said Lori, with her eyes sparkling. And as Walli watched the girl leaving with a spring to her walk, she thought to herself, *"If only more solutions in my life were so simple."*

The next morning Lori awoke very early, to a beautiful day. She hadn't said anything to Beth, yet, because Beth liked to sleep until the gong sounded. *"I'll spend a few minutes alone and then see if I can get her up."*

Julie opened her sleepy eyes and saw Lori, already dressed, going out the door. It puzzled her, because she sometimes went out to exercise and stretch, all alone and she wondered what Lori did. She got dressed and followed her.

Lori was getting a canoe ready with life jackets, and paddles. She looked up and was surprised to see Julie approaching.

"Oh, ...Hi, Julie," she said.

"Hi. Going for a ride?"

Lori said, "Yes, want to come?" thinking Joann was not very far behind her.

"Is it okay?"

"Yes," said Lori. "I've already asked Walli.

"Well, for how long?"

"Only 'till breakfast."

"Where's Beth?"

"Still sleeping."

"Well, okay." Julie came a little closer, saying, "You steer? Right?"

"Usually," said Lori.

Julie said, "Ready?"

Lori couldn't believe it, ...but Julie started pulling the canoe out into the water. Numb and slightly dazed, Lori helped. They stepped in, got settled, and started out.

Lori was in a state of shock, that Julie was sitting in front of her, but she paddled, automatically.

"Which side do you want me to paddle on?

"It doesn't really matter," said Lori. "Switch, whenever you get tired."

This confused Julie, because when Joann was steering, she was always saying, "Paddle on the left! Paddle on the right! Hurry up, and paddle on the left, again!" Her favorite command, was "Paddle backwards!"

And with Joann, Julie was always frantically busy and apprehensive because she heard quite often, "Now look what you made us do!"

But this canoe was already moving forward, smoothly, in a straight line, and Julie hadn't even gotten her paddle wet, yet. She felt the canoe surge ahead with each of Lori's strokes. She looked back for several seconds, to see that Lori was paddling on the right, and that she wasn't switching madly, from side to side. She took long strokes, and turned the paddle, a little at the end of each stroke. Walli's lesson about how to 'J' paddle-stroke, suddenly seemed to make sense.

Julie started paddling on the left and the canoe picked up speed. It made her feel good to know that she had an effect. She never really knew before, because they crashed so much and didn't seem to get very far. She had never gone this far, this fast, and they weren't even trying to race. It was exhilarating!

This was so different. Lori didn't chatter away and everything was so quiet. When Julie accidentally banged her paddle against the side of the canoe, it made a loud noise. She vowed to do better, because she realized that Lori's paddling hardly made a sound at all. She could only hear the water dripping off Lori's paddle as she moved it forward, above the water, for her next stroke.

It seemed like just a few minutes had passed and already they were far from camp. The creek narrowed slightly and the trees made a canopy overhead. The sunlight streamed through, here and there and Julie felt like she was in a 'make believe world'.

Lori was deep in thought, wondering if Julie was having as good a time as she was. The morning was perfect. She loved the misty curtain of sunlight, and she craved the silent beauty all around them. That it was Julie with her, made the day even more perfect.

Julie's hair fell across her face a little, and she stopped paddling to fix it. She put the paddle across her lap for a minute while she smoothed and tucked wayward strands behind her ears.

155

The canoe kept moving. She could feel the power coming from Lori. Usually, by now, Joann would be screaming, "Paddle Julie! I can't do this all by myself!"

She was curious to see how long it would take Lori to tell her to paddle, especially since they were coming to the first tight curve. So, she just sat there, resting.

Lori said nothing and Julie realized that it was quieter than ever. She felt so serene, yet excited somehow, to be out in the wilderness and not be afraid. She looked down into the clear water and watched the bottom as they passed by.

They got to the sharp curve, and the bow of the canoe just started turning to go around it. Julie looked back, and Lori was still calmly stroking and steering, ...no big deal. Julie thought, *"She learned this a lot quicker and a lot better than the rest of us. That's for sure."*

Lori paddled all the way around the curve. Then Julie felt Lori stop paddling, but the canoe was still coasting from her efforts. It got completely quiet even though they were still silently gliding along.

Julie was reluctant to break the spell. It was hypnotic. *"So, ...this is canoeing,"* she thought. *"I love it."*

Then Julie looked up ahead to the right, and couldn't believe it. A doe and two baby fawns, full of little white spots, were at the water's edge. Julie looked back, to show Lori and saw her already watching them. Julie realized that was why she had stopped paddling.

The doe was drinking and one fawn started 'pronging' around in little stiff-legged jumps, with its head down. It bumped into the doe, on its 'brand new legs' and fell down. It got up and bounced around some more, and fell down again.

"He's just glad to be alive," thought Julie, smiling and stifling a chuckle. *"Me, too."*

Unbelievably, the deer had not seen the canoe yet. *"Because we're so quiet,"* thought Julie, *"and neither one of us has moved a muscle."*

The canoe had stopped silently gliding, and was dead still in the water. She and Lori got to watch them for about 30 seconds more, before the doe picked her head up, looking, and 'cocking' her ears, in their direction. She snorted a cough-like noise at them and stomped her front hoof.

When that didn't scare the girls away, she raised her tail and turned quickly to leave. Julie was surprised to see that the underside of her tail was bright white. The doe started running and the babies followed. She leaped exceptionally high, over a little bush, and the babies followed, ...not as high, but with their tiny tails up, waving like flags, too.

"They're so-o graceful." said Julie, in a whisper.
"Yes, they are," sighed Lori, remembering another very beautiful, high leap.

Julie just sat there, thinking, *"I've never seen deer, running free, before. That was special."*
Lori stretched a little and said, "Guess we should go back."
"Do we have to?"
"Yes, I promised," said Lori.

They turned the canoe around and started back. As they rounded a curve they met Walli and Fletch.
"Hi girls," they said. See anything interesting?"
Julie was ready to tell them all about the deer, but Lori said, "Mostly...just quiet beauty..." ....and Julie wondered why she didn't tell them more. Then, re-living it as she was paddling along, she decided it *was* more meaningful just shared between the two of them.

Later, as they were putting the canoe up on the rack Julie said, "Lori, I just want you to know that this morning meant a lot to me. It was very special. Thanks for inviting me."
"You're welcome," replied Lori, wishing she was brave enough to say *"Let's do it again, soon, ...just you and me..."*

But Beth and Joann came down to the beach, with Joann shouting, "There you are! Some nerve, sneaking off and leaving us behind!"
Lori just smiled and drawled, "Aw, ...you two sleepy heads would miss breakfast every day if the gong didn't ring. Come on everybody, I'm starved!"
Heading up the beach, Julie thought to herself, *"Boy, Lori sure kidded Joann right out of her usual, five-minute-long, 'whining' guilt trip that I would have heard. Cool!"*

157

Touch Football II

Rory came through the center-restroom-area of the cabin carrying her football.

"Hey, Lori. Want to play catch later, before swimming starts?"

"What time?"

"Right after lunch. Okay? About 1:15?"

"Okay," said Lori. "I'll meet you out front. Is it okay if Beth comes?"

"Sure."

Later, during lunch, Julie noticed that Lori and Beth were in a private, animated conversation. Lori kept making slow hand motions, showing Beth the palm of her right hand and pointing out the 'pads' of her fingertips. Then she'd do a hand and arm motion, like she was throwing.

After having such a great early morning, canoeing with her, Julie found herself wondering if Lori was having a lot more fun at camp than she was. She watched as they left quickly after lunch and then she started to follow them.

"Where are you going?" asked Joann.

"Oh, uh...maybe for a walk." She didn't know where they were headed and she would've felt stupid, saying, "to follow Lori and Beth."

"Aren't you going to read with me today?"

"No, ...at least, not right away. I'll come find you later, okay?" And she left Joann staring after her, standing in the doorway of the mess hall.

Julie saw Rory and her buddy, Meg, walking with Beth and Lori, heading down the path to the field. They were tossing the football around with little passes. She followed, but found herself wondering if she could get close enough to hear the things they said to each other.

The girls started running out for little passes, and catching them as they went along the path. When they got to the field, they started running out farther, for longer passes.

When Julie got to the edge of the field, she sat down in the shade of a big tree and they didn't notice her. Compared to most of the little passes that had been thrown in the football game she'd played in, she was surprised at how far these girls could throw, ...especially Lori and Rory. She chuckled at how their names sounded, together. *"And,"* she decided, *"they weren't afraid to catch the ball, either."*

She had to admit that she was 'scared' of the ball. *"It could easily hit me in the face, or the chest, or break my fingers."* With these thoughts in mind, she watched their 'techniques'.

Beth threw 'wobbly' passes but Rory could throw a good 'spinner'. Lori showed Beth again, about 'rolling the ball off her fingertips' like she did at lunch. But now, Lori had the ball in her hand, and it all made a lot more sense.

Julie thought, *"Hm-m, wonder if I could do that?"*

Just then Rory yelled, "Throw me one!" and she took off running. Lori tossed it to her and the ball didn't wobble at all. Rory caught it easily, turned, and ran back closer, towards Lori. After she threw it back, she said, "How about a really long one?" and she took off running at top speed, diagonally away from Lori.

Lori took a few 'get-set-steps' and threw the ball hard and really far. It went up and up and out and out. As the ball reached it's peak, and started down, Julie could see that if Rory kept running fast, she and the ball would get to the same place at the same time.

Rory made it under the ball in time and caught it.

When she threw it back, it fell short of Lori, but Meg went and got it. Julie looked at how far away Rory was, and realized that Lori's pass had been really far, ...like the ones she had seen the school quarterback, Brad, throw.

Rory came in closer and yelled, "Nice pass! Is that your best shot?"

Lori laughed, and motioned with her left hand, for Rory to run directly away from her. Rory took off.

Lori waited, and then took her 'set up' steps, and then, leaning way back, she 'let fly' an absolutely awesome pass. It went off on a rocket-like trajectory.

Julie caught her breath and watched it going really high, and far. *"Wow,"* she thought, *"she really hurled that one."*

Rory was running fast. The ball finally started reaching its peak height, as Rory kept looking up and back over her shoulder. She ran harder. The ball started its descent and Rory ran even harder. She was 'pumping her arms' forward and backward for more speed.

With outstretched arms, she jumped and reached up high for the ball, but it sailed over her fingertips. The ball bounced on the ground, out in front of her. She slowed down, and went to pick it up, shaking her head because she couldn't believe she'd missed it...

Julie realized that Rory was incredibly far away from where Lori was standing. But then, Lori started running diagonally toward Rory, indicating with an outstretched arm, that she should throw a pass back to her. Rory waited for Lori to get in range and then threw her a high pass.

"I bet Lori threw that pass at least a half-a-football field!" thought Julie. *"And, it was straight!"* She wondered if Brad could throw that good and she

159

laughed, thinking, *"She should be on the footb..."* and she stopped herself from saying it. *"...but she can't, because she's a girl."*

The unfairness of that, took her attention away from them, and she just sat there, staring into space.

Beth had walked over to her, and was saying, "Hi Julie! Want to play?"

Julie 'popped' back into the here and now, and said, "What? Oh! Hi, Beth. Uh, well...I don't play very well."

Beth said, "Are you kidding? I saw you run for that touchdown last week."

Meg came up, and said, "Yeah! Be on our team!"

So, it was Meg, Rory and Julie against Beth and Lori.

Beth kicked off toward Julie. Julie picked up the ball after it bounced on the ground, ran forward, changed direction just as she got to Beth, and ran around her, all the way for a touchdown. It was just as easy and just as much fun as she remembered.

Julie didn't know how to kick, so Rory punted the 'kick-off' ball to Beth and Lori.

Lori caught it, and headed up the field. All three opponents, Julie, Rory, and Meg, were trying to cut her off. Lori ran right at them, and then, at the last second, 'zigged' left, 'zagged' right, and went right through them all, for a touchdown.

"Darn!" thought Julie. *"She's tricky. She doesn't 'just change direction'. She does a little wiggle, somehow."* She pictured the move, analyzed it, and decided that Lori was doing a fake move with her head and her shoulders, to one side, and then going the other way.

Beth kicked off to Rory's team, and Meg picked it up and started running for a TD. Julie tried to block for her, but Beth caught Meg, and tagged her.

On their first down, Meg centered the ball to Rory, who handed it to Julie, and said, "Run!" Julie took off, and saw that only Lori was between her and the goal. Julie 'zigged', and tried to go around her, but Lori caught her.

"Darn!" she thought, again. *"I forgot to do the 'head and shoulder' thing."*

Meg ran hard, on second down, and got past Beth, for a score. Upset with herself from the previous play, Julie thought, *"I should've been able to make that touchdown past Lori."*

Then it was time for them to kick off to Beth and Lori, again. Rory punted it, and Beth caught it. Julie ran after her and tagged her pretty quickly.

"Hah!" she said under her breath. "I *can* catch them."

On the next play, Julie's job was to 'rush' the passer, which was Lori. Beth centered the ball to Lori, and started running out for a pass. Meg and Rory, both, guarded Beth, closely, running on either side of her. Lori couldn't safely throw it to her yet, so she was saying, "Get open! Get away from them!"

Meanwhile, Julie was supposed to be tagging Lori. It was an 'eye opener' for her, because Lori would 'feint' one way, and run the other. Julie kept up the chase, and finally got so close that she was sure she was going to tag her. She reached out, leaning...

Lori did a feint left, and a feint right, and finally moved left. Julie had over-extended her reach, and gotten off balance. Then, unbelievably, she fell down, and couldn't believe that 'Lori was gone'.

She turned around to see Lori throwing a long pass to Beth. Beth was running at full speed, with her hands outstretched in front of her. The ball came down right over Beth's head, into her 'basket-like' waiting hands. She caught the ball, and made a touchdown. Julie could see that she was all smiles.

"Darn," thought Julie. *"There's more to this game than I thought. When the guys play, it just looks like they're all going 'splat' or 'crunch', blocking each other and falling down. But, there's a certain 'finesse' to it. Funny",* she thought, *"I never thought I'd use the word, finesse, to describe football. Even though it's played on a huge field, it seems like it's often, just a game of 'inches'."*

Now, she had two personal goals to achieve...one, to catch Lori and tag her, and the other was to escape when Lori was chasing her.

The game went on, and finally, Julie found herself running back with a 'kick-off', trying for a touchdown, with Lori coming at her to tag her. Julie did a 'feint' left, then changed direction, and 'floated' around Lori.

After she made the move and before she was even six steps away, she heard Lori saying, "What a great move! You faked me out pretty good on that one, Julie."

Somehow, that compliment meant more than the rest of the long run to the goal line for the touchdown. Feeling very good about herself, Julie now hoped to achieve her other goal, ...to tag the elusive Lori.

"Please kick it to Lori." thought Julie, when Meg got ready to do the kick off.

But the ball went to Beth.
"Oh heck." said Julie, silently.
Then, Beth lateralled a sideways pass to Lori.
"Oh, Good!" thought Julie, and she took off on the chase.

161

Meg and Rory cut Lori off from the left side, so Lori headed down the right side of the field.

Julie ran right at her. She made a little face as she ran, sort of all scrunched up in total concentration. Lori was watching Julie's body, generally from the waist down, to see which way to fake her out.

First, she faked right, but Julie didn't fall for it. Then Lori faked left, and Julie didn't fall for it. In fact, Julie was almost running in place, now, with lots of little steps, so she could go either way, in a split second. Lori was almost up to her, and feinted left, and went around the right side...

Julie fell for it a little bit, but recovered and ran directly sideways at Lori really fast, reaching and leaning, and coming almost close enough to tag her. "I've got you, now!" she said.

It would've been a simple tag, but Lori happened to look up at Julie's face and saw that funny little scrunched up, 'super-determined' look. And without warning, she suddenly felt her knees going weak as her giggles began deep down inside her. As she lost leg power she thought, *"Oh, no-o..."*

Julie had planned on tagging her as Lori passed by, and then, without any other body contact at all, just neatly going behind her. But when Lori slowed down a little, Julie's 'tag' turned into an unavoidable, full-body, 'crash' tackle. Both girls tumbled over and over each other, and ended up in a heap, with Lori sprawled on the bottom. In-between 'belly' laughs, and in spite of the fact that her cheek was pressed hard against the ground, Lori managed to say, "You...got me..."

Julie, still all business-like, gracefully rolled off Lori to a sitting position, saying, "Yes, I did! And I could do it again, too!"

....which made Lori laugh so hard that she couldn't even begin to get up.

And then, Julie noticed Lori's cheek still smushed in the dirt. She pictured how silly they must have looked, she relaxed a little, leaned back on her hands, and started laughing, too.

Lori sat up, finally, still chuckling. As she was quietly admiring Julie's smiling, dirty face and enjoying her delightful laugh, she was thinking, *"I don't think I've ever heard her laugh, before.* As their eyes met, and held for a long moment, Meg came up with the others and said, "Nice tackle, Julie! We win! And, it's time to quit!"

"When's our next game?" said Julie, looking up at her from the ground, still very much unaware of her smudged face and dirty knees.

Lori, sitting, with her arms wrapped around her knees, was just shaking her head, and chuckling to herself. *"I knew she'd be good at sports if she tried."*

Meg said, "Hey, Julie, you're not becoming a 'fanatic' are you?

"Yeah, we might have to call you 'Julie, the Jockette'..." teased Rory.

"Don't you dare!" said Julie.

Meg tagged Julie on the shoulder, and said, "You're it!", and took off, running.
Julie caught her about twenty-five yards down the field toward the path.

Lori still sat on the ground wiping dirt off her cheek, thinking, *"It's a great day!"*

Canoe Race

Lori sat in the canoe with Beth, calmly waiting for Walli to say, "Go." The race would be 'upstream' for about almost a mile as the crow flies, but about two miles with all the curves in the creek. One of Boots' assistants had been assigned to the finish line. Gerri was stationed about half way upstream, in case of any problems. After the race there would be a picnic with swimming, and then a leisurely drift back downstream to return to camp. Once Walli got them started, she would bring up the rear in her own canoe with a small motor on the side-rear, to keep tabs on any stragglers.

All of the Falcons had been up 'Shady Creek' several times in canoe class, so it was just a matter of who could paddle the hardest for the longest time, with a major emphasis on 'steering' around the many sharp curves.

Beth sat in the front. Lori would steer and be the power paddler. Four canoes sat ready. Ceil and Vivian were just getting in theirs. Buddies from swim class stayed together for this event. The race was handicapped, so that Ceil and Vivian were to be in the first canoe and get a full ten-minute head start. Julie and Joann, and Liz and Nancy were in the next two canoes and got a five-minute head start, ahead of Jen and Lu and Beth and Lori, who sat in the third row behind them.

Lori looked around at the set up and saw Julie in the front position. Joann would steer. Then she happened to look to her left, and saw Jen, in the front and Lu, aft. It struck Lori as funny because Lu had this 'determined' look on her face, and was intently staring sideways at her, across ten feet of water.

"Now what?" thought Lori. *"She still thinks I hurt Jen? Or that I have a 'thing' for Jen? Hmm, ...seems as if she wants to really stare me down this time."*

Lu let go of her paddle down low, and put her right hand on her hip, and 'glared' even harder.

Since the 'lead' canoe was still not even 'set', Lori decided to 'play the game'. She ignored the slight rocking of her canoe caused by Beth adjusting her position, and just kept on looking at Lu. *"This is almost comical,"* thought Lori, *"because I can look at her with my 'long distance focus' and see everything past her."*

She heard Julie nervously checking with Joann about some plan for 'serpent curve' number three, and Lori pictured it. It was the sharpest series of curves that ran in deep gullies of 'still-moving' water between very steep, five foot high banks on each side. It was often called 'the serpent' because the creek doubled back on itself so many times.

Joann was saying, "Well, you'd just better pay attention!"

The 'stare down' was still going on and Lori was thinking, *"...I'll have to do some serious steering, and maybe even some 'back paddling' on that one. And, Beth will have to do her thing, up front, paddling really hard at times. That's going to be an interesting spot today if it gets jammed up by anyone."*

Meanwhile, she still stared through and beyond Lu. Consciously, she narrowed her gaze and focused in on Lu's face, and saw what? *"What, exactly, was Lu trying to prove, anyway?"* From the set of her chin which jutted out, her big frown, and her hand on her hip, Lori figured, *"She just wants to 'best' me at this moment."* Lori's inner self, somehow, wouldn't let her turn it into a non-contest and just let Lu win, so she just sighed a little and continued the stare.

Lu, frowning as hard and mean as she could, looked continuously at Lori. It aggravated her to death that Lori just gazed 'unconcernedly' back at her, with those 'damnable' calm, green eyes. *"She'll look away first, soon,"* Lu assured herself.

But Lori didn't, and it was as if time stood still, ...too still. Lu began to fidget a bit. Lori didn't move a muscle.

Lu decided to change her mind about here and now as the *best* time to do this. She picked up her sunglasses and put them on and turned to talk to Jen, as if nothing had been going on.

Lori smiled to herself as she heard, "Ready! Set! Go!" Ceil and Vivian started out. They got pretty far upstream, in the ten minutes they were allowed.

"Ready! Set! Go!" Liz and Nancy, and Julie and Joann started paddling hard. They were pretty evenly matched except that Nancy could steer much better than Joann. The two canoes soon crashed their sides together. Liz and Nancy were trying their best to get away from Joann and Julie's veering canoe. Joann was saying, "See? You have to paddle harder, Julie!" Finally, they all seemed to get going straighter and were moving pretty fast.

After what seemed an eternity, Walli said, "Ready! Set! Go!"

Lori dug in deep and hard with her paddle, twenty times or more without having to just steer, and encouraged Beth to "Keep doing what you're doing!" The creek was widest at this first stretch and it was the best place to pass the other canoe if possible. After several minutes they pulled a little ahead of Jen and Lu.

She heard Lu mumble something, but only heard, "...ain't over yet."

Beth did a great job of uninterrupted paddling and after about fifteen minutes they started catching up to Julie and Joann. Liz and Nancy were up ahead, chasing after Ceil and Vivian, who were still in the lead...

As Lori pulled up alongside Julie and Joann's canoe, she said, "Pull, you 'swabbies'! Pull!" Julie laughed, and 'back splashed her with her paddle. Lori got even with her, drenching Julie with forward swipes of her own paddle, saying, "Take that, you landlubber!" And with continued hard strokes, she and Beth pulled ahead.

Donna Kelli

After a couple of minutes, Lori looked back and saw that Lu and Jen had also passed Joann and Julie and weren't very far behind. Liz and Nancy were just ahead, and Ceil and Vivian were still leading the pack. Lori pulled harder. She felt good because the race was on and she loved the challenge.

Soon, she and Beth pulled up behind Liz and Nancy. Lu and Jen were still back about a hundred feet, but they were keeping pace.

"This is going to be some race," Lori said. "Lu and Jen seem to be doing great."

As they approached the next gentle curve, she steered to the inside. Liz and Nancy lost it a bit, and turned too wide. They didn't give up, though, and paddled furiously. The race got exciting as the canoes bumped and paddles noisily banged the sides. Everybody was straining so hard that when they got splashed, it felt good.

She and Beth paddled steadily and they not only passed Liz and Nancy, but zoomed right by Vivian and Ceil, who were doing some serious resting. For the first time, she and Beth were in the lead. After they rounded the next curve, Lori eased up a little and said, "Ease off, Beth. Rest and take some deep breaths." They coasted for a short while.

They heard the shouts of everyone behind them, and Lori looked back. "Guess who is just behind us, Beth! Liz and Nancy, and Lu and Jen!" She laughed to herself because this was getting to be interesting and fun. "Go, Beth! Go! They're catching up!"

She and Beth kept up the faster pace and increased their lead. Lu and Jen caught up with Liz and Nancy. As Lori approached the next curve, which was much sharper, she saw the two canoes behind them just rounding the last curve. Lu and Jen were passing Liz and Nancy on the inside. Lori steered hard right around the next curve, and then told Beth to rest a little. They coasted for a couple of minutes, as they tried to catch their breath.

Lori looked back to see Lu and Jen, coming around the bend. "Here they come, Beth. Let's get going," she said. They reached the beginning of 'The Serpent', and there sat Gerri in her canoe. After warm "Hellos," Lori paddled slower and steered hard. Beth switched to her other side, and paddled hard around the difficult, very narrow curve. "Yea, we made the first one!" said Beth.

They didn't stop paddling until they rounded the second hairpin curve. Then, when they reached the end of the long, narrow straight part, Lori looked back to see how close Lu and Jen were. They were coming on strong. She steered hard left, and Beth did her part. They made it around the next sharp corner, and Lori said, "We can take it easy for a minute."

"Good!" said Beth.

Lori looked back after a couple of minutes and saw the bow of their canoe coming. She and Beth pulled hard, until they were completely around curve number four, and then they paddled easier for a while.

Lori looked back again, but there was no canoe coming around the curve. "I wonder what happened to them?" she said. "Maybe they had to rest a little." Lori stopped paddling to rest also, and Beth sagged forward putting her head on her forearms. As it got quiet, Lori realized that the noise of the main group of canoes seemed 'way, way back'. "I bet they messed up on the sharp curve, just before the serpent, Beth. Listen to how far away they seem."

"Yeah, too bad. It would be more fun if everybody was up here paddling like mad. It's exciting then."

"I wonder what happened to Lu and Jen." said Lori. They should be coming around the curve by now."

Suddenly, a tall, running figure came up over the bank and leaped way out over the creek at them, landing feet first in the water right next to their canoe and pushing down on the side of it, upsetting it, violently.

As the canoe started over, it tipped Lori forward and she pushed herself toward the attacker, Lu, who was now just about completely underwater, with her hands still pushing down hard on the side of the canoe. Lori landed heavily on top of her, pushed on her shoulders and made sure Lu's head went under.

Beth hadn't been looking, and she tipped over hard with the canoe and ended up in the water, too. The canoe turned completely upside down and Beth went under.

This was the deep, slow water and the bottom was about twelve feet down. It was visible in the clear water but Lu couldn't touch bottom to push upwards.

Lori was firmly holding her down but didn't even have her own face in the water, yet. She was kicking hard, balancing to keep her position atop Lu, and holding on to Lu's shoulders with a vise-like grip, to keep her in place just below her.

"Beth! You okay?" Lori asked, as Beth surfaced.

"Yes!" she said, as she hung onto the bow of the upset canoe, swimming it away from Lori. "Who *is* that?"

Lu was desperately scratching at Lori's wrists and forearms, trying to get loose. Lori didn't answer Beth. Rather, she took a deep breath and pushed down even harder with her entire body weight to cause Lu to go even deeper.

Leaning forward, Lori passed over Lu's head, and dove down behind her. Lu thought she was free and started pulling for the surface. But on her way toward the bottom, Lori got hold of Lu's waist band at the back of her shorts, and dragged her down even more. Being a 'non-floater' it was easy for her to head deeper. And Lu, being similar, was easy to take downward.

Lu was kicking and clawing for the surface. Lori was well below her and behind her, when she finally turned her loose. She felt safer down there because otherwise, Lu might've tried to climb up 'her' like a ladder, to get much needed air.

Lu didn't make it to the surface before she breathed in. From near the bottom now, Lori pushed upward and broke the surface about four feet behind the girl. Lu's face was finally above water but she was choking and flailing, and tiring quickly.

Lori watched her for several more seconds and then, feeling that Lu was pretty much, 'out of fight', she swam up, staying behind her, and grabbed the back of her collar. She did the side stroke and pulled the choking girl to shore.

Beth was already there. "Help me, Beth. Let's get her up the bank."

Slipping and sliding, they pulled Lu out.

"Oh my God!" they heard from downstream. Jen, sitting in the bow, had finally maneuvered their canoe around the curve.

Lori paid no attention to her. "Let's get her on her stomach, with her head lower than her feet."

When Lu was finally lying prone, she vomited some lake water out and coughed violently.

"Oh, my God, Lu! Are you all right?" screamed Jen, pulling her canoe up closer to the bank.

Lu moaned, opened her eyes and lifted her head up. She weakly propped herself up on her elbows, and held her head on her hands.

They could hear the rest of the group just over the high bank, finally getting closer, with paddles banging the sides of canoes, and excited shouts about 'where to steer, and how to paddle'.

Lori went to Beth and helped her beach their canoe and dump the water out. Then, with their canoe sitting ready, Lori knelt down and sat back on her heels, and ran her fingers through her hair to fluff it a little.

Beth didn't know what to say. But remembering the time on the dock when she was sorry she had spoken, she remained silent, waiting to see what Lori had in mind.

Lu spoke first. "You damned near...drowned me!" she said between lingering coughs.

Lori said nothing.

"I said, you damned near drowned me!" Lu twisted around, and sat up, glaring.

Lori just looked at her as if she hadn't spoken, thinking, *"There's no talking this out with her right now."*

Then, Lori lazily looked over at Jen.

Jen said, "You think you're too good for us! Don't you?"

Lori just shook her head slowly and stood up, wondering, *"Will we ever be able to settle this?"*

The other canoes came around the corner. "Look! There they are! They wrecked, too! They're not so far ahead, now! Hurry!"

Lori said, in a calm voice, "Come on Beth, let's join them."

They got in their canoe and noticed that all the other girls were wet.

"Hey! Did you guys tip over, too?" asked Lori.

Lots of voices chimed in, telling of their big 'jam-up' when Liz and Nancy got turned sideways at the curve, and they had a big crash. Everybody fell over.

When Walli came by the spot in her motorized canoe, she saw Lu and Jen getting in theirs. *"Strange."* she thought. *"Jen isn't wet, ...and Lu looks sick."*

"Are you girls alright?' she asked.

"Yeah." mumbled Lu.

"Are you sure?"

"I said yeah, didn't I!"

"Hmm," thought Walli. *"I'd give a lot to know what went on here. Maybe, someday, I'll persuade Lori to tell me. Too bad Gerri came back to help the others, instead of following these four."*

Meanwhile, as they sat in their canoe away from the others, Beth turned completely around, and sat facing Lori. She asked quietly, "What was that all about? Is this still because of me aggravating Lu at volleyball that time?"

"I doubt it," said Lori. "I think Jen keeps egging her on. I didn't tell you, because it's embarrassing, but Jen asked me to be her 'girlfriend'."

"What did you say?"

"I told her I couldn't."

"What did she say?"

"We didn't get to really finish... Lu came running, and..."

"Oh, that was that same day!"

"Yeah. I guess we just have to expect 'anything' from them, ...so be on guard, okay?"

"Okay," said Beth.

Lori asked, "Do you care if we lose?"

"Um-m, uh, no, not really, ...why?"

"Well, we know we could've won, right? So, how about, if we just 'play' with these girls and bump them some, and fool around in the shallows ahead?"

"Sounds good!" said Beth, relieved that Lori was smiling a little.

For the rest of the race Lori and Beth joked and kidded with everybody in the main group, gently running them almost into the bank here and there, grabbing onto the other canoes and 'hitching a ride' and generally being 'pains' to them. Everybody got soaked again and again, from all the splashing. Paddles swept sideways into the water could send water pretty far.

Liz and Nancy officially won, and were ecstatic. Lu and Jen hung way back, arguing a lot, yelling at each other, and came in last.

On the way back, after the picnic, the rest of the girls really got into Lori's 'playful, mischievous' mood. Nancy got out of her canoe, climbed up a high bank and ran and did a cannonball jump. She landed fairly close to Lu and Jen's canoe, soaking them both, and making them even madder than they already were.

Next, Nancy chose Lori and Beth's canoe, to 'bomb'. She landed right near them and half-flooded their canoe. Then, Lori and Beth got completely cut off, and playfully tipped over by Ceil and Vivian, who laughed themselves silly. And then as Julie and Joann came by, Lori caught on the back, and acted like a 'sea anchor'. She slowly tilted them precariously to the side, for a long while, and then, gleefully, turned them completely over.

Both, Joann and Julie descended on Lori, and dunked her twice. Julie noticed all the scratches on her wrists, and forearms, but something told her 'not to ask'.

As Walli cruised slowly by, she also noticed the deep scratches. *"Curiouser and curiouser,"* she thought, as she got splashed from the side.

On her way to help Beth 'dump the water out' for the umpteenth time, Lori thought, *"Camp can be so much fun!"* And still in her playful mood, she planned ahead. *"I think I'll smush a marshmallow on Beth tonight at the campfire."*

That night, Lori took time to catch up with her dad.

Hi Dad,
Today was an exhausting day. We had a canoe race up Shady Creek. Lots of things happened, like getting splashed, getting turned over, and lots of horsing around. Usually, we're not supposed to do that, but now, everybody knows how to swim, and canoe, and handle themselves. It was great fun. Also, I have some interesting stuff to tell you when we go for that coke.
Then we had a softball game against the Owls. We won!

As camp starts to get near the end, I'm getting sad. Of course I'll be happy to see you, but this place has been one of the best experiences of my life. Too tired to write more, now. Goodnight, Dad.

After lunch the next day, she continued...

Hi, I'm back. Well, we just had our archery contest this morning. Julie won two second place ribbons! I'm happy for her because she didn't know anything about archery when camp started.

My regular buddy, Beth, won a few ribbons, too. And so did I. I'll show them to you when I get home. Dad, I can shoot pretty far, now. Fletch, our instructor, lets me use her bow after class sometimes, just for fun, ...and it has some awesome power.

Guess I seem busy, huh? ...always saying 'bye'. Sorry, but we're doing a skit tonight, after dinner, and I have to go 'rehearse'.

Joann and lots of other girls have been trying their best, for two weeks, to get Julie to do a ballet dance for us. But, Julie says "Absolutely not!" Oh, well.

Lots of love,

Lori

Tracking

The next day, it was the first activity right after breakfast. The girls were deep in the woods along a trail they hadn't yet hiked. There was nothing familiar, anywhere.

Katie said, "We won't be very far ahead, so if you get lost just stop and blow your whistle. We'll hear you." Then she passed out six referee-type whistles. "Okay, you last six girls see if you can 'track' us. We'll be bending grass down, maybe leaving footprints, maybe not. We might 'accidentally' break a small branch, or even drop an object on the trail. Gerri will stay right here in case you need to come back."

She continued, "We'll walk for about fifteen minutes, and then we'll hide. See if you can 'read the signs' and find us where we stop. Then we'll switch, and let you girls leave the 'signs'. Lu, you have a watch, so don't get started for nine minutes." Katie left, with Liz and Nancy, and Ceil and Vivian to 'mark' a trail...

When it was time, Lu and Jen decided they should lead. No one disagreed, so they did. They walked pretty far along the path and around a curve before they both squatted down searching for signs. Beth came up and leaned over Lu's shoulder to look at 'the sign', too.

"Get away from me!" Lu shouted rudely.

Beth was startled and stepped back.

Jen said, gruffly, "Yeah! Don't crowd us!" ...and Beth stepped back another few steps.

Joann and Julie unconsciously stepped back, also, even though they weren't as close as Beth was, and just looked at each other wide-eyed.

Lori stepped in front of Beth and said calmly, but firmly, "You know, this is supposed to be a group thing."

Lu said, "Well, I don't like the way she was 'hanging over me'."

Lori said, "Maybe we can just relax a little here, ...and get on with tracking them."

"Yeah!" chimed in Joann and Julie.

Both Lu and Jen glared, first at Lori, and then at Beth.

Then they stood up and hung back, talking quietly, while Julie and Joann led the way and found the first footprint. Beth walked along with them and spotted some crushed grass even farther ahead. Lori was keeping an eye on Lu and Jen when all of a sudden, they turned and ran through some bushes and quickly disappeared into the woods.

The others looked up when they heard them making noise as they ran. Lori and Beth just looked at each other and Julie and Joann looked to them for leadership, asking, "What should we do?"

Lori said, "I guess they just want get ahead somehow, to be first. We can go on, or would you rather go back and inform Gerri?"

"No, ...No..." everybody said.

Lori said, "Okay, then, let's go. I hope they don't lead us on a false trail."

"How will we know?" asked Joann.

"We won't," said Lori.

Beth led off, with Joann and Julie almost beside her but a half-step behind. Nobody wanted to scuff up a sign. Lori was looking around and gazing deep into the woods, but there was no one near them.

"Here's a broken twig!" said Beth. "We're on the right trail."

A few minutes later, Julie found a footprint turning off the trail. There were no other signs so everybody turned into the woods. Joann spotted a clump of mountain grass that was squashed, so they continued on, single file, with Beth now leading.

It hadn't been hard for Jen and Lu to keep hidden and stay near them because the girls were usually talking. Suddenly they both jumped out at Beth, pushing her sideways into the brush, and falling on her. In the process, they knocked Joann backwards into Julie.

Lori cursed under her breath and headed around Julie and Joann. Both Jen and Lu were hitting at Beth. Lu was punching hard.

Lori grabbed Lu by the left shoulder and pulled her up and backwards, and spun her around. As Lu was spinning, she swung hard with her right fist at Lori's face. From her dad's coaching Lori was already ducking down, and as Lu's arm passed by overhead, Lori drove her own right fist, deep and hard into Lu's solar plexus area.

Lu collapsed to her knees holding her stomach, and wide eyed, because she couldn't catch her breath at all with her nerve center paralyzed. Then she sagged all the way down, and lying on her right side, doubled up in a fetal position.

Lori turned to Jen, but Beth was slapping back at her. However, when Jen tried to scratch at Beth's face, Lori spun her around and almost punched Jen's face with a hard right fist. At the last second she changed her mind and punched her in the mid section, too, sending Jen into a crumpled heap.

As the two girls writhed around on the ground, Lori was thinking, *"You were right, Dad, ...it works!"* When she was younger, she had never been able to hit him hard enough to disable him like this, so she wasn't really sure before.

173

Beth, Joann, and Julie came up, and stood over the two gasping girls. "What's the matter with you two?" demanded Julie.

"Yeah!" said Joann. "What are you trying to prove anyway?"

They couldn't answer, and wouldn't have, even if they had the breath to speak. So Beth just looked at Lori to see what was next...

Lori was looking intensely back at her, scrutinizing her face for any injuries, asking, "Are you okay?"

Beth nodded, "Yes."

Then Lori sighed, and asked, "Julie, would you and Joann try to find the trail, please? Meanwhile, Beth and I will help them along behind you. But, if you can't find it, we'll blow a whistle, and they'll come find us, okay?"

Julie frowned and didn't understand why Lori would help them at all, but she said, "Okay."

Lori took Lu, and Beth got Jen up. Julie couldn't figure out why they were letting them even touch them. Then she realized that they were probably afraid of more punches. She also saw a little bit of new respect in Joann's eyes. She wasn't saying one word, for the first time in her life.

Lori motioned for Beth to go ahead a little, and Beth knew Lori was going to try to talk to Lu. She chuckled to herself because if ever there was a good time, it was now. Lu still wasn't breathing right, and she didn't seem to be strong enough to make any more threats.

With Lu's arm unwillingly across her shoulders Lori kept her walking, but very slowly. Finally, she stopped and eased Lu to a sitting position. They were all alone.

"Lu, I don't understand what the problem is, but if you want to fight me, let's name a time and a place."

For a few minutes, Lu didn't answer. Finally, she said, "No, I don't want to fight *you*. It's, ...it's just that...

Lori didn't speak.

"It's just that Jen likes you, you know. She thinks you're beautiful and I know I'm not. And you're so good at everything, that I thought that if I could show you up at something... Well, if I could, ...then she might like me better."

"What's this thing with attacking Beth?"

Lu sighed. "Jen...it was her idea, over and over, to 'beat up Beth', but there never was a chance."

"But why?"

"Well, she knows you and Beth are better than friends, and she wanted to show you that Beth was not as good as...as you seem to think she is."

174

Lori said, "Lu, ...thanks for being honest. But Beth and I are best friends, and nothing more. Personally, I think you deserve somebody who treats you better than Jen does, ...but, ...that's for you to decide."

Both girls were quiet for a long minute. Lori asked, "Lu, do you think I want Jen as my girlfriend?"

"She said you did."

"She wha-at? Whew... this presents a different kind of problem." Lori thought for a minute and said, "Lu, you know where they keep the rowboats, right?"

"Yes."

Well, I'm going to ask Jen to meet me there tonight, just after it gets dark. If she says 'yes', I'll nod to you, later. If you can, go turn one boat upside down and get under it. Then, maybe you'll get to know the truth...that is, *if* you're interested."

Lu just sat there, very dejected. At last, she looked into Lori's eyes and saw calm 'sincerity'. Finally, she said, "Okay."

Lori helped her up and they continued on. Pretty soon, Lu said, "I can walk okay, now," and she pulled her arm from around Lori's shoulders. They hadn't gone twenty steps, when they heard a whistle being blown somewhere just ahead of them.

When everybody converged on the bedraggled group, Ceil said, "Boy! You guys are terrible trackers! We left all sorts of clues!"

Lori looked at Beth and she still seemed fine...no scratch marks showing up...no swollen face. Jen was sullen and sitting down. Jen looked up at Lu, but Lu looked away and acted as if she didn't want to talk to her.

"It's our turn, now!" said Vivian.

Julie sensed that Lori was mentally still involved with 'the incident', and that she wasn't in the mood to be jovial, or to lead. And she knew that Beth probably wanted to go talk to her. Julie would've preferred to quit, and listen to what they would say. There were lots of questions she wanted to ask Lori. She'd never seen girls fight before, and she could still picture Lori coming to help Beth. It was over so quickly!

"Yeah! Leave us some good clues." said Nancy.

Julie waited, but it seemed like nobody was going to report Lu and Jen. *"Maybe it's over,"* she thought. She stepped up and spoke for her group. "Let's get this show going, okay?" and she took off her whistle and handed it to Nancy. "I didn't blow mine so it's still clean."

Katie knew something was not right because Lori seemed distracted and withdrawn, as if she didn't care whether she participated, or not. And here was Julie speaking up.

She said, "Okay, Let's go!" but she still looked at her new group. Julie was acting as if nothing was wrong, but, ...and then, she saw Jen rub her stomach. And as she watched Lu, she saw her holding her stomach once, also. Realizing that some things have to be worked out between campers, she chose not to intervene.

"Okay," she said, now let's be careful not to leave any marks for the next ninety feet or so." And the somber group followed her lead into the woods.

Called to the Office

Lori walked into the main office. Mrs. 'Z' and Walli were waiting for her. She was surprised to see Walli because Katie had been the counselor for 'tracking.' *"This must go all the way back to the canoe races,"* she thought.

"Hi, Mrs. 'Z', Walli."

"Come in, Lori. Please sit down," said Zee.

"We've been watching you for a couple of weeks now, to evaluate your progress here."

Lori could feel it coming, ...a bad report home to Dad, about Jen and Lu. "Yes ma'am," she said, and looked down, 'steeling' herself for the criticism.

"We have a situation here that we need to resolve," said Zee.

Lori looked up, waiting.

"Gerri can't be here for the last two weeks, except in the mornings. Her father is ill and when he gets out of the hospital, she'll have to give him constant care in the afternoons for a few months. Her sister will be with him in the mornings."

"Oh, I'm sorry," said Lori, frowning deeply, and looking down.

"We need another 'Counselor in Training' to help cover her duties."

Lori looked up at her, frowning a little.

"You're scheduled to leave this coming Sunday, after the Dance and all. But, if you're interested in staying on until the end of camp, and helping us, we'll waive the tuition for the last two weeks." 'Z' paused a minute, and then continued, "You'd be expected to work with Walli, on the waterfront each afternoon during the time your cabin is scheduled to swim, and also, instead of Arts and Crafts, and then in addition, help with some team sports. Would you like to do it?"

Lori couldn't believe what she'd heard. "Uh, yes, ma'am! I certainly would," said Lori, smiling. "I love it here." Then she added, "If my dad will let me."

"We always check with the parents first, Lori, in case of a 'no' answer."

"Really?"

"Yes," said Zee. "One other thing, our C.I.T.s usually sleep in a separate cabin."

"Oh-h," said Lori, clearly disappointed. She looked down.

Zee and Walli looked at each other. Walli shrugged.

"Well," said Zee, "since you'll be 'watching out for Gerri's girls', maybe you *should* stay there. Part of your responsibility will be to help the new girls get settled in."

Lori beamed at her. "Great!" she said. "Can I call my dad?"

Later, she found Beth. "Beth! Guess what?" "I get to stay at camp for two more weeks! I've been asked to stay on, as a C.I.T.!"

"Oh?" she said, with a surprised look on her face. And then, frowning, she said, "Oh-h...," feeling bad that she couldn't stay any longer, and that she hadn't been asked.

Lori was sorry she'd been so excited for herself after she saw Beth's face. But Beth recovered, and hugged her, saying, "Great!"

Lori hugged her back, and said, "Maybe we'll both get to come back next summer!"

"I hope so!" said Beth.

"Come on, let's go see if we can check out a canoe for a while, okay?"

"Sure!" said Beth, 'getting happy' again.

To be a C.I.T

After lunch, Zee stood at the microphone with Gerri and Bigfoot behind her. She announced the decision about Lori, and asked her to stand up. Just about everybody clapped for her and Lori looked around the room, grateful for their acceptance. She felt embarrassed, but very happy. Rory cheered the loudest and gave her a big wink. Lori felt the red blush begin creeping up her neck.

Lu and Jen just stood there. They both would be here for the next two weeks.

Lori thought, *"They probably think I'm going to try to boss them around, now. I wonder if they will go to the counselors now, and complain about this morning?"*

Beth clapped, and smiled at her. Joann, who was leaving to travel with her parents, stood there straight-faced, not clapping. When Lori made eye-contact with Julie...strangely, it held. Julie was clapping hard, with her hands raised over her head, and smiling, and Lori could feel herself relaxing, more. Then she watched as Julie turned and noticed that Joann wasn't clapping. She gave her a little nudge and frowned at her until eventually, Joann clapped a little.

Finally, it was over and Lori was thankful for that.

After the meeting the Falcons and the Hawks had 'clean-up' before they could have free time. When all the work was done, Julie told Joann that she would see her later, and walked over to Lori.

"Excuse me, Lori?"

Lori turned from chatting with Beth, and said, "Oh, Hi, Julie."

"Could I see you in the Arts and Crafts room?"

"Uh, ...sure..." Lori turned back, and asked, "See you in a few minutes, Beth?"

"Sure." Then Beth left to go do one of her very favorite things, ...read.

As they entered the room, Julie said, "Congratulations, on being selected as a 'C.I.T.' That's quite an honor!"

"Thanks."

Julie went to the clay sculptures rack and said, "This is Rocky's head, that you did."

Lori chuckled. "Yes, it's supposed to be. How'd you know?"

"It looks just like him."

"Really?"

179

"Yes, ...and when I saw your model, I went out and sketched him. Want to see?"

"Sure."

Lori looked at her sketch, and said, softly, "Wow! You really *are* artistic! You even picked up the 'light in his eyes."

"Thanks," said Julie. Then, "...Uh, ...Lori? You know, ...Joann's leaving."

"Yeah, ...sorry...Beth, too."

"So, ...would you..."

Lori looked up at her, as Julie was looking down. Then Julie looked up, into green eyes that slightly overwhelmed her, and continued softly, "...like to be my partner?"

Lori's heart skipped a beat... *"For a lifetime..."* she felt like saying.

"Y..." Nothing came out. "Yes," she managed. "I'd like that."

Julie smiled at her and Lori felt herself melting inside.

"Good!" said Julie, and she took Lori's hand, and said, "Let's go!"

Lori felt herself 'numbly' following her 'elusive elf' out into the sunlight, and knew that she'd probably follow her anywhere. When they got outside, Julie said, "I have to go find Joann, now. We're reading a good book, together. Bye."

"Bye," said Lori, heading toward the cabin, feeling like she was floating along...

"Oh, Julie, wait!" she said, turning back.

Julie stopped, and headed back, thinking, *"Oh, good. Now, maybe she'll tell me what happened with Lu."*

When she got close, Lori asked, "Would you do me a favor, please?"

"What?"

"Will you, quietly, go ask Jen if she'll meet me by the rowboats tonight, right after dark?"

"Are you sure you don't want Beth to ask her?"

"Yes, I'm sure. Will you do it... and not tell *anyone* else?"

Julie was completely curious now, but she said, "Well, okay, I guess."

"Terrific. Thanks a lot!" said Lori, and she turned and left.

Julie stood there, thinking, *"Oh great! Now I know even less than I used to know."* She sighed and started walking, wondering how she could ever get Lori to confide in her. *"Maybe when we're 'partners'..."* she hoped.

*

Confrontation

At dusk, Lori went out of the cabin and headed toward the rowboats. "Are you in there?" she asked.

A low, muffled "Yes," came from underneath.

"I don't know if she'll show up," said Lori, "but I'll just sit here quietly for a half hour and see."

"Oh, she'll come," said Lu. "I told her I was going to see the horses and she was glad I was going."

After about ten minutes, Jen appeared. She was very cautious and looked around for Beth, or anyone else, thinking she might be ambushed.

"Hi," said Lori.

"Is Beth around?" asked Jen.

"No. Want to talk?"

"What about?"

"Oh, a few things, ...mainly about you and I," said Lori.

Jen came and sat down beside her and leaned back against the rowboat.

Lori asked, "Jen, are you looking to fight me?"

"Uh...No! Why do you think that?" she said, looking truly surprised.

"Then, what?"

"I just want you to...you *must* know I like you a *lot*, Lori."

Lori looked at her in the semi-darkness and wondered what she would do, if this terrible, unthinkable moment ever came between her and Julie.

Jen took her silence as 'maybe she had reconsidered', and went on. "I told you before, I'd *really* like you to be my girl. But why did you punch me so hard, today?"

Lori said gently, "Because, you deserved it... And, if you'll remember, when we talked about this before, I told you I couldn't be your..."

"Why can't you?"

"Jen, it's still not *in* me to be your girlfriend."

"You could try."

"I can't force myself to love you, Jen."

"You love Beth."

"No, I like Beth a lot. We're very, *very* good friends. But, I don't have the kinds of feelings for her that you're talking about."

"You act like you love her!"

181

"Yes, I guess I do love her, ...as a *friend*. I'd do anything for her, ...but not like you mean."

"She loves you."

"That's your interpretation, Jen. You know she has a boyfriend back home."

Jen was quiet for a moment. Then she said, "Congratulations, on your C.I.T. thing. Will you be my 'buddy' for the last two weeks?"

"What about Lu?" asked Lori.

"Oh, ...Lu... Well, I might tell her to go home."

"You can do that?"

"Yeah, pretty much... She'll do anything I tell her to."

"...Like jump on canoes, ...and attack Beth in the woods?"

Jen let out a cynical laugh. "Yeah... I wanted her to get rid of Beth somehow...you know, just make her quit camp and go home. I didn't know she was leaving early, anyway."

"You know, somebody could've really gotten hurt with all that stuff, Jen, ...like Beth!"

"Yeah, I guess, ...but she didn't! And Lu can take care of herself. She's pretty strong."

"Yes, she is. And, she's good at lots of things. Do you know that by her actions, she seems to love you, ...and I mean more than just being friends."

Jen shrugged and said, "Lu's Lu. And I'm me. I've never loved her and I never will! ...So, ...will you?"

"What?" asked Lori.

"Be my buddy for the last two weeks?"

"I can't, Jen."

"Why not?"

"Well, I've already been asked," said Lori.

"By who?"

Lori hated to answer, for fear that Jen's venom might now be directed at... Finally she said, "Julie."

"That little snip? Look, Lori, I, ...I *love* you. Don't you understand?"

"Yes, ...I, ...I'm sure I do, Jen. Look, this is hard to say," continued Lori, gently, "but, ...I don't love you back."

"But..."

"Jen, I'm honestly trying *not* to hurt you, but I can't accept your love. I don't know how to deal with it."

"But..."

"No, Jen, ...I'm really sorry, ...it's your feelings and unfortunately, your problem."

"But I like you a lot," said Jen.

"You have strange ways of showing it," said Lori. "Jen, please, I don't know what else to say to you... so, let's just end this, ...as friends, okay?"

"I was right...you *do* think you're too good for me..."

"No, Jen, I never, ever thought that." Lori stood up and said, "Goodnight, Jen. See you later." And she walked away, realizing she was all sweaty under her arm pits. *"Boy, I need my shower tonight,"* she thought. *"This 'personal relations' stuff is stressful, and I don't know how to ever reach an understanding with Jen."*

Jen got up and slowly walked away in the opposite direction...

With Lu

The next morning, Lu came up to Lori in the mess hall after breakfast, and said, "Got a minute?"

Lori said, "Sure." She followed Lu outside.

"I just wanted to tell you "good-bye.""

"Good-bye? Where are you going?"

"I've decided to go home. I called my parents and they're coming to get me on Sunday."

"Oh, I'm sorry," said Lori.

"Yeah, me too. But it's better this way."

"Oh," said Lori, not wanting to pry.

Lu waited for Lori to say more, and began to feel uncomfortable with the silence.

"Jen's staying," she said. "And I don't, ...uh, ...I don't want to be around."

Lori just looked at her, and nodded that she understood. Then she asked, softly, "Are you okay?"

"No, not really. You know, ...I feel like such a fool. She really had me 'wrapped', if you know what I mean."

Lori frowned, slightly.

"I did almost anything she wanted. Somehow, I thought I could make her love me. Now, I'm glad she doesn't. She has a real 'mean streak' in her and I never saw it."

"I'm sorry," said Lori, looking down.

"Do you know she actually had me believing that you were constantly flirting with her? ...Behind my back, of course. And, she convinced me you thought you were a 'know it all' ...which she didn't mind, but that you and Beth were laughing at *me* every chance you got."

"Really?"

"Yes, really. And, the worst part of all was that she said, "Beth was the real problem. She was your girlfriend, but only until we could make her leave camp. And Jen couldn't like me, until *after* she got you out of her system."

"Sounds very complicated," said Lori.

"Yeah, it is. I'm going home, and see if I can't live a 'simple, teenage life' for the rest of the summer. I feel like I've been part of a sick soap opera. She told me so many lies!"

"Seems like it," said Lori.

"Well, ...anyway, thanks for what you did last night, ...and I'm sorry I, ...I caused you, ...so much...uh...so much..."

Lori gently interrupted, saying, "Maybe we can be better friends, next summer. You *are* going to try to come back, aren't you?"

"I don't know, ...right now I feel so..."

"Maybe there's someone else back home..." suggested Lori. And she wondered if Lu knew any other...other... 'gay' girls. *"That word sure doesn't come easy to me."* she thought.

Lu shrugged, thinking. "Yeah, there's a new girl at school named Jennifer. She seemed sorry I was leaving for the summer. Maybe I'll call her and start seeing her."

"Good," said Lori, chuckling inside and thinking, *"J, J, J, and more J's."* ...adding, "And maybe you could convince her to come to camp with you. It can be *great* fun, here."

Lu looked up and saw the beginnings of Lori's genuine smile, ...and the twinkle in her eyes. She knew that Lori probably had more fun at camp than most of the other campers.

"Depends," said Lu, wondering what it would be like to have Lori Hunter as a friend, instead of an enemy. "Do you usually *wrestle, ...half-drown, ...or punch...many campers in the stomach,* each summer?"

Lori chuckled out loud and felt the beginnings of a blush. Then, looking down as the blush deepened, she jokingly said, "Only the 'bad asses' Lu, only them." And then looking up at her, she said, "...never my friends." Still smiling, she put her arms out, offering a hug to the taller girl.

Lu took it, without hesitating.

"I'll miss you, Lu," she said, still grinning. "Life just won't be the same."

"Bye, Lori. Have a great...year." Lu turned and walked away.

Lori knew she was crying.

The Dance

The old bus, full of boys, finally arrived. Most of the girls in the camp had primped and preened for an hour or more and were very excited about meeting them.

As the boys filed out of the door the girls were looking them over and commenting to their best friends on what they "liked or disliked." The semi-circle of girls kept moving forward and gradually closed in on them.

But not Lori, ...she just looked. She thought that for the most part, they looked young and pimply-faced. Beth stayed beside her, quietly taking in the scene.

"Why do girls act so giddy?" Lori wondered aloud, as the giggling and pointing seemed pretty childish to her.

A sudden, "Oooohh!" filled the air and she saw a special guy stepping out of the bus. He was taller, looked much more mature and was definitely handsome.

"Well, at least I agree with everybody else on this one," she decided.

His name tag was too far away to read, but she heard several girls saying "Hi, Greg!" She and Beth looked at each other and smiled.

"Now, *he's* good-looking!" said Beth.

"Yes, he is! Very!" She figured that he'd probably end up with Julie by the end of the night. She remembered all the boys at school who always seemed to be trailing behind her.

She always seemed to know where Julie was in a crowd and out of habit she glanced over to see if Julie was showing any reaction. Joann and Julie had their heads together talking quietly. They were smiling but she couldn't tell much.

"Okay, Girls and Guys! Finish introducing yourselves, and let's move into the mess hall!" said Mrs. Z, in her loudest voice. Many started drifting slowly in that direction.

Five or six girls crowded around 'Handsome,' but Julie wasn't one of them... not yet, anyway. Lori kept looking, but for the moment she couldn't find her.

"C'mon." urged a voice beside her. Beth had taken her hand and was pulling her. "Let's go inside."

"Okay," Lori said, still searching the crowd for Julie. Finally, she saw Julie and Joann walking on either side of a tall, blonde, big-boned, very muscular guy with huge shoulders. He had a definite 'swagger' to his walk.

"See anyone you like?" asked Beth.

"Not really..." she lied, thinking of Julie. Suddenly she felt like she ought to go talk to a boy, ...any boy! ...just to not seem 'shy', or worse yet... 'different!' *"Well, almost any boy,"* she thought, as a very fat boy walked by. He was apart from everyone and looked 'lost'. *"Oh well, what the heck,"* she decided.

"Let's say 'Hi' to him," she said to Beth.

Beth looked at him, ...and then back at her with a shocked expression, but she shrugged and crossed her eyes, and said, "Okay, why not?"

They chatted with Billy enough to find out that he was very self conscious and not sure of himself, at all. He had a bruise on his left eye that was almost completely faded out.

"So-o, ...what happened to your eye?" asked Beth.

"I got punched," said Billy, with his head down.

"Oh, ...by who?"

"By Mickey, ...that blonde guy over there." It was the guy with Julie and Joann.

"Did you deserve it?" asked Lori, frowning.

Billy blushed deeply, smiled, and said, "No. He's just a bully, ...and I forgot to duck."

The girls laughed at his smile. Lori decided Billy knew his limitations. Not like some people she knew, ...and she decided he was okay. Very shy, but okay!

As they entered the mess hall, Mrs. Z. was announcing the rules for the evening. "Enjoy yourselves! But not to the point of getting into or causing trouble.

Treat each other with respect.

No fighting.

No swimming. No boating or canoeing. Stay away from the lake.

No leaving the area right around the front and side of this mess hall."

"Any problem from even *one* person will end the evening immediately! And, the bus will leave! With all boys aboard, I might add!" That comment got moans and groans from the crowd.

Mrs. Z. continued, "The dance is scheduled to end at 10:45. We have good music, cold punch, and the cookies are plentiful. Have fun!"

The music started. The male and female counselors were scanning the room. So was Lori. Julie was across the room, already dancing with the blonde guy.

"Want to dance?" asked Billy.

"Not just yet," said Lori. She smiled at him and said, "I'll be right back," and she headed toward the punch table, mostly to go check to see how much of a 'good time' Julie was having.

She was met half way across the room by a red haired boy, slightly taller than her, with a huge smile on his face, who said, "You're looking for me, I hope."

She had to stop walking, or crash right into him.

He had assumed a dance position, and when he heard no response from her, he reached down and took her right hand in his left, and put his other hand on her waist, ...respectfully keeping a large space between them.

Slow music was playing. He leaned his upper body slightly forward. Lori stepped backward. They were dancing, and she didn't really know how it had happened. Only seconds had passed!

He smiled again, and said, "I'm Winston."

Still Lori said nothing. She was praying she wouldn't step on his feet.

"And you're Lori," he said, reading her name tag.

Lori looked at his face and thought, *He looks just like Hattie! He could be her brother, ...they look so much alike."*

She smiled, finally.

"Thanks," he said.

"What for?"

"The smile..." he said. "You're very pretty."

Her feet stopped dead. She couldn't get used to that kind of compliment.

"No...don't stop! ...please...

And she once again found herself moving. "You, uh, look just like a friend of mine," she said.

"Is he handsome, I hope?"

"She! She's rather nice looking. You could pass for her 'brother'."

"Good," he said, smiling. They danced the entire song without speaking and then he asked her if she wanted some punch.

"Yes, please."

"Okay. Will you wait for me by this window? I'll be right back." Lori nodded, and he left.

"I haven't even looked for Julie for awhile," she complimented herself. *"Winston was easy to be with,"* she decided...even though they hadn't talked much. *"Just be with him, mentally as well as physically!"* she told herself. *"Enjoy the dance!"*

She tried to imagine him as a boyfriend, ...and it didn't work. *"Just a friend,"* she decided. She let out a big sigh, just as he handed her some punch.

"Bored?" he asked.

"No," she said. "Just thinking."

"About what?"

"Um...what's it like at your camp?"

He started describing it, and it sounded very similar to theirs. Only it was farther away than she'd thought. It would take the bus almost an hour to wind through the mountain roads. She found herself looking away from him and scanning the room.

"I guess I am boring you," he said.

"Sorry, I was just wondering if my friend, uh, my friend, Beth, was dancing."

"Is she?"

"Yes. There they are."

"Wow! She's dancing with Billy! We all had bets that he wouldn't get one dance."

"Why? ...just because he's fat?"

"Yeah, and because he's so shy. Come on," he said, reaching for her hand again. "Let's dance."

The music was fast and he danced well. In fact, she found that it was getting to be fun. They stayed on the floor for several fast songs in a row. She could tell what he expected her to do, because he had a nice strong lead. As she twirled under his arm and then back again, she thought, *"I might take Dance class next year...and check out lots of different kinds of dances."* She was really loosening up, anticipating his moves, and not worrying at all, anymore about stepping on his feet. Her natural agility made it seem easier and easier, and now, she was completely enjoying the rhythm and the flow. Her face glowed, she smiled constantly, and her eyes danced. She was almost in a 'zone', like when she played basketball. She was in her own private little world, with just Winston and the music, oblivious to other people and what they were doing or thinking.

They stayed together the entire first two hours, and danced almost every dance.

Occasionally other boys would cut in, but Winston was back before the music ended...

They were dancing to a very fast song, and he was turning her under his arm for two and three turns in a row, now. She was having a great time, and her eyes sparkled.

The person in charge of the music began the slow song, exactly at the end of the fast one. They didn't leave the floor, and he started her off again. This time, he held her a little bit closer, as they danced smoothly.

"This is the first time I've been this close to a boy," she thought.

"May I cut in?" a deep voice said.

They stopped dancing and Winston reluctantly stepped back.

And there stood 'Handsome'...

189

Winston didn't turn loose of her hand until she looked back at him. Finally, he said, "I'll see you in a little while." Then he turned and walked away.

Lori suddenly felt unsure of herself and felt like running out of the room. She took in a slow, deep breath and willed herself to stay.

He took the dance position, and felt her rigidity.

"I'm Greg," he said. "Relax, ...I don't bite."

"I'm...

"Lori," he finished for her. "I know. I've been watching you."

"You have? Why?" she asked, truly puzzled.

"Because you're one of the only girls in this room who hasn't seemed to notice that I'm even alive... And, you seem to be enjoying yourself...a lot!"

"Oh?" said Lori. "You need everyone to look at you?"

"No... just you." he said quietly, and eased himself closer to her.

She noticed his cologne. It smelled a lot like soap, ...nice and clean. She finally began to relax, and he pulled her a little closer. She was almost touching her forehead to his cheek. He eased her closer, and then, they *were* touching.

She seemed to float along, with his every move, and she lost herself in the music. "He's good," she thought. He held her very close, and she allowed it. The insides of their feet were touching as he led her in a tight spin. The room went 'round and round'.

The music ended, and he said, in her ear, softly, "Don't leave me."

"Huh?"

"Don't dance with anyone else right now...please? Some people are outside. Let's go out for a few minutes, okay?"

"Well..." she looked around the room for Beth. "I ought to tell my friend" she said. But she didn't see Beth, ...and she didn't see Julie. But Winston was beginning a fast dance with Joann.

"Okay," she said, finally.

He held her hand securely as he led the way through the crowd.

Outside, the night air was cool and refreshing. There was no moon, but the night sky was brilliant with stars. A few couples were standing around talking quietly. A male counselor and Bigfoot were on duty outside.

He led her off the porch and onto the beginning of the path that led to the lake. He stopped by the first huge oak tree, and turned to face her.

"Been to camp before?" he asked.

"No. Have you?"

"Yes," he said. He took both of her hands in his, and said, in a husky voice that she could barely hear, "I want to kiss you."

There was something hypnotic about him and she didn't pull away.

He leaned forward a bit and pulled her closer. Slowly he bent lower, and then softly, his lips touched hers.

She froze.

He kissed her gently and then leaned back to look at her. When she didn't move, he leaned forward slowly, and kissed her again.

She felt her heart pounding, but she told herself *"to relax a bit, and just 'experience' the kiss."* It lasted a long time and she was thinking that it was especially nice.

He gently enfolded her in his arms and held her even closer. His lips parted slightly, and he touched the tip of his tongue to her lips. He seemed to be trying to part her lips. She let him, and she felt the tip of his tongue touch her tongue.

She felt a sudden twinge in the familiar place, and her heart soared. *"...Oh, God, ... Thank God!..."* she thought, *"...I'm normal! ...My body can 'like' a boy!"* Then, her mind went numb.

The kiss ended, and he said, "That was nice..."

"It was," she agreed.

He started another long, slow kiss and she felt herself kissing him back.

He had nice lips, soft, and gentle. And she started trying to picture his face.

But, in her mind, another image started creeping in...*of Julie*, ...of her kissing *Julie* like this, ...so close, ...touching, ...so close. And the twinge became an ache. She felt Greg's hardness as he drew her even closer.

She wanted something...she needed something*!* *"If only it could be..."* She felt herself sort of swooning, and he held her tighter and tighter. He kissed her deeper...

"Lori?" She heard Julie's gasp, behind her.

Lori weakly pushed away from Greg's embrace, and looked in the direction of the voice. Julie and Joann had walked over, she guessed, to check out who 'Handsome' was kissing...

They just stared at her, in awe. The moment was broken.

"Excuse us," said Joann, fidgeting. Then Julie just looked down at the ground, and then back toward the mess hall, without ever looking Lori in the eyes.

"We didn't mean to interrupt," continued Joann. They quickly turned, and headed back toward the dance as fast as they could walk...

"I guess we'd better go back," said Lori, in a weak voice.

"I can't..." said Greg. "Not just yet."

Lori didn't comprehend, immediately, but then, she knew. "Oh," ...she choked. The night hid her deep blush. She felt guilty, ...like she was a tease or something.

"Sorry," she said in a small voice.

"Yeah, me, too, but can I see you again?"

"I...uh, I don't see how."

"Are you going to be at camp until the end of summer?

"Well, yes, but..."

"I'll find a way," he said.

When they returned to the hall she introduced him to Beth. Then he asked her to dance some more.

Julie and Joann weren't the only ones watching them intently. Thanks to Joann's love of gossip, all eyes now seemed to be on them as they slow danced. All the girls' eyes, that is. And Lori saw envy in some of them, and curiosity in others. She closed her eyes to shut out the stares.

She started to think about Julie, and wondered what she must be thinking, when Winston cut in and she suddenly felt carefree, again. She looked over at Greg, as he backed away. His eyes were still locked on her, as other girls were coming up to him, hoping to dance.

"He's intense!" Lori murmured to herself.

"That's the truth!" said Winston. "He can have any girl he wants! It's very hard to be around him...to compete. Don't like him too much...okay? He's dangerous."

"Okay," said Lori, remembering the feel of him pressed up against her.

They danced two fast dances together, and Lori knew now, for sure, that she definitely liked to dance.

"LAST DANCE!!" announced Mrs. Z. "A slow one, *by special* request," she added.

Greg immediately cut in, and smiled at her. He held her at a respectable distance, but only for a short while, and then he edged closer. She was trying to decide if she liked him to do that, when Winston cut back in.

"Not with *my* girl, you don't!" he said.

Greg, at first, started to refuse the intruder, but he finally stepped back.

Winston smiled at him, and danced away with Lori. Greg stood there a moment, scowling, and then left the dance floor. Lori didn't let Winston hold her very close at all. This part was not fun. She hoped that the guys wouldn't be enemies after the dance.

"THAT'S IT, FOLKS!!! THE BUS LEAVES IN TEN MINUTES!! BE ON IT!!!" said a male counselor's deep voice.

Winston kept Lori's hand and led her to the farthest back corner of the mess hall, and turned to face her.

"Did you kiss him?" he asked quietly.

Looking down, she hesitated to answer.

"Will you kiss me?"

192

"I, ...uh,"

"Please...kiss me goodnight."

"But it's so bright in here!"

He led her outside through the nearest side door, and surprisingly, they were alone. He took both her hands and pulled her closer. He was only slightly taller, and he leaned forward...

And she could feel his lips, lightly on hers. And then, they were not. She wondered at the kiss. *"What was that?"* she thought.

And he was saying...

"Thanks, Lori! C'mon, walk me to the bus?" He held onto one hand and they started walking. "You're staying at camp until the next dance, aren't you?" he asked.

She said, "Yes."

"So-o!" There you are!" Greg met them as they rounded the front corner of the building. "Winston!! I'm going to have to knock some sense into you!"

"You could easily do it..." smiled Winston. "...but think of my poor, squashed nose! And, anyway, you can't have *every* girl, you know."

Greg ignored Winston, looked into Lori's eyes, and said, "I meant what I said before."

She thought back, and remembered his promise, "to find a way."

"What? That you feel 'undying love' for her? Come on, Greg! Forget it! Lori's going to be my girl." He turned toward Lori. "Will you write me?" he said. "The mail comes every day."

Lori wasn't answering either of them. She was busy just turning her head back and forth between them, as they talked.

Several of the girls watched as Lori approached with a boy on either side of her, each, trying to get her undivided attention. As they neared the bus, Lori realized that all the other boys were on the bus, already, and the counselors were waiting for the last two.

"Come on, Guys!!"

"Sorry, but I have go," said Greg.

"Yeah, he's 'sorry', alright!" said Winston.

They entered the bus amid hoots and hollers.

With her escorts suddenly gone from her sides Lori felt very much alone. As she looked around, hoping to see Beth, she saw a few girls talking to boys at the windows, as the bus started to roll. The rest of them were waving, and walking with the bus a little, as it moved along...

"Bye, Girls!" "Don't forget us!" yelled many voices from within the bus.
"We won't!"
"We'll see you at the last dance!"
The group of girls chorused... "Bye!" The bus pulled away and even though she looked after it, waving, like the rest, she didn't feel like part of the 'throng' of girls.

Then, as she was picturing Winston and Greg verbally abusing each other, all the way back to their camp, the group of girls turned and headed directly toward her. In a matter of a few seconds she found herself in the center of a 'loud crowd'.
Questions were being shouted at her from all directions.
"What's he like?"
"Is he as 'sexy' as he looks?"
"Do you like him?"
"How did he kiss? Good?"
"Will you try to see him again?"
"What did you talk about?"

Her head turned this way, and that way, as the questions flew at her. She was very uncomfortable in the midst of the little mob!

"OKAY, GIRLS...ITS LATE!!!" said Mrs. Z, exceptionally loud.
"CABINS FIVE AND SIX, THE ROBINS AND THE EAGLES...ITS CLEAN UP TIME. THE REST OF YOU, GET TO YOUR CABINS. YOU CAN TALK ALL NIGHT IF YOU WANT TO, BUT LIGHTS OUT IN THIRTY MINUTES!!!!"

Moans and groans greeted the announcement, but mercifully, the attention was diverted from Lori momentarily, as some girls started to leave.
Beth had come up close to her elbow and asked, "Are you okay?"
She nodded.
"Then, let's get out of here..."

A few girls followed close behind them, wanting to hear every word. But the two partners didn't talk. They went straight to their bunks and started gathering up their towels, bathroom kits, and their pajamas. The girls who didn't belong in their cabin, hung around just inside the door, and some others gathered outside by the windows, still hoping to hear something.
Jen came up to Lori's bunk, with a leer on her face, and started to say something, but Julie and Joann arrived, saying, "C'mon, Lori! We *all* want to know about you and Greg." Jen closed her mouth, and stepped back a bit. More

girls crowded around and started sitting on the surrounding bunks. Even Jen sat down, squeezing in on Julie's bunk.

Lori was again, the main object of attention, and feeling very tense.

Beth came and sat down on Lori's bunk. "Might as well get comfortable," she shrugged, patting the bunk, for Lori to sit down. "They're determined."

Slowly, Lori sat down, and everybody started again.

"Is he nice?

"Did you really kiss him?"

"Did he try to get fresh?"

"Wait! Wait! One at a time!" said Joann.

Lori looked from face to face, ...wide eyed faces. *"Well,"* she thought, *"I seem to be 'one of the girls' now..."* But she wished they'd all go away, so she could just lie back and sort things out.

"Is he nice?" asked Joann, in a pretty loud voice.

The room got quiet, ...real quiet. Even the girls just outside the windows were completely silent.

Lori cleared her throat. "Yes, he is..." she found herself saying. But somehow, she couldn't picture his face at this very instant.

"Is he a good kisser?" Impatiently, but quieter than mice, they all waited for the answer to *that* one.

She looked at the questioner. It was Julie, and Lori felt a blush start to creep up...

"Yes, ...He's an...an 'excellent' kisser," she ventured.

"Did he put his tongue in your mouth?"

"Did he try to touch your breasts?"

"Did you let him?"

As the chorus of questions came at her, Lori slowly put her hands up to silence them.

"Look," she said, finally, and in a low but firm voice. "There's not much to tell, ...really. I'm sorry... And now, if you'll excuse me, please, I need to go to the bathroom, ...and...I need to get my shower, before lights out." She picked up her kit, and started walking away from them.

"Wait, Lori!"

"Aw, Nuts!"

"Jerk!"

"Bitch!" ...she heard behind her.

Jen came up behind her, as she entered the bathroom area, and said, for her ears only...

"So-o, ...you like *excellent* kisses, huh?" And then she was gone.

195

Donna Kelli

"Oh, God," thought Lori, *"everyone is going crazy! And Jen! I thought she'd be 'over it', by now. And at least, ...at the very least, I thought she'd be done with her comments! That girl is...stubborn!"*

As she was showering, Beth joined her at the same showerhead. Jen came and showered right beside her. Nancy and Liz came and showered next to them on the other side, and they tried to draw her out.

But she 'soaped up' and kept her face under the shower as much as possible, Soon, almost everybody from both cabins ended up in the showers, and it was crowded, and noisy. She ignored all the questions. After awhile, they finally started talking about their own experiences of the evening. She finished, then went and dried off.

Later, Beth joined her, as she brushed her teeth. "You okay?"

"Yeah, I guess so."

"Quite a night!" said Beth.

"Yeah, ...that it was...we'll talk tomorrow, okay?"

"Sure."

They returned to their bunks, and gradually, everyone else finished their nightly routines, and began to settle down, ...but only after they were convinced Lori wouldn't talk about it at all, ...not even a little bit.

Lori simply said "Good night," to all the faces that still looked her way, "Good night," to Beth, and then she remained silent.

Later, as she was lying down, the lights went out and she heard...

"Lori...pleasant dreams!" "Yeah," others joined in.

"We know what you'll be dreaming about!"

"Let's tie her to a tree until she tells us!" said a 'brave' voice, in the dark.

"That could be 'scary'... Lori thought. *"This is not fun."*

"Leave her alone!" ...came a voice from Beth's bunk. "Go to sleep! Tomorrow is another day!"

After many more muffled remarks, it got quieter. Nancy and Liz were whispering quietly on Nancy's bunk. Joann and Julie were done whispering.

Lori was alone with her thoughts, at last!

The Night

Finally, when the cabin was perfectly quiet, Lori started thinking about the kisses. *"Greg's kisses were very nice, ...especially, the last one! He definitely knew what he was doing."* She remembered being pressed up against him, and decided, *"I bet he's had sex with lots of girls. He knew just what to do. And, Winston's probably right about him being dangerous."* "No," she decided, *"he is dangerous. I didn't want to stop kissing him,"* she admitted to herself.

"But Winston, now, ...he didn't know much. His kiss had been barely a pressure on my own lips. Nothing much to even let me feel as if I had been kissed."

She started to re-live the dancing part, and her mood lifted. Winston sure knew how to dance! ...much better than he could 'kiss'. She started recalling all the different turns he knew how to do. *"I learned a lot of neat dance steps, tonight,"* she thought, happily.

"Lori?" a voice whispered.

It was Julie...and she was...*right there...*bending down...beside her bunk!

"Lori...can I get in? ...can I talk to you?"

Like a confused 'zombie', Lori moved over, and finally raised the light blanket to let her in. Her mind was racing with lots of questions, like *"...why? ...what's the matter? ...are you okay?"* But she was 'tongue-tied'.

"Thanks!" whispered Julie, as she lightly entered the bed. "I, uh, ...I know you don't want to talk about... I know you're a very private pers...Sorry! I'm just rambling on. Look... I don't really know very much about sex with boys," she whispered close to Lori's ear. "But boys seem to like me, ...and I *do* have a boyfriend, but I've never, *ever* kissed a boy like you did, ...you know? ...like so... so..."

"Uh, ...no, ...how do you mean?" she whispered back, lying there as stiff as a log.

"Well, he kissed you for a long, long time, ...and, ...and, ...he was...holding you *so close,* ...and, ...well, ...it was like you were in the movies, or something."

Lori said nothing.

"What does a kiss like that feel like?"

After a long silence, Lori said, "It's hard to explain..."

"Well, I've had three boys kiss me," said Julie. "And they were all 'sloppy' kisses, ...and," she sighed, "they, ...well, they *all* tried to put their hands all over me."

"Oh," said Lori, finally breathing out, and relaxing, somewhat. She'd only had two kinds of kisses, and they were as different as night and day. But now, it seemed like she might be a little more experienced than Julie, somehow. She turned on her side, to face Julie. And even though she couldn't see her features at all, in the dark, she asked, very guardedly, "What part do you want to know about?"

"Well," said Julie, I..."

At that very moment, Lori realized that their knees and forearms were touching. She froze once more, wondering if Julie would notice, ...and then she felt the twinge, ever so slightly. "Oh God, ...I can't do this," she barely murmured.

"Oh, please!" whispered Julie. "Everyone at school thinks I know so much about boys, ...but I don't, ...really!"

Lori sighed, "Can't you ask Joann?"

"She doesn't know anything much. She's never even kissed any boy, ...not even tonight."

"Did you?"

"Yes," said Julie, "I kissed Mickey, that blonde guy."

The faint, powdery aroma filled Lori's nostrils.

"Oh, ...uh, ...how was it?"

"It was okay, but I didn't think it was very special. It might have been my fault. Maybe I don't know how to kiss that well. I wanted him to stop." She paused for a long time. "Why was Greg's kiss so special? What made it so *excellent?*"

Lori didn't know exactly where to begin... She didn't really *want* to begin.

Finally, she whispered very softly, "Well, ...well, ...he seemed sure of himself you know, ...but he wasn't obnoxious. He...".

Julie scooched closer so she wouldn't miss any of Lori's low whispers. And now, they were touching almost the entire length of their legs.

Lori's body responded immediately, and she had a hard time concentrating on anything else. "He, ...held me close, ...when we danced," managed Lori. "And I got used to him, ...being *close,* ...you know?"

"Have you ever danced that close to a boy before?" asked Julie.

"No,...that was my first time....Uh, ...Julie?"

"What?"

"You know, ...I, ...uh, ...I'm a *very*, ...uh, private person, ...and if I'm going to tell you any more, ...you have to promise not to tell anyone."

"I've noticed!" she said. Then she paused briefly and agreed, "Okay."

"No, ...I'm *serious*...not even Joann!"

After several more seconds passed, "Okay. I promise! ...I'll be the only one who knows anything."

"Do you think she's asleep?" Lori asked, wondering if Joann was attempting to listen.

"Are you kidding? If she was awake, there'd be three of us in this bunk!"

"Oh, Jeez," said Lori, not even wanting to picture that.

"Don't worry! She's asleep! And I won't tell her *anything!*"

Her words were met with silence.

"*...anything, ever, at all!*"

"...Okay," Lori sighed, finally.

"So-o...were his lips soft?"

"...Yes..."

"It was a really long kiss, ...right?"

"...Yes..."

"And then?"

"Then, ...he kissed me again..."

"Then what?"

"He, ...uh, kissed me some more, and then, ...he, ...well, he...touched his tongue to my lips..."

"Ugh..." said Julie, and then she was quiet, thinking about her own experiences. "Was it gross?"

"...No, ...he only used the very tip. And, ...actually, ...it was okay, ...after I got used to it."

"Did you feel anything?"

"Like what?"

"Well, ...when someone kisses you, and if it's a *good* kiss, you're supposed to feel something, ...right? I read that in a book..."

"Well, ...yes, ...I do, ...I *did*."

"What did it feel like?" asked Julie.

"Boy," sighed Lori, "...it's a good thing you can't see my face right now."

"Why?"

"Because it's red," said Lori, turning her face more into the pillow.

"C'mon, ...tell me. What did you feel?"

"I'm too embarrassed."

"C'mon, Lori, please...it's just me..." ...and Julie put her face even closer to her ear.

199

Lori was now acutely aware of her light powdery aroma, and of her 'tooth paste' breath. Her lips were, ...she was just, ...*so close...*

"Please?"

"Oh, God..."

"It can't be *that* bad..." said Julie.

"It *is...* " said Lori, as the feeling began pulsing for real.

"What did you *feel*?"

"Throbbing!" ...she felt like shouting. But, she took a long, jagged breath and said, in a very quiet voice, "Well, ...a, ...a..."

"A what?"

"...like, ...a...'tingling'."

"A tingling? ...where? ...in your lips?"

"...No..."

"Where?"

...Silence,...

"...Lori?"

"In betw...in betw...my legs."

After what seemed an eternity, Julie said, ... "oh-h..." in a meek little voice. And after another long silence, she cleared her throat a little... "...uh, ...when did it *start?*"

Lori's mind was in pain., thinking, *"Why did I ever agree to do this?"* But she sighed heavily, and said, "...as he touched me with the tip of his tongue." She could vividly remember that. She sighed again.

"And, ...and, ...when did it end?"

"...it ...didn't..."

"It didn't? Why?"

"Well, ...he kept kissing me."

"With his tongue?"

"...Yes..."

"What did he do, exactly, ...did he lick your lips?"

There was no response, and Julie could tell that she was really pushing Lori, now, but she couldn't stop. By trying to understand, she was trying to feel something, too, ...and at least be able to recognize a good kiss if she was ever lucky enough to get one.

"Please?" she begged.

Lori took a deep breath, and whispered softly, "Well, ...he put the tip of his tongue on my lips, ...and then, past my lips, ...and, ...slightly into my mouth, ...and, ..."

"And?"

"...and, ...he lightly touched the tip of my tongue with his."

At that thought, Julie felt a twinge sensation in her own pubic area. "Uh, did you like it?"

Lori squirmed in spite of herself. "...yes."

"Then what?"

"You and Joann came up."

"Oh, no! ...I'm sorry!"

There was an uncomfortable silence now between them, and finally Julie offered, "But, I think I feel what you felt."

"Wha-a-t?"

"Yes, ... a little ripple, or something."

"Where?"

"You know-w-w, ...between my legs."

"Really? Right now?" Lori didn't know if maybe Julie was just trying to make amends for being so inquisitive.

"Yes, really!" she whispered, indignantly. And after another silence, "When did your ripple sensation go away?"

Lori didn't answer.

Julie allowed for a short silence, but no response at all meant... "You still have it?" she asked aloud, incredulously.

"Sh-h!" said Lori.

"Sorry!" she whispered. "Um, ...uh, ...how long will it last?"

"I don't know," she fibbed, "...probably when I stop thinking about it."

Julie sighed deeply. "All that...from a kiss?"

Again, Lori was silent. Her mind reverted to Julie, and how she could picture Julie and herself kissing right now. Julie was so very close! And she smelled so-o good.

"Did he touch your breasts?"

"No, ...why?"

"Mine sort of tingle right now, ...just from talking about this."

Lori remembered Julie floating on her back, in swimming class, and pictured her nipples turning into hard little buds. And her own body, which was already throbbing, began aching for real, ...and begging for release.

"Look, ...uh, ...Julie," she moaned, "we'd...uh, ... better get some sleep."

"Yeah, ...okay, ...and...

"What?"

"Thanks, ...a lot!" And Julie put her hand on Lori's shoulder and brushed her lips against Lori's cheek, in a 'girl to girl' casual kiss, saying, "Good night, Lori." Julie left and quietly slid into her own bunk.

Lori turned completely on her stomach, buried her face in her pillow, ...and at last... 'touched' herself and pressed. She immediately exploded into an orgasm. Her legs stiffened and she gasped into her pillow in spite of her self. She tried to be very quiet and she tried not to move as the waves of spasms continued.

After long minutes passed, her body began to relax. *"Boy! That was close!"* she thought. She finally allowed herself to get into a more comfortable position. She felt weak and completely 'spent'. *"I forgot to say goodnight,"* she realized.

Though not talking, both girls lay awake awhile, still contemplating what had happened, this night. Julie was very curious about her own sensations, but couldn't explain them. And Lori was amazed at how her body reacted much more to Julie's being near her, than to Greg's very intense kiss.

Lori fell asleep first. Julie could hear her deep, even, breaths. *"How can she just go to sleep, if she's tingling, like me? She had to feel it more, because she was the one who kissed him! Strange..."* Julie tossed and turned, and finally dozed off.

Saturday Alone

Lori looked at the clock. "6 a.m." Everybody was still sleeping after the late night, last night. Saturday. No schedule today until long after breakfast.

This morning felt like Sunday to her, and she just wanted to be near the lake...alone. Somehow, certain spots seemed to be as solemn to her as a church. She hadn't done anything 'wrong' last night, but somehow she thought, maybe, she should apologize to God.

She dressed in shorts and a blouse and went to sit up against a pretty maple tree that was far from the cabins, but close to the water. It was a very calm and peaceful morning, ...but inside, Lori was disturbed.

"Who am I? ...What am I?" she wondered.

She had danced and had fun with two boys, and had kissed them both. Greg's kiss was memorable, but then she remembered why. *"...Because he had a great way of kissing, and then, later, she was imagining herself kissing Julie, instead of him."*

"Maybe, if I didn't know Julie at all, I would like Greg a lot." So-o... she didn't *hate* boys, or even 'dislike' them.! *"That's good!"*

After being with him, she knew she could like having a 'neat guy' kiss her. *"That's great!"*

She just liked Julie better. *"That's not so good."*

"To thine own self be true." ... she remembered reading, somewhere. And now, she knew the truth. There was no doubt about it. She was very much attracted to one special girl, ... more than she was attracted to *any* of the guys she knew, ...even Greg, who had a lot going for him. She sighed heavily, and...and... She knew *for sure,* deep down, in her soul, that she would really like to hold Julie in her arms, and, ...softly, and ever so gently...kiss her *on the lips*! "Amen, to the truth," she whispered.

"Would that be a sin?" she wondered. *"Probably..."* she decided, sighing heavily.

Then, she thought about Lu and Jen. *"I suspected that they didn't think too much about boys. And, now I know they like girls better."* She interrupted her own thoughts to ponder the word 'girls' with an 's'. *"I wonder if I could feel this way about any other girl?"* She closed her eyes, but couldn't 'see' anyone but Julie.

"Anyway, back to Lu and Jen," she thought. *"If there are three of us 'sinners' in this small camp, and a 'Jennifer', back in Lu's home town, ...then,*

there has to be a lot of 'girls who like girls' in the entire world! Whew," she thought, *"lots and lots more! Who could they be? Where are they all?"* She tried to think of anyone else here at camp. She didn't really know lots of girls that well, to even make a good guess, ...but Rory came to mind. *"What about the counselors?"* Well, she hadn't paid much attention.

Then, she tried to remember if there was anyone back at school. Just guessing at possibilities, she could count two or three. And then the girls on the different park teams... *"Of course, the girl in the construction shoes."* And she could count two more real 'possibilities'!

"Maybe it's just a phase, ...a teenage phase. But, if it is a phase, how long will it last? I'll have to read about it. And, since there is a word, like 'gay' to label people, how long has it been used?"

"God can't be mad at 'all of us', can he? I mean, ...well, He made us what we are, right?" Nevertheless, tremendous feelings of guilt overtook her, and Maude's disapproving face flashed in her mind. She closed her eyes to pray.

She tried remembering the Ten Commandments, and only one ran through her mind... 'Thou shalt not covet thy neighbor's wife.' Well, ...at least Julie wasn't anyone's wife.

She remembered a Catholic movie 'confessional scene'. The dialogue started out with, "Bless me Father, for I have sinned."

She bowed her head, solemnly, and prayed, earnestly, "Bless me Father *if I have sinned."*

Deep down, during her silent meditation, she found herself asking, *"Have I?"* She didn't 'sense' an answer. She had not ever been taught that God was 'cruel'. As a result, part of her was having a hard time believing that God condemned 'love and kindness' toward anybody. Nevertheless, she prayed for 'forgiveness', several times.

Finally, she took a deep breath. "Amen." she said, still very confused, but feeling better than when she first woke up.

Dear Hattie

Dear Hattie,

Thought I'd better write you, since I'm not coming home yet. I've been chosen to be like a counselor for the last two weeks, helping out on the waterfront.

It's great for me, since you know I'd rather be here than with Maude. Camp has been so much fun. You know how I love to play! I wish you could come next year!

I met a boy at the dance last night, who could pass for your brother, ...and boy is he nice! His name is Winston, and he's a really good dancer. I met another boy named Greg, and that's a story I'll have to see you to tell you about.

We've been having our 'end of the session' contests in lots of activities. We just finished our 'Race day' in swimming. I got a few blue ribbons, and my friend, Beth, got one for winning the backstroke. She won a couple of second place ribbons, (red) for the crawl stroke and the underwater race. We each got to enter 3 races! Our cabin did great! The contest was racing against the whole camp, and lots of girls didn't know how to swim at all when we first got here. I hope I can help Walli, (the waterfront director) to get the new girls to swim pretty well in the next two weeks.

Camp ends tomorrow for a lot of girls, and I'm not looking forward to all the sad 'good-byes'. You've heard of the 'buddy system', right? My best buddy, Beth, has to leave. Her parents need her home, to help out, because her Mom is going back to work. Julie Conners, from school, is here, and we'll be partners for the last two weeks, 'cause her buddy's leaving, too.

Hope your summer has been fun! Miss you, lots!

Love,
Lori

Sunday 'Good-byes'

The mood of the day was 'blue'. Lori was at Beth's, bunk, while Beth packed up the last of her stuff. She had lots of things from Arts and Crafts. Luckily, Mrs. Watson had given them all a bag to use, but Beth was still overloaded.

Gerri was visiting each girl to help her 'get it together', and she gave Beth a big hug, and said, "Thanks for all your help in swim class! Walli and I are recommending you for C.I.T. next year, if you're interested."

Beth's eyes lit up. "If I'm interested? Yes, I am very interested! Thanks, Gerri."

Lori and Beth did a little Indian dance all up and down the center aisle, whooping and shouting at the good news. They had already exchanged addresses and now started planning way ahead. In the middle of a lot of other people's sadness, they were completely happy.

Gradually, everybody headed to the mess hall for breakfast. Some girls carried their things, with buddies helping out. Others wanted to wait until later, and get their stuff after they showed their parents around the camp.

As usual, there was an early church service, for all those who wished to attend.

Later, Mrs. 'Z' 'did her thing' at the microphone, and had them remembering all the good times they'd had together. She mentioned little things about most of the girls who were leaving, and they realized that she 'knew' them, even though she wasn't around them a lot. They were leaving a friendly place, and most of them hoped to return next summer.

Since lots of parents were arriving early this morning, and lots of 'good-byes' were waiting to be said, Zee ended the formalities.

Jill came up to Lori and Beth and took their picture in front of the mess hall. She made them do some close-up poses and promised to send them copies. Then, she took one of Gerri with her entire group. All the Falcons and the Hawks from cabins three and four, had become close friends. Jill used up all of her film as Rory and Meg, and Ceil and Vivian got everybody to pose this way and that.

Afterward, Lori walked Beth to the parking lot and met her parents. Then she left them alone, because Beth wanted to take them on a tour of the camp.

Beth said, "I'll come give you a hug before we leave."

"Okay." said Lori. As she returned to the mess hall, she thought, *"I'm really going to miss her. We've talked about a lot of things. Julie and I have never really been able to 'talk' much."* She had the weirdest sensations...first, sadness about Beth, and then exhilaration, at the prospect of really getting to know Julie better. "Talk about mixed emotions," she said aloud.

She had to change gears quickly though, because a few girls with tears in their eyes were headed her way.

Donna Kelli

Letter Home

Dear Dad,

I've been doing the counselor in training routine for a few days now. It's pretty great! I still get to be with my same group, except we have some new girls. Beth, Joann, and Lu went home. Beth will probably get to be a C.I.T. next year, also, but only if the enrollment is up. It was tough to tell her good-bye.

I've been helping the new girls with all the 'camp stuff'. One girl cried for most of two nights. And another girl wouldn't take a 'gang' shower for two days. I don't think I was that bad, and now, I guess I'm more used to it.

Julie's my new buddy, but we don't get to do much together. I have to work a lot now, and I miss Arts and Crafts almost every day. Sometimes I miss things, like a hike or a softball game. Julie gets to go to them, ...she just doesn't have a buddy for those activities. We're not together for Archery either, because she's helping the new girls learn to shoot, and so am I. She's doing a mural for the wall in the Arts and Crafts room, like a 'collage' of our activities here. So, she spends extra time there, and I guess she doesn't mind missing some events, either. We'll always get to be buddies for swimming though, because I'm here at the waterfront. It's going to be interesting to see if she can learn the 'butterfly stroke'. She's doing great in the others.

As much as I love what I'm doing, I guess I miss the old routine a little. I miss talking to Beth.

On a happier note, I get a new privilege. I'm going to learn to use a rowboat. We have two, and the waterfront counselors usually use them to patrol the lake... The rest of the counselors only get to go boating during their free time. Well, time for breakfast, and I'm starved. I'll get this in the mail. It will probably be my last letter, but I'll call you next week.

I miss you!

Lots of love,
Lori

Mailbag

When Lori took her letter in, to mail it, she was surprised to get mail. She opened up a very wrinkled letter from the boys' camp.

Dear Lori,
I hope you will be there for the last dance. I can hardly wait to see you, again. They won't let us call you girls from here, but we keep asking. I miss you a lot, and really had a great time dancing with you.
Sorry this is a short letter, but guys watch me all the time, waiting to see if I write you. They would steal it, add some pretty bad things to it and mail it to you, just to see your reaction. Think about being 'my girl', okay?
I like you a lot!
Winston

Lori read the letter and then chuckled to herself, because she could picture Winston cramming the letter in his pocket a few times, just to hide it. He was a gem of a guy, but she was still in a sad mood, and couldn't seem to shake the doldrums.

Within minutes, she was trying to figure out how to work more time with Julie into her busy schedule.

Donna Kelli

Can You Canoe?

After helping Walli with the new girls in swim class, Lori asked if she could take a canoe out for a while, and help Julie. When she got a 'yes' answer, she felt her spirits rise and she actually smiled for the first time all day. She waded over to Julie, and asked, "Care to go for a canoe ride?"

Julie, feeling pretty bored for the past hour, looked at Lori's happy face and found herself thinking, *"She's really something! Especially when her green eyes just light up, and she smiles like that! How can I refuse such an offer?"* She said, "Sure! Let's go!"

"Ever thought about sitting in the back, and steering?" she asked Julie as they stood in the clear, shallow water getting the canoe ready.

"Yes, I tried it once with Joann, but I like it much better in the front," she said, remembering their early morning trip.

"Walli told me that some of us are going to do a 'fun' thing, called 'gunneling' before camp is over. It means having to take a canoe by yourself for a short ways, so... would you like to 'learn the stern'?" she drawled, smiling.

"Sure," said Julie.

After several minutes of showing her how it felt with another person in the canoe, Lori got her to try it alone. It was more difficult to keep the canoe going straight ahead, but somehow, Julie finally turned the canoe around, and came back with a brilliant smile.

"This is great!" she said. "I didn't think I could do it."

Lori smiled back at her, thinking as usual, *"Your smile... is what's really great."* "Congratulations." she said.

"Get back in and let's go for a little ride, okay?" suggested Julie.

"Okay, you steer," said Lori, and she climbed in the front.

They paddled around the shore line of the lake and when they got out to the sand spit, Julie turned toward the little dock. There were several girls lounging there and they started kidding with the twosome.

"Hey, Lori, got room in there for me?" asked Rory.

"No way."

"Well, how about we race to the blue buoy? If I win, you have to get out and let me take your place! Okay?"

Before Lori could ask Julie if she wanted to do it, Meg said, "Ready! Set! Go!"

And Rory did a racing dive off the dock.

Julie felt frustrated, because she didn't know what to do.

"Paddle backwards, on the right..." said Lori, in a low, but firm voice.

Julie did, and the canoe seemed to turn on a dime. She looked, and Lori was paddling hard forward, on the left.

"Okay, now, just paddle forward on the right."

Julie did, and they finally got moving and gradually picked up a little speed.

Lori said softly, over her shoulder, "It's okay to just steer, whenever you want to. It's better to keep us straight than to go off course."

Julie steered often and Lori just kept paddling. They were going pretty fast now, but Rory had a good lead on them. Julie was trying to judge whether or not they could even catch up, much less win. It didn't look like it.

But Lori kept up the pace and said in a loud voice, "You're doing great, Julie!"

And in spite of the fact that she was getting tired, Julie felt the rush of excitement, pumping in her veins. She dug in harder, and asked, "Can we change sides, now?"

"Sure!" said Lori, and she switched to paddling on her right without missing a beat.

Julie switched, too, and new muscles came into action. The canoe surged forward a little faster. The girls on the dock were cheering, loudly for their choice, and Julie looked back for a second. She was surprised to see only a few girls left on the dock. Lots of them had dived off and were swimming after them, far behind the canoe. They wanted to be part of the action, too, it seemed.

On shore, a little groups were gathering, shouting, "Lo-ri! Lo-ri!" or "Ror-y! Ror-y!" or "Ju-lie! Ju-lie!"

Julie got so excited that she shouted, "Lori, paddle harder!"

Lori started chuckling to herself but she said, "Okay!" And she tried to paddle even harder. They caught up with Rory's feet, and held the pace, but couldn't pass her.

Finally Rory touched the buoy and turned to face them, smiling broadly. They zoomed right past her and coasted up to the beach.

The onlookers were cheering, "Yea, Rory!" and "Great race!" and "You guys almost won!"

"Okay, you slowpoke!" taunted Rory. "Get out of that canoe, and let a real..." she had to dive sideways, because Lori had stepped out of the canoe, and was coming at her fast, to try and dunk her. They only wrestled under water a moment. Both came up laughing.

"All right, you landlubber," said Lori. "If my partner can stand to have you aboard, I guess you won!"

Julie stood in knee deep water, watching them, thinking, *"Lori and Rory are good friends, even though they compete against each other. I never kid with girls like that. I certainly could never have done it with Joann. She would've been screaming at me the whole way, and then blamed me for losing."*

211

"What do you say, partner, can you stand to have this poor, worn out, 'dock dawdler' in the same boat with you?"

Julie laughed, and said, "Aye, Cap'n."

The beachfront got very noisy as all the swimmers from the dock arrived and started kidding around.

As they were turning the canoe around, Lori said, softly, "You did great, Julie! That was so-o 'fun'. Thanks." Then, she turned to Rory, and said, pointing her finger playfully at her, "Have her home in time for dinner."

"Or what?" kidded Rory.

"Believe me, you don't want to find out, you 'swabby.'"

Julie liked the way Lori had, of making her the center of attention, even though all the action was really between the two of them. After Rory climbed in and they had paddled out from shore, Julie said, "Congratulations. You swam a great race!"

"Yeah, I did, didn't I?" Then she said, "Paddle for the dock! I want to tell Meg something."

Julie thought, with a sigh, *"Somehow, it's just not the same."*

Later

That night, while lying in her bunk, Julie decided that she hadn't seen Lori smiling all that much all summer. She didn't know if she had with Beth, but she remembered a day when Lori was laughing so hard, her sides seemed to be splitting. Of course, it was *at her,* and she didn't appreciate it at the time, but now she wished she could see her smile and laugh more often. She knew that Lori was usually calm, but intense, and spent an awful lot of her time helping and teaching others.

She started thinking back to all the different things she had learned by Lori's patient willingness to 'be there'. Her fear of the water was the most important to overcome. And archery had been a 'bear' until Lori helped her.

Now, that she knew how to swim, canoe, ride horseback, play volleyball, and even football, she vowed to add some fun to Lori's life, whenever possible, for the last week and a half of camp.

"Goodnight Lori," she said. "I had fun today in the canoe." ...silently thinking, *"...until you got out..."*

"Me too, Julie. Sleep well." Lori, more contented than she had been for days, fell asleep immediately.

Just 'Cavorting'

"Handicap! That's the word!" said Julie. "Let's race to that white buoy! And your handicap is that you can't kick! At all!"

"You always want an advantage," said Lori.

"Every chance I get!" laughed Julie. "Ready! Set! Go!"

Julie churned up the water, and she took four breaths, while doing a better than average, 'racing crawl' stroke. Lori peeked at her as she took her own breaths. *"If she wasn't concentrating so hard on beating me,"* she thought, *"she'd be doing a very smooth, 'pretty to watch', stroke. She's come a long, long way."*

Julie pulled ahead of Lori in the last few yards and touched the buoy.

"Hah!" she said, happily, looking and talking through water streaming down her face. "The 'Great Julie Conners' won again," she announced, turning to an 'imaginary crowd', "over that 'very wimpy', not to mention, 'ugly, ugly' Lori Hunter! An-d, she could do it again, ...and a—gain, ...and, a—glub..."

Lori had silently slipped below the water, and once submerged, swam forward. She grabbed Julie's heels and up-ended her. Julie twisted around underwater and came up already in motion, splashing at her, furiously.

Lori, not splashing her back at all, let her get very close. Suddenly she reached out and tagged Julie, and said, "You're it!" and dove sideways under water. Julie swiped at her trying to make the 'tag back', but missed.

"Darn her!" Julie didn't know how to swim fast, under water, so she took off after her, doing the crawl.

Lori surfaced in front of her, just out of reach, rolled over, and began doing the back stroke. She saw one 'wide open' clear, blue eye' keeping tabs on her as Julie caught each breath. Swimming just hard enough, to stay ahead of Julie, she taunted her... "Here comes the 'Great Julie Conners', churning up the water like an old 'egg beater'. She could swim faster folks, but her ego is dragging her under."

Forgetting to look behind her, Lori bumped into another girl, who had been wading out deeper, while talking to a friend. Lori stopped, and apologized immediately, but then Julie caught her. Lori felt Julie grab her around the neck and shoulders, and try to push her under. Lori took a quick breath, went under, and headed out farther and for the bottom, which was about six feet down. Julie hung on tightly, and ended up deeper in the lake than she had ever been. Lori let out some of her air and sank lower. Then she turned completely around and sat on the bottom of the lake.

Looking with her eyes wide open, Julie couldn't believe it when she saw Lori just sitting there, calmly, like an Indian chief with her legs crossed.

"Ooh, she makes me so mad, sometimes!" she thought, pushing off, and heading up to get air. Then, she remembered something and she dove back down as best she could. When Lori finally looked her way, Julie pointed at her and motioned, "You're it!" and headed up as fast as she could go.

Lori pushed off the bottom, and the chase was on.

Sitting on the beach, watching them, Jen scowled, and clenched her jaw.

Jen, Again

Basketball was played on an outside court. It was one of the sports that only some girls liked. Julie was not one of those who did. Normally, she would've gone to Arts and Crafts an extra time, but she came to watch today because Lori was her buddy, now.

This was a full court 'pick-up game' between some of the better players in camp. Lori and Rory ended up on the same team, but oddly enough, Jen ended up guarding Lori. Julie, who didn't know that much about the intricacies of the game, could tell that Lori was having a good time, as usual, but compared to the others, she seemed to only be playing at 'half-speed'. She seemed to be able to do whatever she wanted.

Julie watched her 'coasting' up and down the court. Lori was running, but not in a 'heavy-footed' way. Somehow, she always seemed to be in position easily. Wherever the ball was, Julie would look up and Lori wasn't far away. Rory could throw her the ball and Jen never seemed to be able to intercept the pass. Lori could always get there more quickly, or out jump her.

She watched as their team passed the ball around, giving the other girls chances to shoot. Whenever they missed, either Lori or Rory seemed to be able to get the rebound, and set up again, for another chance at the basket.

Just now, Lori had the ball and wanted to drive to the basket around Jen. She faked left, and went right. Jen fell for it, and Lori did a nice easy lay-up, off the backboard.

"I know how Jen feels," thought Julie. *"It's that maddening little 'shoulder-head' thing..."* Then, talking to herself, she added, *"...and her hips and legs go the other way."*

Later, Jen's team scored a few three pointers, and caught up.

The next time Lori faced Jen, she faked left, and hesitated. Jen went left, and then leaned right. Lori went around her to the left, and scored with her other hand. Julie was impressed because she couldn't do much of anything with her own left hand, except ballet.

But Jen was getting frustrated, and it showed.

The game went on, and Julie was getting a little bored until she saw Lori again, with Jen between her and the basket. These were the most interesting parts to her, and she tried to guess what Lori would do.

Lori faked right, faked left, and went around Jen to the right. Jen was fooled into leaning the wrong way, again, and leaned back too late to guard Lori or steal the ball. Completely determined however, she reached out with both arms, and grabbed around Lori's waist, pulling her off balance and off course. Due to

Lori's forward momentum, Jen ended up falling sideways and being dragged backwards, but still trying to hold on tight. Her grip wasn't strong enough to remain waist-high, though, and her arms dragged all the way down Lori's legs, finally wrapping around her knees, and keeping her from taking any more steps.

Lori's forward motion carried her even more through Jen's grip and Jen now held both legs tight to her chest, just above the ankles.

Lori crashed down very hard, on top of her. Her left knee hit Jen in the forehead, and then Lori's fall continued forward. She had already released the ball and put her hands out, trying to land in a 'push up' position, but another girl's leg was in the way. Lori was only able to partially 'catch herself.' Her right shoulder and the right side of her head crashed on the court. Then she didn't move at all.

Julie screamed and ran to her. Fletch had been refereeing, and told everybody else to stay back. There were two girls unconscious on the court. Jen was laid out like she was dead. Lori's knee had helped drive her head down hard on the ground.

Lori groaned and began moving, slightly, saying, "Oh, my head." She tried to sit up, but couldn't.

Fletch got Julie to stay by Lori and keep her down. Jen was still 'out'. Fletch sent Rory for the nurse, an ambulance and some ice, and then, clenching her teeth, said, mostly under her breath, "That was a deliberate tackle."

Julie said, "I know."

Fletch hadn't realized she'd spoken aloud. "Yeah, well how about if we keep it between you and me, for now, Julie. Okay?"

"Okay," said Julie, feeling madder than she could ever remember being in her whole life.

The ambulance came from the hospital and Zee coordinated everything. Fletch climbed in and Julie was allowed to go with Lori. Jen's new buddy, was just that, very new. There wasn't enough room for her anyway.

The doctors decided that Lori had, at the very least, a concussion but they were hoping it was only a mild one. She had to stay in the hospital overnight for more tests in the morning. She wasn't fully conscious yet, and one doctor felt that she was in a coma.

Julie asked if Zee had called Mr. Hunter. Fletch told her she had.

"Could I talk to him?" she asked.

"Not likely," said Fletch. "Maybe after Lori's out of danger."

Julie begged to stay at the hospital with her.

Fletch needed to go back to camp, so she cleared it with Zee, and said, "Okay, but be a help around here, not a hindrance, okay?"

217

Jen was put in a different room. *"Good thing,"* thought Julie. *"I might poison her or something, in the middle of the night."* Then she laughed at herself, because usually she never wanted to hurt anybody. *"Still, that Jen, ...she's something else! She deserved what she got, ...but Lori sure didn't."*

Julie went to the nurses' station and asked what she could do for Lori. The nurse on duty asked her to stay by her and let her know if she woke up, got a fever, or the chills, or started vomiting.

Julie went back and sat in a recliner chair by the bed, and read magazines for a few hours. The nurse would come in about every thirty or forty minutes to check Lori. There was no change. Lori was 'out', and probably would be for the rest of the night.

"Try to get some sleep," said the nurse.

"Maybe in a little while," said Julie.

Dazed and Confused

Lori's first realization was, as if she were coming up through a dense fog. And then, of the pain, ...severe pain, and throbbing...mostly, she thought, over her right ear ...And dizziness...a terrible swirling feeling inside her head. And then, nausea! ...automatically she tried to roll over on her side in case she vomited. But her body wouldn't respond. It seemed as though she weighed tons, and worse yet, nothing worked. Gradually, the nausea passed.

She tried to remember something, ...to remember anything, ...and all she got was a sharp pain in her head. Involuntarily, her face slightly winced at the pain. She felt something softly stroke her forehead, ...a hand. It was a hand. *"Who?"* Again a stabbing pain with another fleeting scrunch downward, over her eyebrows.

"Lori?" a voice asked, from far, far away. "Lori! Are you okay?"

She tried to open her eyes, and, ...nothing. She felt like a lead weight, ...glued to the ground. The ground! She remembered lying on the ground! Her thoughts swirled. *"...Who? ...Why? ...Wh..."* ...and then the hand lightly stroked her forehead again.

"Oh, Lori, please, please, be okay," said the voice, now a little closer.

"Julie? ...Ju-lie!" ...registered in her brain, and her shoulders jerked.

The voice begged, "Please, open your eyes!"

She tried to open them to see if it really was Julie, ...and, ...nothing! It was as if her thoughts were isolated in a deep, dark hole, and her body was a mountain, a heavy, very heavy, immovable mountain. Then, she just needed to sleep, and she faded back into the welcoming cloudy haze...

Sometime later, she felt the hand on her forehead, ever so light, ...so tentative, ...as if her forehead would break.

"It's all her fault!" said the voice. "If only she hadn't...oh Lori, you *have* to be okay!"

And Lori slowly started to remember, ...falling, ...falling, ...somewhere hard...

And here was Julie, trying to get her to wake up.

"I'm awake..." she said, slowly in her mind. *"I am ...awake!"* She tried to mouth the words, and, ...nothing...

Donna Kelli

"Paralyzed!" she thought. *"I must be paralyzed! I can't move anything!"* She demanded her eyelids to open. She strained to concentrate on that one thing. And for her effort, her head throbbed in pain. *"Well, at least, ...I can feel, ...and I can hear,"* she thought slowly, deep down in her foggy world. Nothing else seemed to hurt, so she thought, *"maybe nothing's broken, ...except my head,"* she mused, wryly, but painfully...

"You should have your dad here, but you've only got me."

"...only got her?" She wanted to tell Julie "Not to worry ...that deep down, she was fine!" ...but she couldn't. She was somewhere else, somewhere in a very murky, different world.

And then she felt the hand lifted, and Julie was gone. *"What? Where are...? Oh, don't go!"* she wanted to say.

She strained to hear Julie's footsteps, and determined that she was going toward the dim light that filtered through her closed eyelids. Toward the entrance of the cave! *"We're ...in the cave!"* she thought... *"Don't ...go!"* she shouted inside herself. But only a barely audible moan escaped her lips.

Hearing it, Julie came back immediately and sat beside her.

"Lori? Are you okay? Does your head hurt bad?"

And Lori felt frozen in time. *"Yes..."* she said in her mind, *"...it hurts pretty bad. Can't you hear me? I'm here! I'm awake, but I can't seem to move...please ...don't leave..."*

And her own ears heard nothing but Julie, sighing softly, in sympathy and frustration.

After a few minutes, Julie said, "I'll be right back."

And Lori "saw" her shadow briefly obscure the light.

"This is ...silly!" she thought. *"I should be ...helping her! She's ...probably ...going to get ...firewood. Wait!"* she tried to say, ...and then she knew she was alone. There was no sound except her own breathing.

It seemed like hours passed. *"Cold!"* she thought, *"I'm cold!"* And she wondered if Julie had left her to go back to camp to get a doctor. And then she heard footsteps...

"I'm back!" she announced, as she came closer. "I told the nurse you moved your eyebrows, a little, and you moaned." Julie came back and sat down beside her. She leaned forward and said, almost in a whisper, "Lori? Wake up, ...please! I'm so worried about you! Please be okay..." she pleaded, as her voice trailed off into nothingness.

And Lori was completely frustrated because Julie couldn't seem to hear her shouting... *"...I'm ... I'm awake! ...I just can't open my eyes!. Where's the nurse? Is she here, in the cave?"*

No answers seemed forthcoming.

"Why can't I get up?" she wondered. She wasn't sure if she could feel her legs or feet. She tried to wiggle her toes, ...and, ...'nothing'.

"I felt Julie's hand, ...but, ...I can't seem to feel my..."

And there it was again, ...Julie was beside her, ...stroking her forehead... "Oh, Lori, I hope you're not dying! They said you definitely have a concussion, but that you'd probably be okay. They don't seem to be terribly worried, but you look so, so... Lori? Can you hear me? Can't you blink your eyes, or something?" ...and her hand moved to Lori's cheek.

Still in the depths of fog, Lori felt Julie staring into her closed eyes.

"I can blink," she thought. *"Blink!"* ...she commanded her eyes. *"Blink!"* But she wasn't sure if they did.

"I guess you're just really 'knocked-out' *good!*" said Julie. "I wonder if that's the same as being in a coma?" she murmured. "When that tree bumped my head, I almost got a concussion, but it wasn't this bad..." And she slowly got up and went to look out the window. "It's getting dark out," she said.

Finally, Julie came back and took her same place. "I wonder what time it is?" she said softly, to herself. She couldn't quite see the clock in the semi-dark room.

And Lori wondered, fuzzily... *"What time, ...of what day?"* ...and her body convulsed slightly.

Julie said, "Lori? It's me, ...Julie, ...I'm here! Are you okay? You just *have* to be okay. Oh, you're shivering! I'll go get the nurse." And she was gone.

The nurse came into the room, checked Lori, and said, "She'll do that, off and on. Try to keep her warm with this extra blanket if you can. I'll be back to check on her in about forty minutes. I have to make my other rounds now. If you really need me, come down the long hall to the right."

Julie put the blanket over Lori, then returned to her other side, and sat on the bed.

This time, Lori felt Julie sit down and felt the bed give a little. *"Bed?"* she wondered. *"...where am I?"*

She felt Julie's hand checking her forehead.

"You're still shivering. I'll just stay here, and..." She lifted the blanket and moved closer, and lay full length beside her, to share her own body warmth.

Lori felt Julie stretch out next to her. She could feel Julie's legs touching hers... *"My legs! I can feel my legs! ...at least the right one! Hmm, my knee hurts...and my shoulder, too. Maybe I'm not paralyzed! So...Why can't I move*

221

anything?" Then, she felt herself trembling... *"I really am shivering!"* she realized.

Feeling her shiver again, Julie draped one leg gently over Lori's legs, and put her arm across her waist. Then, she rubbed Lori's left arm briskly, trying to warm her up.

"Cold! I'm so cold!" thought Lori, as her body shivered.

"Don't worry, ...I'll keep you warm... Just ...don't die." Julie moved even closer, and partially covered Lori with her own body. Her face was under Lori's chin, ...and Lori could feel Julie's forehead against her cheek. Then Lori felt herself fading again, back down into the fog. It was like grayish-black smoke, and it swirled all around her.

Later, she felt the fog disappearing and a smooth hand, was caressing her face.

"...Who?" She recognized Julie's powdery aroma. *"Am I dreaming?"* she wondered. *"Could this be happening? ...Julie's so close... and I'm so far."*

Julie was saying, "You and Beth kept me warm in the cave, remember?" And she ran her fingers lightly across Lori's forehead.

Lori became very conscious of how much of Julie's body was touching her, and how good it felt. And when she remembered that Julie's face was so close to hers, she thought, *"If only ...I could hold her, too."* Then she felt her new friend, 'the tingle', stirring, down 'there'. *"Well, Jeez, ...that part ...of me ...is not ...broken..."* she thought, and knew she was laughing somewhere, *"...probably in my almost dead head."* Then she wondered how she could chuckle inside, without a sound outside. Her mind was racing, but in slow motion. *"I'm sick..."* she thought. *"Sick in the head! Here I am, half- dead, and I'm reacting to Julie like a sex maniac...no...a pervert! Because she's only doing this as a friend...a true friend, trying to keep me warm ...just like Beth would've done."*

Guilt and intense shame washed over her. She felt prickly hot goose bumps go down her back and legs. A tear rolled out of her eye, and down her cheek.

Julie felt it as it reached her forehead. "Lori? You're crying! Does it hurt? Are you awake?"

"...Yes, ...I am awake in here and I'm even getting a little warmer." thought Lori. *"Shame must've made me blush clear down to my toes."* But she still couldn't move.

"My poor Lori," whispered Julie. "You're so helpless... Funny, ...all along, I've been sort of the 'helpless' one, ...and you've been the 'all American' girl."

Lori felt Julie give a big sigh.

"You know, if you were awake, I don't think I could lie this close to you, ...you know, ...like, ...like we're ...snuggling." After awhile, she continued... "The way you look at me sometimes, Lori... I don't know, ...it makes me feel like, ...like when my boyfriend looks at me, ...only, ...different. It's deeper, ...more intense, ...and then, it's gone, ...that look. It's so personal, ...like you're looking into my soul...and then, you look away."

Julie sighed again. "What do you see in there, Lori? Can you see into other people's souls? Do you look at anyone else like that? At Greg?...at any other girls?" Then Julie was silent, thinking to herself.

And Lori was now numb inside, as well as outside. *"She knows! She knows! Oh no! I might as well die, because... Oh Lord, ...I can never look at her again!"*
"Lori, can you feel me here next to you?"
Lori listened, ...afraid of what was coming next.
"Can you hear me at all?" she heard softly in her ear.

Julie could see Lori's profile against the light in the hall, and was thinking to herself that Lori had ...nice... "You know," ...she said, in the softest voice ever... "you have ...nice lips."
And Lori felt light fingertips smoothing over her bottom lip.
"And I love the color of your eyes..." she whispered even softer. "I can get 'lost' just looking into them... and, ...it's a *good* thing you can't hear me, or I'd just *die."*
Lori couldn't believe her ears, ...or the very light touch across her lips! If Lori wasn't already 'paralyzed', she would be now! She was frozen in fear! ...fear that Julie would realize she was awake, inside, ...and...
Then Julie's soft, caressing touch 'feathered' up to Lori's eyelashes.
"And your lashes, ...they're so long...and so dark..."
It felt funny to have her eyelashes touched. *"Oh God, ...don't blink now!"* Lori ordered her eyes.
Julie seemed fascinated with the little upward curl of the ends of the lashes, as she ran the tips of her fingers back and forth, ever so gently, with slightly trembling hands.
Then Lori felt herself leaving, once more, as everything got fuzzy and 'very far away'.

Sometime later, as she slowly faded back in to the 'here and now', Julie was saying, in a whisper...
"Do you know how incredible you are to look at? You know, I try *not* to look at you in case you 'catch' me staring! Yes, 'catch me', with ...those, ...absolutely haunting, hazel-green eyes, ...just calmly looking out from under these beautiful thick lashes. Funny, ...I can picture them now, even though your eyes are closed. Do you know that almost every girl I know at camp wishes she had your eyes and eyelashes?"
Lori's mind began racing, and numbing at the same time.

223

Julie's fingertips moved to Lori's cheek. "And your skin... it's so soft...so different from my boyfriend's. Julie's hand seemed to pause, ...and then she murmured, "I've been wondering, ...what it would be like to..."

Lori felt Julie scoot up a little, ...and then, ...she felt Julie's cheek softly on her own. *"Oh Lord,"* thought Lori, *"...if this is what it's like to...if I'm dying...I'm ready."*

"Oh God," thought Julie, *"...don't let her wake up now,"* as she moved her cheek across Lori's and murmured, "...*so-o* smooth."

When Lori didn't move at all, Julie propped herself up on one elbow and slowly bent over, until her lips were very close to Lori's. Hardly breathing, she came to within a hairs-breadth of 'touching lips', and slowly she began moving her face back and forth a little.

Lori could feel the energy of Julie's lips, *right there*, above her own! She could feel her soft breath, and she could feel her own heart skipping beats.

And then, ...Julie's lips were touching hers, ...light and feathery, ...and then, ...gone.

Lori's heart was pounding.

Julie's was, too, so she didn't notice.

Julie leaned back and gazed down at Lori. "You know, you look, ...well, ...'striking'. Somehow I think you feel 'less than pretty', just because you're such a tomboy, and so good at sports. But, ...I think you're gorgeous." And Julie leaned down again, ...to softly press her lips to the corner of Lori's mouth. "Do you know you have a cute little dimple here when you do a certain little smirk?" ...and Julie lightly kissed the spot, again.

Lori felt her own body from the inside out, ...turning inside-out. And then, she felt herself slipping away, again, back into the fog, and thought, *"...No-o... I want to sta-a-y."*

As she came 'back' once again, Julie's lips moved to 'feather' across hers, and then, Lori's fuzzy thoughts became completely paralyzed. She couldn't think, ...she could only feel, ...Julie's lips brushing hers ever so gently.

Again, Julie stopped, and leaned back. "Funny, ...I'd die if you woke up, but I wonder what it would be like to have you... *kiss me*. You know, ...like a real kiss, ...like you and Greg had."

And Lori felt Julie's lips melting ever so softly, down on her own. And even though her lips couldn't respond to Julie, part of her was throbbing... Then, she felt Julie's soft lips, ease back again, and begin to just 'play', lightly across hers, She felt like a guitar, and all the strings were vibrating. Her special friend was now pulsating. Her mind was trying to analyze the wonderful feelings, but it was hopeless.

She felt those soft lips once more, and the pleasure started coming in waves, and then, without warning, ...Julie's soft tongue played leisurely across her bottom lip, and back again... Lori felt muscles deep inside her trembling, and erupting, ...and becoming an incredible spasm. She saw beautiful colors, ...brilliant gold and intense purple.

"Oh, ...Julie," she thought, "...you are ...my...". and she almost stopped herself from finishing the thought... *'world'."* "*She couldn't be her 'world'..."* ...but, small tremors still pulsated from within her, reminding her that her body definitely thought so.

And then, Julie stopped kissing her. "I'd better stop this," she said in a husky voice. "I feel so...so...warm and sexy...no...I hate that word... I feel so... Anyway, this can't lead anywhere. I wonder what two girls would really do for sex anyhow?" She sighed one last sigh, and then Julie scooted back down and put her face on Lori's shoulder again.

"At least you seem warmer now. You've stopped shivering. Let's try to get some sleep," said Julie, seriously. And then, Lori heard her chuckle... "Yes, *you* try to go to sleep now, and we'll forget this ever happened, won't we?"

Then, serious once again... "God, I hope you're gonna be all right..."

"All right?" thought Lori, "If I was ...anymore all right, I'd be in the spirit world. Maybe, ...maybe I'm there already. Oh, Julie, if only I could give you the wonderful feelings you just gave me... Thank you," she thought, as she felt Julie snuggle closer to get comfortable. "This would be a nice way to live. ...to live and to love. This is the best night of my life." ...and of that, ...she was sure. And as she re-lived the wondrous thing that had just happened to her, she thought., "I didn't even have to 'touch' myself ...to reach that...that 'peak'!" Lori was very much in awe of the power of Julie's presence, and especially, her kiss.

And as sleep was impossible for Julie, she was thinking... "This is the worst night of my life! What if Lori dies? People in deep comas die sometimes, don't they? The nurse doesn't seem to be overly concerned, but..." She reached up and touched Lori's cheek. "I'm so sorry, Lori. This never should've happened to you."

While Lori was thinking, "Maybe what I feel for Julie isn't so bad after all. And, she doesn't find me disgusting, like I thought she would. If this guilt could just leave me," ...but she knew it probably never would.

Awake

When Lori opened her eyes, it was morning, and Julie was asleep in a big chair.

After looking around, she realized she was in a hospital room. Her head hurt something fierce and she was thirsty. She tried to sit up and everything went blurry.

"Oh, ...wow," she said.

Julie opened her eyes and looked over at the bed. "Lori...?"

She jumped up and went to Lori's side.

"Can you help me to the bathroom?"

"No, you're not supposed to get up. I'll get the nurse..." and she was gone.

Later, after the nurse left, Julie came back in. "Lori? How do you feel?"

"My head is killing me, but the nurse gave me a pill. What happened? Why am I here?"

Julie came close and sat on the bed, as she had been doing, and reached out to touch her forehead. "Want some ice?"

"No thanks, but your hand is cool, and it feels good."

Continuing to softly 'smooth' her hand on Lori's forehead, and her hair, Julie told her the story, bit by bit. She finished with, "So here we are. And Jen is still 'knocked out'. Boy, ...I'd like to knock her out, all over again."

Lori had been looking at Julie's face, all during the story. She started chuckling when Julie said, 'knock her out', because she had gotten her scrunched up look, that meant she was feeling tough.

"Well, I *would*!" Julie said, ...first taking offense, ...and then smiling back.

"Thanks," said Lori, frowning at the pain in her head.

"For what? I didn't do anything."

"For being willing to fight my battle for me, ...that's special. And, for being here. That's even more special."

Julie didn't know what to say, so she just shrugged and looked down. Somehow though, she felt a new tenderness leaving through her fingertips to Lori's brow.

Lori closed her eyes and cherished the moment. Both girls were silent for a few minutes.

"Hi Julie," whispered Zee, tip toeing in. "Is she asleep?"

"No, she's not," Lori whispered back. "And, she wants to go back to camp."

Zee and Julie laughed, glad that the ordeal seemed nearly over.

Two days later, after lots of tests revealed no damage, a few phone calls from her dad and several people at camp, the doctor finally released her.

Lori never tried to see her, in the hospital, but Jen ended up having the most severe concussion. Her tests were inconclusive and she remained in a semi-coma. Her mom came and stayed with her and then took her home several days later.

Julie wished she could've been in on the conference that Zee had with the woman. She tried to picture Zee saying, "Your daughter is a menace to society. She does mean things to people and she's not welcome back at Camp Foxmore, ever."

"Well, anyway, that's what I would've said," she thought. She knew Zee was very tactful and undoubtedly got the message across without being so direct.

Skit Night

Most nights there was some type of group activity. If it was a 'sing-a-long' Lori would join in, even though she didn't sing well. The Falcons and the Hawks had done their last, 'fiasco' of a skit, over a week ago. Tonight, was the Herons and the Blue jays' turn to perform, and their skit was about a goofy new teacher trying to control her class.

Lori was there physically, but mentally she was far, far away. She'd only been back at camp since yesterday, and everyone was forcing her to 'take it easy'. Several of the new campers had chipped in and bought her a straw hat, with a wide brim. She had to admit, it helped a lot when she was standing in the hot sun, waist deep in water for a good part of the day.

Actually, she felt fine. She didn't even have any headaches as a reminder of her ordeal. What she did have, however, were memories of Julie, tenderly lying in bed with her in the hospital. *"I'll cherish that night, even more than back in the cave,"* she thought, *"because she was touching me. It was her idea."* She closed her eyes, and started remembering.

"Lori? Are you all right?" It was Zee, worrying about her.

"What? Oh. Yes, I'm fine. I was just... just... thinking."

"Would you like to 'turn in'?"

"No, thanks, Mrs. Z, honest."

"Well, okay. But if you need anything, just let me know, ...maybe I can get it for you... okay?"

Lori sighed, a big sigh, and nodded, saying "Thanks." But, she was thinking to herself, *"If only you could, ...I'd be eternally grateful..."*

Bareback

Finally, Zee was convinced she was 'just fine'. So, for two days, during free time after lunch, Lori had been allowed to practice riding bareback around the ring. She loved it, because she could really feel how Rocky's motions began and ended with each different gait. It was harder to stay mounted, but her legs were getting used to 'squeezing tight.'

As she came around the ring, she heard, "There you are! I've been wondering where you were. My mural is done! Want to come see it?" There was Julie, walking her 'light-footed' walk, towards her.

"Sure. But first, do you want to ride bareback for a few minutes to see how 'neat' it feels?"

"Oh, ...uh, ...well..."

"Come on over to the big rock. You can ride with me. He's strong enough to easily carry us both."

Julie hesitated for a minute. Lori nonchalantly guided Rocky to the rock and turned to look at her.

"Oh, ...okay... But, if I fall off..."

"I won't let you. Here, you can sit in front. Put your leg up, and give me your hand." Lori helped her get seated, and felt how stiff Julie sat. "Here, hold on, tight to his mane," said Lori. "Squeeze your knees up against his body, and you won't feel like you're going to fall off."

Rocky started walking slowly, and Julie hung on for dear life waiting for something bad to happen.

Meanwhile, Lori became intensely aware of Julie's closeness and of her own familiar, light, powdery, aroma. Her friend immediately started coming to life... but Lori paid it no attention. It was much more important to keep Julie safe.

Then, as she looked over Julie's shoulder, she became immersed in the clean smell of her shampoo. In order to hold the reins, and keep her from falling off, she wrapped both arms completely around Julie. *"...I've always wanted to hold her close, again,"* she thought, happily, *"...and my wish is coming true, right now."* Then she became even more acutely aware, inch by inch, that almost the entire length of their legs was touching. Her heart started beating faster at the intimacy, and she felt little ripples of pleasure. She tensed slightly.

"Are you okay?" asked Julie, worried that the horse was going to do something sudden.

"Yes. I'm fine," managed Lori, taking a deep breath. "Let's try to relax, so Rocky won't feel our nervousness." She guided Rocky around the ring, thinking, *"When we studied Pavlov's 'conditioned response' in Science, I didn't expect I'd*

229

ever be having one. This is getting ridiculous... All I have to do is get near Julie, and my body responds. I wonder if I'm 'over-sexed' or something."

Julie began to feel more and more like she was safe, because Lori was holding her securely. And gradually, she began to relax. Lori felt completely content, tight up against Julie. *"This is the closest I'll ever get to her again, in this lifetime. I'm actually hugging her, while she's 'awake'...and she's not pulling away..."* she thought, contentedly, not wanting it to end.

After a while, though, she was beginning to feel guilty about the pleasure she was enjoying, and thought Julie was probably getting bored.

"Want to try to canter?" she asked.

"Will I fall off?"

"No, hold tight." And Lori shortened her grip on the reins even more, and held Julie tightly to her.

After Lori coaxed Rocky into his 'rocking-horse' gait, Julie began to feel, and appreciate the amazingly comfortable rhythm. After cantering half way around the ring, she realized she wasn't going to slide off and she relaxed into the horse, and leaned back into Lori's arms, more and more.

After twice around the ring, she said, "This is super! Does he always canter like this?"

"Yes," said Lori. "I love it!

"Me too! I'm not even bouncing! My hips just 'roll' a little!" said Julie.

"Let them roll more, if you can. It means you're making it easier on him."

Lori tried to practice what she had just preached, and consciously rolled her hips with Rocky's rhythm. Both girls relaxed by degrees, into the horse, and seemed to ride more and more like one person.

As Lori felt her hips slowly undulating with Rocky and with Julie so close, her body responded more and more. *"Oh, Lord..."* she thought. Rocky easily kept the pace, without further urging from her, and she began to enter the 'lone zone', almost worry free. She got more and more 'trance-like' as pleasing sensations became the center of her thoughts.

Julie had faint stirrings of arousal but never having reached a climax, she thought it was because of the male animal she was so close to. Lori was quiet, and Julie just decided to enjoy the ride. After all, who could tell when Lori would just say it was over? Besides, she didn't think she could do this 'bareback thing' by herself. She felt very good, being held snugly in place, by Lori's arms and legs.

She hadn't realized it until now, but she felt Lori's breasts pressed up against her back. The rise and fall of the horse's gentle gait, caused Lori's breasts to rise and fall a little, against her body.

"It's a good thing she can't see my face," she thought. *"I know I'm blushing."*

She took a deep breath, and decided it felt pretty nice. She nestled back a little more against Lori, and sighed deeply.

At that exact moment, Lori's body finally began to convulse, and Julie felt Lori's arms and legs holding her tighter.

"Oh, I'm sorry." said Julie, tensing up, a little.

When Lori didn't respond, Julie asked, "Did I lean too hard on you?"

Lori was in her own world, and didn't hear all of what she said, but she murmured, "No, ...I'm fine..."

Julie relaxed again and Lori was able to gradually recover. After several minutes, Lori asked, "Are you ready to quit and show me your mural?"

"Not really, but I guess we ought to, huh?"

"Yeah, we probably should. I still have to brush him and all," said Lori.

"I'll help you."

"Great."

After they cooled him off, and were brushing him down, silence fell between them. Lori felt the old insecurity coming over her, just like that first day of camp. Her mind raced, trying to think of a subject that wouldn't bore her partner. Finally, she thought, *"Talk about boys."* So, she cleared her throat, and asked, "Do you miss your boyfriend?"

Julie was still feeling uncomfortably aroused. "I guess," she said. But she was distracted by Rocky's penis, beginning to relax and hang down.

Lori happened to look up, and saw where she was looking. When she checked, she was not surprised at its length. She had gotten used to it from being around him. But Julie was clearly hypnotized by its ever increasing size. Lori pretended not to notice Julie's fascination and just kept her eyes straight ahead, and continued brushing Rocky's back. After some minutes, his organ was hanging down as long as she had ever seen it.

She and Beth had often talked about it, and so she finally said, "Look at that. Do you believe how long his penis is?"

Julie looked over at her to see Lori, too, curiously gazing down, under Rocky.

"I've never seen anything so huge," added Lori, not meeting Julie's eyes.

"Me, neither!" said Julie, clearly in awe. "Joann and I saw him do that a little bit, before. We used to joke about it, ...but I didn't know it could get so long. Kind of makes me feel strange, like, ...I don't know, ...like interested in sex, and all."

"Yeah, I know what you mean," said Lori, still very much aware of her own, sensitive areas.

"Did you ever wonder about boys' penises? I mean, the size, and everything?" asked Julie.

"Oh, definitely," said Lori. "I'm going to take Sex Ed. this year."

"Really? Do you get to see pictures of nude boys?" asked Julie.

"I don't know, but I plan to look at every book I can find. Sex is interesting."

"Maybe I'll take it too, if my parents will let me," said Julie, looking back up at Lori. "And then we could share anything we find out."

As she and Julie started walking back to the cabin, Lori was thinking, "I know she felt all 'melted' inside, too. But it was all about Rocky, ...not me." The old silence fell between them once more, and Lori thought, *"Oh well, at least we talked for a few minutes, even if it was about horses and boys."*

Julie was wondering if it would again take all night, for this troublesome feeling to go away. At least it should be gone by morning, like last time. But, she remembered how long she tossed and turned before she could finally get to sleep. She wondered if Lori had the same tingling, but she was too embarrassed to ask, just now.

As they got close to the cabin, some campers started talking to them. Both girls were glad for the interruption in the subtle, mounting pressure between them, as to who was going to speak first.

'Flipped'

"Don't be afraid," said Lori, earnestly. "I promise you that if you keep breathing out slowly, like you usually do, and you do it the whole time, no water will go in."

"But I've never done a back flip," said Julie.

"Just look way back, reach back with both arms and pull yourself around and down toward the bottom. If you keep arching your back and pulling hard with your arms, you'll come up pretty quick."

"Are you tricking me?" asked Julie, putting a hand on her hip.

"No, watch, I'll do it again." Lori looked back at the sky, arched her back, reached back with both arms, gave a little jump, and rolled underwater into a back flip. She pulled hard with both arms, and almost immediately she was coming up, right where she used to be standing.

"Well, ...what do you expect! You're ...part dolphin!"

"Come on, Julie, just do one of those 'ballet-style backbends, pull hard, remember to swim and breathe out your nose, ...and you'll do it."

Julie just looked at her. Lori could be exasperatingly, patiently stubborn. "The things I do for you, Lori Hunter..." she said, arching her back easily until her hair was in the water. "Now what?"

Lori just looked at her, thinking, "She looks like an ice skater doing a back bend and spinning in place." "Okay, now take a deep breath, and reach back. Good! Now give a little jump backwards and pull hard."

Julie took a deep breath, but she didn't 'go'.

Lori watched her chest go up and down as Julie took a few more deeper breaths. Lori just rolled her eyes and slowly shook her head at herself. "Ready, Set, Go!" she urged.

Julie gave a little jump, pulled hard and turned underwater. She came up looking through all the water running down her forehead. "I did it!" she smiled. "Did you see that? I did it!"

"Yes, you did, and you made it look so easy," smiled Lori. "Can you do it again? We could both go together, like synchronized swimming."

Julie liked that, and she tried it again, ...this time, with Lori. "Oh-h. I forgot to breathe out, that time! My nose hurts."

After she recovered, Lori asked, "Can you 'cup' your hands, like this?"

When Julie did, she came close, tentatively put her hands on Julie's slim shoulders and asked, "Can you give me a boost?"

Julie gave a big grunt, and lifted her hands a little.

233

Lori did a back flip a little bit high in the air. She came up, laughing. "That was great!" "Want me to 'do' you?"

"Do me? No way! I remember when you 'did' me," Julie continued, with one eyebrow raised high, and her forefinger pointing accusingly. "There I was, trying to swim past you, and you picked me up on your shoulders for the whole world to see! I *still* owe you for that one, Lori Hunter."

"Ah... you 'ballerinas' are all 'bluster'. You're probably *afraid* to do a high back flip, Julie Conners, ...Julie *Marie* Conners," said Lori, with a little smirk and a twinkle in her eyes...

"Oh yeah?" said Julie, putting both hands on her hips. "Well, just 'cup' your hands and I'll show you a flip. You think you did a flip. It was more like a *flip flop*."

Not responding to the barb, Lori intertwined her fingers. Julie approached her, and put both hands on her shoulders. Lori loved the feel of her. "Okay," she said. "Let's see this magnificent back flip by the great Julie Conners. Ready? One! Two! Three!"

Just as Julie pushed hard with her right foot, Lori let her fingers come apart. Julie went nowhere but down.

"Oh-h, Lori! Darn you! And I fell for it!" She gave a big shove, and pushed Lori backwards.

"No, c'mon. I'll do it right," said Lori, laughing. "I promise."

"You'd better."

When Julie pushed hard this time on the count of three, Lori really gave her a high boost. Julie went about three feet up into the air, arched beautifully, and flipped neatly down into the water.

"Wow!" she said, coming up. "That *was* great! Do me again!" she said smiling at Lori.

Lori put her hands together, thinking, *"I'll do you, ...till I die. And, isn't it great?"* she asked herself, happily as goose bumps shivered down her back, *"I've gotten so many of those brilliant smiles that I've lost count."*

Walli watched them playing. "Lori's a good teacher." she thought. "She's still teaching, even after her duty time is up. She and Julie make a good twosome. They don't have as much time together as regular buddies have, but when they do get together, they sure seem to enjoy it."

Uncle John

Zee answered the phone, "Camp Foxmore."

"Hello. This is John Hunter, Lori Hunter's uncle. Can I speak to her?"

"She won't be near the phone, until noon. Is this an emergency?"

"No. I'll call back just after noon. Thanks. Bye."

When Lori came into the mess hall, for lunch, Zee called her over.

"Lori, your uncle John called earlier."

Lori frowned.

"It's probably one of the boys from the dance," Zee said, smiling. He's not the first to call and tonight I'll probably get lots more 'uncles and cousins' calling." Talking mostly to her self, she added, "I'll have to call Jeff and tell him it's okay for them to give their real names."

Lori didn't know what to say.

"He's going to call back soon. Do you want to talk to him?"

"I don't know which one he is for sure, but, Yes, may I?"

"Yes. I'll call you."

Three other girls got phone calls during lunch. The mess hall was in a dither.

Then Lori got called to the phone. On the way across the room she was thinking, *"They probably drew straws, to see who could call, in what order, using the counselor's phone."*

"Hello?" she said.

"Lori? It's Greg.

"Hi."

"I heard about you being promoted. Good for you!"

"Thanks."

"Sorry I couldn't call sooner... The counselors weren't going to let us, until we all signed a petition."

Lori chuckled and said, "I thought you guys might dream up a scheme."

He paused and then asked, "Can I see you soon? Real soon?"

"I don't think so."

"Please, just for a few minutes?

"I don't know how."

"Can you sneak out at night?"

Lori pictured that. "No," she said.

"I have a car. At least I can borrow one. Can we meet?"
Lori didn't answer.
"Don't you want to see me?"

Lori knew she had to see if she liked him at all, or if, ...she was, ...if Julie was...
"Yes," she finally said.
"Where?"
"Can you drive to our parking area on Sunday and be a 'visitor'?"

"Would they let me?"
"I don't know. Will your camp let you leave?"
"I'll find out," he said.
"Me, too."

"I'll call you back around dinner time, okay?"
"Okay, ...bye," she said. Then she went and found Zee. "Mrs. Zee," she said, "that was Greg."

Zee nodded, remembering him well.
"He'd like to come see me. Is there any way he can visit on Sunday?"

Zee was dumbfounded. "His idea?"
"Well, his idea to meet, ...my idea to meet here."

Zee admired her simple, direct honesty. Most girls would be planning a 'sneak'.
"Meet here? Where?"
"...Maybe in the parking lot?"
"Do any of your friends know?"
"No, just you and I."

Zee thought for a minute and said, "Then, how about if you ask Bigfoot to sit in her car for fifteen or twenty minutes, and chaperone you from a distance. And tell Greg to come here an hour before regular visiting hours."
"Thanks, Mrs. Zee."
"See you later, Lori," smiled the wise administrator.

Lori went back to the table to hear 'tons' of questions being asked of her. She forced herself to look up at their faces and smile a little. These girls were getting to be her good friends and she couldn't just shut them out.
"Was it Winston?"

"Was it Greg?"
"Are you going to sneak out to meet him?"
"What did he say?"

She decided to answer as best she could.
"No."
"Yes."
"No."
"Not much."
She kept up almost as fast as they asked, acting very nonchalant, and they got bored with her pretty quickly. When the next girl came back from the phone, they closed in on her and forgot about Lori.
"That was easy enough," she thought.

Through it all, Julie just looked at her, and figured she'd talk to Lori, later. She knew better than to ask her right now. Lori Hunter was the most private person she'd ever met.
She sighed, thinking, *"We've been 'buddies' for almost a week, and we don't 'talk' together, like Joann and I used to do. Of course,"* she admitted, *"Joann liked to gossip and jabber about herself a lot. Lori doesn't do either one. Also, Joann was forever getting excited about 'what might happen, in the future'. Lori doesn't do that, either. Lori's just, ...just, ...she does so much more, instead of talking about it."*
"Well, I'll have to figure out something she likes to talk about. I've never even found out all the things that went on with Lu and Jen, and Beth and her.

"Julie! Telephone!" said Mrs. Z.
Lori thought to herself, *"It's Uncle Mickey time."*

Free time

Julie sat on the beach and waited for Lori to finish her last swim class. When Lori finally came and sat down beside her, Julie said, "I need to talk to you."

"What about?"

"Us."

"Us?" repeated Lori, thinking *"Oh Lord, ...maybe I talked in my sleep."*

"Yes," said Julie. "Are we real buddies or buddies in 'name' only?"

Lori was thoroughly confused and said, "How do you mean?"

"Well, we never talk much. Joann and I used to talk all the time, and I miss it."

"Oh... uh... what do you want to talk about?"

"Lots of things! Greg and Mickey! All that stuff that happened with Jen and Lu when we were tracking that day. Even school!" And then, indignantly, Julie added, "You don't even know that I've been asked to be a C.I.T. for Arts and Crafts next summer!"

Lori smiled and said "Really? Congratulations! You really deserve it! That means we'll both be back next year!" She couldn't stop smiling. "Did you call your parents yet?"

"No, they already know. I wanted to come tell you, first," she admitted.

"Thanks," said Lori, "and any time you want to know anything, just ask..."

"Okay, what happened that day? Why did they attack Beth?"

Lori took a deep breath and explained, "Well, they ...uh, that is, Jen wanted to be my...uh... 'buddy'... and she and Lu tried to make Beth want to quit camp and go home."

"I don't understand," said Julie. "Lu was Jen's buddy. Why would Lu help her become your buddy. Didn't they get along?"

"No, they didn't," said Lori. "Not really. That's why Lu went home early."

"Oh," said Julie. "I see." But she didn't. "When Lu left, did it have anything to do with me asking Jen to meet you at the row boats?"

"Yes," said Lori, worried at how far this questioning would go.

"Did Jen ask you to be her buddy that night?"

"Yes."

"What did you tell her?"

"I told her I couldn't, and that I'd already been asked by you."

"Oh," said Julie, feeling glad that Lori had agreed to be her partner. "So Lu went home, ...and Jen tackled you because she was mad at you, right?"

"Right," said Lori as she stood up and tagged Julie on the shoulder. "You're it!" ...and she headed into the water.

Julie didn't respond immediately because she wanted to ask Lori about a thousand more questions. "Darn!" she said. "That girl is always ready for..." and she chuckled out loud, "a good time!" She jumped up and followed her into the water. "Listen, Lori Hunter, we're not playing tag. You need to work on your, ...on that thing you call a handstand. So, 'Miss Teacher' ...let's see your best form!"

Lori didn't care what they played, so under the water she went.

"Point your toes!" shouted Julie, as she tried to force Lori's toes to point more toward the sky.

When Lori came up, from standing on her hands underwater, she wiped water from her eyes and asked, "What?"

"Point your toes, more."

"I was."

"You have to point them *more!*"

"Oh, like you 'fru fru' ballerinas? ...who point your toes, so hard, that they can say 'hello' to your heels?"

"You'll pay for that!" said Julie, starting to wade after her, with her 'scrunchy' look.

"Not likely..." laughed Lori. "You 'ballerinas' can't swim fast...or even *wade* very fast... You look like you're always dragging your 'tu tu's.'"

Julie took a big dive at her, but Lori stayed just out of reach. Then, Julie stopped, and said, "Okay! I give up, ...for now. Let's race, walking on our hands!"

"Okay."

"You can only use one hand!"

"What?" said Lori. "No way!"

"C'mon, 'Hoppy'... give it your best shot, ...cause the 'one and only' Julie Conners, is going to leave you, way, way behind!" And she dove under, thinking contentedly, *"She kids with me now, like she does with Rory."*

And as Lori 'hopped' along, trying to keep her balance, she thought to herself, *"I love acting 'nutty' with her!"*

With Greg

"Hi, Lori," said Greg, leaning across the seat and opening the car door for her.

"Hi," she said.

"It's good to see you."

"You, too."

"I've been thinking about you, a lot, Lori, like every day. It's hard to concentrate on things."

She knew exactly what he meant, because it had been happening to her too, a lot, lately. She smiled and said, "Yeah, I read somewhere that adolescent males think about girls, a almost all the time."

"We do," he admitted.

"Don't worry. They say you'll grow out of it."

"Lori, look at me, please."

She met his gaze, and saw pretty, dark blue eyes, with long, black lashes. *"Too long for a guy,"* she thought. He had lazy, sleepy-looking eyes... *'bedroom eyes'* she remembered from a romantic novel she'd read.

"I like you a lot," he said.

"You don't really know me."

"Yes, I do. You're fun. You're capable. You're smart and carefree. And you're not silly, like those other girls."

"Really?" she said, feeling almost like she was going to laugh. She was wondering how many young girls had heard this same 'line' from him.

"Yes, really. And, you act much more mature."

"And how can you tell that?"

"By your kiss."

Lori didn't say anything. Then, she said, "I suppose you'd know. You're 'experienced', right?"

"I guess."

"Well, I'm not."

"Will you be 'my' girl?"

"Why?"

"Because, I like you a lot. I'd say 'love', but I don't use that word lightly."

"How many girls have you said it to?"

"None."

"None?" You can get all those girls to have sex, without saying 'love'?"
"What do you mean, all those..."...he paused, and then admitted, "Yes."

"I don't think I could do that at all."
"What?"
"Have sex with you, with or without the 'love' commitment."

"Lori, please don't talk about having sex with me."
She laughed. "Why?"
"Look what you do to me," he said, glancing down.

She looked down and saw that his jeans really bulged. She immediately thought of Beth and Ronnie, and petting. "But...I didn't touch you."
"You don't have to. Just being near you makes me so 'hot.' I've been like this all morning, just thinking about you."
Lori didn't know what to say. *"Could it be true? Could he feel about her the way she felt about Julie?"* She looked into his eyes, searching for some truth.

"And if I think about your lips, ...I begin ...to throb... And if I think about your tongue, I just...Oh, God!" He grabbed for a paper napkin, somewhere under the armrest, and reached down in his jeans with it. He closed his eyes and made a face like he was in pain, and held himself as he climaxed.
Lori felt like bolting! Automatically her right hand went to the door handle. She didn't know what to do, so she just stared at the floor while he sat there, momentarily frozen in an almost fetal position.
She did know how powerful the mind and emotions were, because she vividly remembered how she'd throbbed, and needed release before, and couldn't stop it from happening! Especially the time Julie climbed in her bunk and was lying so close to her!
But, she didn't think he really loved her. And, she began to wonder, how many girls had seen him do this 'stunt'? She was glad that Bigfoot was just across the parking lot. *"To her, it probably just looks like we're talking,"* she thought, still looking down.

After he recovered, he left the paper napkin in his jeans and sat up straighter.

"Was that supposed to impress me?" she asked, softly.
"No...no, I'm sorry...did it?"
"No. It scares me."
"Don't be afraid of me, ever...not ever."
"You could...hurt me with that."

Donna Kelli

"I suppose I could, ...but I never would. I'm not into 'force'. I'd hoped you'd know that by now."

Lori sighed. She was curious about him, but she still wanted to run and glanced to her right, out the window.

"Don't leave. *Please,* don't go. I *need* to talk to you."

"About what?"

"I can't come to the last dance. We're moving and I can't stay. I'm leaving camp. I have to help my dad close down our store."

All of a sudden Lori had mixed emotions. She had thought she might at least get to dance with him once more. Now, she might not ever see him again.

"Where are you moving to?"

"To Lennox, about a half hour from where you live."

Lori was silent. She hadn't told him she lived in Grove City. Winston had asked her while they were dancing, so she knew how he'd found out.

"Lori, will you give me your phone number? Can I call you?"

Now she really had mixed emotions. "Did she want to see him?"

Lori considered it some more, and he waited, silently. She finally asked, "Are you into sports?"

"Why?" he asked. It wasn't at all what he expected to hear.

"Are you?"

"Yes."

"Which ones?"

"Basketball and Track."

"Okay," she said. "Call me and I'll come watch you play."

"You will?" he said, smiling. "What's your number?"

After she gave it to him, he said, "I'll call." Then he looked down, and said, "Sorry about this. I just, ...couldn't ...couldn't..."

"...help it?" she finished for him, thinking of how she barely got Julie out of her bunk in time...

"Yes," he said, with a pained look. "Lori, I won't try to hold you, or even touch you, but will you kiss me, 'good-bye'? I'm leaving camp in two days."

Lori hesitated... and then, as he leaned toward her, she did want to feel his lips again. She met him half way, and their lips touched, very softly.

"He really does have a nice kiss," she thought.

He kissed her a little harder, and she felt herself responding.

She leaned away finally, and said, "I'd better go."

"Will you be my girl?"

"I don't even know what that means," she said, opening the door.
"I'll call you. You won't be sorry."
"Bye," she said, looking at him, possibly for the last time ever.
"...only until later." he said. Then he smiled and started the engine.

She walked away thinking, *"I still feel the same way about him. He's intense. He definitely has an excellent kiss, and now at least I'll be able to remember his face."*

Bigfoot was standing, by her car. "Well, how did it go?"
"Okay," said Lori. "He's leaving camp soon and can't come to the last dance.

Thanks a lot, for being here for me. I really appreciate it."
"No big deal," said the counselor, as they walked toward the mess hall.
Lori was wondering, *"Could she be right?"*

Gunneling

Walli took all the girls from cabins three and four who had passed their swim tests, and had them sit in shallow water. Bigfoot sat on the beach with the new girls who hadn't passed yet.

Walli stood in knee-deep water. She climbed into a canoe without saying a word. Then she indicated a 'sh-h' sound, and put her forefinger up to her lips to shush them up. This lesson would be taught silently.

She paddled out a few feet and turned the canoe so that the bow was pointing 'down wind' along the shoreline. Then she put her paddle in the bottom of the canoe. She carefully stood up on the rear seat. Then she turned and with her back to the wind, faced front toward the bow. She balanced herself by putting her arms out to each side.

The canoe drifted a little, but when it was basically, very still in the water, she began. She bent her knees and bounced her weight downward. Her arms, up and out to her sides, bounced slightly with her. Her downward motion caused the rear part of the canoe to go down in the water a little. Then it quickly bounced back up. At the same time, the bow came out of the water a little and then slapped back down with a loud sound.

She repeated the motion over and over, keeping her balance. To everyone's surprise, as she bounced the canoe repeatedly, it started moving forward. It veered off to the left a little, in the front, because of the wind, but it was definitely going forward.

Still without a word, she got down, paddled closer and got set again. This time she stepped up on the seat and then very carefully climbed up higher on the small, triangular 'gunnel' area of the back tip of the canoe.

The stern of the canoe was deeper down in the water now and the bow was sticking up out of the water. The wind could easily push it around now. While precariously perched there, Walli waited patiently until the canoe was heading down wind.

When the canoe was calm, she began to 'gunnel' it, with tiny little bounces. She had a very hard time keeping her balance, but occasionally she would get going pretty good. Finally, she lost her balance and fell in the lake making only a small splash.

Everybody clapped and cheered loudly. And, everybody was ready to try it without any further instruction. The only thing Walli said was, "Buddies. Four to a canoe. Take turns."

Foursomes got the canoes in the water and the scene got wild and comical immediately. Even though each girl had been trained to walk down the center seam, some forgot to keep their balance and were falling out of their canoes before they even got to the back seat.

Everywhere in the near vicinity the onlookers on the beach immediately heard, "My turn!" Crash! Splash!

"Now it's my turn!"

Lori and Julie teamed up with Ceil and Vivian because they were almost always 'nutty'. Ceil went first. She got one foot up on the back seat and then over the side she went. The very *big* girl made a great *big* splash for the appreciative audience.

Next, Vivian, who was even larger, did everything slowly and carefully. She finally managed to get up on the back seat, but she was facing the wrong way. And there she stood, balancing herself and trying to decide what to do next.

Julie was already doubling over in laughter.

Lori had tears running down her cheeks. "I *have* to get a camera!" she said.

Then, in between chuckles, Lori shouted, "Yea Viv! You can do it!"

Vivian looked over her shoulder and figured she couldn't turn her feet around. So, she put her arms out wider for balance and decided she'd do the bouncing thing...she'd just do it going backwards.

Everyone in the water, in the other canoes, and on the shore stopped what they were doing to watch her because the canoe looked like it was already in big trouble. It was almost sinking in the rear and the bow was pointing nearly straight up. Some people had their mouths open in wonder.

Vivian finally did a big bounce downward and water poured right in on her feet. Her eyes and her mouth opened wide in genuine surprise. She looked down and her ankles were already underwater. The canoe was a 'goner'. The bow pointed to the sky as the biggest girl in the entire camp toppled into the water with a huge 'belly wop' splash. The canoe shot forward and broad sided Rory's canoe, tipping her off balance and into the water. And Viv's 'tidal wave splash' tilted Nancy's canoe and flipped her out, too.

Everybody was laughing and clapping and cheering Vivian's antics. When she came up from the deep, she ignored all the applause. She looked at Walli, and with a perfectly straight face, said, "This canoe leaks something fierce! Do you have a better one?" Somehow she was always entertaining!

"Yea Viv!" shouted Lori. "You did it! You wiped out all your competition!" And then she kidded Rory with, "Whatsamatta, Rory? Can't take a little bump?"

Rory started pushing her canoe back to shore, smiled and yelled back, "It ain't over 'til it's over, Hunter!"

Julie was next. Lori helped her tip all the water out. Julie paddled out, put the paddle in the canoe, and stepped up on the back seat. She started bouncing the canoe, little by little. She went along for awhile and then coasted.

Lori watched her ballet-type grace and balance, thinking, *"She's a natural for this event."*

Julie mounted higher up behind the seat onto the gunnel, and started again. Her elf-like figure seemed to belong there. She propelled the canoe along effortlessly, at a very fast pace. She looked like she was just playing and having fun. In fact, she was, and having a great time.

Lots of people noticed and cheered for her. She coasted to a stop and did a little 'ballet curtsey' from her perch. Then she stepped down on the seat and motioned to Lori that it was 'all hers'. She sat down on the seat and paddled and steered back toward shore.

Lori got in and paddled the canoe away from shore and away from everybody else. She got positioned up on the back seat and tried it out. Once she got the hang of it, she coasted to a stop and mounted the gunnel. Being heavier than Julie, it was a little harder to keep her balance, but slowly she got the canoe moving.

Then she got into a rhythm and she really got it going. She felt like she could bounce the canoe all the way out to the little dock. Instead, she stopped and paddled back so Ceil could have her next turn.

Rory wanted to race her, and said, "Hey Lori. First let me get my sea legs, and then I challenge you."

Walli heard the challenge and said, "Races start in thirty minutes. Practice 'til then. The top two in each race get to go again until we have an overall winner."

The races were wild and crazy. When Rory raced Lori, they tied for first place. Rory said, "I'll get you yet!"

Lori said, "Nah, your feet are too funny to do this trick for very long."

For once, Rory couldn't think of a smart-alecky comment to fire back at her.

Julie listened to their constant teasing of each other. She didn't like being left out today, but she didn't know how to be a part of it right now. So she just concentrated on watching other people's mistakes.

The races went on for a long time. At last, in the final heat, the contestants were Sue, Meg, Julie, Rory and Lori. They all started out well, and the canoes were slapping along to loud shouts, hoots, and hollers.

Sue lost her balance and fell in. Her splash caused Meg's canoe to veer sideways, careening a bit into Rory. Meg kept her balance. Rory survived the little bump, too and stayed ahead of Meg.

Rory's canoe had gotten a little off course and so she 'accidentally on purpose' bumped hard into Lori. Lori stopped 'bouncing' for a minute and rode out the attack. Meanwhile, Julie surged ahead. When Rory finally had to step down on the back seat to keep from falling in, Lori started bouncing again. Frustrated, Rory really worked hard and stayed even with Lori. They were bow to bow, and both were giving it everything they had.

Julie stayed way out in front, and won the race easily. She acknowledged the cheers with a wave of her hand, and sat down on the back seat. She turned around to watch the fierce competition going on behind her, for second place.

Lori's face was very intent but happy. *"She's really happy when she's going all out!"* thought Julie. *"Just look at that face!"* Lori was smiling and kidding with Rory, yet her whole body was in to it.

Rory was doing her best also, and she pulled ahead of Lori a few inches at the finish line. She'd won second place!

Julie still watched Lori, surprised that Lori's face stayed happy. Julie was even more surprised as Lori said, "Great race, Rory! You really had the rhythm going!"

"Well, she's definitely not a sore loser!" Julie decided. *"And she's not making up any excuses, either."*

As she was deep in her own thoughts, two of the new campers waded by her and said, "Isn't Rory the greatest?"

"Yeah," said the other one, "but Lori had her beat until Rory deliberately bumped her. She could beat Rory in any really 'fair' race!"

Julie chuckled to herself and thought, *"I don't doubt that!"* Then she added, *"Any day, any time!"* Somewhere she heard her name being called to come and accept her blue ribbon for first place.

Basketball Buddy

Julie planned to read after lunch during her free time. But before she could get out the door to go sit under a tree, Rory asked, "Seen Lori?"

"Yes. She left with a basketball under her arm." said Julie.

"Come on, Julie, come with me. Meg and I want to play, and if you'll play with Lori, we'll have two against two."

"Oh, I don't like basketball," she said, remembering Lori being tackled by Jen.

"Please? It's only a half-court game."

Julie sighed, and said, "Well, okay." She had been working on another project in Arts and Crafts and hadn't really done anything energetic yet, today. "But do you promise you won't tackle me?"

Rory laughed, and held up two fingers. "Scout's honor," she promised.

When they got to the court, Lori was surprised to see her, and smiled. Julie was surprised that Lori would even want her to play, so she felt a little better. Lori took her aside, and said, "Try to always watch me when I have the ball, because I plan to toss it to you a lot. Don't be fooled if I don't look at you, okay? Just always be ready!"

"All right," said Julie.

"And when I get it to you, try not to take the time to bounce the ball. Just turn and shoot. Don't worry if you miss. Just keep shooting, okay?"

Julie nodded, but couldn't picture herself making even one basket, the way Lori and Rory played. They bounced the ball all over the court and jumped so high and all, that she figured she'd just be there taking up space.

The first surprise she got was when Lori came dribbling the ball right by her, on her way to the basket. Julie felt the ball put up against her stomach, and reflexively grabbed it before it fell to the ground. "What do I do?" she thought. Nobody was guarding her because both Rory and Meg had committed to guarding Lori.

She hesitated, looking after Lori.

"Shoot!" she heard from Lori.

Julie was close enough, so she looked at the basket and shot. It missed. Lori jumped really high, and tapped it in.

"Boy, that was fast," thought Julie.

A few minutes later, Lori did the same thing, and Julie found herself holding the ball again. She turned and shot. The ball rolled around and around the rim, but it finally went in.

Lori watched her, waiting to see if she'd smile. Julie's face was a stunned mute look of amazement, silently saying, "It went in. I don't believe it!" And, finally, she smiled, shaking her head.

"Good shot Julie," said Lori.

Rory and Meg made several baskets, because they had only Lori guarding them. To get around her, they just kept passing it to each other.

Julie felt she should be doing more, but she didn't really want to bump anybody, and she didn't want to get bumped either. Lori seemed to be able to slip between people and never touch them. *"She's like a ghost,"* decided Julie, as she tried to keep her eyes on her, and watch the others, too.

Speaking of the ghost, Lori leaped high in the air, and intercepted a pass from Meg to Rory. Before she came down, she lightly tossed it to Julie.

Julie didn't have to be told, ...she turned a little, and shot. As the ball went 'swish', in the net, she said, "I made it!" as she was jumping up and down. *"This could be fun,"* she thought.

The next pass almost hit her in the chest, because Lori looked like she was setting up to shoot. Looking up, and seemingly concentrating on the basket rim, Lori then 'shot' a pass to Julie without so much as a glance in her direction. Julie almost caught it, but it fell out of her hands and bounced once. She grabbed it and shot. Again, it went 'in'. When she looked at Lori in disbelief, Lori was smiling at her and saying, "Good shot, Julie," as if it were usual.

"She's tricky. I'll have to be really ready all the time."

She didn't have to wait long. Lori came bouncing the ball casually toward the basket, with Meg guarding her. As Lori dribbled the ball faster, feinted around Meg, and was 'going in for a lay up shot', she bounced the ball to Julie, but kept right on running. She even jumped up as if she still had the ball, and Meg jumped right with her.

Julie was surprised when the ball hit her in the stomach, but she managed to catch it. "Darn," she said, mad at herself for not expecting something. She turned and shot it, and missed. "Darn," she said, again. Then the ball came right back to her because Lori got the rebound, and tipped it back to her. She had to catch the ball right in front of her nose. "Darn, darn, darn!" she said, and she shot again. She missed, again.

"Well, damn!" she said, and before she knew it, the ball was tipped back to her, once more. Lori watched as Julie made her funny little scrunched up face, and Lori knew that meant she was concentrating.

Julie shot once more. It hit the backboard just right and went in. "There!" she said. "Finally!"

Watching Lori became a habit, and as the game went on, she was ready for every pass that came her way. She was not expecting it, though, when Meg got in front of her, just in time, and blocked her next shot. Julie wondered if she should've passed that ball back to Lori. *"Next time, I'll just do that and see if she's paying attention,"* she thought.

She was surprised to learn that they were out of time. Meg came up to her, and said, "I didn't know you knew how to play so good, Julie. You did great! And, that was fun!"

"I did?"

"Yes, you most certainly did," said Lori, coming up behind her, and smiling. "Thanks for playing."

As they walked back to the cabin, Rory, Meg, and Lori were 'ragging' on each other, about how bad they looked, or how pitiful a certain jump shot was. Julie was thinking back to the game. *"Lori did all the running around, and jumping, and stuff, ...and I didn't even sweat, hardly. But she didn't yell at me to do more. Somehow, it wasn't rough, like I thought. And, I have to admit, it was fun. I wonder what Mom would think, if she'd seen me doing that. Or even worse yet, what would she think of me playing football? Hmm...maybe I won't tell her about some of my activities here."*

'Just 'Do It'

Lori was, 'as seemed usual' these days, often very deep in her own thoughts. *"There's just not much time really alone,"* she thought. *"I can hardly ever, just 'be' with Julie." Most of my time is taken up at the waterfront. And then, if Julie comes down after class, we only get to play around for a little while. Those times are the very best part of my life here at camp."* Then, she began to think about the row boats, ...and the lake.

"I wonder if she'd go?" she thought. *"I wonder if I have the courage to ask her?"*

She helped Walli for several hours, and then went up and joined in the Arts and Crafts class. After about a half hour, Julie held up a drawing she'd made of some flowers, and said, "What do you think?"

"Very colorful, and nice to look at," said Lori. And she came back with, "How do you like this very fine art?" knowing, full well, that she was one of the worst 'artists' in this class. It was a drawing she'd just sketched of the lake, and the beautiful maple and oak trees surrounding it.

Julie looked at it with an appreciative eye and then said, graciously, "It's pretty."

"Well, I know it's pretty awful. But anyway, the real lake *is* pretty," said Lori. "And, it's *very special* at night."

"It is?"

"Yes. It's quiet, and it's dark. The lights from the paths don't get in your eyes, so on a clear night, you can see a 'zillion' stars."

"You've been there at night?"

"Well, only from the shore, ...with Beth, during a few campfires." After a pause, she continued... "I'd like to go again, ...but out *on* the lake. I'd *love* to take out a rowboat, and just drift around." Her heart was pounding. It was 'now or never'!

She opened her mouth to speak, and her tight throat made a funny sound. Clearing her throat, she said, in a low whisper, "Let's do it... Let's sneak out tonight, and ...just do it!"

"Oh...I don't *think* so!" said Julie, in a muted voice. "What if we got caught?"

"It would be *worth* it," whispered Lori, and she meant it. "And besides, there are only a few days left. What can they do? ...*expel* us? I don't think so. And besides, we *won't* get caught. We'll just go for a little while."

251

"I don't know," said Julie, slowly shaking her head 'no'. But she got a little 'sparkle' to her eyes, and said, "I guess it *could* be fun."

Lori just looked at her for a minute, and then said, "We could leave about an hour after lights out, if everyone is asleep."

"How will you know?"

"I'll go around and check bunks," she said, with more bravado than she felt. She actually dreaded the thought, of bending down by someone's head, to 'check her breathing' and having her demand, "Lori Hunter! What are you doing?"

"Check bunks? Oh... well. ...uh... I'll think about it and let you know later tonight if I'm brave enough to go."

Nodding her head, Lori was afraid to show any sign of elation but she was thinking, "At least she didn't say a definite "No!"

That Night

That night, as Julie and Lori were brushing their teeth, Julie suddenly whispered, "Okay, ...I think I'm brave enough." Then she left quickly and went to her bunk.

After lights out, Lori got into her bunk as 'wide awake' as she'd ever been. She had criss-crossing thoughts about the whole plan. *"Oh well, I'll just play it by ear. Hopefully, Julie won't change her mind."*

The minutes ticked by. She checked her watch for the umpteenth time. *"Time is passing so slowly!"* she agonized. After another half hour passed, she finally got up and headed toward the bathroom. On the way, she listened for anyone who might speak to her, hoping against hope that no one would.

She actually 'went to the bathroom' while she was there. *"I needed that,"* she thought. And then she made the trip back, slowly, listening beside each bunk for the sound of deep breathing.

Finally, she sat down on the side of her bunk that faced Julie's. Then, instead of getting under her blanket, she leaned forward on one knee and bent over Julie's pillow. "Are you awake?" she whispered.

"Yes. Is anyone else awake?"

"No, everyone's sleeping. How about if you go in the bathroom, and then, if you don't hear anyone moving around, ... just go out the door, ...and wait in the shadow of the first oak tree. I'll be right behind you."

"Okay..." said Julie, and she got up and went to the restroom.

Lori waited for another 'eternity' until finally, she saw Julie's quiet form move out through the door. She grabbed Julie's blanket, and her own, ...tucked them under her arm, and said, under her breath, "Here goes nothing." With her heart in her throat, she followed Julie outside.

They hid in the shadows for several minutes. Then, surprising herself, Lori took Julie's hand. Without a word, she led her from the shadow of one tree to the shadow of the next. Again, they watched and waited. Getting to be 'self conscious,' Lori turned loose of her hand and whispered, softly, "C'mon, let's head to the next tree."

"It's *far*..."

"Just walk fast. We'll be okay."

Finally, they reached the boats. Lori went to the one in the shadows. "Help me with the boat," she said, tossing the blankets in the bow. They lifted and dragged, until it was in shallow water. As they walked the boat out a little deeper, Lori saw that Julie, up by the bow, was about to get her shorty pajamas wet.

"Get in, and sit in the stern," said Lori. "I'll push us off. Just leave room for me to pass by, as I climb in." Julie climbed in quietly, and sat very still.

"Here, catch this blanket and wrap it around you."

"Thanks," whispered Julie. "I didn't realize how chilly it would be."

Lori pushed off smoothly and firmly, and quietly hopped in the stern beside Julie. And in her agile way, she moved to the center of the boat, turned around and sat down.

"She hardly made the boat tip," thought Julie. *"It's that 'cat' thing."*

The boat coasted pretty far before Lori picked up an oar. She knew that sound carried very far over water. As she placed the second oar in its oar-lock, she whispered, "I hope I can row quietly." Carefully, she turned the boat a little and headed out toward the middle of the lake.

Julie continued to sit pretty still, but was looking all around over her shoulder, back at the lighted pathways. She was very nervous, yet excited. She was sure they would get caught. In fact, she had resigned herself to it. She just didn't want 'getting caught' to be her fault. *"No klutzy moves, tonight!"* she said to herself. She wondered if they did get caught, if 'Zee' would call her parents tonight, or wait until tomorrow. Then, she spent a long time trying to figure out how to explain it all to them.

After several minutes of slow, quiet strokes, Lori stopped rowing. She had watched Julie in the darkness the whole way, and saw how nervous she was. *"I'm glad I had to exert myself rowing,"* she thought, *"or I'd probably be too tense to move a muscle."* As it was, she felt comfortable and warm, in the cool night air. She tipped the oars up and set the handles in the bow without a sound.

Keeping her voice in a whisper, she said, "I'll fix a blanket...stay where you are, for just another minute." She folded the blanket several times into a thin pad. Next, she put it on the bottom of the boat, with part of it reaching up and over the low back seat, so that it formed both a seat and a back rest.

"Okay," she said to Julie, "move your knees a little, so I can put this part wider."

Then, she said, "Now, you can sit 'right here', and she pointed to the blanket part in the bottom of the boat. Then, you can lean back against the seat. But first, let me have that other blanket, okay?"

Julie, distracted from her worrying, did it all. Then she looked up at the stars. "Oh, my gosh!" she whispered. "You're right! I can see them much better from here than from shore. They're beautiful!"

Lori sat next to Julie. "Are your legs cold?" she asked, spreading the blanket over her own legs and offering half to Julie.

"Where did you get *this* blanket?" asked Julie.

"Off your bunk."

"You're *too much*, Lori. I can't believe you *did* that!" Then after a short silence, "But, yes, my legs are freezing." She pulled the blanket over herself, and tried to tuck it under. It was too narrow, so she scooted closer to Lori, and then tucked it under her knees. She shivered in spite of the cover.

"Cold?" Lori scooted closer, automatically, to keep her warm, and the two girls were 'touching', the entire length of their bodies. Lori took a deep breath, and let it out slowly, thinking, *"I'm here. This is where I want to be..."* She smiled into the darkness and tilted her head back. "Wow, just look at that sky..." she said, sighing heavily.

"Is that Mars?" asked Julie.

"Where?"

"Over there..."

"Are you pointing?"

"I'm too cold to point."

"Oh, sorry. Where are you cold?"

"My feet. They're freezing! See?" She put one cold foot on Lori's leg.

"Jeez! You're like an ice cube!"

Lori sat up, tucked her top part of the cover around Julie's shoulders and reached under the blanket. "Where's your foot?" she whispered. Julie bent her leg and put it up over Lori's knee. And Lori put warm hands on her foot. She was so intent on getting Julie warm that she didn't even hesitate about touching her. She just hoped that Julie wouldn't get really cold and want to go back to the cabin.

Lori rubbed her foot briskly, but gently, stimulating the circulation. And it brought back memories of the cave. She did the heel first, then the instep and then her toes.

"That feels good," said Julie. "I think it's thawing out a little. When my feet and legs got wet, I got chilled."

Lori rubbed her ankle, too, and then somewhat up the calf of her leg.

"That felt great," said Julie "Do you mind doing my other foot?"

"Cross it over," said Lori. She held the other ice cold foot cupped in her hands. Again, she rubbed briskly at first, but then she slowed down, realizing that she liked what she was doing, ...and didn't want it to end. After a while, she asked, "Getting a little warmer?"

"Some," said Julie.

Lori started 'slowing down' her hand motions even more, and thought about the foot she held in her hand. She made long, slow strokes over the instep and under the arch. *"A very high arch,"* she thought. Then she reached under the heel. *"Smooth,"* she thought, *"her whole foot is smooth and soft."* She let her fingers slide up and over the toes, and then, 'between' her toes.

She felt her 'special friend' beginning to awaken. She smiled and thought, *"I'll suffer, even if it aches. I'll gladly suffer...just don't let this end yet."*

Julie was lying there, looking at the stars, grateful for Lori's 'warming up' of her feet. She was really cold, ...and it felt, *so* good. Gradually, she found herself thinking more about Lori's touch, than how the stars looked. She closed her eyes, and shut out the world, thinking, *"Lori has a nice way of massaging. It's so relaxing..."* She turned a little more on her side, to be more comfortable, and to make it easier for Lori to reach her calf.

With no words spoken, Lori moved her fingers up on Julie's ankle for awhile, and then on up to her calf. Julie's lower leg was smooth to the touch. *"My special friend thinks so, too."* Lori thought, feeling 'the feeling'. She went from the calf, to her toes, very softly, several times. When she slipped her fingers in-between Julie's toes this time, she thought, *"This is 'very sensual' to me,"* ...and her friend began to ache and throb. *"I wonder if Julie thinks the same thing, or if she's falling asleep?"* Afraid to ask, she just continued allowing her fingertips to, ever so gently, explore Julie's toes.

Julie felt a twinge between her legs, and knew at once what it was. As soft fingers caressed her foot and then slid up over her lower leg, she felt it again. When Lori caressed her toes and then slid between her toes, she felt it even more... *"Oh God,"* thought Julie, *"Lori's hands are making me feel so good..."* Remembering her first boyfriend, she wondered, *"Why couldn't Allen make me feel this feeling? His massages were so different, ...rougher, and more abrupt."*

She wanted to have it go on and on. Her mind was now attached to Lori's caress.

"She really is 'caressing' me," she thought. *"This isn't 'just a massage'. I wonder if she realizes what she's doing, or if she's just 'dozing off'?"*

As Lori's soft hand slid up her calf again, she wished it would caress her whole leg, but it didn't. Lori's hand returned to the soft underside of her arch.

"Uh, ...would you mind doing my upper leg for a little while?" Julie whispered.

Lori was getting close to reaching a climax, from just touching her 'lower leg'. She was afraid that if she touched her anywhere else, she'd go into a spasm and then Julie might figure out what had happened to her.

"...Okay," she managed to whisper. She let her hand slide up and over Julie's knee, thinking, *"The calf of her leg is smooth, but her upper leg is 'silky smooth'.*

Julie turned toward her even more, ...draping her leg partly across Lori's lap.

"Oh, Lord," thought Lori, ...and she began to caress Julie's thigh with long, tender strokes. *"I wonder if she can feel the 'love' in my touch?"*

Julie was amazed at the little ripples of pleasure she was feeling in her pubic area. She closed her eyes, and just appreciated the wonderful feeling. Then, she shivered, a little...

"Are you still cold?" asked Lori, afraid Julie would say, "Yes. Let's leave now."

Suddenly, Julie wished Lori was up close to her, lying down. "Yes," she said. "My shoulders are. Can you get back under the cover with me?"

Lori tucked the cover all around their legs and leaned back, with Julie's leg still draped across one of her own. She was sitting taller than Julie... "Here," she offered, "I can put my arm around behind you, and rub your shoulders."

Julie came into her arms without a word, ...and Lori found herself holding her as if they were 'cuddling'. *"Like the cave,"* she thought, blissfully. *"Only, she's awake now, and she doesn't seem to mind."* She began caressing her shoulder with her free hand, and then, she couldn't help 'enfolding' her, closer and closer. Julie melted into her shoulder, and they stayed like that for a long while, ...each quietly thinking how 'exquisite' that moment was...

Julie was afraid to admit to Lori, what she was feeling. She just didn't want the feeling to disappear, and she knew, that if Lori moved away from her, it would be over. She thought about Lori's lips... and remembered how she' had 'toyed' with them, when Lori was 'helpless' in the hospital. And now, ... she wished Lori would kiss her.

Lori was very much aware of Julie's perfume-like, 'light, powdery aroma', and softly, buried her nose in her hair, thinking, *"And I thought Greg made me swoon."*

Julie tipped her head back a little and murmured, "Lori, ...my nose is cold."

Lori put her lips on Julie's nose, ...and kissed it gently.

Julie tipped her head a little more and brushed Lori's lips with her own. She felt Lori moan, and then, she felt soft lips kissing her, ...gently, ...so gently. Julie lay very still, amazed at the sensations of Lori's lips on her own. Then she wrapped her arms around Lori, pulled her even closer, and began kissing her back.

Lori felt it building and getting dangerously close, as she was thinking, "Julie's lips are *incredible*." It was going to happen, now, ...and she just couldn't stop it... She entwined her legs with Julie's, marveling at the feel of bare skin against her own. She pressed her leg tighter over Julie's and held on tight. She trembled as she climaxed, long and deep, still kissing Julie and holding her tightly in her arms.

Gradually, as she 'came down' off her 'best one, ever', she realized that Julie was 'not there' yet.

Lori eased back a little and then began again, ...kissing Julie's pouty lips. Julie responded, kissing her back, more and more with a sense of abandon and deep feeling. After several long kisses, Lori felt her own friend coming to life again. *"This is unreal,"* she thought.

Lori allowed the tip of her tongue, to lightly touch all along the outline of Julie's top lip. Then she slid her tongue across her bottom lip. Very slowly exploring, she touched the tip of her tongue to each corner of Julie's mouth.

Finally, she felt the tip of Julie's tongue, barely peeking out between her lips, and Lori allowed their tongues to softly touch and melt together.

Shock waves went through them both and they clung to each other tightly...

Lori, not believing she was going into a second, smaller one, so soon...

Julie, in complete amazement at what Lori was doing to her body. Her climax was so overwhelming, that she moaned...from somewhere deep in her chest, and she didn't even realize that she had the little boat rocking. Then neither of them moved for a very long time...

Finally, Lori asked slowly, "Are you still cold?"

"Mm-m... Keep me warm a little longer."

They both were so content that words weren't necessary for a long, long time... Neither one wanted the spell that seemed to be cast over them, to be broken. Lori was wishing they owned a place like the camp, where they could be close like this, every night if they wanted.

Julie wished that tomorrow wouldn't come, because tonight, something miraculous had happened to her body, ...and her mind, too. She had a lot to think about. Another thing had become important to her that she never expected. She'd been made to feel like the most important person in Lori's world. But when dawn came, Lori would belong mainly to the camp again.

"It's clouding up," said Lori, wistfully. "We should go back."

Julie thought, *"Maybe it won't rain. I don't want to move."* Not really wanting to, she said, "Okay."

Lori rowed back very quietly and they beached the boat. They moved silently up to the cabin and carefully opened the door. They went into the bathrooms and Lori breathed a sigh of relief, that they had not been missed.

Julie got back to her bunk, first. As Lori slipped into her own, she realized that they hadn't even said 'goodnight'. She reached out as far as she could reach, and touched Julie's bunk. With her finger tips, she tapped lightly. Julie turned over, and touched her hand. Lori took her hand and squeezed it gently. Then, very reluctantly, she released it.

Without another sound, they were 'unto themselves' and their thoughts. Separately, they re-lived the evening, over and over. Eventually, they both fell asleep.

It seemed like the gong sounded only fifteen minutes later.

I've Been Thinking...

The gong seemed aggravatingly loud this morning to both girls.

When Lori looked over at Julie, suddenly, she felt strange. They'd been so close last night, yet now, in daylight, it almost seemed like it must've been a dream.

Julie's eyes finally met hers, but only for an instant. Then she quickly looked down and blushed.

Lori looked away, feeling just as embarrassed. She got out of bed and headed to the bathroom with her towel and toothbrush kit. Along the way, she answered questions about the upcoming dance, put to her by the new girls, but she felt like her head was in a fog. She didn't want to be responsible for them this morning. If only she could talk to Julie, ...privately. She looked in the mirror, and saw a 'troubled' Lori, looking back at her. *"Come on! Get with the program."* she ordered herself. And gradually, she started paying attention to her 'groupies'.

Julie sat at a different table during breakfast, and Lori understood.

The day was torturous for Lori. Everything seemed to be going too slowly. Lunch time seemed way overdue. Then swim class seemed dull. She was asked by three different girls if she was 'okay. *"Lovesick. That's what I am,"* she thought, smiling. *"I knew she'd have a nice kiss. I just didn't know how 'incredible' it could be."* Meanwhile, Julie was nowhere to be seen. *"Probably hanging out in Arts and Crafts..."* she decided.

Julie had thought about last night, all morning, and was having problems, too. She couldn't concentrate on much of anything else. Whenever she thought of Lori, she thought of her caresses and her kisses, and she began to feel the tension building in her pubic area. The discomfort had stayed with her all day.

And this time, it was Julie's idea. After avoiding her all day, she came up to Lori after dinner, and asked quietly, "Can we go out on the lake tonight?"

Lori just looked at her, then opened her mouth to speak, but nothing came out. She just nodded mutely, "Okay..."

Late that night, they followed the same routine and met outside again. Carefully, and quietly, they maneuvered out onto the dark lake. Once there, Julie said, "I've been thinking about last night, *all day*."

"Me, too," said Lori.

"Let's lie down..." said Julie.

They fixed the one blanket as a pad, like before, and got under the other one. Sitting 'side by side' Julie said, softly, "I was more comfortable last night..."

And Lori understood. So she put her arm behind Julie and brought her in closer. As they got settled, and then snuggled, Lori thought with a long sigh, *"This is truly where I belong."*

They both relaxed and got more comfortable. Julie tipped her head back, and offered her lips for a kiss. Lori kissed her softly, and then stopped. Julie pulled her down, gently, until their lips melted together. The feeling of the kiss gradually imprisoned them, ...and neither one wanted it to end.

Finally, Lori pulled away slightly and paused...

Julie edged closer, and whispered, "C'mere..." She lazily slid the tip of her tongue across Lori's bottom lip...

...and Lori loved it. She felt herself going into that 'twilight' zone again, and couldn't help it. She remembered that cute little pink tongue, and now, it was actually licking her top lip. She wanted more, and somehow, Julie knew. She drew little circles on Lori's closed lips. And then shyly, tentatively, inserted the tip of her tongue between them, searching. And when Lori responded, Julie began drawing slow little circles around the tip of Lori's tongue.

Lori kissed her back, delicately exploring every part of her lips, and even running the tip of her tongue along the edge of her teeth. Julie allowed the exploration, and then sought more of Lori's tongue with her own, sliding her tongue a little deeper, and then deeper...until their lips became locked in a bruising kiss.

Lori started caressing Julie's shoulder and arms, and then, ...caressed her face. Julie moaned with pleasure. Such tenderness, yet such intensity, just overwhelmed her. It seemed impossible, but they kissed more deeply and then clung to each other as if their lives might otherwise end. The kiss took on a 'life of its own'. They were lost, ...in a different time, and a different space. There was nothing else...no one else.

Julie's tongue ventured even further, and began caressing Lori's on the underside. As Lori moaned in pleasure, Julie finally started shaking and trembling all over, and she held Lori closer than ever.

Simultaneously, Lori felt muscles tightening everywhere, from her nipples, to her belly, and deep, deep inside, ...from the front to the back... The climax was like a bucking horse. So was Lori, and so was the boat.

Julie gave up trying to figure out what her body was feeling... She only knew that it was the most wonderful thing that she'd ever experienced... even better and more intense than the night before.

They remained motionless for long minutes after it was over. Lori hated that it was over so soon.

"Do we have to go back yet?" asked Julie, feeling the same way.

"No."

"Then let's stay..."

They looked at the sky, for awhile, and then Lori turned back to Julie. She smoothed soft fingertips over cheeks, and over her forehead. After awhile, she reached around and stroked her shoulder. Then, she caressed her arm, down to the wrist and back, several times. Once, as she was touching her arm very lightly, she accidentally brushed her finger tips against a soft breast. She stopped, ...wondering if Julie was mad.

After several seconds, Julie whispered, "More..."

Lori caressed her arm, and then, once again, allowed her fingers to brush against Julie's soft breast. Her own body responded with a few twinges 'below'... *"Absolutely unreal,"* she thought.

Julie didn't pull away, ...so Lori allowed more of her hand to caress her breast. Julie turned slightly, ...more on her back, ...and then there was no arm in the way at all. Lori gently ran her fingers over Julie's breast, and marveled at how her body was so soft, and yet firm. She ran her fingers over her nipple, and felt it harden into a small, little button. Her own body responded by beginning to throb.

Julie turned even more and arched her back a little. Lori caressed each breast tenderly...arousing both nipples into little hard mounds... She cupped one breast in her hand, and felt its fullness. Julie moaned softly.

After some time, Lori put her hand on Julie's bare stomach, just under her pajama top, and began to slide her hand upward a little, on silky smooth skin. Then she hesitated, suddenly unsure.

"Yes..." whispered Julie.

Slowly, she continued moving her hand upward. And at long last, Lori touched Julie's bare breast.

Julie felt as if she'd gotten a mild electric shock and murmured something unintelligible to herself.

Lori caressed her breast lightly, and her own body parts went wild and raged once again. She clamped her legs together, weathering the little mini climax all by herself...

When she recovered, she began drawing slow circles around Julie's nipples, and Julie moaned again. Lori could picture them...little and pink. She caressed the smooth skin, all around and under the nipple for a long time. Finally, she held one tight little rosebud between her fingers and, on an impulse, pinched slightly, and then a tiny bit harder...

"Oh God..." moaned Julie, and she began to climax in jerking spasms. She rocked the boat and once again, little waves were heading toward shore. Lori just drew her in close and held her, tightly. Finally, Julie lay still, ...for a long time.

Julie seemed 'spent', but apparently, she was not 'done'. Calmly, and deliberately, she turned, and began to unbutton Lori's shorty pajama top. With the last button undone, she deftly moved the material to each side and said, in a whisper, "Lie back more, and relax."

And Lori did.

Julie rubbed her own hands together to warm them up, and then she started 'feathering' one very smooth hand, this way and that, on Lori's stomach. She lightly drew imaginary figures here and there, never touching very high up.

Lori's breasts were exposed to the cold night air and her nipples contracted tightly. She began 'living for the moment' that Julie would touch them. It didn't happen, and now Julie began stroking Lori's sides, as well as her stomach.

Julie caressed up and up and then stopped, just short of the under side of each breast. They began to 'have a mind of their own'. They ached for attention, but Julie seemed to be in no hurry at all.

"She's teasing me, " Lori realized.

Julie just continued, 'playing', lazily.

Then, in a graceful motion, Julie moved to sit astride, over Lori's hips. She placed both hands gently on Lori's stomach, and lightly, slid them upwards.

Lori found herself arching her breasts higher and higher to the sky. *"Is she going to touch me, this time?"* she wondered. Lori even considered 'begging'...but she stayed silent, and still.

Soft fingertips reached nearly high enough, fluttered, and then moved back to her waist.

"Surely, she will, this next time!" she thought. And she believed she heard herself moaning, softly.

Finally, smooth hands slid higher and higher, all the way up to her breasts. She felt soft fingers caressing around her breasts, but gently touching only the under sides. Julie was, lazily and slowly, driving her crazy... cupping and stroking the sides, and all around her upper chest. She caressed every part of her breasts, except...except...

And then, she felt a light finger-tip, 'brush' over her nipple, ...first on one breast, and then, the other. And then, once again. Waves of pleasure coursed through her body. She never wanted it to end...

But, then, Julie stopped. Lori kept her eyes closed, and waited., murmuring, softly, "...don't stop."

Julie scooted backward. She opened her own top, and leaned forward. Lori felt bare breasts on her stomach. Julie slid her warm body up a little, ...and then back down again.

Lori remembered her dream. She pictured Julie in her dream, ...and then she *needed* Julie to slide up and up. It became a focused goal. In her mind, she urged, *"Oh, yes, please, slide up higher."*

Donna Kelli

Soft, warm, velvety skin went higher and higher, almost up to her breasts, and down again. Lori felt her like her entire body was about to short circuit. Finally, finally... as their nipples touched, Lori went berserk. She crushed Julie tightly to her bare chest. She breathed out all her air in one soft moan, saying, "Ju-lie-e"

Julie smothered Lori's next moan with an 'all consuming' kiss. And as her own body reached the point of no return, she extended her legs out behind her, on top of Lori's. She wrapped her arms around her and held her tighter and tighter, until her own uncontrollable spasms were over.

Minutes passed, and Lori came out of it, completely 'done in'. Julie was still on top of her but, strangely, she didn't feel heavy. Lori's last coherent thought was, *"Bare skin feels 'electrifying'..."*

Some time later, she heard a whispered voice, saying... "Lori? Lori, ...wake up. Please, wake up."
Lori opened her eyes, saying, "What?"
"Sh-h..." whispered Julie. "We've almost drifted up against the little dock."
Lori sat up, and put her hand out to keep the boat from banging the dock. She pushed off a little and said, "Sorry, I fell asleep."
"I did too," said Julie. "It must really be late."
Lori sighed. "As much as I hate to, I guess we'd better get back."
Julie said, "I know."

They quietly retraced their steps, and finally, climbed into their bunks.
Lori very quietly whispered, "Goodnight."
She heard back, a muffled, "Goodnight, Lori."

Lori could've sworn she'd hardly closed her eyes when, once again, the gong began to sound.

264

Before the Dance

Talk about excitement! Almost the entire camp was transformed, from thinking about playing and winning end of the year races and contests, to great hopes for a good time with the boys. Liz and Nancy were putting on make-up in front of the bathroom mirror in cabin three. Ceil and Vivian were sort of 'preening' but since they hadn't met anyone at the first dance, they didn't have high hopes. A lot of the new girls were having the nervous jitters.

Lori was already dressed in a dark blue, full-skirt and a silky, baby-blue blouse. The low-cut 'sweetheart' neck complimented her tan. She went over to the window and looked off in the distance, out over the lake, thinking... The entire day had been weird. Julie had avoided looking her in the eye, and, she hadn't even talked to her directly.

After being out on the lake almost all night, for two nights in a row, Julie looked tired. Lori felt tired. Most of all, she felt dejected. After their incredible intimacy, Julie was acting like a stranger.

Lori really didn't care if she even went to the dance. She'd much rather, just go somewhere quiet and be with Julie...to hold her, again. Yet, she didn't dare look at Julie for very long. Not with all these girls around. She knew she'd probably look like a 'lovesick puppy'.

To be sure, she had initially been 'infatuated' with her. But now, she just liked so many things about her. Now, it was more than infatuation. She was definitely in love with Julie, ...and even more than that, ...deep down, she felt she would love her forever.

"Could it be possible that Julie felt the same ...and was afraid to look her in the eye? Maybe that was it!" Lori's heart skipped a beat and she almost smiled. *"Or was she 'over it'?...and ready to get on with her life?"* She didn't know how to solve this problem, ...the biggest one in her life, so far. *"If I could only talk to her, I'd know,"* she thought.

"Oh, well," she sighed, *"try to think about the dance."* She *was* looking forward to seeing Winston. He had written her twice, about 'saving all her dances for him. *"And, it was fun, once she got moving on the dance floor,"* she admitted. Of course, Greg wasn't going to be there, and Lori still had mixed emotions about that.

She'd hoped to spend more time with him. *"And,"* she admitted, *"she wanted to kiss him for one of those long, long kisses, at least once more. That is, when she was in the mood. And the parking lot meeting didn't qualify."* She wanted to figure out how his kisses compared with Julie's. Of course, Julie's kisses were branded in her brain. She would remember her lips for the rest of her life.

Yet, there were several questions. *"How exactly, did Julie feel about her?"* They had never said, "I love you, or even, I think I love you." She had belittled Greg for having sex without a love commitment. Then, she'd done the same thing. It all just happened. She felt the love and said it in her head, but somehow, the words never were spoken. Not by her, ...and not by Julie. *"The two of us have never been much at conversing,"* she thought.

And, the other questions. *"Could she feel more attracted to Greg if she knew him better? What if Julie didn't love her? What if those incredible moments together, turned out to be just a 'novelty' to Julie?"* *"Then, I'd be empty inside,"* she knew.

"If that happened, would Greg, ...could Greg replace some of that loss? How much?"

Then she saw Julie coming...

"Hi, girls," said Julie, coming in the door right near Lori. She breezed by her, went in the bathroom and stood close to Liz, looking in the mirror for one last check.

"Now, I'm just 'one of the girls'," thought Lori. And, more than ever, she felt like staying in the cabin alone, rather than go to the dance. But, she knew that Winston would come looking for her. *"Would Julie? Would she care?"*

The group started passing her by, going out the door. When Julie got next to her, she only said, "Come on, everybody." The 'everybody' was Lori.

"This is bad," thought Lori. *"She can't, or won't even say two words to me."* Lori was the last one out as they headed for the mess hall.

Last Dance

When the boys' bus arrived, it was like old home week. Those who knew each other had lots to catch up on.

Winston greeted her, just naturally, with a big smile and a huge hug. He didn't try to kiss her, 'Hello'.

She smiled at him, glad to see his happy face. *"He will be good for me tonight,"* she decided. *"Is that the kind of person she should marry in the future?"* she wondered. *"Someone who always brightens your life?"*

Winston wanted to know all about everything. They talked for about a half hour. He was genuinely interested in how much she liked the horses, and that she'd been offered C.I.T. for the coming year, also. That news had already made it to the boy's camp.

"I'll be back, too," he said, "but not as a C.I.T.. Too bad we live two states apart or I'd ask you for a date.

Lori laughed.

"And, I'd ask you to go steady."

Lori just looked at him.

"Not ready to go steady, huh? Well, at least be my steady date for tonight. Promise to dance almost every dance with me, ...especially the 'last dance'.

Lori nodded, "Yes."

He asked, "Want some punch?"

She nodded, smiling. *"At least he's romantic. And all for one person. That's nice. He's not like Greg who will probably be 'wow-ing' lots of girls his whole life."* She remembered how the girls chased after him at the first dance. *"How can a guy refuse girls all the time? And, in a few years, would he refuse all the women as he got older?"*

"Probably not..." she answered herself, aloud.

"You don't want it, now?" asked Winston.

"Yes, ...yes, I do," she said, smiling. "Sorry, I was just thinking ahead, and, ...and I'm sorry to see camp ending."

"Me, too," he said.

The music was good, like before, and they danced several dances in a row. Lori lost herself in the beat and the moving. It was great fun and she wished she knew how to dance every kind of dance there was. *"I'll learn them all,"* she decided.

When a slow dance came on they settled in comfortably, cheek to cheek.

267

"If only, I could be dancing with Julie," she thought. She closed her eyes for awhile, imagining.

When she finally looked up, there were Julie's eyes looking at her, around the side of Mickey's shoulder. Lori forgot to dance, and Winston bumped her toe.

"Oops. Sorry," he said.

A fast song started and he turned her under his arm, twirling her in and out, in and out. She lost track of Julie. Before the song ended, he suggested, "Let's take a break. Want some air?"

As they walked to the door, she looked for Julie. She had seen her only a few minutes before, but now, she was not inside. When she and Winston got outside, Lori saw Julie standing by a tree talking with Mickey. It was the same tree, she had been near, with Greg. They weren't touching, but Lori's insides knotted up and she felt angry.

"Cold?" asked Winston.

"No," she managed. "I'm okay." But she was wondering if their time in the boat had really meant something to her, or if Julie had just 'used' her to practice on.

"Do you miss Greg?" he asked.

"No, ...*no!*" she said. And she thought, *"that's not why I'm angry."*

"Okay, don't get upset. I was just asking."

"Oh, sorry," she said. "I..."

"I'm jealous, you know," he said softly.

Slowly she said, "...oh-h." and realized, silently, *"Me too...Oh God, ...me too."*

"Lori, look at me, please. You haven't really looked at me all night.

She forced herself to concentrate on him.

He took both of her hands and looked into her eyes.

Lori was thinking, *"He wants to kiss me."*

"We have fun together, don't we?"

"Yes," she agreed.

"Do you like me at all?"

"Like you? Yes, I do."

He moved a little closer. "Do you think you could love me?"

"I don't know, Winston, I..."

He leaned in and pressed his lips to hers. Her first inclination was to back away, but he put his arms around her and pulled her closer. She hadn't shut her eyes for the kiss and looked off into the distance, and saw Julie, on her tip toes, kissing Mickey.

"Live in the here and now," she'd learned in Philosophy class. *"Enjoy the moment."* She turned her attention to what her lips were feeling. *"Tenderness."* She sighed a little. Winston pulled away and when Lori didn't move, he kissed her, again.

Closing her eyes, she thought about his lips. They felt 'okay', but they weren't Julie's. *"He's going to make someone a great husband..."* she thought, *"but, not me."* The kiss lingered on, and she wondered, *"Why can't I just like him a lot? If I loved him, my life would probably be so simple."*

She felt his hardness pressing against her, and not wanting to be a tease, Lori ended the kiss. "Let's go in and dance some more."

"In a minute, okay?" he said.

"Sure," she said softly, understanding. She looked over at the two male counselors on duty, just outside in front of the mess hall, and thought, *"I guess they're seeing a lot of kissing tonight."*

They returned inside and after she'd danced with Winston for only half a dance, Billy cut in. For a big, heavy guy, he was light on his feet.

"You can really move," she said.

But, after one fast dance, Billy said, "I'm hot. Can we go outside to cool off?"

"Sure," she said, "but this isn't...you're not going to try to kiss me, are you?"

"No, Lori. Honest."

When they went outside, she didn't see Julie or Mickey. She walked around front to the counselor and asked him, "Have you seen Mickey?"

"Yes," he said. "He and a girl were around by the side door, about five minutes ago."

She didn't see Julie anywhere, but she saw the same man out front, and the other counselor out patrolling along the path that led through the oak trees toward the beach.

She hadn't seen Julie come in and she and Billy had just come out of that side door. She had to check once more. "Excuse me, Billy. I have to see if I can find them."

He started looking, too, around the outside, but didn't see them, so he finally followed her in the front door. Lori had breezed through the mess hall, leaving Billy pretty far behind. Lori was sure Julie was not inside. Neither was Mickey. She flew out the side door and saw a little path going to the rear of the building. *"She wouldn't, would she?"* Her heart sank. *"She just couldn't."*

As she went around the corner, out of the floodlighted area and into the semi-darkness, she saw Mickey several yards away, struggling with Julie. He was bending down, trying to kiss her and she was saying, "No! Mickey, *stop* it! You're hurting me!"

Stunned by what she saw, Lori's heart 'leaped into her throat', and she couldn't even utter, "Stop!" or "Let her go, Mickey!" She looked behind her, wondering if Billy would figure out where they all were, or if she had time to go get the counselor.

Mickey said, "Shut up, you *bitch!* I'll *really* hurt you if you yell!" And with a sudden wrestler's move, he easily threw Julie down on her back and ended up lying on top of her.

When she heard a muffled cry from Julie, Lori started running toward them. Mickey didn't see or hear her coming. He was busy holding both of Julie's wrists up behind her head, with his right hand. His left hand was grabbing at her breast while his mouth was completely covering hers, muffling her sounds.

As she got closer, Lori slowed down and put her whole body into the 'sequence of steps' to her most powerful soccer kick, and blasted him in the ribs with the point of her right shoe.

"Un-h-h!" he grunted at the pain and let go of Julie's wrists, lowering his right elbow in a reflex action, to cover his rib cage.

But he was still on top of Julie. So Lori took a step back and just as he started turning his head to see who had hit him, she took a big step and kicked him hard, on the right temple.

"Uh-h! Shit!" he said, covering his head with his right forearm. He finally rolled off Julie and up to his knees, turning to see who was attacking him. *"A girl!"* he thought. He couldn't believe it.

Finding her voice, Lori yelled, "Get away, Julie!"

Julie rolled over and started crawling, but she was still too close to him for Lori to just run away and save herself.

To further distract him from Julie and before he could stand up, Lori stepped forward and kicked him hard, up under the chin. He grabbed at his throat with both hands, making 'gurgling, gagging' sounds, and his eyes were bulging now in disbelief and anger.

"Run, Julie! Go get help!"

But Julie stopped up against a tree, watching as if she was in shock.

Mickey forced himself to a stand, and leaned toward Lori, ...groping menacingly...

She heard her dad saying, "Don't let him hurt you!" Fighting the urge to run, and with her own heart racing wildly, she stood her ground. Just as he grabbed for her, Lori hauled off and punched him, with a solid right fist, square on the nose. As she felt it go 'crack' and the blood spurted everywhere, she said, "Yuck!" and thought, *"Jeez, that hurt!"*

Mickey stumbled backward a few steps, moaning, in his 'now-gutteral' voice, "Oh-h-h...*Shit!* ...My nose! You... *bitch!...* " Then he started for her.

"Uh, Oh! For sure I'm dead now!" thought Lori, stepping backwards as she rubbed her aching knuckles. Her mind screamed, *"Run!"* But once again, she heard her dad's voice repeating, "Don't let him hurt you! Disable him at all costs!" So, taking a big breath, Lori steeled herself to face him once more.

Mickey, still powerful, lurched at her with his fists clenched, saying, "Now you'll pay!"

Just as he started his swing at her, Lori took a big step right at his hulking figure, and kicked him, up between the legs, with all her might. She was only wearing flat black shoes, and her instep felt his testicles 'squash'. He screamed a shrieking noise, grabbed at his crotch, and doubled over, starting to fall forward. Lori quickly stepped backward to avoid his body weight.

Before Mickey could fall very far, Billy came running out of the darkness and hit him with a 'bone crushing' shoulder block. Mickey went flying to the side, about ten feet. Billy went and rolled him over on his back, and plopped his 275 lbs. down, knees first, on Mickey's belly, and then slugged him with a hefty left hook to the eye.

Lori knew that Billy owed Mickey a shot or two, so she relaxed a little.

The counselor came around the corner, and saw Billy, over Mickey, with his right fist already in motion.

"Billy? Billy! Stop!"

Billy didn't stop the right fist to the jaw, and it made a loud noise. But then, out of breath, he looked up at Jeff, and said, "He tried to...tried to rape her, you know? That girl right there..." He pointed at Julie.

Julie was still, backed up against the tree with her arms pulled in close, just staring, wide-eyed at everything that was happening. Jeff could see that she was scared.

Lori went to Julie and without even thinking, put her arms up to hold her. Julie leaned in to her and Lori held her tight. Julie started to cry, and Lori just held her tighter.

"He... he..."

"It's okay," said Lori. "He can't hurt you now."

271

Through her tears, Julie saw the counselor and Billy struggling, getting their shoulders up under Mickey's arms, and starting to drag him toward the corner. He was too big to carry. Mickey had blood all down the front of his shirt.

Lori and Julie didn't move. "Are you okay?" asked Lori. "Did he hurt you anywhere?"

"No, I don't think so... maybe just some bruises."

Lori caressed her back, silently.

"I'm okay. Just embarrassed," said Julie.

"Embarrassed?"

"He just picked me up so quick, ...like a sack of potatoes." She started crying again. "He put his hand over my mouth and carried me around back, ...and I, ...I couldn't stop him. He, ...he was so strong," she said, sobbing harder.

Lori just stood there, quietly embracing her. Finally, when Julie's spasmodic sobs eased up a little, Lori leaned back and touched Julie's face with soft fingertips. As she trailed them slowly along Julie's cheek, she said, "I was so scared he'd hurt you."

"Me, too," said Julie.

Lori said, softly, "I hate to move, but maybe we'd better go face the wrath of the counselors."

"What do I say?" asked Julie, as she let Lori guide her toward the corner.

"Tell them what you just told me."

Zee, Bigfoot and Walli almost crashed into them as they came around the corner.

"Julie! Are you alright?" asked Zee.

"Yes, I think so."

"Did he hurt you?"

"No, not really," said Julie, brushing herself off.

"Let's go in the infirmary so the nurse and I can check you," said Zee."

As they entered the side door of the mess hall, everybody started to crowd around them. The other counselors cleared the way, and made a path for them. They slowly made it across the room to the Infirmary door. Winston tried, but couldn't get close enough to get Lori's attention.

Not one camper, or any of the counselors wanted to leave the mess hall, for fear they'd miss something. They had all seen Mickey dragged in.

Billy had blood on him, also, from Mickey's nose, and suddenly his reputation as a quiet, shy, 'nobody', was changed forever. There were three other boys from his school, besides Mickey, there at camp, to carry the heroic tale back to everybody.

"Wow! Did you see how bad he beat up 'Big Mick'?"

"Yeah, and it wasn't even over Beth, or Joann! It was over a girl he didn't even know, ...some girl named Julie."

"I never knew he had it in him."

When Billy walked out of the infirmary with Jeff, everybody started crowding around him. Winston was the closest, demanding, "What happened? Is Lori okay?"

"You will *all* have to wait," said the counselor. "I need to see him alone, outside."

But Billy nodded, "Yes," to Winston.

Outside, Jeff was having a hard time, believing what Billy was telling him. "The girl did it?"

"Yes sir, most of it."

"Did he hit her?"

"No, ...he didn't have, ...she didn't give him a chance, you know? She kicked him real hard in the ribs, ...and then in the throat. Then she punched him in the nose, ...and kicked him in the 'nuts'. That's when I tackled him, and then you came around the corner, you know?"

"Come on, Billy. You don't have to make up stories. It's okay, if you beat him up, especially after what he tried to do!"

"Sir, I *didn't* do it all. I *wish* I had been the first one there, but she ran really fast, you know? And, ...and ...I bet she has blood on her, too."

The counselor just looked at him. "Go get on the bus and wait for me. Don't talk to anyone, not even any counselors, until I get back."

Jeff went back in the infirmary, and saw Mickey on the cot, still 'knocked out'. The nurse had already checked him over and had an ice bag applied to his nose. She and Mrs. 'Z' and were still in the back room talking to Julie.

Lori sat calmly observant, on a little stool in the corner.

He looked at her calm green eyes, and thought, *"No way! No way, she could've done all that."* As he walked closer, he saw little blood spatters on her blouse. He tried to figure out if she just could have been close to Billy, when he hit Mickey.

"Hi, Lori?" "My name is Jeff. Glad to know you," he said, extending his hand to shake hers.

She calmly looked at him with a curious expression and then, slowly extended her hand. When he had hers snugly in his, he turned her knuckles 'up'. Two knuckles were all red and swollen. He gave her a gentle hand- shake, and said, "Incredible. You're a remarkable young lady."

Lori looked down, but said nothing.

Zee and the nurse had taken Julie into the back room and verified that she still had her underwear on, and it wasn't torn. She had told her story twice, about being carried out back and thrown down on the ground.

"He didn't have time to do more than throw me on the ground, before they attacked him," she said.

"They?" asked Zee.

"Lori and Billy."

Julie had to relate the whole story beginning with Lori's attack. The tale was hard to believe. Julie had a hard time believing it herself. 'Calm, cool, collected' Lori, had become an intense, fighting whirlwind, ...and made Mickey completely helpless, in a matter of twenty or thirty seconds. It had happened so fast. Then she remembered another encounter with Jen and Lu that had ended just as fast.

Zee looked at the nurse and shook her head, slowly. "Wonders never cease," she said. "And Billy? What did he do?"

"He tackled Mickey, and hit him in the jaw twice."

"Not the nose?"

"It was hard to tell, but Mickey's nose was already a bloody mess before Billy ever got there to tackle him."

"Julie, can you keep this story from becoming 'headline news' until tomorrow?"

"How do you mean?"

"Well, we have lots to do tonight, like, get Mickey into the ambulance and call your parents. Then, we'll call the Police, who will need to hear your story before anyone else does. We'll write reports, ...and...we have a camp full of girls who will probably be up all night."

"I'll do my best, Mrs. 'Z'."

Jeff met Zee, as she came into the infirmary out of the back room. He stopped her, whispering, "Zee, you're not going to believe what I found out."

"Yes, I believe I already know."

"Lori?"

"Yes.

"Do you believe it?"

Zee sighed, and whispered, "To look at her over there, you wouldn't believe it possible, would you?"

"No."

"Well," she sighed, "believe it.

Jeff just looked at her.

Do you know how long before the ambulance arrives?" she asked.

"Soon."

"And the Police?"

"I thought we'd wait until you reached her parents. What if they won't let her press charges?"

"Jeff, I want the police called now. At least they can make a report."

"Okay."

Zee asked the nurse to call the police, and then she sighed an even bigger sigh. "I've never had anything like this happen here before. I guess the rumors will be grandiose before they leave on Sunday. And, both of our enrollments will probably be down next summer."

Jeff said, "I know."

"Well," said Zee, louder, "I guess we'd better go out there and tell them."

"Better you, than me," said Jeff. "After you tell them, I'll get the boys on the bus, and get them on their way. Then I'll wait here for the ambulance and go to the hospital with Mickey."

Zee looked around, and asked, "Is everybody ready to face all the questions? Let's go out together and I'll tell them what happened. Then, I'll dismiss the dance crowd. Julie? Lori?" Zee wanted everybody to see that Julie was alright.

The two girls nodded and got up and moved toward the door, but waited for Zee to go first.

The room got very noisy as Zee worked her way to the microphone. Then suddenly, you could hear a pin drop.

"Ladies, and Gentlemen," she began. "We've had a bad thing happen tonight. Mickey tried to attack, ...yes, ...he tried to rape, Julie." The room got noisy and Zee waited until it was quiet again. "He gagged her with one hand and carried her, against her will, around behind this mess hall. No doubt, he would have succeeded with the attack, if it were not for Lori and Billy. They stopped him completely, before he had a chance to do anything more than throw her down on the ground."

Controlled cheers stopped her speech for several seconds. But nobody wanted to miss anything, so they were immediately attentive, again.

"Lori was the first to reach them and she kicked him, and...

"Let her tell us!" was the request from one boy, and the group agreed. "Yeah! Let Lori tell us!"

Zee looked at Lori, and raised her eyebrows, silently asking her if she wanted to tell what happened.

Lori shrugged. Finally, she stepped forward. The campers cheered, wildly. She waited patiently for them to quiet down.

"Well," she began, in a slow, deliberate voice, "I saw Mickey and Julie outside, talking and then, they disappeared. Billy and I looked everywhere, inside and outside. As I came around the back corner, I saw Mickey trying to, ...uh, kiss Julie. She said, "No." And he said, ...uh, "*Bitch!* ...If you scream, I'll *really* hurt you!"

The crowd buzzed for a full minute, and then got quiet and waited for her to continue.

"He threw her on the ground and fell on top of her. I ran up and kicked him in the side. Later, when he stood up, Billy put a flying tackle on him and then punched him, twice, in the face, very hard. I think he knocked Mickey out with the first punch. I don't think he even felt the second one.

The room burst into noise. Everybody wanted to know where Billy was.

Jeff said, "He's on the bus. Tell the girls 'goodnight' and then you can see him."

It was the quickest 'goodbye' in dance history.

Except for Winston. He 'captured' Lori, giving her a gentle bear hug. And, he wouldn't let go. It almost made Lori cry. *"I wish he was my brother,"* she thought.

"Lori, are you okay? Really okay?"

"Yes. I'm fine, honest. It's Julie that got roughed up."

He accepted her answer and memorized her phone number. "I'll call you! Bye!" And he dashed out to catch up to the others.

Billy

As all the guys piled on the bus, they crowded around Billy. He had been sitting in the dark, wondering if he was waiting to be arrested. Instead, he found himself the center of attention among guys he'd never really thought of as close friends.

They seemed to think he'd done it all, to Mickey, ...or at least everything but one kick in the ribs. He couldn't figure out why Lori would leave out all the good stuff. So, after they told him what they knew, he said, "Wait! Wait, let me tell you guys what *really* happened!"

No matter, he was still their hero. They could picture a 'weakling' girl, kicking and kicking at Mickey, but he was the one who finally 'knocked him out'!

Donna Kelli

After the Fight

All cabin counselors were up very late that night, answering questions about rape, and trying to get girls to understand that they had to be careful, ...not just a little careful, but *very* careful. Also, that it was better to go places in a group, or to double date. And, the campers, themselves suggested that if the camp had any more dances, it would be smart, if 'buddies' went outside to 'get some air' at the same time, even if only one of them was with a boy.

Julie hadn't been able to reach her parents. They had been traveling and weren't scheduled to be home until the morning.

Zee called Lori's dad and gave him a brief summary. Then she handed the phone to Lori and left the room.

Lori didn't say much, at first, ...just that she was okay, and hadn't been hurt at all. Then, as she was thinking about the fight, and re-living it in slow motion, she confided in almost a whisper, "I think you'd be proud, Dad, ...except, I only punched him once. No, the rest were all kicks. No, he didn't... You once told me, "If you're ever in a fight, where you could *really* get hurt, ...*win!*. No matter, what! Even if you have to pick up a 2x4, and 'whack' somebody!"... remember? Well, I didn't have a 2x4, so I just kept going, until I was sure he couldn't hurt me back."

She sighed, and said, "Yeah, it *was very* scary... And I can see why you said 'never hit a girl in the face'. Dad, I felt his nose 'squash,' and he bled so much! It was gross... I hope I never have to do that again... That's right. Sure! Well, I'll call you again tomorrow night, okay? I love you, too. Good night, Dad."

After everyone was back in the cabin, Lori made a firm comment, for all to hear, "...that Julie had been through enough for one night, and that neither she nor Julie would answer any questions." Finally, after showers and lights out, each girl was left to her own thoughts. It was after midnight.

Lori leaned out of her bunk a little, and whispered, "Julie. Are you alright?"

Julie turned toward her, and said, "Yes, ...I think so. But I can't stop thinking about it."

"Me, neither."

"Goodnight, Lori."

"Goodnight."

After thinking and thinking, Lori was just dozing off, when she felt her cover lift. She moved over, and Julie 'slipped in'. Lori turned on her side, facing Julie, and felt Julie nestle her back up against her. They fit together, like it was something they always did. Reflexively, Lori put her arm over Julie and snuggled her up, even closer. No words were necessary. In her own little cocoon, Julie felt safe. They finally slept.

At 1a.m., Walli came by with a flashlight, to see if Julie was crying. When she saw them in Lori's bunk, she thought, *"Good. Maybe they'll both sleep all night."* And she left, thinking, *"But I'll check again around 3 a.m."*

Donna Kelli

Aftermath

Late Saturday afternoon, Julie was in Zee's office, speaking to her parents for the third time. Mainly, they just wanted to be sure that she was alright. They were arriving Sunday, by car, as originally planned.

When Julie hung up, Zee got a phone call from Jeff. He was at the hospital and brought her up to date on Mickey.

"It looks like he planned it, all along. He kept her talking out near the side door, until one counselor left to check along the path toward the lake. Apparently, Mickey had already 'checked out' the area behind the mess hall. And, when he saw his chance, he grabbed her around the mouth with one hand, and just picked her up and carried her, with his arm around her waist, sideways on his hip, around the corner."

"All of Julie's story checks out. But Lori, as we both know, left out 95% of her part. He's a mess, I'll tell you. I'll get you a copy of his medical report. You won't believe it! His dad can't believe it either, ...that a girl in a skirt did this to his son! And, he wants to get a look at her... I'll make sure I come with him. We'll stop by later and do the reports, okay?"

"I'll be here," said Zee. "However, I'm not sure Lori should have to see him."

"I think he'll sneak back another time, if we don't let him."

"No. I'll inform the Ranger. He's not to come here."

"Okay. Well, that will have to do. Could you please get Lori or Julie to come to the phone? Billy's here, with me, and he'd like to speak to one of them. And could you get on another phone, to listen, in case it's important, later."

"Julie's right here with me. Hold on. I'll have her pick up in the nurse's office."

"Hi. ...Julie?"
"Hi."
"This is Billy. Are you okay, and all?"
"Yes."
"Well, uh, about Mickey, you know? His parents came and saw him already. They flew in this morning."
"Anyway, Mickey looks *bad*...like a bear beat him up ...or something! His head is all puffy, and everything, where she kicked him on one side of his head, you know? And, where I hit him on the other side, by his left eye, you know? And it's all black and blue and swollen, too. His head looks so big, and lumpy, and lopsided! Even his eyes, are turning blackish-blue, ...you know?

280

"He probably has a concussion, you know? And, his throat...he talks like an old man."

"Jeff calls it 'raspy' or 'horse,' or something. I guess my other punch dislocated his jaw, 'cause they have to put wires in it, tomorrow... They couldn't do it yet, because ...oh yeah... his *nose*...it was broken, for sure!...you know? And the doctor set it just before lunch. And, would you believe ... he has two cracked ribs? ...and his...ball ...uh, ...his testicles are so swollen, that they can't operate on 'em yet. I heard the doctor tell his dad, that he might have to...to... Well, he may be called, 'Mickey-one-nut' for the rest of his life, you know?"

Julie had just been listening, blushing at the last words, ...and a little distracted by all the '*you knows*'...and when Billy paused, she said, "Oh, I guess I'm kind of sorry for him."

Billy said, "I'm not! You know, I came with Jeff, to apologize, sort of, you know? ...cause I felt bad. But you'll never believe what happened!"

"The 'nose doctor had just finished setting his nose when his parents came back from lunch. They have lots of money, you know? And Mickey even has his own lawyer, you know? ...to keep him from going to jail last year for beating up a younger kid. Well, anyway, Mickey was tellin' his dad, "Aw Dad, you don't have to worry about the police. Girls don't tell."

His Mom got mad, and said, "Why would you say a thing like that?"

And, when Mickey didn't answer her, she said, "You mean...you mean, you've ...you've attacked girls before? ...and ra..."

"She didn't even finish talking, Julie, you know? She was *so* mad! You're not gonna believe this! She walked right up to his bed, right by his face, you know? And slapped him across the face, on his nose bandage, you know? And probably broke it again! Boy! Did he scream."

"Then she said, 'I want that girl to press charges! And she told her husband, he'd better get Psycho...Psych...a *head* doctor for him', you know? And she left, ...and went back to the hotel."

Then, Jeff and I came downstairs. And I don't feel bad at all anymore, 'cause I think he raped at least one other girl. I'm going to try and find out when I get back home, before school starts, you know? So, ...are you?"

"What?"

"Going to press charges?"

"Oh, ...I don't know. My parents won't be here until tomorrow."

"Uh...okay, Julie. Well, tell Lori, 'Hi, and Bye.' for me. Do you know her phone number?"

"No, I don't."

"Can you give her mine?"

"Sure." She saw a pen and wrote it down.

He asked, "Are you coming to camp, next year?"

Donna Kelli

"I don't know yet, but, ...thanks, Billy. Thanks for helping me!"
"Aw... that's okay. I owed him one, you know?"

The Last Night

She had made it through Saturday's activities like a zombie, and Lori felt miserable. She wasn't crying exactly, or getting all 'stuffed up,' but tears just seemed to roll out of her eyes. She'd been lying awake in the dark for over an hour. Tomorrow meant heading home. Life here at camp had certainly been interesting. And, it had passed by pretty fast. She seemed to have been busy almost every minute and she didn't want it to end. She dreaded living her life without Julie in it, and who could tell what would happen, now.

"Here I am, back to thinking about my 'messed up' life..." she thought. *"If only..."*

And then Julie came into her bunk, without a word. Lori shifted a little to make room.

As Julie touched her face with soft hands, she felt the tears on Lori's cheeks. "Lori?" she whispered as she held her tight.

They remained together, softly caressing and consoling each other, wordlessly.

"Funny," thought Lori, *"here we are, so very close together. I can lose myself in her sweet aroma, and live for this moment in time, just enjoying the nearness of her... and, my special friend isn't haunting me, at all."*

Julie nestled closer.

"We're both afraid of tomorrow," Lori knew.

After a long while, Julie softly kissed Lori's 'pouting' lips, ran her fingers once more over her cheek and left, as quietly as she had come.

Goodbye

They didn't look at each other much, or talk at all, the next morning. They sat apart at breakfast, and Lori left the room first.

Later, Julie came from the mess hall slowly. She walked with her head down.

Lori was sitting, alone, at campfire circle. As she got closer, Julie said, "Let's walk a little." They headed for the path around the lake. Neither of them spoke for several minutes.

Finally, Julie began... "Lori, my parents will be here in about thirty minutes. They'd like to... Will you come to meet them?"

Lori nodded.

"Then, we're going on to my uncle's house from here. Will you be okay, ...going back on the bus?"

Again, Lori nodded.

As they walked near the lake, Julie began... "Lori, I've learned to like you a lot, ...in fact, ...I, ...uh, ...well, ...I... You're a very special person..."

Lori said nothing, so Julie hurriedly continued...

"But, ...camp is over, ...now, ...and I have to go back to my 'old life'."

More silence greeted her.

"And, ...uh, ...and I don't know what to do about you, ...about us, ...about so much that's happened."

Lori said, "I know..."

Julie said, "I can't do this... Can't we just forget what happened?"

Lori felt like saying, *"No, I'll never forget! Could you?"* But instead, she just looked at Julie for a long time. Then she said, quietly, "Julie, you can fool yourself, and deny to the world, ...but not to me. What we felt, and what we have together is wonderful and powerful."

Julie said, "I just don't..."

"You're going to miss me, Julie... You're going to miss... 'us'." Lori turned to walk away.

"Wait," said Julie.

Lori turned back and looked at her.

Julie looked down, and got very quiet. "I think I feel love for you."

Lori just stared at her, and stepped closer. "Real love?"

"Yes."

They had never said "I love you." to each other. And here, in the middle of this terrible 'goodbye' Lori was hearing it. She was glad, and then very sad, in the same second of time.

"But I'm scared."

"Not of me..."

"No, ...of ...what everyone would say."

Lori sighed heavily, and finally said, "You're right..." And because she knew it would be best for Julie, she managed to say, haltingly, "Maybe, ...maybe it *would* be best, ...if...we just...just, ...stayed away from...each other."

Julie started to cry softly.

Lori wanted to comfort her, but didn't dare, because the embrace she would give her wouldn't be a quick, 'bye I'll miss you' type. And, there were parents and campers walking everywhere.

"I care so much for you, Julie. I wish I could hold you, but I'm going to just walk away. You're right, ...it's for the best."

Lori turned away from her, and started back toward the mess hall, wishing through her own tears, *"...that the world was different."* ...wishing *"that people could understand..."*... And then she realized, *"that even she didn't understand how it all fit together."*

"It just hurts so bad. If only Julie wouldn't care about the consequences. If only she'd call me back... If only we could go be together once more, and lie in each other's arms...just once more, ...far from, ...from..."

And then, she realized, *"...they would always have to 'hide in the darkness' ..."* and suddenly, ...she saw her dad's face, and felt completely defeated. *"How could she even begin to explain her 'new found' self to him?"*

After several minutes of walking very slowly, she entered the mess hall.

It wasn't long, before Lori was hugging everybody, and everybody was alternately, laughing and crying. Although her tears were from being 'heartbroken', she fit right in with the others. She thought that Julie had already left, and so she was stunned to look up and see her standing right in front of her.

"Lori, I'd like you to meet my parents. Mom, Dad, this is Lori."

Through blurry vision, Lori saw a grown up, more mature, beautiful version of Julie.

"Hi," she said, blinking away the tears. "You look just like...uh, ...Julie looks just like you."

Mrs. Conners extended a warm handshake and a nice hug. Julie's dad said, "So, you're the girl who helped save Julie from the flood? And, from Mickey?"

Donna Kelli

He pulled her close, giving her a big bear hug. "Well, we both want to thank you! Julie's very precious to us!"

Lori just looked down, embarrassed, but thinking, *"To me, too."*

"I told you she was shy about compliments," said Julie, smiling and crying at the same time.

There was a moment of awkward silence.

Finally, Julie said, "Well, we have to get going."

Lori looked up. Julie came close and gave her, what was at first, a tentative hug, that turned into a desperate, 'I think I'm drowning' type embrace. There were tears rolling down her cheeks.

Lori was numb, but she realized Julie was trembling, deep inside. Lori held her tighter, feeling her own tears, again. Finally, Lori relaxed her embrace.

"Bye, ...see you at school." Julie said, stepping back...

"Yeah," said Lori, her arms feeling empty, "...see you."

Julie turned and headed toward the door. Her parents both said, Goodbye, Lori," and turned to follow her. Mrs. Conners stopped, and looked back. "Come over soon, Lori, okay?"

Lori just nodded, and then stood there, as if in a trance. She heard others in the room shouting, "Goodbye, Julie!" ...but it seemed to come from far, far away.

Some time later, Meg tugged on her elbow. "Come on, Lori. I want you to sign my camp brochure."

Lori turned, to go with her, but still looked back.

Meg was saying, "Next year, I'm bringing a camera and an autograph book. That's a good idea, don't you think?"

Lori hadn't heard a word.

The end

Coming soon...

...more wild adventures with Lori and Julie

in

UNBIDDEN DESIRES

Donna Kelli

About the Author

Donna Kelli writes for women of all ages. She hopes that her novels will bring new experiences to many, and bring back pleasant memories for others. She would feel especially pleased if her work helped others to feel completely accepting of themselves.

Donna resides very contentedly in Virginia, with her cherished partner-for-life, and when not working on her next novel, she enjoys dancing and sports of all kinds, wood-working, and visiting and playing with family and friends.

You may E-mail your comments or questions to:

DonnaKelli1@AOL.com

9 780759 669536